The Collected Supernatural and Weird Fiction of Barry Pain Volume 2

The Collected Supernatural and Weird Fiction of Barry Pain Volume 2

Seventeen Short Stories & One Novel of the Strange and Unusual Including 'Celia and the Ghost', 'The Reaction', 'The Four-Fingered Hand', 'The Unknown God' and 'The Octave of Claudius'

Barry Pain

LEONAUR

The Collected
Supernatural and Weird
Fiction of
Barry Pain
Volume 2
Seventeen Short Stories & One Novel of the Strange and Unusual Including 'Celia
and the Ghost', 'The Reaction', 'The Four-Fingered Hand', 'The Unknown God' and
'The Octave of Claudius'
by Barry Pain

FIRST EDITION

Leonaur is an imprint of Oakpast Ltd

Copyright in this form © 2022 Oakpast Ltd

ISBN: 978-1-915234-56-8 (hardcover)
ISBN: 978-1-915234-57-5 (softcover)

http://www.leonaur.com

Publisher's Notes

The views expressed in this book are not necessarily
those of the publisher.

Contents

Celia and the Ghost

Through half-closed eyes that were still heavy with sleep, Celia saw that the dawn had come—the early dawn of a summer morning. The decision to which she had come the night before floated vaguely on the surface of her mind. She could see the letter that she had written and addressed to her mother; she had put it on the mantelpiece under the spotted engraving of some tiresome cathedral. She could hear the footsteps of the bored policeman passing slowly in the street below.

The letter was as follows:—

Dearest Mother,—I love you, and father, and my brother. That love comes of nature, and nothing could ever alter it. But I am going away. Early in the morning, before anybody else in the house is awake, I shall start. Don't be angry or frightened. I am not going to commit suicide, or do anything disgraceful. I can take care of myself, and I have with me five pounds that I have saved. I shall write to you, too, so that you will know I am well and safe. But I am going, because I must.

I wonder if you will understand. I don't think a girl of seventeen ought to be sick of life as I am. I am sick of the quarrels and sordid economies of home. I am sick of the drudgery of the office, and the tea-shop luncheons, and everything. I have no liberty.

I do not live—I only execute orders.

So, I am going, without any very definite plans, to see if the world has anything better for me. Perhaps it has not, and then no doubt I shall return, when my money is spent, and father will have the pleasure of calling me a fool and an idiot, as he does most days. But I shall have been alive for a little while.

Your loving and unhappy Celia.

No, she did not repent of the decision. Soon she would get up, but there was plenty of time; nobody in the house would be moving for hours yet. Her body was suffused with a pleasant and equable warmth. Her mind tasted already the strong joy of freedom.

And on no account, she told herself firmly, must she go to sleep again.

∗∗∗∗∗∗∗∗∗∗∗∗

Bright sunlight, and London all behind her. She must have been walking for hours, and her sensible shoes were white with dust. But she did not feel tired; she was filled with a sense of exhilaration, almost of triumph. Sitting on the stile that led to the field-path she ate hungrily the apples and biscuits that she had bought. Not for years, she thought, had she breakfasted so deliciously. And where she was, she neither knew nor cared. At the next village she would make discreet inquiries, and if there were a railway-station and a train that went seaward she would take a ticket. She had been too wise to take a ticket at any London station, lest capture should follow.

She glanced at a diminutive, thoroughly inexpensive, gun-metal watch. In about one hour and a half, she calculated, Mr. Abrahams, portly and white-whiskered, would be demanding the stenographic services of Miss Melrose, and he would be informed that Miss Melrose had not arrived at the office. Whereupon Mr. Abrahams would request that his soul might be blessed and become apoplectic. His sweet son, Mr. Sam Abrahams, aged twenty-two, would also be disappointed. Celia recalled with disgust that Mr. Sam Abrahams distinctly leered, and that he had once put his grimy hand on her shoulder. Ugh!

And at that moment another hand touched her shoulder, ever so lightly. Celia sprang to her feet, thus dropping an apple and the greater part of a biscuit.

"So, you've run away, little girl, have you?" said a man's voice.

Well, yes, Celia admitted, it was a pleasant voice. And she liked the looks of the young man who stood on the other side of the stile. Not handsome, perhaps, but interesting—which, in Celia's view, was so much better. Yet it was necessary to show that Miss Melrose knew how to take care of herself.

"How dare you speak to me?" she said, with breathless firmness. "If you don't go away at once I'll—"

"Useless for two reasons. Firstly, there is no policeman for you to call. Secondly, there is no necessity to call him. Unconventional I may be, but I would not dream of hurting or offending you in any way, little runaway."

8

He knew that she had run away? He might take steps to send her back again. Clearly this man must be managed.

"Why do you say that?" she asked, shyly. "What makes you think that I have run away?"

"The satchel on your back, the dust on your shoes, but above all the ecstasy in your eyes. May I have this?" He picked up the biscuit.

"But I've bitten it!" exclaimed Celia.

"That's why," said the young man, calmly. "I'll give you the apple, though I am not the serpent nor even Paris."

"Don't understand," said Celia, as she took the proffered apple.

"No? Did you never hear of the prize of beauty?"

"But I'm not," said Celia, blushing.

"After you had gone to bed last night," said the young man, "your father and mother were speaking of you, and they agreed that you were a dangerously pretty girl. Of course, their devotion to you may prejudice them in your favour, but I must say that I agree with them."

"You were not there last night. You can't have been. I don't know you. In fact," she added, a little feebly, "I ought not to be speaking to you."

"No," he said, "you don't know me. But all the same I am a friend of the family. Also—as I should possibly have explained before—I am a ghost."

At this surprising statement Celia was compelled to laugh.

"A ghost?" she said. "You're a very substantial ghost. Do ghosts wear flannel suits and straw hats, and appear at nine in the morning, and eat what's left of my biscuit, and then smoke a Russian cigarette, as you're doing? A ghost, indeed! Whatever do you mean?"

"I am a ghost," he repeated, "just as surely as you are Celia Melrose." She was a little startled to find that he knew her name. "It is as easy for a ghost to be solid and opaque as it is for it to be vaporous and transparent. It is as easy for it to appear at nine in the morning as at midnight. Also, there are two kinds of ghosts. The story-tellers speak only of one kind of ghost—the ghost of what has been. That's ignorance. I belong to the other kind. I am the ghost of what will be. Coming events cast their shadows before. It is true that I am solid, but I am also just such a shadow."

"A shadow of what?" said Celia, almost in a whisper. For she loved no man and yet longed to love, and this type of man—if he had not been only a ghost—appealed.

"The shadow," he said, gravely, "of your lover, your husband, the

9

father of your children. You will love me as I shall love you—and what more has the earth for anybody? I will tell you more. In a year's time you and I will be standing here by this stile. The man that I shall then be will have forgotten, and you also will have forgotten—"

"Never!" exclaimed Celia. "It's far too extraordinary. I shall remember this to my dying day." But even as she said it, she looked at the man, and commonplace clothes could not prevent her conviction that she was indeed speaking to a being of another world.

"You also will have forgotten," the man repeated, calmly. "Why do you doubt me?"

"Oh, I don't know," said Celia. "You knew that I had run away. You know my name. That was all right. But then you went on to speak of the devotion of my father and mother. Mummy's fond of me, I know, though she's sometimes cross. Matter of fact, when I ran away, I made my letter to her just as nice as I possibly could. But my father's temper's awful. You don't know the things he says to me. I simply couldn't stand it any longer. Why, if I'd thought they both cared for me very much I wouldn't have dreamed of running away."

"There is a saying, Celia, that to know everything is to forgive everything. Your father teaches music, I think."

"Yes—it's his profession."

"And the poor man's a real musician. He has not been successful as a composer so far, and he does not know—as I do—that success will come to him before very long. Meanwhile, he teaches the piano to duffers. Think what that means. Every day, on the average, his true and sensitive ear is tortured with seven hundred and eighty-six wrong notes. I include Sundays, when he does not give lessons, or the average would be much higher. And he goes through this continuous martyrdom for the sake of those he loves—your mother, your brothers at school, and you, Celia.

"Then he is a poor man. He is bothered always with debts and money troubles. He had to pawn his watch to buy your last birthday present. He just manages to keep on the right side of bankruptcy. The wonder is that he has not been driven into raving lunacy. As it is, his temper and language are frequently deplorable—but his whole life speaks more loudly than his language and contradicts it."

Celia's pretty mouth twitched a little, and there were tears in her eyes, but she controlled herself.

"Oh, dear!" she said. "I didn't know. I wish you hadn't told me about the watch. What a beast I've been! And it's not true that he's always in a temper. Often, he says things in his grim sort of way that make us laugh. Ghost, you seem to know everything—tell me what I can do."

The ghost smiled an enigmatic smile. "All that a runaway can do," he said, "is to enjoy the perfect sense of freedom—the escape from drudgery and routine—so long as the money lasts. I think you have five pounds and some small change. Up to that point you can live your own life, develop your individuality, assert your claim to put yourself outside the circle of—"

Celia stamped her foot. "Stop talking that nonsense!" she said, angrily. Perhaps she had just a touch of her father's temper.

And still the ghost smiled enigmatically.

"You must admit," he said, "that it would have been easier to tell you what you might have done if you had not run away."

"What?"

"One thing has already occurred to your mind, I think. You make thirty shillings a week, you know, at the office. But I will tell you of another thing. Bad temper is infectious. When your father is furious your mother is cross and you are sulky. Good temper is infectious, but not so instantaneously. Still in three days an invincibly equable temper will make its effect. One more point—it is just as easy to talk, to be entertaining, to take a little trouble, in the home circle as it is when other people are present. Believe me, Celia, it is vulgar to have 'company manners.'"

"Yes, you may call me vulgar," said Celia, mournfully. "I'm such a lot of worse things as well that it doesn't matter much. But I never meant any harm. Really, I didn't. It was only that I didn't think, or didn't know, or looked at things the wrong way."

"That is quite true," said the ghost, gravely.

"Goodbye, ghost. I'm going home now—at once. They'll be angry with me, and I'll endure it. I suppose I've lost my job in the City, haven't I?"

"I think Mr. Abrahams generally sacks people who absent themselves without good reasons. But in your case the son, Mr. Sam Abrahams, might intercede with success. He is sometimes kind to pretty girls, you know, and he always expects them to—to pay for it."

"Then I will get work elsewhere. And now I must telegraph home so that they won't be anxious. Can you tell me where the nearest telegraph office is?"

"I could, but I can give you better help than that. All ghosts—

the ghosts of the future just as much as the ghosts of the past—have strange powers. I will give to you a power that no human being has had yet, though at some point in their lives every man and every woman would give all they possess—and many would even give their lives—to have that power."

Celia looked at him with big eyes, spellbound.

"What is that power?" she asked.

"Simply," he said, in his ordinary voice—and perhaps he was the more impressive because he was never for a moment histrionic—"simply the power to put back the time of the whole world for a few hours, so that the things which happened in these hours will not have happened at all."

"Yes, I see," said Celia, excitedly. "But it's impossible. How do I do it?"

"Move back the hands of your little watch. I promise you that the time of the whole world shall move backward with them."

"I've been told," said Celia, "that it's bad for a watch to move the hands backwards. But I don't care; I don't care if it breaks. I believe in you. I'm going to do it."

And she did. Perhaps it was really bad for the watch, for it made a knocking sound. It knocked louder. It knocked as the engine of a motorcar knocks just before it sends in its resignation. And then—

★★★★★★★★★★★★

And then Celia, with slowly-opening eyes, recognised that it was only a knock at her bedroom door. She heard her mother's plaintive voice.

"Celia, you've already been called once. Why don't you get up? The bathroom's ready for you. And you don't want to be late at the office."

"So sorry, mummy," Celia called, cheerfully. "I'll get up at once and hurry like anything."

There had been times when she had met such appeals with a certain acerbity.

She sprang from her bed and stretched her arms wide, her head thrown backward. What a blessed sense of relief! So, she had not really run away. She had not really hurt the people she really loved. She had fallen asleep again after all, and had dreamed the most delightful dream that she had ever known.

The letter she had written to her mother was still on the mantelpiece under the spotted engraving. Celia took it down, and spoke to it as if it had been a living being.

"Do you know what I'm going to do with you, you silly piece of iniquity?" said Celia. "I'm going to put you in prison—in my despatch-case. And in the luncheon hour I'm going to tear you to pieces and throw you over Blackfriars Bridge into the dirty Thames. There!"

She opened her despatch-case. It was rather a good one; it had been a birthday present to her from her father, as Celia remembered. It was at present the guardian of, amongst other things, five one-pound notes, and these Celia took out and placed under a hairbrush on her dressing-table. Then she threw her letter into the despatch-case and shut and locked it.

Then followed a swirl of blue dressing-gown and a dash for the bathroom.

She dressed, her gun-metal watch assured her, in very good time, considering what a lot of hair she had to brush. Just before she went, she took the one-pound notes from the table and put them in a very pretty hiding-place.

As she entered the breakfast-room she heard her father's voice.

"I don't believe they'll cut the light off. I shall get Levison's cheque at the end of this week, and then I can pay. However, I'll go and see them about it."

Celia greeted her parents with more cheerful warmth than usual, helped herself to quite a good deal of porridge, and sat down. Her mother looked at her curiously.

"You're looking very pleased at something or other, Celia," said Mrs. Melrose.

"I know," said Celia. "I had a simply lovely dream last night."

"Good," said her father. "Lovely dreams and Mr. Melrose's fees for tuition are about the only two things that have not gone up in price lately."

"And the dream was partly about you, father. Listen. You're going to have a great success as a composer. It's certain."

"A long time ago," said Mr. Melrose, "I dreamt that I saw a red and blue monkey playing the flute part from the 'William Tell' overture on the E-flat clarinet. It hasn't come true yet, but it may. So may the success."

"It's quite certain," said Celia, "and it's to come before very long. The ghost said so."

"A ghost?" said her mother. "Why, that sounds more like a night-mare."

"But it wasn't. He wasn't a bit like any other ghost."

"And possibly," said Mr. Melrose, "the success won't be like any other success. How goes the time?" His hand went instinctively to an empty watch-pocket and dropped. He glanced at the clock on the mantelpiece. "Twenty minutes, and then I start teaching the 'Moonlight Sonata' to the younger Miss Levison." As he went out, he put his hand for a moment on his daughter's head. "Never mind, Celia," he said, "you're a good girl to dream nice things about me."

"Your father seems in much better spirits this morning," said Mrs. Melrose.

Celia assented. She could not remember that he had said anything particularly sunny, but his manner had been more cheerful than usual.

"He had a good night," Mrs. Melrose went on, "and that makes all the difference. It rests the nerves. It's all a question of the nerves. That's how it is that sometimes in the evening, when his nerves have been on the rack all day, he seems—well, almost irritable."

This was a mild but beautiful understatement.

"I know—I understand," said Celia. "And all the pupils will learn that 'Moonlight Sonata,' or at any rate part of it. The last movement exceeds the speed limit, I fancy, though I've forgotten the old thing. By the way, I've got five pounds towards the housekeeping." Her right hand dived into her blouse and produced the notes. "I've got everything I want for myself, and this is left over. It's been gradually accumulating."

"Oh, Celia! This is very good and kind of you. But I don't think your father will ever—"

"He must. If he won't let me pay even a little bit of my own expenses here, I'll go and live somewhere else and break my heart."

"I think, then, I'll just run up and give your father this before he goes out. It might rather—er—alter his plans for the day. But, Celia, why don't you give it to him yourself?"

"Couldn't," said Celia, and looked suddenly mournful. "I couldn't explain, and I might begin to cry."

"But that's silly, child. Why, what on earth could there be to—"

But Celia had already escaped from the room.

At the office later that morning Sam Abrahams, who was not averse to a speculative investment, informed Celia that he intended to take her out to luncheon that day.

Celia did not even take the trouble to make a polite excuse.

"No, thank you," she said, glacially.

"All right," said Sam; "don't get cross. No one's bitten you."

Having thrown the shreds of her runaway letter into the Thames, Celia lunched alone in the Embankment Gardens. And for lunch she had biscuits and apples, but there are no ghosts in the Embankment Gardens.

★★★★★★★★★★★★

If you ever meet the famous composer, Mr. Hubert Melrose, do not speak to him of the song with which he first achieved popularity. He may tell you that the song was muck, or he may express himself more strongly, but in any case, he will be annoyed with you.

And this is a little ungrateful of him. The song, which was published a fortnight after Celia's dream, had a good melody, dignified and a little ecclesiastical. The words were suitable for singers of either sex, and the accompaniment was within the reach of the vicar's daughter. Its success was instantaneous. In a fortnight the publishers ceased to waste money on advertising it, as the song went by itself; only by the most strenuous efforts could they produce it as fast as they could sell it. And they became most polite and friendly to Mr. Hubert Melrose, and said that they had always been confident of his ultimate success— a fact they had previously forgotten to mention.

And then other compositions by Mr. Melrose, which had been published and had died years before, walked out of their tombs and followed in the song's triumphal procession. These were for the most part more ambitious and important work, and when the critics said that it was a pity that a composer with the genius of Hubert Melrose should waste his time in writing popular ballads, Mr. Melrose smiled with a malicious joy. Prosperity and a tactful daughter had improved his temper.

By Christmas he had given up tuition altogether, and was devoting himself solely to composition. And since he required a secretary who understood business and had a fair knowledge of music as well, Celia worked for him and abandoned Mr. Abrahams.

"And a good thing too," said Sam Abrahams. "There never was any spirit of give-and-take about that girl."

One day Celia's father said to her: "It's just come back to my mind that a week or so before I published that putrescent song of mine you barged into breakfast one morning with a prophecy that I was to have a big success. You dreamed it, you said. It would interest me to have an account of that dream. I wish you'd just sit down and type it out."

"I'll try," said Celia, doubtfully. She put a sheet of paper into the

15

machine, and for a few minutes stared at it blankly.

Then she got up.

"It's no good," she said, "I've forgotten absolutely every single thing about it. And I wish I hadn't."

Later in the evening she tried again, but in vain, to recall her dream. The ghost had told her the truth.

So when, a few evenings afterwards, she met at a dance the young man whose ghost she had seen in that dream she did not recognise him. Nor did he recognise her. They had to be introduced in the usual way. They danced every dance together that they did not sit out together, and he took her down to supper, otherwise neither showed any special mark of preference for the other. Celia went home in a taxi-cab, which seemed to have touches of the seventh heaven about it.

And after that events moved rapidly.

In the following summer, on a sunny morning, Celia walked in the country on the outskirts of London with the young man whom she was very shortly to marry. She had been engaged to him for countless ages, she said, but it can only have been a few months, since he was the same young man that she met at that dance. When they reached the stile at the footpath across the fields Celia sat down to rest and to eat biscuits from a paper bag.

"I think I'm a greedy pig," said Celia, seriously.

"I'm sure of it," said the young man, with equal gravity.

And then they laughed at their own folly, as very happy people often do, and Celia dropped the greater part of the biscuit which was then in action. In an absentminded way the young man picked it up and finished it.

Suddenly Celia sprang to her feet. "This has all happened before," she exclaimed. "I feel absolutely sure of it."

The young man smiled enigmatically.

"Quite likely," he said. "Perhaps we met long ago, some time when I wasn't there."

"No, I think you were there and I wasn't. But I wish I had been."

And as she said this, she looked so perfectly adorable that it became imperative for the young man to kiss her.

"Oh!" said Celia.

"You're terrible; suppose somebody had come past just then."

"Somebody didn't," the young man said, philosophically, and lit a Russian cigarette.

Mala

1

It was Saturday night at the end of a hard week.

I was just finishing my dinner when I was told that a man wished to see me at once in the surgery. The name, Tarn, was unknown to me.

I found a fair-haired man of thirty in a faded and frayed suit of mustard-colour, holding in his hand a broken straw hat. His face was rather fat and roundish; his build powerful but paunchy. The colour of face and hands showed open-air life and work. His manner was slow, apathetic, heavy. His speech was slow too, but it was the speech of an educated man, and the voice was curiously gentle.

"My wife's ill, doctor. Can you come?"

"I can. What's the matter with her, Mr Tarn?" He explained. I do not regard child-bearing as illness, and told him so. I told him further that he ought to have made his arrangements and to have engaged a doctor and nurse beforehand.

"In her own country they do not regard it as illness either. The women there do not have doctor or nurse. She did not wish it. But, however, as she seemed to suffer—"

"Well, well. We'll get on. Where do you live?"

"Felonsdene."

"Eight miles away and right up on the downs. Phew! Can I get my car there?"

"Most of the way at any rate—we could always walk the rest."

"We'll chance it. I'll bring the car round. Shan't keep you a minute, Mr Tarn."

I kept him rather longer than that. There were the lamps to see to, and I had directions to give to my servants. I did not take my driver with me. He had been at work since eight in the morning. When I re-entered the surgery, I found Tara still standing in just the same pose and place, as if he had not moved a hair's-breadth since I left him.

17

"Ready now," I said, as I picked up my bag.

He took out a pinch of sovereigns from his waistcoat-pocket, seven or eight of them.

"Your fee, doctor," he said.

"That can wait until I've done my work. Come along. Shall I lend you an overcoat?"

He thanked me but refused it, saying that he was used to all weathers. The night was fairly warm too. He sat beside me on the front seat. The first six miles were easy enough along a good road, and I talked to him as I drove. I omit the professional part of our conversation—the questions which a doctor would naturally put on such an occasion.

"So, your wife's a foreigner," I said. "What nationality?"

"She is a woman of colour—a negress."

"Ah!" I said. "And you live up at Felonsdene. To tell the truth, I didn't know anybody lived there. I remember the place—came on it two years ago or more when I was roaming over the downs. There was a farmhouse all in ruins—and, let me see, was there a cottage? I didn't come upon anybody living there then. I remember that, because I was thirsty after my walk and couldn't get a drink."

"There was no one there then, and there is no cottage. We came last year. Part of the farmhouse has been repaired."

"Well, you've struck about the loneliest spot in England. Who's your landlord?"

"Eh? It's mine—I bought it. Two acres and the farmhouse. Had trouble to get it—a deal of trouble."

"And who's with your wife now?" I asked.

"Nobody. She's alone in the house."

"Well, that's not right," I said.

"We have no servants—do everything ourselves. The nearest house is a farmer's at Sandene, three miles away, and we've had no dealings with him. It couldn't be helped, and—she's different, you know. I was not long in coming to you. I caught the mail-cart as soon as I reached the road, and got a lift."

"Still, I'm thinking—how am I to get on?"

"You'll find I can do anything a woman can do, and do it better. I am more intelligent and I have no nerves. You must pull up at the next gate, doctor. We strike across the downs there."

We had done the six miles, mostly up hill, in twenty-one minutes. Now we turned through the gate, along a turf track deeply rutted. Luckily the weather had been dry for the last fortnight. We crawled up

18

to the top of the crest and then along it for a mile. I saw lights ahead in a hollow below. A dog barked savagely.

"That Felonsdene?" I asked.

"That's it. The descent is bad."

When I got to it, I found that it was very bad. I stopped the engines.

"If we break our necks, we shan't be much use,"

I said. "I'll leave the car here. There's nobody to run away with it."

"Shall we take a lamp?" he asked.

"Better."

He picked up my bag, unhitched one lamp, and extinguished the other, while I spread the rug over the seats. His ordinary slowness was deceptive. When he was actually doing something, he was remarkably quick without being hurried.

He was quick too in seeing a mechanical device—that was clear from the way he handled the lamps. We began the brief descent, and the dog barked more furiously than ever.

"Is that dog loose?" I asked, as we neared the house.

"Yes," he said. "But he's educated. He'd kill a stranger who came alone; he won't touch you."

He gave a whistle and the barking stopped. The dog, an enormous black retriever, came running towards us; his eyes in the lamplight had a liquid trustfulness.

"Heel," said Tarn sharply, and the dog paced quietly behind him, taking no notice of me whatever.

We went through a yard surrounded by a wall of rough stone. By the light of the lamp, I saw that the wall had been mended in places. There was a rough shed on the left, with crates and packing-cases under it. The front door was flush with the wall of the house. It was unlocked, and when Tarn opened it, a bright light streamed out. Within was a small square hall, and I noticed that the light was incandescent gas.

Tarn saw that I had noticed it. "I put in a gas-plant," he said. "Will you come this way?"

He took me into a great living-room. I should think it was about forty feet by twenty. There was a big open fireplace at the further end of the room. The floor was flagged, without rugs or carpets. The walls were the same inside as out, rough stone and mortar; there were three small windows high up in the walls. The windows were newly glazed, the walls had been repaired. There was very little furniture—three wooden Windsor chairs, a couple of deal tables, and some cupboards made from packing-cases.

There was no attempt at ornament or decoration of any kind, and there was no disorder. The scanty furniture was precisely arranged, nothing was left lying about, and everything was scrupulously clean. The timbers of the pointed roof seemed to me to be new. The room was very brightly lit, with more gas jets (of the cheapest description) than were needed.

What struck me most was the smell of the place—a smoky, greenish, sub-acid, slightly aromatic smell. I wondered if it could come from the great logs that smouldered in the fireplace, before which the retriever now stretched himself.

"Queer smell here," I said. "What is it?"

"It comes," he said, "from the smoke of juniper leaves."

"You don't burn those in the fireplace, do you?"

"No. I—I don't think you'd understand."

The words were said gently, almost sadly, without offensive intention. But they annoyed me a little—I did not like to be told by this scarecrow that I could not understand.

"Very well," I said. "Now then, where's your wife?"

He pointed to a door at the further end of the room, on the right of the fireplace. "Through there," he said. "I—I don't know if you speak French."

"I do."

"Mala speaks French more easily than English. She lived for many years in Paris—was born there. You'll find in that room the things a chemist in Helmstone thought might be wanted. If you need anything else, or want my help in any way, I shall be here."

"Good," I said, and passed through the door he had indicated.

I must remember that I am not writing for doctors. All I need say of the case is that it was a good thing Tarn fetched me. It was a case where the intervention of a medical man was imperatively necessary. Otherwise, all went perfectly well. The child was born in a little more than an hour after my arrival, a girl, healthy and vigorous. Tarn did all that was required of him perfectly—quickly, but without noise or hurry, and with great intelligence.

Mala, his wife, seemed to me to be very young. She showed affection for her child, and expressed her intention of nursing it herself, of which she seemed capable. This was all natural—more natural than normal unfortunately—but all the time I was conscious that I was attending a woman of morbid psychology. When I left her asleep, it was to join a man of morbid psychology in the great living-room.

"All well?" asked Tarn, as I entered.

"Quite. Both asleep." My body was tired, and I dare say I ought to have been sleepy myself, but my mind was awake and alert. The unusual nature of the experience may account for it. I sat down and gave him some instructions and advice about his wife, to which he paid close attention.

"Must you come here again?" he asked. I thought it a question that might have been better expressed.

"Yes," I said. "I don't want to pile up the visits, but I must do what's wanted."

"I didn't mean that. I meant that unless you were coming again in any case, I should have to make arrangements for fetching you if the need arose."

I laughed. "Arrangements? Well, you've nobody to send but yourself?"

"There's the dog."

"But he doesn't know where I live."

"I was meaning to teach him that tomorrow. I'd better do it in any case—one never knows what may happen." He sighed profoundly.

"Teach him to fetch the doctor—eh? He must be a clever beggar. What do you call him?"

"He has no name. He's not a pet. You must take some refreshment before you go. Whisky?"

"Ah, a drop of whisky and a biscuit would be rather welcome. Thanks."

He brought out a jar of whisky, a gasogen of soda-water, and some large hard biscuits in their native tin.

"To your daughter's health," I said, as I raised my glass.

He suddenly put his glass down. "Farce," he said savagely. "But it's all farce—this—this fuss. She's born to die, isn't she? It's the common lot. She's hauled out of nothing by blind Chance, to be tossed back into nothing by blind Chance. Drink the health of the seaweed that the tide throws up on the shore and the tide sucks back again? No! Not I!"

The whole thing had been so strange that this outbreak did not particularly astonish me. "You'd be a happier man, Mr Tarn, and a more sensible man, if you would simply accept Nature as you find it. You can't alter it and you can't understand it. You're beating your head against a wall."

This ragged fellow took on an air of superiority that annoyed me. "Yes, yes," he said. "I've heard all that—and so often. It's the point of view of ordinary materialistic science. You are not a religious man."

"Certainly," I said, "I don't pretend that I know what I do not know. Nor am I fool enough, Mr Tarn, to complain of what from insufficient data I am unable to understand. Put in other words, I am neither an orthodox believer nor an atheist. Do I understand that you are a religious man yourself?"

"The religion of Mala and her people is mine."

"Really? You turn the tables on the missionaries. Well, the theological discussion is interesting but it is often interminable; and I have work to do tomorrow. I must be getting on."

"I will come with you as far as the car. But first, doctor, the dog must learn that you are welcome here and that he is never to harm you. Call him and give him a bit of biscuit."

I called him. He looked up from his place before the fire but did not move. Then Tarn made a movement with his hand, and the dog got up, shook himself, and walked slowly towards me. He went all round me, sniffing. I held out the biscuit to him, and he looked away to his master and whined. Tarn nodded, and the dog immediately took the food from my hand.

"Yes," said Tarn, as if answering what I was thinking, "he has never been allowed to take food from any hand but mine. He will never forget you. You can come here at any hour of the day or night now with perfect safety. It's—it's the freedom of the city."

As Tarn climbed with me up to the car, he spoke again on the subject of my fee. "I suppose I should not have offered it in advance," he said. "But it occurred to me that, as I never think about clothes, I looked very poor, and that the place where I have chosen to live also looked very poor. And you did not know me. As a matter of fact, I am bothered with far more money than I want."

"Ah!" I laughed. "I could do with a little worry of that sort."

As he fixed up the lamps, he thanked me warmly for what I had done for Mala, and asked what time he might expect me on the morrow. I opened my pocket-book and looked at it by the light of the lamp. "Well, I've a light day tomorrow, barring accidents. I shall be here sometime in the afternoon."

The drive home was accomplished without incident. I ran the car into the coach-house and went straight to bed. But for more than an hour I could not get to sleep. I was haunted by that man and his wife, building theories about them, trying to account for them. Just as I was dropping off, I was awakened again by a smell of bitter smoke in my nostrils—the smell of burning juniper leaves. Then I recognised that the smell was a memory-illusion, and fell asleep in real earnest.

2

I got back from my Sunday morning round before one. Helmstone was rather full of visitors that day, and there were many cars before the big hotel in the Queen's Road. As my man was driving slowly through the traffic I saw, a hundred yards away, Tarn striding along, in the same shabby clothes, with his retriever at his heel. He turned down a side-street, and I saw no more of him. On inquiry I found that he had not called at my house. He had merely been there, as he said, to give the dog his lesson.

I am a bachelor. I lunched alone on cold beef and beer, and I read the *Lancet*. I intended to remain materialistic and scientific, and not to be infected by that air of mystery and morbidity which seemed to hang round Tarn and his wife at Felonsdene. I had not been in practice for ten years without coming on strange occurrences before, and they had all lost their strangeness when, the facts had been filled in. My after-luncheon visit to Felonsdene was of course professional, but if I had any chance, I meant to satisfy an ordinary lay curiosity as well.

I drove myself, and the track across the downs looked worse in daylight than it had done by night. Still, it seemed reasonable to suppose that what the car had done then it could do now. I could see more clearly now what had been done in the way of repairs to that ruined and long-deserted farmhouse. The pointed roof over the big room where I had sat the night before had been mended and made weathertight. The chimney-stack was new, and so were the window-casements. Adjoining the big room was a building of irregular shape that might possibly have contained three or four other rooms, roofed with new corrugated iron. One or two outbuildings looked as if they had been newly constructed from old materials.

But that part of the farmhouse which had originally been two-storeyed had been left quite untouched. Half the roof of it was down, the windows were without glass, and one saw through them the broken stairs and torn wallpaper peeling off and flapping in the brisk March breeze. On the grass-field beyond the courtyard two good Alderney cows were grazing. Most of the land looked neglected; but Tarn had no help and had everything to do himself. An orchard of stunted and miserable-looking fruit trees was sheltered by a dip of the land from north and east.

The dog barked furiously when he heard my car, and before I began the climb down to the farmhouse, I picked up two or three flints with intent to use them if he went for me. But all signs of hostility vanished when he saw me. He did not leap and gambol for joy, but he thrust his nose into my hand and then walked just in front of me, wagging his tail, and looking back from time to time to see that I understood and was following him.

He led the way across the courtyard, through the open outer door, and across the hall to the door of the big room. He scratched at the door. From impatience I knocked and entered.

Tarn had fallen asleep before the fire in one of the Windsor chairs. He was just rousing himself as I entered. He had taken off his coat and his heavy boots and wore felt slippers that had a home-made look. From the table beside him it appeared that he had lunched frugally on whisky, milk and hard biscuits.

"Sorry I was asleep," he said. "But the dog knew."

"Ah!" I said. "You'd a long walk this morning. I saw you at Helmstone."

"Yes. I told you."

"You should have come into my house for a rest. How's your wife getting on—had a good night?"

"It seems so. She has slept a long time. So has the child. I will find out if she will see you." He passed into the inner room.

If she had expressed any disinclination to see me, I should have been extremely angry; also, I might have thought it right to disregard the disinclination. But Tarn reappeared almost directly and asked me to go in.

I found that all was going as well as possible both with her and with the child. She seemed pleasant woman, unhurt either by excessive work or—as many modern mothers are—by a rotten fashionable life. With me she was reticent, almost sullen in manner; yet she seemed docile and had carried out my orders. The only difficulty was, as I had expected, to get her to remain in bed. With her child she showed white teeth in ecstasies of maternal joy. Before I had finished with her, I heard the rain pattering on the iron roof of her room.

I went back into the great living-room. It was rather dark there, for the sky was heavily clouded and the windows, placed high up, gave but little light. The table had been cleared, and Tarn was not there. I sat down to wait for him, and the dog got up from the fire and came over to me and laid his head on my knee. He was an enormous and very powerful brute, as much retriever as anything, but evidently with another strain in his composition. I felt quite safe with him now, talked to him and patted him—attentions which he received gravely, without resistance but without any signs of pleasure.

Presently Tarn came in from outside. His hair was wet with the rain.

"I've taken up a tarpaulin," he said, "and thrown it over your car, doctor."

"That's very good of you," I said. "I was just doubting if that rug of mine would be enough."

"It comes down heavily. You must remain here awhile, unless you have other patients whom you must see at once."

"No," I said. "This finishes my work for today, I hope. I always try to arrange for Sunday afternoon free, and I'm glad to accept your hospitality. No juniper smoke today."

"There has been—no occasion." He went on quickly to inquire about his wife and child. He was not a man who showed his emotions much, but he certainly left me with the impression that he was fond and proud of the child. He asked several questions about her as he went round the room, lighting the gas-jets, then we sat before the log fire and lit our pipes.

"One's a little surprised to find gas in a place like this," I said.

"It makes less work than lamps. When one tries to be independent and do the work oneself that's a consideration. Besides, it gives more light, and people who live alone as we do need plenty of light. I'm afraid it must all seem rather puzzling."

"Well," I said, "I don't want to be curious,"

"And I don't want to puzzle anybody, nor to enlighten anybody either. Still, you've done much for us—Mala says she would have died but for you. If you care for a very simple story, you can have it."

"Just as you like," I said. "But I should imagine that your story would be interesting."

"I do not think so. A little more than a year ago I was in Paris. Mala was also there. I met her through a friend of mine. I brought her to England and married her. You know how such a marriage is regarded here—how a woman of colour is regarded in any case. Very well, Felonsdene was a place where we could live to ourselves."

He stopped, as if there had been no more to say.

"So far," I said, "you have told me precisely what one might have conjectured. How did it all happen? What were you doing in Paris—and Mala? Who was the friend? How did it come about?"

He spoke slowly, more to himself, as it seemed, than to me. "My friend was an English Catholic, an ex-priest, a religious man like myself. His mind gave way, and he is shut up in an asylum now. He took me to see Mala. Night after night. Sometimes it was miraculous—and sometimes nothing. When the performance went badly, the uncle beat her. We could stop that because it was only a question of money. I remember it all—settled after midnight at a *café* where we drank *absinthe*—the uncle pouncing on the banknotes and counting aloud in French, very bad French, not like Mala's.

"He was very old—a hundred years, he said—he cannot have been her uncle really. A great-uncle perhaps. He was not a religious man at all. He kept patting the pocket where the banknotes were. We put him in a *fiacre*, because he was drunk. We were out of Paris that night—my friend, and Mala, and myself. Next morning, we crossed the Channel, and next night there was a riot at the theatre because Mala did not appear. Did I say where we went in England? I am not used to speaking so much, and it confuses me."

I was afraid he would stop again. "I don't think you mentioned the exact name," I said.

"Wilsing, my friend's own place. High walls, and lonely gardens, but too many servants—they all looked questions at us. Gardeners would touch their caps and look round after we had passed—you can imagine it. It was while we were at Wilsing that I married Mala. And shortly afterwards my poor friend had to be taken away. You see, doctor, he was a very earnest man, and very religious. He had gone too far along a new road, and he was horribly frightened but could not go back. It was too much for him.

"Mala and I had to go away also, of course. I remember hotels that would not take us in. We have been followed in the streets by jeering crowds. Even when I had found Felonsdene there was endless trouble before I could buy it—there is some silly story that the place is haunted. Besides, the house was all in ruins, and too far from—from everything. And yet the owner would not sell."

He paused. "And in the end?" I asked.

"Oh, yes, I got it in the end. I tempted him. Here we have arranged life as we wish it to be, and we practise our religion without molestation. There are consolations."

"The consolations of religion," I suggested.

Suddenly he put down his pipe and stood up erect. He stretched an arm out clumsily towards me. His eyes flashed under the bright gas-jets, and his nostrils quivered. He spoke in a low voice but with the most intense emphasis. "You don't know what you're saying. In our religion there are no consolations. There is only propitiation, and again propitiation, and always propitiation—the sacrifice of more and more as the end draws nearer." He swept his arm round and pointed at the door of his wife's room. "What consolation is there from the Power that there—in there, where you have been—linked love with life only to link life with death again? What consolation from the Power that has closed and sealed the door of knowledge?"

He sat down and remained silent. I was beginning to form some conclusions.

"Then what consolations have you?"

"Linked to bitterness and yet something. For example—I have Mala."

"Your child also."

"Yes, the child too. For a little time perhaps."

There was again a pause. The rain had cleared now and I rose to go. "Mr Tarn," I said, "before I leave you, I think it my duty as a doctor to tell you something."

"About Mala?" he asked eagerly.

"About yourself." He laughed contemptuously. "If you go on with your present manner of life I will not answer for the consequences. I think you are playing, and have been playing, a very dangerous game; the case of your own friend warns you how dangerous it is. This prolonged solitude is bad for you and bad for your wife. This pessimistic brooding over things you cannot understand—which you are pleased to call a religion—is worse still, especially if it is accompanied by any rites or ceremonies which might impress a morbid imagination. I'm not going to mince matters—if you don't give this up, you'll lose your reason."

"What is it you want me to do?"

"Do not be so absurdly sensitive about the fact that you have married a negress. Be a man and not a baby. Go and live in some village and mix with your fellow-men. No novelty lasts more than three months. Before the end of that time your wife will excite no attention at all—the position will be accepted. And if you can't find any better religion than the dismal rubbish that is poisoning your mind at present, then have none at all. It will be better for you."

"It is impossible to take your advice," he said stolidly.

"Why?"

"Because Mala and I are as we were made. We won't argue it."

"Please yourself. I've done my duty. Goodbye, Mr Tarn."

He told me that he was coming with me to the road. The very thin skin of turf on the hard rock of the crest of the hill would be so greasy that the wheels of my car would go round ineffectively and refuse to bite without his weight on the back axle. At the rutty descent on the other side, he would get off and walk by the car to lend a hand if the wheels sank too deep in the mud there. His predictions happened exactly, and I was very glad of his help. At the road he left me; up on the hill his dog guarded the tarpaulin and waited for his return.

Certainly, in some simple practical matters the man was still showing himself sane and shrewd enough.

I dined that night with a bachelor friend in Helmstone who has a good reference library and a vast fund of curious information. He told me to what Power the smell of burning juniper was supposed to be agreeable. He also informed me that Wilsing was the Herefordshire seat of the Earl of Deljeon.

"Poor beggar!" added my host.

"Deljeon?" I asked. "Why?"

"Oh, well—he's in an asylum, you know. And likely to stop there, so they say."

3

I happened in the course of the next week to hear of Tarn from another source.

Tarn had told me that his next neighbour was the farmer at Sandene, three miles away, and that they had had no dealings together. Now I knew little Perrot, the farmer at Sandene, very well. I had attended his robust and prolific wife on three natural occasions, I had seen the children through measles, I had done what I could for the chronic dyspepsia of his termagant aunt, I had looked after Perrot's knee when a horse kicked him. Perrot was a ferret-faced man, a hard man at a bargain and a very good man on a horse. Between farming and horse-coping he did very fairly well.

He was the willing and abject slave of his wife and his numerous children. He was interested in medical matters, of which he had no knowledge whatever, and relished an occasional long word. So, I was not surprised to receive a note from Perrot stating "our Gladys seems to have *omphitis,*" that he would be glad if I could call, and that he was my obedient servant. Tommy, the brother of Gladys, took back my verbal answer that I would call that morning.

Sandene resembles Felonsdene in that both are hollows in the downs, and resembles it in no other respect. Sandene is approached by a definite and well-made road. Its farmhouse and little group of cottages have a cheerful and human look. The inhabitants are busy folk, but they find time to whistle and to laugh. Gladys Perrot, I found, was suffering from a diet of which the nature and extent had been dictated by enthusiasm rather than by judgment. I was able to say definitely that she would soon recover.

Perrot came in from trouble with a chaff-cutter to have a few words with me.

"So, it's not *omphitis?*" he said with an air of relief.

"I should say it was a slight bilious attack. But I don't know what *omphitis* is."

"All I can say is that my poor grandmother died of it. Buried thirty-six hours afterwards—had to be. Makes one careful. That's why I sent Tom down. He had cake at your place, he said. If he asked for it, I shall have to pay him, to learn him manners."

I acquitted Tom. "No," I said, "that was my old housekeeper—trying to make a job for me." Perrot saluted the veteran joke heartily.

"I was up with your neighbours at Felonsdene the other day," I said.

"Ah!" said Perrot, grimly. "Man ill?"

"No. His wife's just got a baby."

"And you attended her. Very good of you."

"You don't know them, do you?"

"Nor want. Not but what he and his dog did me a good turn once. If you like to take the message, sir, you can tell Tarn that Mr Perrot of Sandene would be glad to give him five sovereigns for that dog. So, I would too, and not think twice about it."

"I'll tell him," I said, "What was the good turn?"

"I lost a couple of sheep. And that annoyed me, though they were marked and pretty sure to be brought back sometime. Still, I was annoyed that night, you ask the missus if I wasn't."

"Like a bear with a sore head," said Mrs Perrot cheerfully.

"Well, at half-past nine I was just on going up to bed, when there came a great barking outside and a scratching at the door. It wasn't one of my dogs, I knew, though you may be sure they very soon chipped in. I went out, and there were my two sheep and Tarn's big dog with them. Those sheep hadn't been hurried and scurried neither. They'd been brought in nicely. The dog wouldn't let me get near him. He was what might be called truculent, as some of the best of them are. He was away again before you could say knife."

"He's no sheep-dog," said Mrs Perrot. "Five pounds for the likes of him! What would you say if I talked like that?"

"To my mind," said Perrot, stolidly, "a sheepdog is a dog that's clever and reliable at handling sheep, and I don't care what the breed is—I don't care if he's a poodle. Come to that, Tarn's dog looks like a cross between a retriever and a—a elephant. All the same, he'd be worth five sovereigns to me, and I'd back my judgment too. Tell you why. I expected there was somebody with the dog and I wanted to do the right thing—a drink for a master or sixpence for his man—and I gave a hulloa. There was nobody within call, for I went right out and looked. He'd been sent in by himself, and he'd made no mistake. That's no ordinary dog."

"No," I said, "he's not. I know him. He's rather a friend of mine."

"There—and the missus says he's more like some wild beast. Oh, they're all right when they've got to know you, dogs are."

Perrot followed me out to the car. "There's rather a queer thing," he said, "but I know the medical etiquette—doctors aren't supposed to talk."

"Well," I said, "they're often supposed to talk, but they don't do it."

"Then you can't tell me anything about that—I don't know what to call it—tabernacle, perhaps—at Felonsdene."

"I've seen nothing of the kind, nor heard of it either. What do you mean?"

Perrot could only tell me what Ball had told him. Ball was a labourer whom Perrot employed. Late in the previous October, on a Saturday morning, Ball had gone in to Helmstone to deliver a horse that Perrot had sold, and drew his wages before he went. He rode the horse in and was to walk back. The purchaser of the horse gave Ball a pint. A friend whom he met by chance gave Ball a quart. A few minutes later Ball gave himself another quart, because he could afford it, and started for home. A carter who gave him a lift told him that he was drunk, and though Ball did not accept the theory completely he thought there might be something to be said for it. It seemed better to him to roam the downs for a couple of hours before he faced the inquisitorial glance of Mrs Ball.

When he reached Felonsdene he sat down to rest under some gorse near the crest of the downs before tackling the three miles home to Sandene. He fell asleep, and when he woke, shivering with cold, it was midnight. But he maintained that it was not the cold which woke him; it was music of a sort. There was a drum beating, not loud, but regularly. At intervals a woman's voice was heard singing. "Stopping short and then starting in again on it" was Ball's phrase to describe it. The sounds came from what looked like an outhouse; it had no windows, but light streamed out from the open door. And in the path of the light there was a grey smoke. He crept very quietly and cautiously down to a point from which he might see what was going on in there.

The inside of the building was filled with the grey smoke, but through it he could see many lighted candles, candles as long as your arm, and a kneeling figure—he could not say whether it was man or woman—in a long red garment. The singing and drum-beating had stopped and all was quite still. Then Ball's foot slipped and sent stones rattling down. The next minute Ball was running for his life with, so he maintained. Tarn's dog after him.

As Ball got away, it may be believed that either the dog was chained, or that it was called off immediately by Tarn himself.

"I don't know what you make of it, sir, but it looks to me as if those Tarns were Romans," said Perrot.

"Mr Perrot," I said, "it doesn't do to take much notice of what a fuddled man thinks he sees."

"Perhaps not," said Perrot. "Anyway, it gave Ball a good scare—he's been teetotal ever since and talks of joining the Plymouth Brethren."

Within a brief period from that day my visits to Felonsdene ceased; there was no longer any reason for them. Tarn accepted all that the law required; he registered the birth of the child and he had her vaccinated. The devotion of Mala and himself to that child was beyond all question.

I repeated the very good advice which I had already given him, but he refused to follow it. I think he considered that he had already said too much, and he quite obviously attempted to minimise it. He said that perhaps he had expressed himself too strongly. It was quite possible for a small family to live happily and cheerfully together even in so desolate a spot as Felonsdene. There was plenty to do. Mala had her baby and the house to look after. He had the outdoor work. If he wanted to see what the rest of the world was doing, he could always go into Helmstone; there were plenty of hotels there where he could get a drink and a game of billiards. When I told him what Ball professed to have seen and heard he got rather angry. It was all a lie. Ball had never been near the place. But a few minutes afterwards he said: "I wish I'd let the dog get him."

It was all intended to be very reassuring. But it was not candid and it was vaguely disquieting. It occurred to me to pay a visit one night secretly to Felonsdene to see if I could make out what was going on. But my practice in Helmstone was too heavy to leave leisure for nocturnal expeditions of that sort; besides, it was no business of mine.

Tarn paid my bill—he wanted to pay twice as much—and I regarded the incident as closed. If I were called in again, I thought it likely that it would be to certify the lunacy of either Tarn or his wife.

But the incident was reopened a little less than a year later, and not in the way that I had expected.

4

In the following January I took a partner in my practice. This was a step which I had long contemplated. I was a bachelor, making far too much money for my simple needs and working far too hard in order to accomplish it. I also wanted time for my investigations into the cause and treatment of a certain disease; these investigations have nothing to do with the story of Mala and her husband and would not interest laymen. I have no excuse but vanity for adding that they subsequently brought me some reputation. My partner was a sound and able young man, much interested in his profession, and soon made himself liked and respected. My life became much easier and more comfortable.

In the March following, about four one morning, I was awakened by the barking of a dog in the street outside my house. Presently I heard him scratching at my door. I hurried down, switched on the lights, and opened the door. I had thought of damage to my paint and not of Tarn, of whom I had heard nothing for a long time. But it was Tarn's dog that lay on the pavement outside.

I supposed at first that somebody at Felonsdene was ill, and that the dog had been sent to fetch me. But the dog's appearance did not bear this out. He had evidently come much further than the distance from Felonsdene to my house. He got up when he saw me, but the poor brute was so exhausted that he could hardly stand, and he looked as if he had been starved for days. I called him into the house and got food for him; he ate ravenously. I waited to see if he would try to get out again, but he seemed perfectly content to remain where he was. Finally, he followed me upstairs to my own room, where he stretched himself on the hearth-rug and almost instantly fell asleep. I was just about to switch off the light and get back into my bed again when I noticed the shining brass plate on the dog's collar. I bent down and examined it. On the brass plate, neatly engraved, were my own name and address. It looked as if the dog were to be mine in future. But why? What had happened?

The dog established definitely his relations with the rest of my household next morning. He took no notice whatever of anybody who left him alone. But he would allow nobody but myself to touch him. Even my partner, who understood dogs and was fond of them, had to confess himself beaten. He was taking the round that morning, and I intended to walk up to Felonsdene with the dog. But the poor brute was still so stiff and footsore that I decided after all to take the car. He sat beside me, and I rather think that he knew where he was going. But he showed no excitement when the car stopped, and made no attempt to rush off to the farmhouse. He followed me quietly down the hill.

A saddled horse was tethered in the court-yard, and the outer door was open. In the hall stood Mr Perrot with a penny note-book and a stumpy pencil in his hand. He looked up as he heard my step, and greeted me with his usual heartiness,

"This is a surprise, Mr Perrot," I said. "I didn't expect to find you here. I was looking for Tarn."

"Afraid you won't find him, sir. They all cleared out yesterday morning. I've bought this place."

"Bought it?"

"House and land, furniture and stock, everything except the dog and their clothes. It's a little speculation of mine, and looks like being a very good speculation too. I knew you were going to have the dog— he told me he meant him as a present to you, and according to Tarn I could never have done anything with him. Truculent—too truculent."

"I didn't know he was leaving. How did it come about?"

"Oh, he came round one morning three weeks ago, and asked me if I'd buy his place. I said I'd buy that or anything else if the price were right. And it was right enough because it was my own price; I came and went over everything and said what I'd give, and he never haggled. I paid my ten *per cent*, next day, and completed at the lawyer's in Helmstone afternoon before last."

"Tarn was there?"

"He was. What's more, we had a bottle of champagne wine at the Armada afterwards at his expense, and he drove me back to Sandene in his car."

"Car? I never knew he'd got one."

"Only had it two months, he said. It's a bigger one than yours, sir, and I expect he'll lose money on it. For he told me he shouldn't take it over to France with him, and they're bad things to sell. Yes, I felt like one of the gentlefolk that afternoon—drinking champagne wine and sitting in a motorcar. He must be a warmer man than ever I supposed."

"How was he looking?"

"Well, he was quiet, and yet he was a bit excited, if you know what I mean. He'd new clothes on—oh, quite the thing. It's my belief that he's come into money unexpected, and that he and the wife and baby are off on a jaunt together."

I did not share Perrot's belief, but I said nothing.

"In France they're not too particular, so I'm told," said Perrot. "I daresay they will fit in better there than they do here."

"Did you see the woman and her baby when you were here?"

"No, they weren't shown, and I didn't ask for them. I don't think they were in the house when I came, for I went into each room. But they must have come in by another way before I left, for I heard them in the next room to us. What's more, the baby was laughing and the woman was sobbing."

"What was she crying about?"

Perrot laughed. "Why, women will cry for anything. Toothache perhaps. Maybe he'd been giving her a bit of a dressing-down."

I did not agree with Perrot's conclusions, but again I made no comment. Perrot had to get on his horse and ride back to Sandene. He confided to me that he'd got a tenant for Felonsdene already. Mrs Lane was going to live there with her married daughter and her son-in-law. Mrs Lane was Perrot's bad-tempered and dyspeptic aunt, and so far, she had lived in Perrot's house at Sandene. "But I haven't got room for her any longer," said Perrot. "So, she's taking her *exeatus*" I recommend *exeatus* to the philologist,

Perrot had ridden off, and I was half-way up the hill to my car, when the idea struck me that I should like to have a look at the building which had been used for the curious rites that Ball had described and I turned back again. I found the place; it stood apart from the house, and was boarded on the inside. That curious smell of bitter smoke still hung about it. At one end I could see that some sort of fitment had been removed, and there were splashes of candle-wax on the floor.

Coming out into the sunlight again, I noted that Tarn had done a little levelling and road-making to enable him to get his car into Felonsdene from the lower side of the hollow. This would give him a greater distance to go if he were driving to Helmstone, but by the shorter route which I had taken the approach was quite impracticable for a car.

And then, quite by chance, I noticed among the stunted trees of the orchard something white that at a little distance looked not un-like a big milestone. As I entered the orchard the dog whined and lay down. I supposed that he was tired and left him there. A nearer view showed me a column about three feet square and about four feet in height, neatly built up of rough lumps of chalk. On the top of the column were a pile of ashes and charred wood. It was then that its resemblance to a sacrificial altar, such as I had seen pictured in an old illustrated Bible, first struck me. Among the ashes something gleamed and sparkled. I fished it out with a bit of stick. It was a small circlet of soft gold, evidently not European work, and might have served as a child's bangle. And my disturbance of the ashes had shown me other things.

I found an old wine-case in one of the sheds, and in this I placed all that I had found on the top of the altar. The lower part of the ashes and the top of the altar were still quite warm from the fire. I carried the case up to my car, sweating with the effort and my hurry. I put the case in the tonneau and covered it with a rug, and then, with the dog by my side, I went home as fast as I could drive.

My partner had returned from his round and joined me in my examination of what was in the case. Incineration had been imperfect and we had no doubt whatever. I could state confidently that on an altar in an orchard at Felonsdene the body of a young child had been burned, within thirty-six hours of the time of my discovery, which was precisely twenty minutes past twelve on the morning of 29th March. I returned at once to my car and drove to the police-station, where I gave my information.

The number and the appearance of Tarn's car were well known.

A white man travelling with a coloured person cannot go anywhere in England without being noticed. He and the woman had been in Paris before, and the man had admitted to Perrot, under circumstances which might have overcome his usual reticence, that he was going to France. The inspector who saw me felt sure that Tarn would be found, and the whole mystery cleared up, in a very short time.

Tarn and Mala were never found. They had been seen in the car in the very early morning of the 28th. The car itself was found at Melcombe Cliffs, an unimportant place on the coast about five miles from Helmstone. Inquiries at ports gave negative results; no negress accompanied by a white man had gone by any of the boats; the only coloured person who had gone abroad bore no resemblance to Mala and was satisfactorily accounted for.

The coroner was extremely polite to me at the inquest on the remains of the child. He said that I had given my evidence in a most clear and open manner. I had mentioned circumstances which I thought to be suspicious, and of course it was my duty to mention them. But still I had admitted fully—and he thought it a most important point—that both Tarn and his wife were devoted to the child. It made any theory that they had been guilty of the horrible crime of murdering the child seem very improbable. Tarn had married a negress and was very sensitive on the point; he lived alone; he hated any publicity. It seemed to him more likely that the child died suddenly, perhaps as the result of an accident, when Tarn and his wife were on the point of departure; and that sooner than face the publicity and inquiry, they had taken this quite illegal way of disposing of the body.

Tarn was an educated man and he would know that what he had done was illegal. He would be anxious to avoid detection, and would probably change his plans in consequence. He was also a wealthy man; the abandonment of the motorcar would not mean very much to him. Inquiries had been made on the supposition that Tarn and his wife had gone to France; but they might have gone elsewhere. They might have shipped from Liverpool. A coloured person with the help of a thick motor-veil, a wig, and greasepaints might easily conceal her race for a little while. The absence of any evidence from people at Melcombe Cliffs and the neighbourhood seemed rather to point to this.

Tarn was a gloomy man of rather morbid and religious temperament. He had certainly said some extraordinary things, but the bark of a man of that type was generally worse than his bite. The cremation of the child's body was wrong and illegal, but the jury had nothing to do with that. There was really no evidence pointing to murder; on the contrary, they had heard that both parents were devoted to their child. An inconclusive verdict was given.

It was on 27th March that the child was born; a year later precisely its body was burned. It may have been a coincidence; it may not. I, at any rate, have never been able to accept the coroner's comforting theory. I remember her too well, and the power that she and her horrible faith had over her husband. They loved their child, I believe. But in the propitiation of the Power of evil, the dearer the victim the more potent will be the sacrifice. They must have been insane in the end. And possibly the sea at Melcombe Cliffs still holds the secret of what became of them.

Post-Mortem

1

After dining for the last time at his club, Evan Hurst returned at once to his flat in Jermyn Street. The greater part of his arrangements had already been made, and most of his things packed; but there were still a few details to settle, and he was to leave for the north early on the following morning.

Yet when he entered his room, he did not proceed at once to letter-writing or to business of any kind. He flung himself down in an easy-chair. He felt unaccountably tired. All day he had had business to attend to, necessary no doubt for the carrying out of his somewhat wild and romantic scheme, none the less wearisome to a man of poetical temperament and of poor physique. He was a man of slight build, with fair and rather fluffy hair, a pretty, thin-lipped mouth, and plaintive blue eyes.

To the world in general his lot would have seemed a fairly easy one. He had sufficient means of his own; and no one in any way depended upon him. His volume of poems, *Under the Sea*, published a year or two before, had excited a great deal of public attention and some controversy; what had seemed genius to one critic had seemed insanity to another. He was not unpopular at his club although he was thought to be slightly ridiculous. It was not supposed that he had any trouble of any kind. Women, of whom in his poems he wrote with such knowledge and such fervency, had never really come much into his life.

As he lay there and smoked endless cigarettes, he admitted the truth to himself. It was vanity that was at the root of it. He had seen the talented and remarkable Evan Hurst dwindling down into nobody again. Once it was supposed that Evan Hurst was dead, dead by his own act, and leaving such strange communications behind him, interest would revive. People would speak again of *Under the Sea*, his

39

unpublished poems would be produced, and there would be obituary notices. There would be, for a while at least, breathless interest in the poet and the suicide, and he, alive and not dead, under another name and acting another part, would read and enjoy it all. To carry out his scheme meant many sacrifices, but the fascination of it was too strong for him, and the success of it seemed to be certain.

His sensations were really very much those of a man who actually knows that he is about to die. He had withdrawn a large balance from his bank and transferred it to another bank in the name which he now intended to take, but it was essential if Evan Hurst were to die that he should leave money behind him. That money he willingly sacrificed. It was enough if he retained for his new incarnation sufficient for a reasonable livelihood. It annoyed him far more to think that he must leave also his books, the collections, the furniture and the treasures of his Jermyn Street flat. They had all come together slowly, and all represented in a way his individuality.

The scattering of them by public auction would be like the disintegration of death. He could imagine already the notice in the catalogue of a second-hand bookseller offering that exquisitely-bound set of Huysman's works, "containing the book-plate of the late Evan Hurst." There were prints and engravings that from long affection and study had given him almost a feeling as if he had had a part in their creation. The Durer, a splendid impression, would fetch fifty pounds at least. Men at the club would remember this evening. They would recall that Evan Hurst was there only a few days before his death, and that even then they had remarked how gloomy and silent he seemed to be.

He laughed bitterly and aloud, flung down his cigarette and passed into his bedroom. There for a while he packed energetically, but soon he had to stop for a feeling of intense and almost painful weariness came over him again. After all, there would be time to finish the packing in the morning. He decided to go to bed.

On the following afternoon he left King's Cross for Salsay on the Yorkshire coast.

2

Salsay is a small fishing village that has not yet suffered from the curse of popularity. Evan Hurst put up at the one hotel in the place and constituted its one permanent visitor. Occasionally a commercial traveller would arrive one day and leave on the next, and would talk as much as possible to Evan Hurst. Evan Hurst, in return, would talk as little as possible, consistent with bare politeness, to the commercial traveller.

Every morning he bathed from the shore before breakfast at a point at some considerable distance from the village. Here there was a small cave in the cliffs, a useful shelter if rain came on, and useful to Evan Hurst for other purposes; for it was here that gradually, bit by bit, he collected the slender outfit with which he was to begin the world in his new character on the day that Evan Hurst was supposed to commit suicide.

His plan was simplicity itself. He would go out to bathe as usual, and he would not return. His clothes would be found on the shore, and in the pocket of his coat there would be a letter to the landlord of the hotel leaving no doubt whatever as to his intentions. In the meantime, in a little cave, he would have altered his appearance, put on different clothes, and from there struck out for the nearest railway station. In the evening he would be in Dover, and next day in Paris, without one tie left between what he had once been and what he was now going to be.

He looked forward to the change with pleasurable excitement. It was something more than vanity after all. As Evan Hurst he had begun in a role which he was not competent to sustain; to have continued in it would have been to disappoint the public opinion of him. In a new part he could write as he liked; act as he liked; talk as he liked. There would be no preconceived opinion of him in the world; it would be all for him to make with the benefit of his experience of his past blunders.

He took immense care with the composition of that brief letter to the landlord. It ran as follows:—

Dear Sir,—It would be impossible to explain to you the reasons why I intend this morning to take my life, but undoubtedly some apology is due to you for any inconvenience which my death may cause you. I leave behind me at the hotel a quantity of money which will be more than sufficient to discharge my obligations to you.

Nor have I any explanation to offer to the coroner and the British jury. These good people will return their usual verdict. Not to be interested in so extremely uninteresting a thing as my life has become, would be a clear proof to them of insanity.

I shall swim out so long as my strength lasts, and the end will come under the sea.—Faithfully yours,

Evan Hurst.

He did not quite like it now that he had finished it. The way in which he had introduced the title of his book seemed to him to be a little on the cheap side, but at any rate it was a letter which would call for a good deal of comment. He promised himself much amusing and interesting reading when the English papers reached Paris a few days later.

The morning came at last; grey, overcast, and misty, and more likely to turn to great heat than to rain. Evan Hurst looked at himself in the glass and laughed. He had spent some hours in his room the night before dyeing his fluffy hair. Unquestionably it was an improvement to his appearance. There was no danger that it would be observed on his leaving the hotel; for he wore his towels slung round his neck, and a broad-brimmed straw hat. As he walked towards the cave, he now felt an unaccountable nervousness. True, but few people went that way, and even if they entered the cave his store of clothes was so carefully hidden that it was unlikely that anybody would find them.

Still, there was just a chance, and it would be maddening if just at the last some trifle occurred to balk his scheme. He breathed a sigh of relief when he found everything just as he had left it. In less than half an hour the change was complete; the clothes of that fluffy poet, Evan Hurst, were disposed with a careful carelessness on the rocks above high-water mark, with the letter to the landlord in the pocket of the coat, and Evan Hurst, in his new incarnation, strode away in a blue serge suit, black felt hat, and black boots, carrying a small bag, which contained a change of linen and the articles of his toilet. The rest of his luggage was to be purchased in London.

For the first mile or so his way lay along the beach, and he was careful to walk on the sand, where, in half an hour, the sea would obliterate his footprints. His feelings were at first those of amusement. In every little detail of his clothes, he was so different from what he had ever been before.

He speculated whether he would not perforce become quite a different kind of man under the clothes' influence. Already he felt himself a stouter person, readier to tackle the world and deal with it properly. His satisfaction was intense. He was still meditating on the subject when he reached the path up the cliffs; a perfectly easy and safe path with a few low rocks between him and it. As he clambered over the rocks, inconvenienced by the bag that he was carrying, he slipped and fell, and lay quite still.

The hours passed, and now the sun blazed. The waves had already touched one of the black boots. They crept up to the head and came back with a pinky stain. At last, when the figure was fully covered, it gave a sudden and ungainly movement, and for a little while floated with arms and legs shot out queerly like the limbs of a starfish. The black felt hat had drifted far away, and tossed about on the waves with absurdity. Then, slowly, the figure disappeared from sight.

The Green Light

The man looked down at the figure of the woman on the couch.
The little silver clock on the mantelpiece began to chime; he could
not bear the sound of it. He flew at the clock like a madman, and
dashed it on the ground, and stamped on it. Then he drew down the
blind, and opened the door and listened; there was no one on the
staircase. Silence seemed now as intolerable to him as sound had been
a moment before. He tried to whistle, but his lips were too dry and
made only a ridiculous hissing sound. Closing the door behind him,
he ran down the staircase and out into the street. The woman on the
couch never moved or spoke. It was late in the afternoon; the light
from the low sun penetrated the green blind and took from it a horrible colour that seemed to tint the face of the woman on the couch.
Flies came out of the dark corners of the room, sulkily busy, crawling
and buzzing. One very little fly passed backwards and forwards over
the woman's white ringed hand; it moved rapidly, a black speck.

Outside in the street, the man stepped from the pavement into the
roadway; a cabman shouted and swore at him, and someone dragged
him back by the arm, and told him roughly to look where he was
going. He stood still for a minute, and rubbed his forehead with his
hand. This would not do. The critical moment had come, the moment when, above all things, it was necessary that his nerve should
be perfect and his thoughts clear; and now, when he tried to think, a
picture came before the thought and filled his mind—the picture of
the white face with the green light upon it. And his heart was beating
too fast, and, it seemed to him, almost audibly. He began to feel his
pulse, counting the strokes out loud as he stood on the kerb; then he
was conscious that two or three boys and loafers were standing in a
little group watching him and laughing at him.

One of the loafers handed him his hat; it had fallen off when he
dodged back on to the pavement, and he had not noticed it. He took

the hat, and felt for some coins to give the man. He found a half-crown and a half-penny; he held them in his hand, and stared at them, and forgot why he had wanted them. Then he suddenly remembered and gave them. There was a loud yell of laughter; the boys and loafers were running away, and he heard one of them shouting, 'Let the old stinker out a bit too soon, ain't they?' and another, 'Garn! 'E's tight—that's all's wrong with 'im.'

Again, he told himself that this would not do. He must not think of the past—the awful past. He must not think of the future—of his schemes for escape. He must concentrate his thoughts on the present moment, until he could get to some place where he could be alone. Yes, Regent's Park would do well, and it was near. He brushed his hat with his coat-sleeve, put it on, and walked. He thought about the movement of his feet, and the best way to cross the road, and how to avoid running into people, and how to behave as other people in the street behaved. All the things that one generally does unconsciously and automatically required now for their conduct a distinct mental effort.

As he walked on, his mind seemed to clear a little. He reached a spot in Regent's Park where he could lie down in the grass with no one near him, out of sight. 'Now,' he said to himself, 'I need concentrate my thoughts no longer—I can let them go.' In a second, he had gone rapidly through the past—the jealousy that had burned in his heart, and the way that he had quieted himself and made his scheme, and carried it out slowly. It had been finished that afternoon, when he had lost control over himself, and—

Through the transparent leaves of the tree near him the sun came with a greenish glare. He shuddered and turned away, so that he could not see it.

Yes, he was to escape—he had made all the arrangements for that. He drew from his side-pocket a roll of notes, and counted them, and entered the numbers in his pocket-book. He had changed a cheque for fifty pounds at the bank that morning. The police would find that out, and endeavour to trace him by discovering where the notes with those numbers were changed. That was one of his means of escape. He would see to it that the notes were never changed by himself, or in any town where he had been or was likely to be. He was going to sacrifice those ten banknotes to put the police on a wrong scent. He had plenty of money ready in gold—in gold that could not be traced—for his own needs. He chuckled to himself. It was brilliant, this scheme for providing a wrong scent, for making the very carefulness and astuteness of the detectives the stumbling-block in their way; and it would be so easy to get the notes changed by others—the dishonesty of ordinary human beings would serve his purpose.

His mood had changed now to one of exultation. He told himself time after time that he was right. The law would condemn him, but morally he was right, and had only punished the woman as she deserved to be punished. Only, he must escape. And—yes—he must not forget.

He looked round. There was still no one near; but his position did not satisfy him. Not a person must see what he was going to do next. He went on, and found a spot near the canal, where he seemed to be out of sight, and more secure from interruption. Then he took from his pocket a little looking-glass and a pair of scissors. Very carefully he cut away his beard and moustache, that hid the thin-lipped, wide mouth, and the small weak chin. He cut as close as he could, and when he had finished, he looked like a man who had neglected to shave for a day or two.

A barber would shave him now without suspicion. He was satisfied with the operation. The glass showed him a face so changed that it startled him to look at it. He glanced at his watch—it was time to start for the station, where his luggage had been waiting since the day before, if he meant to get shaved on the way there.

He walked a little way, and sat down again. 'How well everything has been thought out!' he said to himself. All would succeed. With a new name, and in another country, without that drunken, faithless, beautiful woman, he would grow happy again. He had only meant to sit down for a minute or two, but his thoughts rambled and became nonsense, and suddenly he fell into a deep sleep. He had been overtaxed.

An hour passed. The train that he had intended to take steamed out of the station, and still he slept. It grew dusk, and still he slept. When the park-keeper touched him on the shoulder, he half woke, and spoke querulously. Then consciousness came back, and slowly he realized what had happened.

As he walked slowly out of the park, his mind refreshed with sleep, he for the first time realized something else. In the awful moment when he had left the woman, he had broken down, and forgotten everything. The bag of gold was still lying on the table of the room with the green blind. He must go back and get it. It would be horrible to re-enter that room, but it could not be helped. He dared not change the notes himself, and in any case that amount would be insufficient. He must have the gold.

It added, he told himself, slightly to the risk of discovery, but only slightly. His servants had all been sent out and were not to return until half-past nine. No one else could have entered the house. He would find everything as he left it—the gold on the table and the figure of the woman on the couch. He would let himself in with his latch-key. No passer-by would take any notice of so ordinary an incident. He had no occasion to hurry now, and he turned into the first barber's shop that he saw. His mind was as alert now as it had been when he first formed his scheme.

'Let me have your best razor,' he said; 'my skin's tender; in fact, for the last two or three days I haven't been able to shave at all.'

He chatted with the barber about horse-racing, and said that he himself had a couple of horses in training. Then he inquired the way to Piccadilly, saying that he was a stranger in London, and seemed to take careful note of the barber's directions.

He walked briskly away from the shop towards his own house. A comfortable-looking, ruddy-faced woman was coming towards him. A shaft of green light from a chemist's shop-window fell full on her face as she passed, and the horror came back upon him. It was with difficulty that he checked himself from crying out. He hurried on, but that hideous light seemed to linger in his eyes and to haunt him.

'Keep quiet!' he kept saying to himself under his breath. 'Steady yourself; don't be a fool!'

There was an Italian restaurant near, and he went in and drank a couple of glasses of cognac. Then only was he able to go on.

As he turned the corner where his house came into sight he looked up. All the house was dark but for one great green eye in the centre that looked at him. There were lights in that room.

He stood still close to a lamp-post, just touching it to keep his balance. He spoke to himself aloud:

'It's green .... it's green .... someone's there!'

A working man passed him, heard him mumbling, looked at him curiously, and went on.

The great green eye stared at him. and fascinated him. Then other lights darted about, red lights, white lights. Someone must be going up and down the staircase and passages. Had she got off the couch? Was the dead woman walking? How his head throbbed! here were two nerves that seemed to sound like two consecutive notes on a piano, struck in slow alternation, then quickening to a rapid shake—*whirr! whirr!* Now the two notes were struck together, a repeated discord, thumped out—*clatter! clatter!* No, the sound was outside in the street, and it was the sound of people running. There were boys with excited eyes and white faces, and blowsy, laughing women, and a little old ferret-faced man who coughed as he ran. A police-whistle screamed.

In front of the door of the house a black mass grew up, getting quickly bigger and bigger. It was a crowd of people swaying backwards and forwards, kept back by the police.

The police! He was discovered, then. He must get away at once, not wait another moment. Only the green light was looking at him.

'Stop that light!' he called.

No one noticed him. The green light went on glimmering, and drew him nearer. He had to get there. He was on the outskirts of the crowd now.

Why would not the crowd let him pass? Could not they hear that he was being called? He pushed his way, struggling, dragging people on one side. There were angry voices, a hum growing louder and louder. He caught a woman by the neck and flung her aside. She screamed. Someone struck him in the face, and he tried to strike back. Down! He was down on the road. The air was stifling and stinking there. He tried to get up, and was forced back. Ah! now he was up again, his coat torn off his back, muddy, bleeding, fighting, spitting, howling like a madman.

'Damn you! damn you all!'

The crowd was a storm all round him, tossing him here and there. Again and again, he was struck. There was blood streaming over his eyes, and through the blood and mingled with blood he saw the green light looking.

There came a sudden lull. A couple of policemen stood by him, and one of them had him by the arm, and asked him what he was doing. He began to cry, sobbing like a child.

'Take me up there,' he said, panting, 'where the green light is; it's the dead woman calling.'

The policeman stood for a moment hesitating. For a moment the crowd was motionless and silent. Then one of those white-faced boys shrank further back whispering:

'It's the man!'

The Autobiography of an Idea

1: BEFORE BIRTH

I am a literary idea. Unborn as yet, I have not the incarnation of paper and printing ink which will be mine hereafter. I am conscious. I have knowledge without the usual apparatus for its acquisition and storage. I see without eyes, and hear without ears. I move as I will, and material things cannot hinder my movements. They are swifter than light, and just as swift as thought. You know, of course, that if an idea is going to come to you, neither locked doors nor iron walls will prevent it; it arrives inevitably and insuperably; you are to be its parent and make it come into the world.

You may be ranked as a genius because you are its parent, and (this amuses me) you will think that you are its parent because you are a genius. To the large eyes of the imagination, I might be pictured, in my unborn state, as a Puck-like phantom; only the imagination can see me until I select my parent. Ideas have that privilege. Human beings on very slight evidence-believe that they do not select their parents; but, on the other hand, they believe-on no evidence at all—that they do select their ideas. am not prescient, but I fancy that the man whom I select for my parent should be a very happy man.

I am a perfectly brilliant idea. I am new, and I am a master; the world will say it. I shall bring fortune and fame to my parent. Even now—when I am unborn and cannot tell the precise form that I shall take—I exult in my own utter goodness. This is, of course, vain. But then humility is only one of the impositions of the weak majority upon the strong minority, to enable the weak majority to keep up a self-respect to which facts do not entitle it.

I decided to come here. Before me lies a vast mass of building materials, sorted out into houses and the like, and known on the eighteenpenny folding map as "London and its Environs." It swarms. It is too large. Let me see what is immediately before me.

Before me is No. 23 Harriet Terrace, Fulham. It is a new terrace of thirty-pound houses, and there is no external difference, except the number, between 23 and the rest. It is the residence of Albert Weeks, literary hack. Shall I enter, and bid Albert Weeks be my parent? I should bring him money and reputation. He would be able to live in a better house than this; people would come to him and say, "Albert Weeks, where *did* you get that perfectly splendid idea?" He would taste popularity, smile complacently, and subscribe to a press-cutting agency.

Shall I select him or not? He might possibly, after he had become my parent, be unable to reach the same level again. But that disaster rarely happens. Ideas and sheep follow where there are ideas and sheep in front of them; genius is more often chronic than acute. I do not think that I should have to reproach myself with having caused him ultimately the

bitterest failure—the failure of a man who once succeeded. But shall I select him?

Albert Weeks is married, of course, and has three children. His wife is well-meaning, but, I fear, a trifle under-educated. He met her in the old days when he was on a kind of a spree; his love-making was a kind of a spree; there was a touch of sheer spree even in his marriage. It was all irresponsible—enthusiastic—desperate; and the spree is well out of their lives for ever and ever—unless I interfere. They are still heart-fond of each other, though she has ceased to remark on his cleverness and sometimes is almost snappish, and he has no time to pet her because he is so busy for so little remuneration.

The front room in which he is sitting is rather sordid. They call it the drawing-room, sometimes substitute it for the nursery, and habitually use it as his study. There is a quaint gathering of antagonistic furniture. He bought as little furniture as possible at first—because he was no fool and knew that they would have to be economical—and he has added to it since on occasions when he could not possibly afford it. There are, for instance, two chairs from a drawing-room suite—two only. These are covered with pale green velvet, and the velvet is covered with dust.

On the chair nearest to the table at which he is writing stands a chipped cup of cold tea, surmounting the dust and the velvet. The cold tea seems to be looking upward with a grey, patient eye at the gaudy paper lamp-shade, the photogravure of "The Prodigal Son," and the smoked ceiling. It is a room that must always have had crumbs in it. House-flies go long distances in order to die in this room. They have died conspicuously and frequently in it. In one corner broken and bygone bamboo has now definitely despaired of ever signifying refinement; and in the one piano-sconce which is not broken lingers the stump of a candle that has wept its composite heart out over the stained keyboard—wept for the death of the flies, and the despair of the bad bamboo, and the general deadliness of everything.

There is on the table a handsome, black-spotted wedding present of an inkstand. In front of it sits Albert Weeks at work. He is rather a small man with sandy hair, and the frock-coat which he has given up wearing out-of-doors, or when, as his wife says, "there are people." There are not any now, for he is alone in the room. The expression of his face is careful. He has to be careful, because the editor of *The Inner Circle* was by no means satisfied with his last batch of paragraphs, and he cannot afford to be deprived of the guinea a week which he receives from that very fashionable journal.

The editor had said—though more rudely, technically and briefly—that either Mr. Albert Weeks would have to convey a more convincing impression of his intimate acquaintance with high society or *The Inner Circle* would dispense with his valuable services. The words that the editor—who was rather less fashionable than his penny panting paper—actually used were, "More *savvy*, or outside only, my dear boy, and don't you forget it."

What are you to do when you are too good to know the butler, and not good enough for the butler's master to know you? This is what, I perceive, Albert Weeks is doing, writing laboriously:—

"The season is dying fast, and I am sure that most of my readers will agree with me that it has been an unusually brilliant one. So, everybody was saying to me at Lady Ballingham's last night. By the way, Lady Ballingham must have the secret of eternal youth; last night she looked more beautiful than ever. As for her house in Park Lane, I have always considered it to be quite the most charming town house that I have seen in the whole course of my experience. Well, the long round of delightful and luxurious—"

Here he is interrupted, because his worn-out, striving, vulgar, respectable, loving, sharpish wife had come into the room with a blue paper in her hand. "Supper, Albert; come on now. Oh, you ain't touched your tea, and I was particular to bring it. Are you comin'? 'Ennery 'as broke the soap-dish in the nursery; that's what the cryin' was about. This here is Bilderspin's for what he did to the kitchen range. It's high—one-seventeen-six."

That is the last straw. His editor has bothered him. His work has bothered him. He is very tired. A paragraph—which was really coming out very nicely—has been interrupted. Money is very scarce. And supper is mere mutton, and his wife looks rather ill, and Bilderspin is one-seventeen-six. The combination overpowers him. The little man throws down his pen, stamps his foot, and swears like a mad blackguard—swears profusely.

His wife takes a step backward, as if to get out of the room. Then her face becomes twisted, she sits down on the music-stool, and suddenly begins to cry. She is shaken with sobs. "Oh, Albert! Oh, Albert!" she says, over and over again, and then: "How can you be so cruel? Aren't things bad enough without that?"

Then he goes quickly to her, and is remorseful. He is not angry with her, of course. It is only that things are going so badly. He takes her hand. She regains her composure. She is sure that he is quite overworked, but he ought not to give way; on the contrary, he should 'ope for the best. There is a good deal of make-believe cheerfulness over the mere mutton subsequently.

Now, then, shall I make this man my parent? If I crept through that sandy hair into the whitey-grey brain, what a change there would be. He would be conscious that he had got a new, tremendous, imperial idea. He would put down his knife and fork, finish the beer in his glass at one gulp, explain hurriedly to his wife that he was really inspired this time, and rush wildly at the handsome inkstand and his work. By the following midday I should be in manuscript. In six weeks, Albert would be famous.

In six months, he would have real money and no debts, and there would be more money to come. There would be a new soap-dish, new furniture, new dresses for his wife. 'Ennery would have toys and a go-cart; Albert would, on little occasions, have Heidseck. They would be off to the seaside for a fortnight, and do the thing well, and the personal paragraphs would say that Mr. Weeks and his family were spending the winter in Brighton, "where it is to be hoped that this new and brilliant author will not allow his pen to be idle." No, I definitely decide that I will not make Albert Weeks my parent. I am not a philanthropist; I am only an idea. I do not want to benefit Albert Weeks, and I do want to satisfy my own whim. My own whim definitely refuses Albert Weeks.

At the same time, I am in a great hurry to be born. I have knowledge, but it is limited. For instance, I believe that I am an idea for a short story, but I am not sure. I know I am a miraculously good idea, but I do not know in what way I am miraculously good. I yearn to see myself in my final form. I must positively get born. Well, let me examine elsewhere. Here, I observe, the traffic is being partially disturbed by a long funeral procession coming briskly back from the cemetery.

In the first coach is a young man alone. He is in deep mourning. He has drawn the window-blinds down. His hat is placed on the front seat. He himself is kneeling on the floor of the coach; his arms sprawl over the back seat; his eyes are glaring, hot with unshed tears; he bends his head and bites the wrist of one hand. I knew his name at once and something about him. He is the Hon. Charles Turnour Wylmot. Away in the cemetery lies the still body of Maud Farradyce, whom Wylmot was to have married two months hence if she had lived. The agony of his grief would not be doubted by anyone who saw him now.

Yet Wylmot is a man who has always doubted himself. He is haunted with the thought that he is a sham. He once doubted his love for his books, and had himself put up for a sporting club which neither interested him nor desired his membership. The reactionary fit was bitter, but it was short. As with his books so with his writing. In proud moments he believes that he is going to be a leader; he pays for his pride with days of depression when he doubts whether he is even capable of being a decent follower.

As with his writing so with his love. A few weeks ago, he asked himself seriously if he was not merely trying to be romantic, if he really loved this Maud Farradyce who was to be his wife. That doubt went before the pretty yellow-headed girl died. And now he does not doubt his sorrow. Yes, the Hon. Charles Turnour Wylmot shall be my parent. He shall bring me into the world. Now, as he sprawls in that mourning-coach, his wild, aching brain shall become possessed of me. It is a delightful whim.

In I go.

2: BIRTH

The Hon. Charles Turnour Wylmot has, later in the same day, in the solitude of his comfortable chambers overlooking Piccadilly, just recovered from rather an unpleasant fit of hysteria. Albert Weeks would have thanked God for me, but Wylmot positively does not want to be my parent. He would cheerfully sacrifice a year's income if by so doing he could definitely get me out of his head. But he cannot. I am going to be born, and this is the first part of the process.

The trouble is that I am inappropriate-horribly and grotesquely inappropriate; for I have discovered more about myself, and I find that I am a humorous idea. I am the newest, the most delicious, the most inevitably humorous idea that ever has been or ever will be. The bare thought of me brings a deep satisfaction right away down in the very pit of one's appreciations. At first, I am too great for laughter, but the laughter comes. It comes in chuckles; it swells and grows to shaking paroxysms. Here, in this room, but half an hour ago, Wylmot at last reached the full appreciation of me. It had been growing upon him ever since the moment in the mourning-coach when I first came to him.

There had been at intervals sudden smiles over his face, succeeded by an expression of agonised shame and contrition. But at the full appreciation of me he gave up the struggle and began to laugh. He threw back his head; he stamped one foot; he held his sides with both hands; he roared; he howled helplessly. He staggered about the room, doubled up with convulsions of laughter; he tried to stop, but could not; he tried again, and for one moment gravity secured a foothold; then it slipped and off he went once more, worse than ever, roaring, howling, screaming, purple in the face.

His laughter stopped quite suddenly, as great fits of laughter often do, as if it had been cut short with a clean stroke of a knife. He took out his watch, glanced at it, and—just as he had realised the full humour of me—realised the full horror of the situation. Three short hours before he had stood beside an open grave, wherein he did then most truly believe that all his interest and all the brightness of his life lay. He had wanted the world to stop because Maud Farradyce was gone, and there was nothing else of importance. He had heard the robed priest, Maud's cousin, reciting in a voice that tried to be steadier than it was: "From henceforth blessed are the dead which die in the Lord." He had become unconscious then of the service, unconscious of anything but the burning in his heart. Someone had touched him on the shoulder when it was time to go.

That was three hours ago.

And yet he had just finished a fit of the wildest, most uncontrollable laughter. He had been allowing himself to be amused. It was just here that Wylmot had that unpleasant attack of hysteria.

He has recovered from it, and has composed himself. His face is very white now, and he looks rather like a man under a curse. He gets out his writing materials. "Maud," he says softly, "you are not minding, are you? This damned thing has got into my head. I didn't want to think of anything humorous, but this came to me. Maud, it would make the dead laugh it is *too* funny—and I don't want to think about it any That is why I am going to write it all out. Then perhaps I may be able to put it aside. Oh, Maud, don't think that I'm irreverent and unfeeling. My heart is dead and with you. I hate myself for having laughed, but I had to. I will get rid of this idea that's haunting me, and then I don't think I shall ever laugh again."

He sits down, and at the top of the page writes in a large hand, "Ellen." It is the title of the story which is to embody me. He writes fast for half an hour, and then a servant brings in the lighted lamps.

"Will you dine in tonight, sir?" he asks, when Wylmot looks up from the paper.

"Yes—no—I don't know." He speaks a little absent-mindedly, with one hand on his forehead, shading his eyes, as though he held the idea there and were afraid that it would escape. I have no intention of escaping. "I'm busy; if I want to dine, I'll go to the club. That will be all tonight."

"Very good, sir."

The moment the servant has gone, the pen dashes down on the paper again, as though it had gained an additional impetus by being kept back for a minute. He does not dine out; he does not go to the club. He writes at lightning speed, only pausing to laugh from time to time more wildly than ever. He laughs and writes, writes and laughs, on and on, until he finds that the lamps are going out, and glances at his watch. It is five o'clock in the morning, and the stack of paper in front of him is the finished story—me myself—me, the magnificently humorous idea.

He draws back the curtain and lets the wan London daylight into the room. He realises that he feels very exhausted and shaky, goes to the sideboard in an adjoining room, and gets himself some brandy. He drinks two glasses of it in rapid succession; then he goes off to bed. He is too tired for any further emotion. Laughter and tears alike will be a closed book to him until he has slept. He falls to sleep at once, and sleeps long—heavily, dreamlessly.

And I lie on the table in the study, new-born, in a snow-white manuscript incarnation. Will my reluctant parent burn me in the morning?

No, I am safe—safe in a foolscap envelope, directed, sufficiently stamped, whirled about by postal arrangements,

It happened in this way. Wylmot came into the study rather late next morning. He looked beaten, humiliated, tired, and half-starved. He cast one vindictive glance at me, and passed into the next room, where breakfast was ready for him. He was rather a long time over breakfast. When the emotional heart is completely broken up, the ordinary blood-pumping heart will still go on with its work. So, with the other organs. Sorrow postpones appetite rather than destroys it. Wylmot had no dinner on the day of Maud's funeral; he had quite a nice breakfast on the following morning.

He came back to me at last, and I knew that he meant to destroy me. His face was intentionally rigid, the lip set firm, the eye merciless. Yet somewhere at the back of that merciless eye lurked a quite different, milder expression. The fried sole and eggs had done their carnal work; an incongruous geniality was struggling upward in him; he was going through the disgusting experience of feeling the better for his food. However, he poked the fire fiercely; then he lit a pipe, with the air that he did not care about it, but did not think it worthwhile to omit it. And then he picked me up, to hurl me in the fire. As he held me in his hand, his eye rested for one second on the front page.

In that one second my young life hung in the balance. It was a moment of terrible excitement for me. The eye glanced through a few lines, and I felt a shade safer. The eye twinkled. Then I knew that it was all over, and that my future was assured; Wylmot would not burn me. His habit of doubting himself had triumphed once more.

Of course, after that he had nothing to do but to sit down before the fire and argue it out with himself. The story should be published in *The Cosmopolitan*. Why not? It was unhappy, incongruous, wretched that a humorous idea should have come to him yesterday of all days. But he had not sought for it. He had even struggled to the utmost to put the thing out of his head. After all, if there was any harm done—if there had been any sign of want of feeling on his part—that lay far more in the writing than in the publication of the story. He would never put his name to it, of course. No one should be able to say that Maud's lover took the loss of her lightly.

And he would take no remuneration for it. He would forward the amount of the cheque that he received from *The Cosmopolitan* to some charity. Besides, what right had he to keep that story from the public? It might not be—probably was not—so splendidly and amazingly good as he had imagined, but still he knew something of his business, and he knew that it would be likely to be popular. It might cheer many who were ill and depressed, and add something to the sum of human happiness. And he did not think that the critics, with their Athenian longing to see and to hear some new thing, would miss noticing the novelty and spirit of it. Indeed, he had mingled feelings of philanthropy and self-abnegation as he sat down to write on deep-edged paper, a little note to the editor of *The Cosmopolitan*.

To a certain extent he deceived himself. If Albert Weeks had voluntarily surrendered, on sentimental grounds, his honorarium for a short story, there would have been something in the sacrifice. But Wylmot had a private income, more than sufficient for all his needs, and to him the surrender of the cheque meant nothing. His surrender of the reputation which he believed would attach to the author of *Ellen* did amount to something, for he had the weakness *cui etiam saepe boni indulgent*; but it did not amount to very much, because it is an exceedingly rare thing for a single short story to attract any attention at all, and although Wylmot believed in the chance of *Ellen*, he knew that it was not more than a thousand-to-one chance. Nor was there very much in his doubt whether he had the right, for the sake of his personal sorrow, to deny the public an enjoyment.

The real reason that swayed him was paternal love. He had made me and seen that I was very good. He could not commit infanticide. He liked to explain himself, but his curious mixture of intense humility and some subtle vanities always made a desperate business of it whenever the real explanation was some simple thing.

His note to the editor of *The Cosmopolitan* ran as follows:

My Dear Roger—If you will read the enclosed story, you will understand how gladly I could have sent it to you a few weeks ago. As I did not do so then, I do so now—but, as you will imagine, with the greatest possible reluctance. I send it, because I do really think that it is the kind of thing that I have often heard you say you want. The only condition I make is that my name shall not be put to it, or disclosed in connection with it. I send it you today, instead of waiting, because I am leaving England, and I am trying to put my house in order before I go, and to clear up such business as I have on hand. But I am sure you will appreciate how eager I am to get to some place—any place—where solitude and silence are possible. I fear that this will be my last contribution to *The Cosmopolitan*. If it were not so melodramatic to say so, I would tell you that from henceforth I am practically dead.—Yours ever, C. T. Wylmot.

Now I think it must be acknowledged that, for a man who was not, as a rule, a liar, this letter is from a liar's point of view distinctly creditable.

I hold that letter in my own, somewhat corpulent, manuscript embrace. It and I together, in the twilight seclusion of a foolscap envelope, are at present being whirled through postal machinery.

★★★★★★★★★★★★

It is all over. My embodiments have been multiplied, since *The Cosmopolitan* has sold out seven editions of the number which contains me, to a marvellous extent. I have been a phenomenal and unprecedented success. In the library of the country-house, in the rectory, in Mayfair drawing-rooms, in Bloomsbury parlours, in working-men's clubs, in public house bars, in England, in America, in the Colonies—everywhere where English, or an approximation to it, is spoken-I am the subject of discussion. There is a touch of the universal about me, and already the translators are busy. Enthusiastic critics have been more screamingly enthusiastic than ever before about me; the severest critics have unbent. I have the additional attraction of a mystery.

Only two people really know who wrote me—Wylmot, my author, and Roger Birman, his editor—and neither of them will tell. On the authorship of *Ellen* only two people have dared to question Birman: his assistant-editor and his proprietor. Birman has told neither, and quarrelled with both; it is the day of his glory, and he can afford to quarrel with almost anybody. *Canards* on the subject of my authorship have flown over the country in dense flocks. Albert Weeks has, as usual, drawn his long-bow at a venture; and, as usual, missed the joints of the harness. This is his little paragraph on the subject:

"The secret of the authorship of *Ellen* has been wonderfully well kept. There are probably not more than twenty people in London who really know it. When the secret is told, and—unless unforeseen circumstances occur—it will be told very soon, there will be howling and gnashing of teeth among various uninformed paragraphists who have been spreading their rumours on the subject. As an instance of the importance which the author attaches to the secret, I may say that one of the twenty 'in the know' is a butler who became possessed of the information by accident, and that he is to be rewarded for his silence with an annuity of £200. More than this I am, unfortunately, not permitted to say at present."

Of course, I knew from the first that I was exceedingly good, but still it is very pleasant to have it acknowledged. My success is a joy to me; it is also a joy to Birman; it is also a joy—and this is really terrible—to the Hon. Charles Turnour Wilmot. For in this latter case, I fear the reaction. Letters, forwarded by the secret hand of Birman, have come to him from the office of *The Cosmopolitan*. For many editors have been anxious to communicate with the author of *Ellen*, care of *The Cosmopolitan*. He has answered none of them. Yet, just for a minute, he has hesitated. At this time he carefully abstains from any thought of Maud; if such a thought arises, he puts it out of his head again feverishly. That is the trouble—he dare not think about Maud.

★★★★★★★★★★★★

Maud is apparently not to be denied. The power of the dead has come forth. Wylmot's heart and brain are filled with Maud now. He sees her eyes on him, and hears her voice in day-dreams and night-dreams. He is alone in his rooms, doing nothing, frightened, sickened, humiliated; it seems to him that he had once the belief that, with all his faults, he was at least a man of feeling and honour, and that he has now lost the belief, and that he cannot live without it.

He starts from the chair, and paces the room slowly in utter agony; his brows are contracted; his eyes ache; sometimes his hands close convulsively; sometimes he draws a deep breath, like one who is enduring a torture that kills.

It is the reaction. It began yesterday.

Yesterday he noticed that he felt uneasy whenever he looked at the little oil-painting of Maud that hung above his mantelpiece. He thought that must be because the portrait did no true justice to her, or because it distressed him that any other eyes but his own should see Maud's picture. During the whole period of joy in the funny successful story that he wrote on the night that Maud was buried, he had been ready with shoals of euphemistic cheerful arguments to prove that he was acting finely.

Yet, as a matter of fact, the uneasiness that he felt arose from a kind of fear. He decided to lock the portrait away with her letters in the bureau. As he was doing so, his eye fell on the first note that he had ever received from Maud—merely an invitation to dinner, written to save her mother the trouble, written in shy, formal language, and commencing with "Dear Mr. Wylmot." An impulse seized him to look again, by way of contrast, at the last letter that he had ever had from her. It was written in pencil, just at the beginning of Maud's sudden and fatal illness. It began thus:—

"They tell me I am very ill, Charley, and they won't let me write more than just a little letter. They say that they will send you a longer letter themselves all about the illness. Oh, my poor dear one, I must tell you! I got it out of the doctors that they think I am going to die, perhaps. But I'm not! You've made my life so sweet that I won't leave it. I can't die and be taken away from you. Do not be despairing, my lover; doctors so often make mistakes, you know, and I am sure that I shall get better. How could I die when you've made living so well worth while? Oh, dear lover, did any man ever love so finely and nobly as you! I don't deserve you—no, I don't."

The letter shook in Wylmot's trembling hand. It was with difficulty that he read on:—

"I cried so much last night, and you weren't there to comfort me, and I was so lonely. Why—"

He had to stop there. His throat moved involuntarily, and he was on the verge of sobbing. Moving slowly and quietly, he put the letters back in the bureau and the portrait back in its place on the wall. He sat down in front of the portrait and gazed at it—a pretty, yellow-haired girl with mournful eyes, who had loved him well and thought him noble. And God had taken her and left him to the composition of an intensely humorous story. Now that he has lost the belief in himself as a man of feeling and honour, he cannot live without it. Late at night he goes out. He goes down to the Embankment with the intention of killing himself.

He does not do it because he arrives there just in time to stop another man from killing himself. The other man, a stranger to Wylmot, is a young man with sandy hair—to wit, Mr. Albert Weeks.

"I think," says Wylmot, speaking firmly, but with a curious smile on his face, "you had better come back with me to my rooms and talk this over." He stops a passing cab.

"What's it got to do with you?" Weeks begins.

"You happen to have saved my life."

"That's a lie. You saved mine, though I didn't want your damned interference. You pulled me back as I was on the parapet. What do you mean by saying *I* saved *your* life?"

"Ah!" Wylmot says, with the same dreary smile, "that is what I want you to come and talk about. I also had intended to commit suicide. Surely that is sufficient introduction. Come now; get into the cab."

★★★★★★★★★★★★

At Wylmot's chambers the servant, with an anxious expression on his face, let them in. It vanished as he saw Wylmot. He had been nervous about his master, and he was glad to see him no longer alone and looking in better spirits.

"Have you dined?" Wylmot asked Weeks.

"I don't care for it," Weeks answered doggedly.

"No? Nor do I. We will suppose dinner. Francis, bring coffee. Yes, and we will have a bottle of the port." Francis recognised the force of the definite article.

Albert Weeks felt mazed and wondering. Were the events of the last few days that had driven him to desperation unreal, or was this unreal? The two men had drawn their chairs up in front of the fire. Albert Weeks sipped the fragrant coffee and blinked his eyes; he was in a kind of dream. Through it he heard Wylmot speaking.

"Yes, if it had not been for you, I should have drowned myself to-night. The sight of another man on the verge of committing exactly the same act suddenly showed me that suicide was running away. One should not run away. It is not brave, though brave men have done it through sudden panic. You have placed me under a very great obligation to you."

Weeks shook his head. "You saved me too."

"No, no, I saved you from an isolated act. You saved me from an entirely wrong principle. I do not know whether I make myself clear. But I feel the obligation deeply, and I will speak of it again afterwards. In the meantime, you should know my name." He handed Weeks a card.

Weeks glanced at it and said: "I have no card, but my name is Albert Weeks, and I used to live at No. 23 Harriet Terrace, Fulham. I was a journalist. I failed. I used to be on *The Inner Circle* but I got kicked off. Do you know *The Inner Circle?*"

"I've seen the posters, but I cannot say that I've ever read it."

"It's nothing much to read, but it was all I had to live on. I'm married, with children. It was very difficult to get along. Sometimes I got a short thing taken elsewhere, not often. I borrowed a little money on my furniture. When I got kicked off *The Inner Circle*, I couldn't pay the interest due, and so the Jews took the furniture. My wife and the children have gone to her married sister—a Mrs. Warboys. She wouldn't have me, and she grudges the shelter that she gives my wife and children; they'll come to the workhouse. So, I haven't lived anywhere the last two days. Tonight, I sold the last thing I had. It was my mother's wedding-ring. I thought I'd buy myself a good dinner before I died."

"Then why didn't you?"

"Oh, I'd got into the habit of giving my wife anything that I happened to make, so I went into a post-office and sent it off to her without thinking."

"Go on," said Wylmot. "Well, there wasn't much more. In the letter I sent from the post-office, I told her I had a berth to go abroad, and if I *could* make anything I would send it. I've cut my name off the linen. If I'd once got into the river, there would have been nothing to identify me by. So, she'd have got used gradually to being without me. And her married sister would have felt she'd more claim for support if she had no husband."

"Now I must tell you about myself."

"Well, of course, I know a little about you. I've seen signed things by you in *The Cosmopolitan*. I was never one of the lucky ones—they wouldn't take me on the swell magazines."

"Did you read *Ellen?*"

"Read it and roared over it."

"So did I."

"They kept the secret well. I suppose they didn't tell you who wrote it?"

"No, they never told me. Fill your glass again."

Albert Weeks did so. The wine was warming him, giving him a little more self-confidence and geniality.

"This is beautiful port," he said, "really beautiful port. I can't understand why you should have wanted to commit suicide. You have no money troubles?"

"None."

"You live in these comfortable chambers in perfect luxury, with a butler and everything. You can get your, stuff taken by the very best papers. I don't say that you've made a real hit, like the man who wrote *Ellen*, but you must be good to get into *The Cosmopolitan*."

"It's so much better, you know, Weeks, to be a good man than to be a good author. I had done a disgraceful thing. It did not involve public disgrace; it was not, in the eyes of the law, an offence at all. But it took away my self-respect, and I did not feel as if I could live without it. It was driving me mad. I would rather not speak of the details."

"Certainly not," said Weeks.

"Now I want to talk over some plans for you, but I must first write a letter. Will you excuse me?" The letter was soon written, and given to Francis to post.

"Now then," said Wylmot, standing before the fire, "as we have finished our wine we will smoke. A cigar? It seems to me indicated. As I said before, without intending it, you have placed me under a very great obligation. I feel sure that you, as a gentleman, will understand that I should like to show my sense of the position. As some slight acknowledgment of the great service that you have rendered me, I have just sent instructions to my solicitors by which you will, on my decease, receive a legacy of one thousand pounds. You want money now, and I want to give it you, but of course you would not consent to the humiliation of receiving a present of money. A legacy is a different matter; and one can take a legacy."

"I—I do not know how to thank you," said Weeks. "I could not, of course, have accepted a present of money."

"Now I must tell you my plans for you. You love your wife?"

"She and the children are—well, they're naturally the principal thing."

"Now it is quite evident to me that it is your duty to take them into the country for a holiday. You look overworked."

"Oh, I worked pretty hard, but it didn't come to anything. I failed."

"Very likely from overwork. Your wife and children, too, will want a change. You must be away at least two months. When you come back, I will give you a letter to the editor of *The Cosmopolitan;* he will do, I may say, a good deal for me. If you can write, he will let you write. If not, he will find some other remunerative occupation for you. And, I think, you would probably like to discharge any pecuniary obligation that you may be under to Mrs. Warboys."

"I should. But it is impossible. There is no money."

"Oh, some arrangement can easily be made. Why not borrow a hundred from me, giving me your I.O.U.? Even if it is not convenient for you to pay before my decease, the sum to which you are entitled under my will—"

"Stop," said Weeks. "It doesn't take me. You're giving me money; I take it with gratitude. You've saved my life, and you've made it possible for me to go on living. And you've done it all so kindly, treating me as an equal, and no one's been like this to me for a long time—and, damn it, I can't even speak about it!" He rose and turned to the window with a sob in his throat. in.

★★★★★★★★★★★★

Albert Weeks holds a sub-editorial post on *The Cosmopolitan* now. He has a very comfortable little flat in South Kensington. Wylmot did his best to live without self-respect. He lasted a few years, wearing himself out with work. He died of something quite commonplace.

But I am still remembered. I am still the standard of humour to which nothing more recent approaches.

The Eight Stories of the Muses

On a beautiful summer night of last long vacation, a cloud sailed slowly out of the west. The sun was going down; the honest worker had fallen asleep over his books, and in his dream was standing before a booking office in the Bay of Tarentum and asking for a second aorist return to Clapham; the jubilant whist player, holding the situation in his hand, had exhausted the trumps, and was bringing in the rest of a long suit the mere conversationalist had worked in that epigram again, and the mere athlete, who did not believe in that fancy kind of talk, had gone away to drink a little good beer; the fiery bedmaker had just gone round to the kitchens, to tell the men precisely what she thought about them: in fact, everything—except the cloud—was much as usual. But the cloud was extraordinary.

It was granted to me to see that cloud close at hand, to stand in its midst, to hear what was spoken there, while I remained unseen and unheard. I do not wish to speak of myself much, because it seems to me vain and immodest; but I must say that I believe the real reason why I was permitted to behold the Muses, and to hear the stories which they told to one another to while away the summer night, is that my nature is singularly pure, and good, and spiritual, and free from grossness, and beautiful. So, I feel sure, is your nature, my dear reader, although in a less degree.

1: CLIO'S STORY: CHARLES MARIUS.

With the Battle of Waterloo the last hope of Charles was humbled in the dust. Three years afterwards he was found by the lictors seated in a poor third-class compartment in the railway junction which was erected on the site of that scene of carnage, and still retains the name of Waterloo. Charles surveyed them from the window, calmly and un-flinchingly. "Go," he said, "and tell the Carthaginians that you have seen Marius seated in the South-Eastern Express for Charing Cross."

His request was never carried out. It was almost impossible to book through to Carthage, and it was too far to walk. With tears in their eyes, the lictors walked sorrowfully away to the refreshment-room. The train steamed out of the station and arrived a week later at Charing Cross, a little tired, but in fairly good condition. Charles Marius levied two benevolences on the arrival platform, and conferred a monopoly on the bookstall; but he was not looking at all well. The marshes of Minturnse, and a rooted dislike to being called a man of blood, had preyed on his mind, and made him appear haggard and anxious. He was met under the clock by the aged Menenius Agrippa, Socrates, John Bradshaw, the Spanish Ambassador, and others. John Bradshaw was naturally the first to speak.

"As Sergeant-at-Law and President of the High Court of Justice, it is my painful duty to—"

"Stay," interrupted Menenius Agrippa. "I once told a fable to the Plebeians, and it did good. It is not generally known, and it may be of service in the present critical juncture. Charles Marius, you man of blood, listen. Once upon a time the members refused to work any longer for the Belly, which led a lazy life, and grew fat upon—"

"Don't, my dear friend, don't," said the Spanish Ambassador piteously. "We know it by heart. It's all in little Smith."

"But it may do good," said the aged Menenius. "How far had I got? Oh yes—and grew fat upon their toils. But receiving no longer any nourishment from the Belly, they soon began to—"

At this moment a cheerful porter, with a merry cry of "Now then, stoopid!" ran a heavy truckful of luggage into the aged Menenius and bowled him over. This gave John Bradshaw an opportunity to resume his remarks:

"It seemeth to me that the time hath now gone by when the telling of fables might serve the body politick; and seeing what grave charges have been exhibited against you, Charles Marius, you man of blood, and duly proven before me, it behoveth us rather to inquire into the method which shall be deemed most suitable for your execution."

He went on to point out that there were many methods of execution, but that it was most agreeable to the sense of the nation that Charles Marius should be taken to a very small, very cheap, very dirty, very Italian restaurant; and that he should drink there one bottle of that sound dinner-wine Raisonola at eleven shillings the dozen.

"We hereby give our royal word," said Charles Marius; but he was sternly checked by the Sergeant-at-Law.

"We need nothing of your royal word, having in former times had too much of it. I myself will walk first, accompanied by the Spanish Ambassador and Menenius Agrippa. You, Socrates, will accompany that man of blood, Charles Marius, and administer to him the consolations of your philosophy. You others will remain."

The sad procession filed out of Charing Cross Station. Menenius Agrippa looked a little angry, and was brushing the dust from his toga; but the Spanish Ambassador and John Bradshaw were intensely stately and dignified. Behind them walked Socrates and Charles Marius. Socrates began at once:

"'Seeing, my friend, that you are about to be executed, let us speak of execution. For it is well to speak always of the thing which is the present thing. So, setting aside your misconduct under H. Metellus Stanleius in Africa, let us discuss this execution. Now, I have often wondered why to the many it always seems an evil to be executed. For if a will be duly executed, it takes force therefrom. Now, to acquire force is plainly to be reckoned among the good things. Therefore, to be executed must be good and desirable. Or shall we say rather that words have no meaning?"

"Go to the deuce!" said Charles Marius sulkily. "We offered John Bradshaw our royal word, and he refused to take it. So, we won't talk at all."

And he never said another word until they were all five seated at one table in the Italian restaurant. A melancholy waiter of no nationality brought a soiled bill of fare; he also added two forks and a mustard-pot as a kind of after-thought.

"Bring," said John Bradshaw, "one bottle of Raisonola and one glass."

"Ver' well," said the waiter sadly, flicking a dead fly off the table with one end of his napkin. "It will be a shilling, if you please."

"Pay afterwards," said John Bradshaw sharply.

The waiter shrugged his shoulders. "I am ver' sorry, but we mos' always ask for ze monny before we bring ze Raisonola. We haf our orders. You see we haf often had a trouble to get ze monny afterwards from ze heirs. Tree weeks ago two gemmens kom in and order ze Raisonola. They trink it, and die all over ze floor." (An expressive shrug of shoulders came in again here.) "We sweep 'em up, and throw 'em away, and they pay us nossin—nossin at all. It is all so moch loss." His hands were turned outward, deprecatingly.

"Look here, my man," said Menenius Agrippa quickly. "Once upon a time the members refused to work any longer for the Belly, which—"

"Dry up," thundered John Bradshaw. "We must pay," he added. "And it so befalleth that I have not my purse, but the Spanish Ambassador—"

The ambassador explained that he had only Spanish coins with him, which would not be accepted. Socrates hastily added the information that he always took his money straight home to Xantippe, and that if he was short that night there would be unpleasantness.

Menenius said that he had no money, but would be glad to continue his fable. "Let's see. Where was I? Oh, I know any longer for the Belly, which—"

"Do drop it," sighed the Spanish Ambassador pathetically.

"Silence," said John Bradshaw. "Charles, be a man, and pay for your own execution."

Charles offered his note of hand and his royal word.
He nothing common did or mean
Upon that memorable scene.

But the waiter refused them. And the five were compelled to leave the restaurant. There was a crowd round the door. When they had got clear of the crowd, one of their number was missing. It was Charles Marius.

The rest of the story is well known. Charles Marius escaped to St. Helena, and spent the rest of his life in collaborating with Dr. Gauden on a novel called *Eikon Basilike*. The failure of the execution preyed upon John Bradshaw's mind, and in a fit of madness he wrote the time-tables which bear his name. Menenius Agrippa became a diner-out, and acquired the surname of "History," because he always repeated himself. The Ambassador still lives in his castle in Spain.

2: EUTERPE'S STORY: THE GIRL AND THE MINSTREL.

The child came through the forest. The big trees grew close together, and creeping plants hung like heavy serpents from their boughs. The sun found its way through, here and there, among the broad, smooth leaves, and made splashes of light on the red gold of the child's hair. One bird called to another; every now and then there was a flutter among the leaves, or the quick rustle of some small live thing in the tall grasses and brushwood below, and a scented wind kept singing of a land of rest where the good winds go when they die. From far away one could hear the low roar of a lion, as he stood by the margin of the distant morass, looking over stretches of sand and spaces of still water to the line of grey hills that seemed to be the end of the world.

The child was very fair. Her hair was glorious; her eyes were blue; her young limbs were white, and strong, and graceful. Yet one might see a fierce look in the blue eyes, and splashes of crimson here and there on the white limbs, and her breath came quickly; for it was in her nature to torture and to kill, and she knew no better thing. In one hand she dragged along the body of a young wild cat, scarcely more than a kitten. She lived ever in the open air, and she was fleet and fearless. All the morning she had chased it, until it was weary; yet, although it was young, it had fought long and fiercely.

On the hand that dragged it along were the marks of its claws and teeth; thick drops of blood fell slowly on to its body, and its fur was wet and stained. The child wore a living, tortured, fluttering necklace. She had caught the butterflies one by one, choosing those which were brightest in colour, and had threaded a spiked tendril through the soft bodies to make herself the necklace. She liked the tickling fuss and flutter that the butterflies made against her smooth skin, as they hung there and died slowly.

A great purple flower, that grew low down on the ground, lifted its brightness towards her as she passed: "And, oh!" sighed the flower, "she is fair, and sweet would it be if she would take me and wear me gently at her breast." The child did not know the voice of flowers; but she stooped down and tore off the purple petals one by one. From the cup of the flower rolled a big golden bee: he had been sleeping there. For one second, he buzzed on the ground, trying to remember where he was and to understand what had happened. In that second the child had swiftly seized a stone, and so she crushed most of the bee, leaving it enough life to let it feel the agony of death.

She flung down the body of the wild cat, and ran on for a few steps, with a laugh on her red mouth. Then she stopped again where a nest was built in a bush with very dark leaves and little white globes of flowers. In the nest were three young birds: two of these she cast to the ground and killed at once: she held the third in her small hot hands for a second, and a kind of frenzy came on her, and she made her firm teeth meet in its neck. For a little while she stood shuddering, and then she passed onwards, but more slowly. Slowly she came through the forest in her fairness and cruelty, caring nothing for her own beauty, and knowing nothing better than her cruelty.

And it chanced that she came to the place where the minstrel sat in pleasant shade on a mossy curve of a tree's root. In his hands was his lyre, and music came from it like falling water. The child crept into the brushwood, and hid herself, and listened. And the minstrel sang:

Far away is the land where all things go,
The rest of the winds that have ceased to blow,
The peace of the rose whose leaves lie low,
Scattered and dead, where roses grow.
Far away! far away!

There the dead bird takes a song again,
And the steed has rest from the spur and rein,
And the dead man learns that all were vain
All the old struggles, and joys, and pain.
Far away! far away!

And the light on their eyes is a wondrous light,
Where there is not day and there is not night,
Where the fallen star once more grows bright
That fell into darkness out of the height
Far away! far away!

Let me win there ere the break of day,
Ere the first faint light o'er the hills grows grey,
I am tired of my work and tired of my play,
And I'll make better songs in the land far away,
Far away! far away!

The voice ceased; but the music of the lyre still flowed on, and the minstrel looked upwards towards the sky. No word of cruelty had been in the song; but through the music her first knowledge of gentleness came to the child, and she saw that she had been cruel. She crouched there amid the tall rank grasses; her face had grown whiter and whiter; her eyes were strained and piteous, but there was no tear in them. With trembling fingers, she unfastened the living fluttering necklace, and gently killed all the butterflies to spare them torture. Then she flung herself prone on the ground, with her forehead on her linked hands; her red lips quivered a little, but the relief of tears came not.

"Ah!" she moaned, "why was I so cruel? Why did I never know?" The wind played with her hair, moving it caressingly.

As the child lay there, and the minstrel played on and on, the sky above grew darker. There was no need now for pleasant shade. Over the line of grey hills that seemed to be the end of the world rested the storm-clouds, black and purple. Suddenly the air became quite still, as if it were waiting for something. Was it the roar of the lion or the voice of the storm that sounded dimly afar off?

Once more the minstrel raised his voice to song, and anger was in his eyes:

The pure white flower grew up in the way
Where the wild cat's whelp went forth to play.

And the whelp rent the flower for the gold within,
And a child slew the whelp for its soft warm skin.

And the lion slew the child for a draught of blood,
And the river swept the lion away in its flood.

And the gods dried the river in its deep stone bed,
And all from the flower to the stream were dead.

We are things that the gods make sport upon:
We shall have no peace till the gods are gone.

The child had raised herself to watch the minstrel. As he sang the last words the skies seemed to snap overhead; a quick flash shot downwards, like the thrust of ghostly steel. For a moment the child's eyes were dazzled; then the loud roar of thunder seemed to fill the forest and the sky. When she looked again, she saw that the minstrel had fallen forward on his face; by his side was his lyre, with the strings broken and smouldering; from his body, charred by the lightning, delicate strays of smoke curled up. The child came, and knelt by the side of the dead minstrel. She raised his head, and looked piteously upon it, for the beauty had all gone out of it now; then she pressed her little red lips to the blackened lips of the dead man, and went on her way. It was the first kiss she had ever given.

And still she did not weep; but the blood in her veins seemed to be as fire, and strange voices were sounding in her head. When the evening fell, she stood by the edge of the swamp. Out of a dim cavern crept an old lion, and looked at her with green, hungry eyes. His lips curled a little backward. The child called to him: "Come, then! I have been seeking for you! Torture me, and then let me die!"

The lion turned swiftly round, and fled with a howl back into the cavern.

The child wandered on. She ate the black poison berries, but they

73

would not hurt her. At last, when the moon was up, she saw a dark, deep pool, and flung herself into it; but the pool cast her back again on to the shore She was fain to die, and to atone; but the gods knew their business better than to allow it.

And still, she walks through the forest, seeking rest and finding it not, and she speaks to none. Only sometimes at night, when the golden moon comes up behind the low grey hills, she sings in a sweet child's voice a few lines of a remembered song:

> *Let me win there ere the break of day,*
> *Ere the first faint light o'er the hills grows grey!*
> *I am tired of my work and tired of my play,*
> *And I'll make better songs in the land far away,—*
> *Far away! far away!*

And the gods are immensely amused.

3: Terpsichore's Story: The Under-Study.

There was a man once—not very long ago—who was poor, but artistic; and during his life he had rather more than his share of co-incidences. It happened one autumn that he was amusing himself by wandering about a country that was good enough for an artist, but failed to attract many tourists because it did not boast enough places where you had to pay for admission. He had stayed a few days in a little village, where there was one street that went tumbling downhill, sometimes with cottages on each side, sometimes through clumps of stunted trees, sometimes with the open heath all round it. It happened one night that he was wandering down this street, and had reached one of those places where the street turned into a country lane for a time, or rather for a space. He was smoking, and humming to himself a song that he had heard Viola sing a few months before.

Viola had taken very fair hold of the town that season. It was not only that she sang divinely; she was beautiful, and a little mysterious. The numerous stories told about her were rendered probable by her beauty, which was rather wicked; but no one could be certain about them because she was so mysterious. Besides, many of the stories were self-contradictory.

On one side of the road was a cottage, standing by itself, and partly screened by the shrubs which grew in the small garden in front of it. Here the man stopped short, for the lower windows of the cottage were open, and from within he could hear someone singing the very song which he had just been humming. Someone? Why, it could be no other than Viola herself who was singing it like that! He had always been interested in Viola, although he had seen her only on the stage. It was her reputation that she loved splendour and luxury. What could she be doing in this quiet, out-of-the-way village?

He leaned over the low garden gate, resting his elbows on the top of it, and listened until the song's conclusion. The room in the cottage was brightly lighted, and the curtains were not drawn over the window; he had heard rightly; it was Viola. He could see her distinctly. She was standing with her face towards the garden; and the man watched her attentively. The mystery increased. Her dress was brilliant, not the dress that a woman would put on in solitude and in a country village. She was wearing her diamonds too—those diamonds about which every story had been told except the true one. What was the reason for it all? Was this simply her passion for splendour, existing even when the splendour was to have no witnesses. The little, shabby, taciturn old woman who acted as her companion in London was seated at the piano, and had been playing the music for her song. But surely Viola would not have made herself so magnificent simply on her account.

It suddenly dawned on him that he was doing rather a mean thing by watching Viola in this way. He would not look any more, but he would wait, in case she should be going to sing again. That was love of music—not curiosity.

But even as he was making this decision the door of the cottage opened, and Viola came out. She walked straight up the pathway towards the gate on which the man was leaning; there was not the least hesitation about her.

"I wonder how on earth she managed to see me in this darkness?" he thought. "Well, I'm not going to run away. I will wait, and make my apologies to her. I expect she will be angry with me. Well, she should not leave the windows open when she sings, if she does not want people to stop and listen."

As she drew near to him, she murmured a few words in Italian, as if she were pleased about something; he conjectured that much, for he could not understand Italian. Then she astonished him by placing her hands on his shoulders, and kissing him, once, passionately.

It flashed across him for an instant that she had been expecting someone else, and had made a mistake. Now he understood the dress, the diamonds—everything.

"Excuse me, my dear lady," he said, "but you are kissing the wrong face—are you not?" He afterwards thought that he might have expressed himself better, but he was agitated.

She, on the other hand, never lost her composure for a second. She spoke in English, with the faintest possible stammer:

"Yes, th—thanks; it *is* the wrong face. Would you t—take it away?"

He retired at once, walked twenty yards down the road, and then met the full humour of the situation. He laughed a long, suppressed laugh. He went on and on, away from the village, out over the heath, away from the haunts of men. And, as he walked, the humour of the situation vanished again; but the night was full of her music, her queenliness, the fragrant charm of her presence. "Viola," he said softly, "Viola, what a heavenly mistake!"

Three years passed away. The poor but artistic man grew slowly wealthy in those years. The exaltation of that night never left him; he was full of brightness and happiness; his work was all light and strength. He grew popular—partly by reason of his excellent spirits, and partly because of his finer qualities. His luck was proverbially good; but he had enough hope, optimism, and vigour to have carried him safely through the most trying fortunes. His reputation was at its brightest when his death came.

He was in an accident—a commonplace railway accident—an accident that passed over a dishonest commercial traveller in one compartment, and killed the artist in the next. There was a short period, however, chiefly occupied by delirium, between the accident and the man's death.

It was at the end of the delirium that he turned to the friend who was by his bedside, and asked abruptly:

"Have I been speaking of Viola?"

"Yes; of course, I wouldn't—"

"Of course. All the time?"

"All the time."

"Were you surprised?"

"Well, I have known you most of your life, and I never heard you speak of her before—not in that way at all. I did not know that you had been her lover."

"I was not. But once, before she left England, I was—I was her lover's under-study. I have lived on it ever since," he added, after a pause.

Then, through some queer freak of the brain, the humour of the mistaken kiss appealed to him again, and he began to laugh—uncontrollably, as if the thing had just happened.

Laughter was the worst thing possible for him in that state. He died laughing.

4: MELPOMENE'S STORY: THE CURSED PIG

A watchman stood on a lonely tower, looking eastward, and whistling "Wait till the clouds roll by," shredding it in as a remedy against impatience. And that watchman was nothing if he was not classical.

He pondered upon the history of the house. For the master was away from home, having gone to a lonely place not marked on the maps, in order to make atonement for his crime. Ten years before he had eaten a veal-and-ham pie, in which, owing to the inadvertence of the cook, his eldest daughter had taken the place of the veal-and-ham. And the cook's carelessness had been entirely due to absence of mind: he was distraught because his son had just murdered his aunt, and the son had murdered the aunt because his mind was unhinged owing to a sudden depreciation in nitrates, which he had bought largely.

And the gods had caused the nitrates to depreciate because one of the directors hadn't sacrificed anything except one thigh slice, rather fat, for the last two years. And the director hadn't sacrificed anything else, because he got his butcher's meat under contract and the butcher had bilked him. And the butcher had been compelled to bilk him, because the gods had sent a murrain on all the cattle in the world, to punish one pig that they had a spite against.

This was not quite the ordinary curse, descending from father to son with the silver spoons and the mortgages. It went zigzag, like a snipe. Many people had taken snap-shots at it with sacrifices, but they hadn't been able to stop it. Nobody knew where that curse was going to next; so, a general interest in it prevailed. Teiresias had taken a long prayer at it, just as it was hopping from the director to the cook's family, and missed badly. And now the master of the watchman's house by name Eustinkides had fired a ten-years' penance at it. Some thought he'd hit it; others said it was lying low, and would get up again in a minute.

This distressed the watchman. He felt uneasy. It was one of those frisky curses, with an everlasting ricochet about it, going on like sempiternal billiards with a bad cushion. He did not think it probable, of course, that it would hit him. He was in such a very humble position in life. But still he would have felt more comfortable if he could have seen that curse getting to work somewhere else. It was not a pleasant thing to have hanging about the house.

In the meantime, he awaited the coming of Eustinkides. The master had ordered that at the moment when he appeared in sight the hot water should be turned into the bath. For, during the ten years' penance in the place not recognised by the Atlas, he had carefully abstained from all manner of washing, and had not so much as breathed the name of soap. Suddenly the watchman removed his eye from the telescope, and cried: "Listen, ye that are within the house. For on the road is a curious geological formation that walks, and a staff is stuck in a projecting portion of one of its upper *strata*." When it came nearer, and within hearing, the watchman called out to it:

"What ho! old alluvial deposit. How's your ammonites?"

A deep voice answered: "I am thy master, Eustinkides."

"Oh! sorry!" gasped the watchman, and disappeared abruptly. *Whish!* The hot water poured into the bath.

An hour afterwards Eustinkides lay in that bath, and soaked. As fragments of other climates slowly detached themselves from him, he thought of his penance and of his journey home. He had stopped at Delphi and put himself in communication with Zeus. "Could you tell me how to stop this curse, Mr. Zeus?" he called up the communication tube. He waited for some little time, and then a hollow voice replied:

"One pork chop and mashed. Two in order." At this Eustinkides had at first been angry; but afterwards it seemed to him that it might be a mystery. He thought of writing to Zeus to ask for a further explanation, but there was the difficulty about the address. He felt sure it would not do to write:

——Zeus, Esq.,
Up Top, R.S.O.

So, he dried himself slowly, and went into the study. As he sat there, his French cook was announced, to consult with him on the question of dinner. While they were talking, a smell came out of the kitchen and walked slowly upstairs; it was a strong young smell, but it was lazy. It lounged into the study, and sat down under the king's nose.

"Ah!" said Eustinkides, "that is very pleasant. What is that you are cooking downstairs?"

"Pork chops for myself and the watchman," said the cook.

In a moment the words of the oracle flashed across into the mind of Eustinkides. "I also will eat pork chops, but they must not be cut from the animal whereof my servants eat. So go out, and catch another pig, and kill him, and chop him, and cook him, and bring me the result."

So, the cook went out, and caught a butcher who was very careless, and demanded a pig. And the careless butcher remembered that he had killed a pig a month or two before, but he had entirely forgotten what he had done with it. At last, he found it in the coal-cellar, and brought it to the cook. "It's a bit dusty," he remarked, "but that'll all wash off."

"There's something wrong with that pig," said the cook as he prepared dinner for Eustinkides.

"There's something deuced wrong with these chops," remarked Eustinkides as he worked his way slowly through them. However, he felt sure that he was doing the right thing, and carrying out the commands of Zeus, so he did not much mind at the time.

A quarter of an hour afterwards he staggered into a chemist's. "Give us two-pennyworth of any quick sort of death, will you?" he gasped faintly.

"What are you suffering from?"

"Cursed pork," he murmured.

That was precisely it. The pig from which those chops had been taken was the very pig which the gods had such a spite against. Eustinkides was carried home to fulfil his destiny. His last words were: "Apple sauce!"

So, the front end of the curse run into the hinder end, and that smashed the thing up. Wherefore let us all reverence the name of Eustinkides, and refrain from soap and sin.

5: POLYMNIA'S STORY: AN HOUR OF DEATH.

It happened one day that Zeus was in a bad temper—a thoroughly bad temper. When this took place the whole of Olympus knew it. John Ganymede knew it. He had grown respectable and middle-aged. He was inclined to be portly, and still more inclined to give his views on anything to anybody. Just at present he was standing in his pantry, polishing glasses, and talking to the Deputy Cloud-controller.

"There's no pleasin' of him, when he's like that," said Ganymede, shaking his bald respectable head. "Last night he was suthin' awful. 'Ganymede,' he says to me, when I brings him his whisky last thing afore he goes to bed, 'you can pour it out for me.' So, I does. 'And you can put hot water in it.' So, I does again. 'I think a couple of lumps of sugar would improve it—and a little bit of lemon peel—don't you,

Ganymede?' 'Yessir, suttinly sir,' I says, and puts 'em in. 'Grate a little nutmeg on the top.' I were surprised, o' course, but I did it. ' Stick a couple of spoonfuls of Maraschino into it.' All this time he's lookin' as quiet and gentle as a hangel.

"There wasn't no Maraschino, and I had to go down to the cellar and fetch it. I measures it out careful, and says nothing. 'I'll have a large lump of ice in it, and two straws.' I thought his poor 'ead must be going, but it wasn't my place to make no remarks. I just carries out the horder. 'Have you done all that, Ganymede?' he asks, drowsy-like. 'Yessir, suttinly sir,' says I. 'Well, there,' says he, 'you—several blanks—now you can run round, and see if you can find a dog that's such a Zeus-forsaken fool as to drink it—because I ain't going to.' And with that he goes off into his bedroom, screamin' an' laughin' an' swearin' like a maniac. Now that ain't no way to be'ave."

The Deputy Cloud-controller could sympathise. That very morning Zeus had sent for him, and demanded:

"How's the wind?"

"Due East," said the Deputy.

"Then make it due West."

The Deputy bowed, retired, and made it due West. In ten minutes' time he was summoned before Zeus again.

"Make it East and West and South and North all at once," said Zeus.

"I can't," said the Deputy.

"Then consider yourself discharged," roared Zeus.

"Then consider *yourself* a blighted idiot," replied the Deputy indiscreetly, getting ready to dodge a thunderbolt,

"So, I do," said Zeus, who never was very expected. "Go away, and send me someone else to be angry with. You're stale."

The Deputy Cloud-controller had found some difficulty in getting anyone to go.

"What am I to do, Mr. Ganymede?" said the Deputy despairingly. "They all say that it's more than their lives are worth. And the females won't stand his language. I must send someone, or I shall get discharged in real earnest."

"Well, pussonally," said Ganymede, "I should be very glad to oblige you, but leave this 'ere glass and plate I can't. Now, there's the Clerk of the Curses. He's pretty tough. Why don't you send him?"

"So, I would," said the Deputy, "but he's away on his holiday."

"Then there's the Earth-child," suggested Ganymede, looking a little ashamed of himself.

No one quite knew how the Earth-child had come among the gods. There must have been a mistake somewhere; it was pretty generally known that she was to have been born in Arcadia. There was something of a scandal about it, too. But there she was, generally petted and liked, and happy enough among the gods.

"Yes, there's the Earth-child," said the Deputy, and he too looked a little ashamed of himself. They talked together a little while longer, and then the Deputy went away, suffering badly from conscience.

A few minutes afterwards the Earth-child walked fearlessly into the hall where Zeus was seated. She had red hair, and an intelligent face. She was bright, and affectionate, and twelve years old, and not afraid of anything.

"I heard you wanted to be angry with me, Zeus," said the child.

Zeus looked at her grimly. "I should prefer something rather bigger."

"Why do you want to be angry?" the child asked.

"Because I've done everything, and know almost everything, and I'm quite sick of everything."

"Music?" suggested the child.

"Sick of it!"

"Love?"

"Everything—everything, I tell you," said Zeus hastily. "I'm tired of eating, drinking, loving, hating, sleeping, walking, talking, killing—everything."

"I'm sorry for you, Zeus," said the child, with a sigh. "Couldn't you die?" she suggested afterwards, seriously.

Zeus frowned. "No, no—not that," he said. There was a moment's pause. Zeus was thinking; and, as he thought, his face grew very ugly. He was immortal, but to a certain extent his immortality was conditioned. He might die at any moment he chose, and remain dead for an hour. If at the end of that hour any one would put his lips on the lips of Zeus, and draw in his breath, then Zeus would come back to life, and he that so drew in his breath would die. But if no one did that, then Zeus himself would be dead for ever. Zeus had never ventured on the experiment; he knew that no one loved him enough. But he might play on the simplicity of the child. And take her life? No, he could not do that. But he would ask her.

"Earth-child," he said, "will you do something for me?"

"Yes, Zeus—anything that will make you happy again."

81

It was horribly tempting. Should he try this one thing of which he knew nothing, of which he was not tired? Yes, he must.

"I am going to sleep," he said rapidly. "I will turn this hour-glass here, and when the last grain of sand is running out, you must put your lips to mine and draw in your breath. Then I shall wake up again, and be happy."

The child stared at him with wondering eyes. "I will do it," she said.

A minute afterwards Zeus was lying dead, and the child was watching him, and in the hour-glass the sand was running out slowly. Time passed, and the child, as she watched, saw that his face was changing queerly. It was not quite like the face of one who slept. Suddenly she crept to his side, and put one hand over his heart. It was motionless. "Zeus!" she called, in a loud whisper. He did not answer, and she knew then that he was dead.

"But shall I wake him?" she said, watching the running sand.

As the last grains ran out, she bent over him, and did what he had said. He sat up with a gasp, and a look of horror died slowly out of his face. And the child lay prone on the floor, face downwards.

Zeus hardly thought of her. "Take that away," he said to Ganymede, who entered the hall just then. Ganymede went pale to the lips, but he lifted the white burden in his arms, and carried her out. "I wish we hadn't sent her," he sighed to the Deputy Cloud-controller; "I would have gone myself, if I'd known."

"I wish you had," said the Deputy. "Both of us together are not worth her."

Zeus had forgotten her. He could think only of the things he had known in that horrible hour. "I will never die again," he said to himself; and for many nights he could not sleep.

6: Calliope's Story: The Last Straw.

There was once a man, an Athenian, who was the opposite of all that he wanted to be. The gods had made him for a joke, and a very good joke he was; but as a man he was a failure.

To start with, he desired to have a perfect body and then to despise it. He wanted to be beautiful, and strong, and think nothing of it. Yet he thought a good deal of the bent piece of ugliness which was the nearest he could do to a perfect body. For he had nothing he wanted, and could do nothing he wanted. Sometimes he made good resolutions and tried to lead a fine life; then the gods dug one another in the ribs, and rolled about Olympus gasping with laughter.

They knew very well that they had taken unusual pains about that man's physical composition; they had afflicted him with several hereditary taints; they knew that he might make enough good resolutions to pave the whole of well, Westminster Abbey, and that it was a physical impossibility that he should keep any of them. "Let this man," one of the gods had said to Zeus, shortly before the failure was born, "be cowardly, sensual, and brutal." Then Zeus said that he was tired of making that sort. "Oh," the other god urged, "but we'll give him at the same time the emotions and aspirations of a noble mind. Then we shall see soul and body fighting, and the soul will get thrashed every time."

"Now, that is something like sport," Zeus had remarked, as he gave the necessary order.

So, this man went on providing amusement for gods and men until he was twenty-five years of age. Sometimes he, unfortunately, was quite unable to laugh at himself. Then he wrote verses. At other times he laughed at himself very well—often in self-defence, because it made other men let him off easier and then he would tear his verses up.

On that last day he lay in bed in the morning and shivered. He had slept for a little while—he had seen to that before he went to bed—but he was wide awake now, and his head was burning, and his thoughts were of the kind that tighten the muscles of the body and are likely nowadays to lead on to padded rooms. For the day before he had been found out; one act of fatal cowardice on his part—such cowardice as no one could forgive—had cost a girl her life, and this girl was the sister of his own familiar friend. There was plenty of variety about his thoughts.

Sometimes he felt like a murderer. Sometimes he heard the dead girl's brother speaking awful things to him, contemptuous, heart-broken words. There was no hope of concealment, no pretty story that he could tell. It had all been seen and known. In his dreams that night he had been through the whole scene again, but his own part had been altered. In his dream he had been equal to the occasion taken the plunge, rescued the girl, and been welcomed with praise and honour, and he had walked back through the streets of Athens feeling more happy than a god. Suddenly he awoke and recalled the facts. The girl whom he had loved was dead—dead through his own cowardice. It was such loathly cowardice that he shuddered to think of it. All men would hate him, and yet their hatred would be nothing to his own hatred for himself. Every thought was a torture, a knife that went into his heart and brain, fiercely and with regular beat, stabbing and stabbing.

He sprang from his bed, and dressed himself hurriedly. The house seemed to him to be strangely quiet. He called—in a parched, husky voice—and no one answered. All had left him: the very slaves had run away from such a master, and he was alone. No one, he thought, would come near him now. He had served as a laughing-stock for his friends: he was now too despicable to be laughed at. If you wish the villain of your drama to be hissed as villain was never hissed before, make him during the first two acts the low comedian of the piece.

The man was trembling and shuddering. He made a small fire, and crouched down by it. Ah, if he only had it to do again! A million deaths were better than such torture as this. An impulse—irresistible almost—came over him to shriek aloud and to tear with his hands at something. Could he be going mad? The thought horrified him. He fetched wine, and drank it, and tried to calm himself, crouching down by the fire again. Suddenly he heard footsteps, and presently one of his old companions—and the worst man in Athens—stood before him.

"You cur!" said his old companion.

"Leave me alone!" gasped the crouching figure. "Leave me alone, or I will kill you."

"You know that you dare not touch me."

The coward knew it. It was true. The long knife which he had grasped fell from his fingers. "Leave me," he cried again piteously; "you can say nothing of me which I have not said of myself. You cannot hate me as I hate myself. Leave me! leave me!"

Then, with a gesture of disgust and contempt, the worst man in Athens left him. And now the strength of the wine mastered the coward, and he slept. This time dream followed dream, and every dream was cruel. It was late in the evening when he awoke. The only light in the room was that which came from the dying embers of the fire. By that light he saw to his horror the figure of a child standing there—a white-faced child, with awe in her eyes—the younger sister of the girl whose death his cowardice had caused.

"I have a message for you," she said. "As I slept this afternoon she came to me, and bade me tell you that she knows all about it, and that you could not help it; the gods made you so; for the gods are strong, and it is fitting that we should be very patient."

The crouching coward said nothing.

Then the child came quickly to him and kissed his ugly face. "I am very sorry, very sorry for you," she whispered gently; and then she crept gently away.

The coward burst into tears, and, grasping the long knife once more, staggered into an inner chamber, and drew the curtain behind him. The child's kiss was the thing that had just turned the balance. From the inner chamber there was the sound of one who fell heavily, and then all was still—very still indeed.

"The worst of making that sort," Zeus remarked, with a jerk of his thumb in the direction of that inner chamber, "is that they so seldom last. But they are certainly funny. Personally, I shan't sleep for laughing tonight."

7: THALIA'S STORY: THE CAMEL WHO NEVER GOT STARTED

There was once a camel who had got sick of the menagerie business. And this was pardonable, because the menagerie had now been on tour for six weeks, and the trombone in the band had been out of tune all the time. There were other things that made the camel weary. The untamed tigress had a bad cough, and kept him awake at night. The showman had called him the ship of the desert at each performance, and he wanted to be called something else for a change.

On one occasion he had been lying in motionless dignity, and a little boy in a tight suit had asked if he was stuffed. He had been kicked by his keeper, ridden by children, starved by the manager, and jested upon by young men with penny cigars, who sucked intermittent oranges and called one another Chollie. He was sick of the menagerie business, and he wanted to get out of it. So, he made himself disagreeable. As he was passing the band-stand one night, he reached out his great neck and ate the trombone part to "Nancy Lee." This made him want to be a sailor and sing "heave-ho" during the rest of the term of his natural life. But where was the sea? He'd got no sea. He hadn't a notion, as people say.

So, he gave up his mind to being disagreeable again. He knocked down a beautiful child with golden hair, and trod on her, so that she died; and the management had to send her parents a *gratis* admission before they'd stop grumbling. Then the camel took up his position in front of the lion's den, and said sarcastic things to the lioness. This enraged her; and not being able to reach the camel, she ate a portion of the lion-tamer, to show her spirit. Finally, he walked up to one of the elephants who had a dummy tusk, and did a little comic dentist business, insomuch that the audience jeered at the showman, and the showman said several things which were not set down in the printed guide to the show. That night the camel kicked his keeper, out of reciprocity, and then talked very high talk indeed in the still midnight hours to a hyena who had seen the world.

"I am going away," the camel said, with a pathetic gasp which was the nearest he could do to a sigh. "My soul is being stifled—quite stifled—in this place."

"That's the bread," said the hyena decidedly. "We get nothing but bread."

"It's *not* the bread," snapped the camel. "It's the smell, and the low social status of the audience. I am going to seek peace and culture in another clime. I am not happy here; there can be no true happiness in a tent which smells of thirty-four distinct species, and penny cigars on the top of them."

"Well, I hope you'll find them—the peace and culture. I'm not much on pilgrimages myself, but I believe the first thing to do is to get started. Start away."

"I will," said the camel. So, he wandered slowly out of the tent, and was fetched quickly back again, and tied up, and treated with ignominy. He tried it again on the following night, and was kicked till he was more grieved than he could express. He tried it a third time, and then the menagerie management sold him to a circus.

Now, at the circus, the camel was at first exceedingly proud, because he walked in the procession, and cab-horses shied at him; but afterwards he grew very lonely, for want of other wild beasts with whom he might converse. But at last, the circus people bought an ostrich that was very cheap because it had consumption, and the camel's heart was lightened. Now the ostrich was a great romancer, and told stories of passion and bulbuls, of rivers and deserts. And the camel listened to all these stories with glowing eyes.

"I once," he said confidingly, "was going to start on a pilgrimage to find culture, but I was prevented. And after all it would surely be better to return to my old home in the desert and taste the sweets of domesticity." Now the camel had been born in the menagerie, and knew nought of the desert, but he was nothing if he was not a talker.

"I shall lie under the palm-trees, and crop the cocoanuts; plunge into the hot white sands for air and exercise; and I shall take a wife, and she shall build herself a nest, and sit in it, and lay eggs in it."

"My dear sir!" said the ostrich with a blush.

"And then my family will gather round me in the winter evenings, and we shall play round games, and go to bed early, and regularly enjoy ourselves."

"When do you start on your pilgrimage in search of domesticity?"

"I shall start, wind and weather permitting, tomorrow at one p.m."

But he did not start then, because he ate of circus bread, which was so exceedingly diseased that he fell on a bed of sickness. And the circus company saw that he would die, and advertised him for sale very cheap. And he was bought by an ardent young curate who had an enthusiastic but indistinct idea that the poor beast might be utilised to illustrate a lecture on the Holy Land.

Now the curate was a very humane man, and lodged the camel meanwhile at a livery stable. And while he was writing a sermon against all manner of pride, that night a message came to him from the livery stable to say that the camel had very bad spasms, and had kicked a large hole in the ostler. The curate, from force of habit, sent the poor quadruped a pound of tea, a bottle of port, and a tract called, "Mother's Mangle; or, Have you a Penny for the Ticket?" The ostler drank the port, and the camel ate the tea. So much tea made him very nervous, and out of compassion they put a cat in the stable to keep him company.

"Pleased to meet you," said the cat. "Will you sing something?" The cat knew perfectly well, of course, that camels cannot sing; it wanted to make the animal return the polite inquiry, and so get a chance of letting off an erotic song which it had learned in the stables. But the camel was not such a fool as that.

"I dislike music," he said. "I went in search of culture, and never got started. I also went in search of domesticity, and never got started. I am now going on a third pilgrimage—but it will not be in search of music."

"Do you like milk?" said the cat rather inconsequently.

"No," said the camel.

"Do you like being scratched under the left ear?"

"No," said the camel.

"Can you catch mice and kill them slowly?"

"Look here," said the camel, now justly irritated, "you're not the Catechism, and you're not the Census; what's the point of all these questions?"

"I was going," replied the cat, rather aggrieved, "to suggest some object for your pilgrimage, and I wished to see what you liked."

"Well, if that's all," said the camel, "I've quite made up my mind. I am going to search for death. I shall start, if the tide serves, at six a.m. tomorrow morning."

But he didn't, because he died that night. And as he arrived without ever starting, it has been argued by some that he must have been a genius. If he had stuck half-way without ever arriving, he would have been only a camel of considerable talent.

But these things may be otherwise. Things generally are.

8: Urania's Story: Number One Hundred and Three

There was once a man who was very careful. He saluted the sun, spoiled a good floor by making libations, sacrificed freely, and learned by heart what enabled him to remember the distinction between the *dies fastus* and the *dies nefastus*. In fact, he did all that could be done. And his number in the books was number one hundred and three.

Now, at the end of the quarter, Zeus & Co. were going through their books. It was wearying work and dry work. Ganymede was in and out of the office all day with liquors, and Mercury had been run off his legs with messages to the different departments. The clerk was reading out the items in a dreary monotone.

"Number one hundred and one. Dead. Cholera."

"That was a capital cholera," murmured Co., "and did its work well. Go on, clerk."

"Used to live in Eubcea. Killed to spite his sister, because she—"

"That'll do," said Zeus hurriedly; "I remember that case—a stupid woman, a very stupid woman—but pretty. Next, please."

"Number one hundred and two. Philosopher still living because he wants to die."

"Say 'usual formula' when we come to that. It's no good wasting time. Has number one hundred and two got anything unpleasant the matter with him?"

"No, sir."

"Ah, then—let me see—we'll give him a couple of ulcers. Mercury, just look in at the Punishment Department, and order a couple of large ulcers to be sent to number one hundred and two, and look sharp back. Next, please."

"Number one hundred and three. Living and prosperous. Regular in his righteousness. Further details at the Virtue Record Department."

"We ought to give that man some other reward," said Zeus, who sometimes suffered from a slight twinge of justice in damp weather.

"I'm not so sure of that," said Co., who was very healthy, and never got a touch of justice in any weather. "I hate a man who does everything right. It's so infernally hypocritical. Besides, it shows a commercial mind. He only does it in order to get something by it. I hate a commercial mind. I'll guarantee he doesn't do it out of affection for us."

Zeus sniggered. "Well, well," he said, "affection, you know, affection—" But here he was interrupted by the arrival of Mercury.

"Just look in at the Virtue Record," said Co., "and bring the detailed list for number one hundred and three."

Mercury was back again in a minute. "The Virtue Record office is shut, sir, nobody ever virtuous after lunch, sir—shuts at one, sir. The clerk's gone home and taken the keys."

"Well," said Co., "it doesn't matter. The man is obviously a hypocrite, and he's got no business to try and make bargains with us. I don't mind it so much myself, Zeus, but it *is* such an insult to *your* dignity."

"Do you think so?" said Zeus quickly. "Then he shall repent it. I'll teach him to call *me* a pettifogging huckster. I'll teach him to try to bribe *me*. I'll give him a lesson. Pass me those thunderbolts. I'll scorch, and blight, and blast—"

"Gently, gently," said Co. "We may just as well try and get a little fun out of it. We'll see who can torture best—killing barred. You shall go first."

So, Zeus, who had plenty of force but very little skill, went to work in the old-fashioned way. He killed the man's relations, burned down his house, destroyed his crops, wrecked his ships, reduced him to poverty, and afflicted him with the most distressing disease that the Punishment Department had in stock. And yet the man continued cheerful, saying that the gods were just and would yet send him prosperity.

"Oh, this is sickening," said Zeus; "I can't do anything with him. Now, Co., you try."

"You've not left me much to work on," said Co.; "you've taken away all the man has, except his baby son and his belief in us. I will give him something—a little accident—fever—cerebral disorder. See? Then he kills his child you observe? the child whom he loves more than himself. Then I restore him to his senses again. Pretty, isn't it?"

"Yes," said Zeus, a little sulkily, "you've won, Co. What made you think of that?"

"I don't know," said Co. modestly. "It was just an idea. He could not be tortured any worse than that?"

"Oh, I don't think so," objected Zeus. "You let me try again." Number one hundred and three still lay moaning on the floor of the room.

"You can try, of course," said Co.

Zeus still stuck to the old-fashioned plan of punishing by deprivation. There was only one thing left to take away—the man's belief in the gods. So, he took that.

Suddenly number one hundred and three arose. There was a chill smile on his face, and he walked out into the courtyard, and looked at the rising sun. "I was mistaken,' he said. "There are no gods. All is as it chances. Good is chance and bad is chance. Nothing matters any more. I would die if I thought anything mattered. There are no more values. It is the same thing whether I murder my son, who is dearer than life to me, or whether I give alms, or whether I eat my breakfast. I shall never be sorry or happy any more. Sorrow and happiness are vain and foolish."

So, he went back to his house again, and washed his hands calmly, and broke his fast.

"Well, I never!" said Zeus.

"Ah!" said Co., "you must learn the new ways. You're behind the times."

"Very well," retorted Zeus snappishly; "you needn't say it so loudly. I don't want all Olympus to know that."

The End of a Show

It was a little village in the extreme north of Yorkshire, three miles from a railway-station on a small branch line. It was not a progressive village; it just kept still and respected itself The hills lay all round it, and seemed to shut it out from the rest of the world. Yet folks were born, and lived, and died, much as in the more important centres; and there were intervals which required to be filled with amusement. Entertainments were given by amateurs from time to time in the school-room; sometimes hand-bell ringers or a conjurer would visit the place, but their reception was not always encouraging. 'Conjurers is nowt, an' ringers is nowt,' said the sad native judiciously; ''ar dornt regard 'em.' But the native brightened up when in the summer months a few caravans found their way to a piece of waste land adjoining the churchyard. They formed the village fair, and for two days they were a popular resort. But it was understood that the fair had not the glories of old days; it had dwindled. Most things in connection with this village dwindled.

The first day of the fair was drawing to a close. It was half-past ten at night, and at eleven the fair would close until the following morning. This last half-hour was fruitful in business. The steam roundabout was crowded, the proprietor of the peep-show was taking pennies very fast, although not so fast as the proprietor of another, somewhat repulsive, show. A fair number patronized a canvas booth which bore the following inscription:

POPULAR SCIENCE LECTURES.

Admission Free.

At one end of this tent was a table covered with red baize; on it were bottles and boxes, a human skull, a retort, a large book, and some bundles of dried herbs. Behind it was the lecturer, an old man, grey and thin, wearing a bright-coloured dressing-gown. He lectured volubly and enthusiastically; his energy and the atmosphere of the tent made him very hot, and occasionally he mopped his forehead.

'I am about to exhibit to you,' he said, speaking clearly and correctly, 'a secret known to few, and believed to have come originally from those wise men of the East referred to in Holy Writ.' Here he filled two test-tubes with water, and placed some bluish-green crystals in one and some yellow crystals in the other. He went on talking, quoting scraps of Latin, telling stories, making local and personal allusions, finally coming back again to his two test-tubes, both of which now contained almost colourless solutions. He poured them both together into a flat glass vessel, and the mixture at once turned to a deep brownish purple. He threw a fragment of something on to the surface of the mixture, and that fragment at once caught fire.

'This favourite trick succeeded; the audience were undoubtedly impressed, and before they quite realised by what logical connection the old man had arrived at the subject, he was talking to them about the abdomen. He seemed to know the most unspeakable and intimate things about the abdomen. He had made pills which suited its peculiar needs, which he could and would sell in boxes at sixpence and one shilling, according to size. He sold four boxes at once, and was back in his classical and anecdotal stage, when a woman pressed forward. She was a very poor woman. Could she have a box of these pills at half-price? Her son was bad, very bad. It would be a kindness.

He interrupted her in a dry, distinct voice:

'Woman, I never yet did anyone a kindness, not even myself.'

However, a friend pushed some money into her hand, and she bought two boxes.

✱✱✱✱✱✱✱✱✱✱✱✱

It was past twelve o'clock now. The flaring lights were out in the little group of caravans on the waste ground. The tired proprietors of the shows were asleep. The gravestones in the churchyard were glimmering white in the bright moonlight. But at the entrance to that little canvas booth the quack doctor sat on one of his boxes, smoking a clay pipe. He had taken off the dressing-gown, and was in his shirt-sleeves; his clothes were black, much worn. His attention was arrested—he thought that he heard the sound of sobbing.

'It's a God-forsaken world,' he said aloud. After a second's silence he spoke again. 'No, I never did a kindness even to myself, though I thought I did, or I shouldn't have come to this.'

He took his pipe from his mouth and spat. Once more he heard that strange wailing sound; this time he arose, and walked in the direction of it.

Yes, that was it. It came from that caravan standing alone where the trees made a dark spot. The caravan was gaudily painted, and there were steps from the door to the ground. He remembered having noticed it once during the day. It was evident that someone inside was in trouble—great trouble. The old man knocked gently at the door.

'Who's there? What's the matter?'

'Nothing,' said a broken voice from within.

'Are you a woman?'

There was a fearful laugh.

'Neither man nor woman—a show.'

'What do you mean?'

'Go round to the side, and you'll see.'

The old man went round, and by the light of two wax matches caught a glimpse of part of the rough painting on the side of the caravan. The matches dropped from his hand. He came back, and sat down on the steps of the caravan.

'You are not like that,' he said.

'No, worse. I'm not dressed in pretty clothes, and lying on a crimson velvet couch. I'm half naked, in a corner of this cursed box, and crying because my owner beat me. Now go, or I'll open the door and show myself to you as I am now. It would frighten you; it would haunt your sleep.'

'Nothing frightens me. I was a fool once, but I have never been frightened. What right has this owner over you?'

'He is my father,' the voice screamed loudly; then there was more weeping; then it spoke again: 'It's awful; I could bear anything now—anything—if I thought it would ever be any better; but it won't. My mind's a woman's and my wants are a woman's, but I am not a woman. I am a show. The brutes stand round me, talk to me, touch me!'

'There's a way out,' said the old man quietly, after a pause.

An idea had occurred to him.

'I know—and I daren't take it—I've got a thing here, but I daren't use it.'

'You could drink something—something that wouldn't hurt?'

'Yes.'

'You are quite alone?'

'Yes; my owner is in the village, at the inn.'

'Then wait a minute.'

93

The old man hastened back to the canvas booth, and fumbled about with his chemicals. He murmured something about doing someone a kindness at last. Then he returned to the caravan with a glass of colourless liquid in his hand.

'Open the door and take it,' he said.

The door was opened a very little way. A thin hand was thrust out and took the glass eagerly. The door closed, and the voice spoke again.

'It will be easy?'

'Yes.'

'Goodbye, then. To your health——'

The old man heard the glass crash on the wooden floor, then he went back to his seat in front of the booth, and carefully lit another pipe.

'I will not go," he said aloud. 'I fear nothing—not even the results of my best action.'

He listened attentively.

No sound whatever came from the caravan. All was still. Far away the sky was growing lighter with the dawn of a fine summer day.

The Girl with the Beautiful Hair

(By my own unaided intelligence, I chose the exactly right spot
at the farther end of the orchard, and with my own hand I slung
the hammock. Now that the day is hot and luncheon is over,
I take my book and go thither to reap the fruits of my labour.
And, behold, the hammock is already occupied with four large
cushions and one small girl—a solemn and inscrutable girl who
hears to the end a complaint of the cruelty and injustice of her
trespass, and then says kindly that I may sit on the grass.)

"Thank you. I am glad you do not want all the grass as well."

I do the best that I can with the grass, and open my book, and the
voice from the hammock bids me to tell a story.

"What, with no better audience than that?"

It appears that this is the charm. She has never had a story all to
herself before.

"There once was a girl who had very long and very beautiful hair.

("As long as yours?"—"Much longer and much more beautiful.
And if you interrupt me again, I will stop this story, empty you
out of the hammock, tie you to a tree, and teach you as much
as I can remember of the French gender rules."—"Very well,
then.)

As I was saying—there once was a girl who had very long and very
beautiful hair, and she knew it. Her sisters, who were as plain-spoken
as sisters generally are, were in the habit of saying that she was a perfect peacock. Her hair was very much the colour of a chestnut, and
she took the greatest possible care of it. It was a rule of life with her,
when she had nothing else to do, to brush her hair. Frequently also she
brushed it when she had other things to do. She never would have it
cut. She even refused a lock of it to her own mother. When she went
out for walks with her sisters she listened attentively as people passed

her, because sometimes they said things about her hair which she liked very much. Then she would try not to look pleased, and when a girl who is really pleased tries to look as if she did not care, she looks perfectly horrid. Her sisters remarked upon it.

Her father, who was a good and wise man, explained to her how wicked vanity was, especially vanity about one's hair. He showed her that personal attractions, especially if connected in any way with the hair, were worthless as compared with the intellectual and moral attributes. On the other hand, her mother took her to a photographer's and had her taken in fourteen different positions, and they all made such beautiful pictures that the photographer nearly committed suicide because he was not allowed to exhibit them in his shop window.

She reached the age at which every good Christian girl wishes to have long dresses and do her hair up into a lump, but this girl (whose name was Elsa, of course) would not have her hair done up, and stamped with her foot and was rude to the governess. In the end, of course, Elsa had to submit, for it is very wicked for girls of a certain age to wear their hair down. But she became extremely ingenious. She had ways of doing that hair so that it would not stop up, but tumbled down unexpectedly and caused great admiration. She would then pretend to be confused and embarrassed. Now, when a girl who is not in the least confused and embarrassed tries to look so, she looks simply silly. Her sisters told her so. Every single girl friend she had, and many who were only acquaintances, had seen that hair in its native glory. Some of these raved about it to Elsa's sisters, and were surprised that the sisters did not share their enthusiasm.

"She has such a lot of it," the friends would say.

"She thinks such a lot of it," the sisters would answer.

Now, Elsa and her sisters were not the only girls in the world, and they did not know all the rest; consequently, a girl called Kate came to them as something of a novelty. As she was called Kate, she was, of course, quite good. Katherine may be proud, and Kitty, may be frivolous, but Kate is solid. If you ask me if Kate is clever, I reply that she is a good housekeeper. If you ask me if she is pretty, I change the subject rapidly. There was nothing dazzling about this Kate. She was just Kate.

It is a sad truth that it is the people who are naturally the nicest to look at who take the greatest trouble to look nice. The woman who, so far as her face is concerned, makes the best of a bad job, is very rare. Kate was not a beauty, but she was sensible and resigned. She dressed herself very quickly in things that wore well. It was her boast that she could do her hair without a looking-glass, and everybody who saw her hair believed it. But as it happened, when Kate met Elsa, a change came over her.

"Your hair is perfectly divine," she said to Elsa.

Elsa tried to be politely bored.

"So kind of you to say so," she said. "I get frightfully sick of my old wig myself. It's an endless bother."

"And you do it so beautifully," said Kate. "I do wish you'd give me some idea for my hair, so that it wouldn't look awful."

"It isn't awful at all," said Elsa, politely. "I don't think I should change the way of doing it if I were you."

Then she went into elaborate technical details and showed Kate that the thing was bad and that improvement was impossible. Of course, she did not use these words, and was sweetly delicate about it.

Now, that night, as Elsa was having her own hair brushed, a horrible suspicion came over her. She put it aside as a thing perfectly absurd. It might have been a trick of the looking-glass. It might have been her own imagination. It did not keep her awake for a moment. But next morning one of her sisters came into her room, looked at her, and said: "What an idiot you were to have your hair cut!"

"I have not had it cut," said Elsa, furiously. "It's the same as it always was."

"Rubbish," said the sister. "It's three inches shorter at least."

"It's not," said Elsa; "and I wish you'd go away. I can't get on properly while you're hanging about talking."

The sister went away, and Elsa flew to the looking-glass. The cold morning light confirmed her suspicions of the night before. Her sister was perfectly right. Elsa's hair was undoubtedly three inches shorter.

That afternoon Elsa secretly and surreptitiously went to a great hair specialist. She had seen his advertisement, and she felt that here she might at any rate know the worst. He looked at her hair and said that it had become shorter from a shrinkage in the cells, owing to undue epithelial activity of the cranium. It was as well that she came to him when she did. As it was, if she would rub in a little of his relaxative she would have nothing to fear. He then sold her a fourpenny pot of pomatum for three guineas, washed his hands, and went home to tea.

But the pomatum was quite ineffectual. Every day her hair seemed to be a little shorter and a little thinner. This was particularly the case when she had been behaving like a peacock or like a spiteful cat. It reached a point when all her friends who met her exclaimed: "Why,

Elsa, what on earth have you done with your hair?"

Then she would smile sweetly and say: "Brushed it. What did you think?" But inwardly she was a mad woman.

About this time, she saw the advertisement of the Indian hair doctor, and she thought she could but try. I do not think the man was really Indian, I know he was not really a doctor, and I fancy he did not know much about hair. But he said that Elsa's case was extremely grave, and that in another week she would have been entirely bald. She must take a course of scalp friction; twelve applications for three guineas the application. She took them; and at the end of the course her hair was nearly all gone, her temper was quite gone, her money was almost gone, and she did not want to see anybody or to do anything except die.

And then unwittingly she did what was best for herself. To escape the sweet sympathy of her friends and relations she went away all by herself to live in a little cottage in a forest. It is good for a girl who has been seeing too many people to live all by herself for a while. It is good for a girl who has been long in a crowded town to go away into the forest solitude. Your soul must go to the cleaner, just like your gloves.

Now that there was no one to sympathise with her loss, and no one to attract by her beautiful hair even if she had still had it, she could begin to think of other things. And she thought about squirrels, and nuts, and blackberries, and sunsets, and streams that made silvery lines down the green hillsides. And every morning she went all by herself to a cottage two miles off and fetched milk for herself.

The old woman who kept the cows at this cottage was frail and old and always polite, but also, she was always very sad. She had the face of one who never ceased to suffer. After Elsa had been two months in her cottage, she suddenly saw that this woman had always looked really sad. The sadness of other people had never mattered to her in the least before; but now one day she asked the old woman why this was, and if there were anything that she might do for her.

Then the old woman said: "I have a daughter and she was very beautiful. None that saw her ever forgot how beautiful she was. And she fell ill of a strange disease so that her whole face became loathsome. No one but I can bear to look on her, lest their dreams should be haunted for ever."

"And she lives here, this poor daughter of yours?" asked Elsa.

"Yes; she lies in the room upstairs. They tell me that she will now soon be dead."

"I will come up and talk to her," said Elsa, "and help to nurse her, for you must often be away on your farm."

"No," said the old woman, "that is too much for you to do. I tell you that no one but myself can bear it. You must not see her."

"Look," said Elsa. And then she took off the big kerchief that she always wore over her head. "I had pretty hair once," she said, "and I have lost it all. I can bear anything, and I want to help you."

Then Elsa went upstairs into a room which was darkened, and even in that dim light she could see that this old woman's daughter, who was once very beautiful, had now become painful to behold. Elsa was frightened, but tried not to show it, and a girl who is frightened and tries not to show it, very frequently does not look nearly such a fool as she thinks. She remained there a long time, and when she came out her face was quite white, and she wanted to go back to her cottage and cry.

But every day after that until the end came, she went to see the sick girl who loved and adored her. And the end came one afternoon quite quietly. And the old woman did not weep at that time, but she blessed Elsa and went out, for the cows were waiting to be milked, and that must not be left.

Next morning when Elsa awoke it was very late, and the sun was streaming into her room. For a while she lay with her eyes closed, thinking over all that had happened. Each visit to the sick girl had been a separate terror to her, but now she grieved that the girl was dead, and wondered in her mind if there were none other for whom she might find something to do.

At last, since it was a shame to lie so late, she got up, and, behold, masses of beautiful chestnut-coloured hair fell far down over her white shoulders! She rubbed her eyes and said that she must be dreaming. But no, it had really happened. Her mirror echoed the truth. The glory of her pretty head had come back to it as strangely as it had gone. So that afternoon she mused what she would do as, sitting in the garden of her cottage, she made a wreath of white lilies.

And the next day she left her cottage in the wood and went back to her own home; and her sisters were all delighted to see her, and praised her beautiful hair, and were glad that it had grown again so quickly. Yet one of them said secretly to another: "Now she will be as vain and horrible as ever."

But, as it happened, she was not vain and horrible; she was really quite nice, so that the prince who married her loved her as much for the sweetness of her heart as for her angel's face and her beautiful long hair.

The Good Name

There was once a girl of whom her friends—that is to say her enemies—used to observe: "You never would have thought it to look at her."

Nor would you. She had the wondering and affectionate eyes of a child. There was not a vestige of cruelty in her pretty mouth. If there was any vanity in the way she did her brown hair it was the vanity that finds its best means in simplicity. Her voice was low and sympathetic. Her general appearance suggested, if anything, an unusual degree of shyness. The girl had left a trail of broken hearts behind her. She had done all that was mad, and wicked, and shameless, and delightful. But certainly, you would never have thought it if you had looked at her.

She was just twenty-three when she first of all heard of the flower which is called the flower of the good name. Everybody about her believed in the existence of that flower, chiefly, perhaps, because no one had ever found it. It was to be found only by the most virtuous among women. A few unkind words and their chance was gone. The most inconsiderable flirtation and you would never find the white flower. This girl never even looked for it. Her girl friends made a point of going to look for it every Sunday.

Uncharitable people said that they did this in order to improve their reputations. It was a way of saying that they conscientiously believed that they had a chance. But the shameless girl never went to look for it at all. Early on a summer morning she went for a bathe. As she came back from the seashore with her wet hair hanging down her back and not looking quite so nice as usual, she was conscious that she had swum far and that the morning was hot, and that it would be no bad thing to sit down and rest. Her seat was a boulder of granite. She sat there and whistled a tune-which was disgraceful and boy-like—and looked across the meadow before her.

And there in the meadow she found it—a white flower, shaped

like a seven-rayed star, each petal edged with gold and a heart of gold in the centre. She gave an exclamation of surprise, which was slightly vulgar. Then she bent down and examined the flower more closely. Then she picked it and kissed it. What was she to do next? The first thing was to take that flower to some man of science and learning and to get its genuineness fully established. Then she would go and visit all those cats, who, as she was well aware, were in the habit of saying things about her, and she would wear that flower conspicuously so that they might see it. But she would talk only of the weather so that they might think that her finding of the flower was to her but a trifle which she had always known must happen one day or another.

Then she changed her mind. No good woman could have changed her mind with greater rapidity than did this sinful little vixen. No, it was no good. All the learning and science affidavits and sworn statements in the world would never have convinced anybody that she had found the white flower. Really, she could hardly believe it herself. She looked back over her past—she was only twenty-three, but she had quite a good deal of past. As she thought out its tempestuous incidents there were times when she smiled, and times when her eyes grew sad, and once when she closed them altogether. It was beyond belief. It could not be true that she had found the white flower. Well, there it was in her hand, and the gold of its pollen had stained her red lips.

Then the thought came to her that perhaps after all she had found this flower not by virtue of her past but by virtue of her future; not for what she was, but for what she was to become. She took the flower home and pressed it between the leaves of a missal, and said nothing whatever about it. But she was going to be a little saint now, and on this point, she did not change her mind.

Years afterwards, her friends—that is to say her enemies—used to observe: "Yes, but you should have known her as she used to be." Such testimony, and here and there a little gratitude and her consciousness of her goodness were all the rewards that her goodness ever got. And of these, the last was most satisfying. There came an evening when she had watched the sun setting to music and felt too unearthly for anything. That evening she went to her missal and took out the flower and carried it with her to a man of great learning. He immediately fired three Latin words right into the middle of it and one of these words was "*vulgaris*." "It has sometimes been confused," he added, "with the flower of the good name."

"Really?" said the saint, with an intelligent smile, "give a woman a good name and she may as well hang herself."

"I beg pardon?" said the man of learning coldly.

She did not repeat the statement. She went away to find some lonely and appropriate spot where she might cry.

Miracles

1

Best and Bliss, at that time unknown to one another, enlisted at the beginning of the Great War, Best making a declaration as to his age which was untrue, but accepted, for Best was very hard stuff. At the time, Best was building up a small business as a greengrocer, and had recently and indiscreetly married. Bliss was the son of a poor parson. He had just taken his degree in honours at Cambridge, and was reading for the Bar, his expenses being meanwhile defrayed by a wealthy uncle.

The middle-aged greengrocer and the young student met somewhere in France, and became fast friends. Both of them had the gift of rapid observation and memory to a quite unusual and remarkable extent, and they had weird competitions to see which was the better in these respects. Best would collect twenty or more small, miscellaneous articles, and put them on a table. Bliss would be allowed to see them for five seconds, and no more. Without making any written note of what he had seen he was required to say, twenty-four hours later, what each of the articles was, and to describe any peculiarity that any of them possessed. Then Bliss would put Best through a similar test. There was a system of marking and the winner took half a crown from the loser. They were very equal. Neither of them ever got ten shillings ahead of the other.

It was while he was lying in hospital that Bliss thought out the code for thought-reading which the two men afterwards used. It was a very good code, involving no speaking, but certain movements so slight as to be practically imperceptible. But it was not a code that everybody could use. It required very quick observation and a marvellous memory. Later, Best learned the code, and they practised together. Occasionally, they gave a friendly performance, calling it *Miracles*. One of the war correspondents saw it, and gave it rather an enthusiastic notice.

Best and Bliss both did well in France, but at home fortune was not kind to them. Best's friend, who had promised to keep an eye on the business for him let him down, and the business was shut up. He also ran away with Best's wife, and she had taken to drink and miscellaneousness, Best considered that about balanced the account. Best broke the man's nose without showing much interest in the performance.

"More a matter of etiquette than anything else," he said to Bliss.

Bliss's career at the Bar had to be abandoned. His wealthy uncle died, and left all that he possessed to the woman to whom he had long been secretly married. And Bliss said that he supposed that after the war he would have to be a blinking schoolmaster. Blinking was not the exact word used.

"What price *Miracles?*" asked Best.

"What do you mean?" said Bliss.

"We might do it on the halls. We might do it at shows in private houses. It's my belief there's a living in it, and nobody here has come within a million miles of finding out how the trick's done."

"Worth thinking over, anyhow," said Bliss.

And ultimately, they did it. It was then that they took the assumed names, Best and Bliss, by which they are known in this story. They had the right to put certain letters, which both gain and deserve respect, after their real names, but these did not appear on their business card, which simply bore the words:

BEST AND BLISS

"Miracles"

Once more their fortunes turned. At the very first private engagement which they obtained through an entertainment agency, it chanced that Sir Charles Brotherton was present. He came late and left early as was his custom at such functions. He saw only the last part of the performance of Best and Bliss, but he recognised that this was something which he had never seen before, and for which he was unable to offer any explanation. He went up to Bliss and gave him his card. Bliss knew the name. Everybody did.

"If you and Mr Best can come to the office of the *Daily Triumph* for about ten minutes at three o'clock tomorrow afternoon, I think it might do you some good."

Bliss looked at Best. Best nodded.

"Thank you very much, Sir Charles," said Bliss. "We shall be there without fail."

They were punctual at the office and were shown up immediately to Sir Charles's private room.

"I've not much time," said Sir Charles. "Show me the best you can do as quickly as you can."

"Very good," said Best. "Will you ring and have my friend taken to some room where he cannot see or hear what goes on here, and arrange to have him brought back when you ring again."

"Certainly," said Sir Charles. And it was done.

"You will excuse me," said Best, "if I seem to give directions, but will you take some object from your pocket and hide it anywhere you like?"

Sir Charles drew a handful of silver from his pocket, selected a sixpence, and put it under one of the three ink-bottles on his plain roll-top desk.

"And will you also write a telegram which you will permit me to see."

"I will," said Sir Charles. "As a matter of fact, it is a telegram which I shall be sending presently."

"I think that will do," said Best. "If you will leave the telegram on the desk and close the top over it, you can then ring for my friend and we will start."

Sir Charles pulled down the top of the desk, rang, and Bliss was brought in. Best was seated in an easy natural attitude in a chair and did not speak. It was the impression of Sir Charles that he did not subsequently move any part of his body until the trick was over. But this was not quite correct.

Bliss talked slowly, but he began at once.

"Inside that desk, Sir Charles, you have an inkstand of walnut wood with three bottles in it. They are marked on ivory labels fixed to the wood, Black, Red, and Copying. Underneath the bottle marked Copying is the sixpence which you took from your pocket. The date of it is 1918, and there is a noticeable scratch right across it on the other side. You have a good deal of silver in that pocket—twenty-three shillings in all. Eight of the coins are half-crowns, and there is also a blotting-pad inside that desk, and the colour of the blotting-pad is green. On it lies a telegram addressed to Peterson, 23 Shell Street, Brixton. The message consists of the two words, 'Nothing do-ing.' There is no signature on the front of the telegram, nor by the way, is the name and address filled in at the back. You have no less than eleven penholders on your desk, and I notice that you write with a gilt J. But the telegram is not written in ink. That was written with a common indelible pencil, which you took from your lower right-hand waistcoat-pocket."

Sir Charles showed no signs of surprise. "I know something of conjuring," he said, "but I am not an expert. Are you prepared to give me a similar performance tomorrow afternoon at the same time here, when experts will be present who will suggest test conditions?"

"Certainly," said Best.

Sir Charles scribbled a few words on a slip of paper and handed it to Best.

"Good afternoon, gentlemen," said Sir Charles. "Give that slip of paper to the cashier downstairs. Anybody will tell you where to find him."

The slip instructed the cashier to pay Best and Bliss ten guineas, and to take their receipt.

At the next performance there were present two expert illusionists, a man of science who was also a spiritualist, a very good descriptive writer, and of course Sir Charles Brotherton. Best and Bliss gave a more extended and elaborate show, and left when it was over.

"How's it done?" Sir Charles asked the illusionists,

"Code, of course. Couldn't be done any other way."

"What code?"

"Well, we might have to see that show twenty times before we could state that completely."

"Good. Will you two do all that Best and Bliss do in three weeks' time for a fee of two-fifty?"

But they did not like to give a fixed guarantee, and besides they were very busy.

"I see," said Sir Charles, and turned to the man of science.

"Would you mind telling me your views?"

"There is no code at all. The amount could not be transmitted in the time. The gift of Mr Bliss. I take it is analogous to the gift of a good medium. He probably is himself a good medium, though, of course, he may not know it."

There was a shortage of news at the time, and Best and Bliss got two columns in the next day's *Daily Triumph*. A leading article dealt with them judicially. Either these two men had some supernormal gift or they were amazingly clever. In a short time, the public would probably have an opportunity of seeing them on the stage and could then form their own judgement.

The only thing that Beat and Bliss disliked about it was the interview with Professor Moon, the scientific spiritualist, suggesting that they had the gift of mediums, and the floods of letters from those who believed or were trying to believe in spiritualism, which immediately followed. They had been in war. They had seen the real thing. The idea that a dishonest medium should take money from a bereaved mother for pretending to put her in communication with her lost son, moved them to disgust, expressed in very plain and improper terms. They sent the briefest of letters to the *Daily Triumph*, saying that they made no claim to any supernatural gift whatever, and would be extremely sorry to be classed as mediums.

2

They had been in London for a year. Best had thought there might be a living in it. It seemed now that there was something approaching a fortune in it. During that year they had worked very hard and taken no holidays. But they were able to do the provincial tour which the agent had mapped out for them quite comfortably in a four-figure motorcar.

They had played for a week in Manchester. On the fourth night they drove back to their hotel after the show and had a whisky-and-soda as their custom was.

Suddenly Best said to Bliss: "What about that woman in black?"

"Yes," said Bliss. "She's been there every night and also at the *matinée*. Third row of the stalls and the seat nearest the gangway on the right—stage right. Wonder what on earth she does it for?"

"She looks pretty awful," said Best. "Looks sort of as if someone was hurting her. Must have been a good-looking girl in her time too."

"She looks to me about half mad," said Bliss.

They thought no more about the subject until the following day, when a letter was handed to them at the theatre, signed Edna Durnavel.

She said that her only son, Arthur, had been killed in the war. Ever since then she had been trying to communicate with him, but she wished to be sure that the communication was genuine and authentic. And for that reason, her first step was to make herself acquainted with the tricks practiced by mediums. She had spent much money on mediums, and had found nothing—nothing that she could trust.

She had, however, recalled an article which appeared a long time ago in the *Daily Triumph*, in which Professor Moon expressed his opinion that Mr Bliss was certainly possessed of inexplicable and supernormal gifts, and was almost certainly, though perhaps unconsciously, a medium. Professor Moon had said much the same thing about Mr Best. She recalled also that they had written and disclaimed any such gift, but she thought there might have been a reason for that.

At any rate she had now witnessed their performances several times, and all her study of the arts of illusion did not suggest to her any possible explanation, except that they really did possess some such power as Professor Moon had described.

If they were able and willing to put her into communication with her son, Arthur, they would have her undying gratitude. She might add that she was a wealthy woman, and would be glad to pay any fee they asked.

"Nothing doing," said Best.

"We'll talk about it afterwards," said Bliss. "We've got to hurry. The orchestra's started."

"Look here," said Bliss, after the show. "You remember our Mr Arthur Durnavel, don't you?"

"Yes," said Best, "and wish I could forget him. Oh, chuck it. He's dead, anyhow. And there are things that don't stand talking about."

"I can't chuck it," said Bliss. "I've got that woman in my mind. Lucky for Durnavel the Huns got him when they did. It would have been far worse for him otherwise. But I suppose she thought a lot of him. Looks as if she hadn't thought of much else these last years. Suppose we put up something for her? Just to—well, sort of comfort her."

Best had been pacing up and down the room. He paused and said angrily, "I won't touch it. Do it on your own if you must. I won't take any of the money."

"Did you think I meant to take any myself?"

"No, not really. Sorry."

They talked the matter over further, and in consequence Mrs Durnavel received a letter next day saying that Messrs Best and Bliss would, on certain conditions, attempt automatic writing on her behalf if she would come round to their dressing-room after the evening performance.

At the interview Mrs Durnavel was pale and trembled visibly with excitement. Her voice was very low and she seemed to find a difficulty in speaking. She thanked them for seeing her and said she was willing to accept any conditions.

"You must hear what the conditions are first," said Best. "Firstly, you will offer us no money or present of any kind for what we are going to do. Secondly, you will never let anybody know that we have done it. And lastly, you will promise never to ask us to do anything of the kind again."

"I agree and promise," said Mrs Durnavel.

"One more point. If we get a message, it will naturally have a great effect upon you. We think it will be better for you if you go the moment, you have read it. We wish to avoid emotional scenes."

"Yes, yes. Anything you wish."

"We will begin then. Are you ready Bliss?"

Bliss sat down at a little table at which was a writing-pad and pencil. He took up the pencil.

"Quite ready."

Best crossed over to him and made a few passes in the air before Bliss's eyes. This had been arranged between them. Suddenly Bliss's eyes closed. And this had not been arranged.

Best stood behind Bliss to read what he wrote, but Bliss's hand remained motionless. Outside in the dark and dirty passage some girl laughed loudly and uncontrollably.

Then the laughter stopped abruptly. Nothing could be heard but the dim sounds of traffic, like a distant sea. And immediately the hand moved and the pencil began to write. It wrote a few lines very rapidly and then the pencil dropped from the fingers.

Best's round and robicund face showed no vestige of surprise or wonder. Nothing could upset that man's stolidity. Yet the words that Bliss had written were not what had been arranged between them. And there was another point that puzzled Best. He took the sheet from the pad and handed it over to Mrs Durnavel.

"But it's his handwriting," she said, breathless. "My boy's own handwriting!"

She read the message and pressed it close to her. She looked up, her eyes full of tears. But all the tension and twist had gone from the face, and it was only happiness that was overpowering her. Bliss still sat with his eyes closed, quite motionless, his right hand on the table, his left arm hanging limply.

Best opened the door.

"You can find your own way out, Mrs Durnavel?"

"Yes, yes. My maid's waiting for me at the further end of the passage. Goodbye. I can never thank you enough. It's hopeless."

She came towards the door. As she passed the table where Bliss was sitting, with an uncontrollable impulse she bent down and kissed the hand that had written the message. Then she went out quietly.

Best walked quickly to Bliss, and tapped him on the shoulder. "Wake up," he said.

Bliss stood up and rubbed his eyes.

"I think I've been dead," he said.

"Dead asleep. But everything went all right. She's quite satisfied. Here, get your hat and let's get back to the hotel. If ever we wanted a drink, we want one tonight."

As they sat over their whisky-and-soda, Best said: "Did you know that our Mr Arthur Durnavel called his mother 'Dearest,' and signed his letters to her 'Chick'?"

"I didn't."

"You wrote it anyhow."

"And what else did I write?"

"Oh, the usual things. It was alright."

"I didn't write a word of it," said Bliss. "And I don't know who did."

Best remembered every word of that letter perfectly, especially this sentence:

> Within one hour we shall be happy together.

He thought of it next morning when he read in the newspaper the account of Mrs Durnavels death in an accident to her motor when she was returning from the theatre. Bliss was not given a chance to see the paper that morning.

The Four-Fingered Hand

Charles Yarrow held fours, but as he had come up against Brackley's straight flush they only did him harm, leading him to remark—by no means for the first time—that it did not matter what cards one held, but only when one held them. "I get out here," he remarked, with resignation. No one else seemed to care for further play. The two other men left at once, and shortly afterwards Yarrow and Brackley sauntered out of the club together.

"The night's young," said Brackley; "if you're doing nothing you may as well come round to me."

"Thanks, I will. I'll talk, or smoke, or go so far as to drink; but I don't play poker. It's not my night."

"I didn't know," said Brackley, "that you had any superstitions."

"Haven't. I've only noticed that, as a rule, my luck goes in runs, and that a good run or a bad run usually lasts the length of a night's play. There is probably some simple reason for it, if I were enough of a mathematician to worry it out. In luck as distinct from arithmetic I have no belief at all."

"I wish you could bring me to that happy condition. The hard-headed man of the world, without a superstition or a belief of any kind, has the best time of it."

They reached Brackley's chambers, lit pipes, and mixed drinks. Yarrow stretched himself in a lounge chair, and took up the subject again, speaking lazily and meditatively. He was a man of thirty-eight, with a clean-shaven face; he looked, as indeed he was, travelled and experienced.

"I don't read any books," he remarked, "but I've been twice round the world, and am just about to leave England again. I've been alive for thirty-eight years, and during most of them I have been living. Consequently, I've formed opinions, and one of my opinions is that it is better to dispense with superfluous luggage. Prejudices, superstitions,

113

beliefs of any kind that are not capable of easy and immediate proof are superfluous luggage; one goes more easily without them. You implied just now that you had a certain amount of this superfluous luggage, Brackley. What form does it take? Do you turn your chair?—are you afraid of thirteen at dinner?"

"No, nothing of that sort. I'll tell you about it. You've heard of my grandfather—who made the money?"

"Heard of him? Had him rubbed into me in my childhood. He's in Smiles or one of those books, isn't he? Started life as a navvy, educated himself, invented things, made a fortune, gave vast sums in charity."

"That is the man. Well, he lived to be a fair age, but he was dead before I was born. What I know of him I know from my father, and some of it is not included in those improving books for the young. For instance, there is no mention in the printed biography of his curious belief in the four-fingered hand. His belief was that from time to time he saw a phantom hand. Sometimes it appeared to him in the daytime, and sometimes at night. It was a right hand with the second finger missing. He always regarded the appearance of the hand as a warning. It meant, he supposed, that he was to stop anything on which he was engaged; if he was about to let a house, buy a horse, go a journey, or whatever it was, he stopped if he saw the four-fingered hand."

"Now, look here," said Yarrow, "we'll examine this thing rationally. Can you quote one special instance in which your grandfather saw this maimed hand, broke off a particular project, and found himself benefited?"

"No. In telling my father about it he spoke quite generally."

"Oh, yes," said Yarrow, drily. "The people who see these things do speak quite generally as a rule."

"But wait a moment. This vision of the four-fingered hand appears to have been hereditary. My father also saw it from time to time. And here I can give you the special instances. Do you remember the Crewe disaster some years ago? Well, my father had intended to travel by the train that was wrecked. Just as he was getting into the carriage he saw the four-fingered hand. He at once got out and postponed his journey until later in the day. Another occasion was two months before the failure of Varings'. My father banked there. As a rule, he kept a comparatively small balance at the bank, but on this occasion he had just realised an investment, and was about to place the result—six thousand pounds—in the bank, pending re-investment.

"He was on the point of sending off his confidential clerk with the money, when once more he saw the four-fingered hand. Now at that time Varings' was considered to be as safe as a church. Possibly a few people with special means of information may have had some slight suspicion at the time, but my father certainly had none. He had always banked with Varings, as his father had done before him. However, his faith in the warning hand was so great that instead of paying in the six thousand he withdrew his balance that day. Is that good enough for you?"

"Not entirely. Mind, I don't dispute your facts but I doubt if it requires the supernatural to explain them. You say that the vision appears to be hereditary. Does that mean that you yourself have even seen it?"

"I have seen it once."

"When?"

"I saw it tonight." Brackley spoke like a man suppressing some strong excitement. "It was just as you got up from the card-table after losing on your fours. I was on the point of urging you and the other two men to go on playing. I saw the hand distinctly. It seemed to be floating in the air about a couple of yards away from me. It was a small white hand, like a lady's hand, cut short off at the wrist. For a second it moved slowly towards me, and then vanished. Nothing would have induced me to go playing poker to-night."

"You are—excuse me for mentioning it—not in the least degree under the influence of drink. Further, you are by habit an almost absurdly temperate man. I mention these things because they have to be taken into consideration. They show that you were not at any rate the victim of a common and disreputable form of illusion. But what service has the hand done you? We play a regular point at the club. We are not the excited gamblers of fiction. We don't increase the points, and we never play after one in the morning. At the moment when the hand appeared to you, how much had you won?"

"Twenty-five pounds—an exceptionally large amount."

"Very well. You're a careful player. You play best when your luck's worst. We stopped play at half-past eleven. If we had gone on playing till one, and your luck had been of the worst possible description all the time, we will say that you might have lost that twenty-five and twenty-five more. To me it is inconceivable, but with the worst luck and the worst play it is perhaps possible. Now then, do you mean to tell me that the loss of twenty-five pounds is a matter of such importance to a man with your income as to require a supernatural intervention to prevent you from losing it?"

"Of course, it isn't."

"Well, then, the four-fingered hand has not accomplished its mission. It has not saved you from anything. It might even have been inconvenient. If you had been playing with strangers and winning, and they had wished to go on playing, you could hardly have refused. Of course, it did not matter with us—we play with you constantly, and can have our revenge at any time. The four-fingered hand is proved in this instance to have been useless and inept. Therefore, I am inclined to believe that the appearances when it really did some good were coincidences.

"Doubtless your grandfather and father and yourself have seen the hand, but surely that may be due to some slight hereditary defect in the seeing apparatus, which, under certain conditions, say, of the light and of your own health creates the illusion. The four-fingered hand is natural and not supernatural, subjective and not objective."

"It sounds plausible," remarked Brackley. He got up, crossed the room, and began to open the card-table. "Practical tests are always the most satisfactory, and we can soon have a practical test." As he put the candles on the table, he started a little and nearly dropped one of them. He laughed drily. "I saw the four-fingered hand again just then," he said. "But no matter—come—let us play."

"Oh, the two game isn't funny enough."

"Then I'll fetch up Blake from downstairs; you know him. He never goes to bed, and he plays the game."

Blake, who was a youngish man, had chambers downstairs. Brackley easily persuaded him to join the party. It was decided that they should play for exactly an hour. It was a poor game; the cards ran low, and there was very little betting. At the end of the hour Brackley had lost a sovereign, and Yarrow had lost five pounds.

"I don't like to get up a winner, like this," said Blake. "Let's go on."

But Yarrow was not to be persuaded. He said that he was going off to bed. No allusion to the four-fingered hand was made in speaking in the presence of Blake, but Yarrow's smile of conscious superiority had its meaning for Brackley. It meant that Yarrow had overthrown a superstition, and was consequently pleased with himself. After a few minutes' chat Yarrow and Blake said goodnight to Brackley, and went downstairs together.

Just as they reached the ground-floor they heard, from far up the staircase, a short cry, followed a moment afterwards by the sound of a heavy fall.

"What's that?" Blake exclaimed.

"I'm just going to see," said Yarrow, quietly. "It seemed to me to come from Brackley's rooms. Let's go up again."

They hurried up the staircase and knocked at Brackley's door. There was no answer. The whole place was absolutely silent. The door was ajar; Yarrow pushed it open, and the two men went in.

The candles on the card-table were still burning. At some distance from them, in a dark corner of the room, lay Brackley, face downwards, with one arm folded under him and the other stretched wide.

Blake stood in the doorway. Yarrow went quickly over to Brackley, and turned the body partially over.

"What is it?" asked Blake, excitedly. "Is the man ill? Has he fainted?"

"Run downstairs," said Yarrow, curtly. "Rouse the porter and get a doctor at once."

The moment Blake had gone. Yarrow took a candle from the card-table, and by the light of it examined once more the body of the dead man. On the throat there was the imprint of a hand—a right hand with the second finger missing. The marks, which were crimson at first, grew gradually fainter.

Some years afterwards, in Yarrow's presence, a man happened to tell some story of a warning apparition that he himself had investigated.

"And do you believe that?" Yarrow asked.

"The evidence that the apparition was seen—and seen by more than one person—seems to me fairly conclusive in this case."

"That is all very well. I will grant you the apparition if you like. But why speak of it as a warning? If such appearances take place, it still seems to me absurd and disproportionate to suppose that they do so in order to warn us, or help us, or hinder us, or anything of the kind. They appear for their own unfathomable reasons only. If they seem to forbid one thing or command another, that also is for their own purpose. I have an experience of my own which would tend to show that."

The Scent

There was no one but myself in the smaller of the two smoking-rooms when he entered. I had picked up an evening paper, and was boring myself with it for a few minutes in front of the fire, before going on to bore myself somewhere else. He walked rapidly to the fireplace and rang the bell, and then turned abruptly to me.

"Hullo! How are you! Didn't know you were here." Then he caught sight of the evening paper in my hands and asked me for God's sake to put that thing down. I put it down and asked him what was the matter. He was very pale and had just the appearance of a man whose nerves were suffering from over-strain.

"I must tell you," he said abruptly. "I'm glad I found you. It's the most perfectly—"

He stopped there because the waiter who answered the bell had just entered. He ordered some brandy and resumed again.

"You will laugh your head off by the time I have finished my story, ghastly though it is. You won't believe a word of it. See here."

He picked up the paper which I had thrown down, opened it rapidly, and handed it to me with his finger on one particular paragraph. The paragraph referred to an inquest on a somewhat commonplace suicide in Soho. The suicide, an Italian judging by his name, had flung himself from a window on the first floor, and had broken his neck on the pavement. Evidence was given by those who knew him that he had been very queer in his manners of late, and the usual verdict had been returned.

"Well?" I said.

"It's God's mercy that I wasn't a witness at that inquest."

"What does it matter?" I replied. "I suppose you saw the accident. You are required to go and say that; it doesn't hurt you. Nobody thinks any the worse of you. It may be a little tiresome, but there is nothing to bring you to this condition, even if you had really given evidence, which it seems you haven't."

The waiter brought the brandy. He drank it, ordered another, and continued more quietly.

"I am afraid I have let the thing prey on my mind a little. I confess that I have had a shock. The story, is not at all what you imagine. I did not witness the accident; it was only within the last two hours that I heard of it, but I know how it was that it happened."

He paused. I selected another cigar, lit it, and said nothing. He continued:

"You know me well enough to know my interest in anything which is a little out of the way. I will even run some slight risk to meet and talk with a man who is not as other men are, or, better still, a woman who is not as other women are. I have a fancy for human curiosities; I should like to take a museum and collect them."

"Yes," I said, "I know that. You will get yourself into trouble one of these days."

He went on speaking.

"About a week ago I went down Wardour Street and saw an Italian looking in at a shop window. I did not know that he was an Italian at the time. The national characteristics were not very strongly marked in him. He was quite well dressed, rather like a well-to-do young City man. His head was abnormal. The breadth from the end of the eyebrow to the ear was enormous. His eyes were not of the same colour; his skin was like parchment; he continually moved the tip of his nose. His nostrils opened and shut. He looked to me to be a very queer beast indeed, and I meant to talk to him.

"After a while he went into a restaurant. I waited ten minutes and then went in after him. I sat down at the same table, and, by way of opening a conversation, knocked over his glass of claret, breaking the glass. Then, of course, I apologised and ordered a waiter to replace it. He at once countermanded the order, and turned to me, saying in excellent English, 'Pray do not trouble. I had quite finished with it.'

"'But,' I said, 'you must let me. Your glass was untouched.'

"'Yes,' he said, 'but I never drink it.'

"I looked amazed. 'I could explain,' he added, 'but it is a little difficult to understand, and it would bore you.'

"'The only things that I care about,' I replied, 'are the things which are not ordinary, and are a little difficult to understand. Unless you are a dipsomaniac, triumphing over temptation, I fail to see why you should order wine which you have no intention of drinking.'

"'Your explanation is wrong,' he replied. 'I ordered the claret because I wanted to smell it.'

"As he seemed to find that conclusive, I observed that even that did not clear the thing up.

"'You must know,' he said a little impatiently, 'that with some people the scents of different objects have curious results. The possibilities implied in the sense of smell are enormous. In most people they are undeveloped; in very few are they at all understood. The connection between a scent and a memory has been noticed. I have seen a woman who smelt wallflowers for the first time for ten years burst into tears. The scent of *eau de Cologne* is supposed to be refreshing, and that of ammonia to be vivifying, and that of ether sickening. No scent possesses the very curious attraction for a human being that valerian does for the lower animals.

"'The whole art of obtaining a new sensation by the use of scents is absolutely unknown to most people. Most women divide scents vaguely into opaque and transparent; most virtuous women prefer the transparent. But that is really as far as they have gone. As for the effect of those scents which are not pleasant to anybody, and therefore are generally called by an unpleasant name, there seems to be no knowledge at all.'

"'I knew a case,' I said, 'of a gardener who had to work in a hothouse filled with lilies-of-the-valley. He fainted away.'

"My Italian friend took up the story.

"'And when he recovered consciousness, he was angry and entreated to be put back again?'

"'Yes,' I said, 'but how did you know it?'

"'Because I know the effect of different scents.'

"I was more fascinated than ever, and made him talk for a long time. Several times he seemed to be hesitating whether or not to tell me something, and I urged him on. It came at last. He had got a secret. He had invented a scent and was assured of the marvellous power of it, but not of the whole of its effects, afterwards or immediate. These he was investigating. 'And,' he added impressively, 'it gives one an entirely new way of living.'

"'I wish,' I said, 'that you were a poor man wanting money with which to carry on your experiments. If I offered to finance you perhaps you would let me witness some of them. I love nothing better than to see something new.'

"'I do not want any money,' he answered laughing. 'My workshop is near here, and I will show it to you if you care to take the risk of coming.'

"'I will come,' I replied, 'with pleasure.'

"And we both walked out together. He took me up a side-street, and then up a precipitous staircase to the first floor of a dingy-looking house. He had three large rooms there, opening into one another. He made me wait in the first, which was somewhat poorly furnished as a library, and he went through into the others. After about ten minutes he came back and fetched me through the second room, where a lot of things were cooking over tiny little spirit lamps, and into the third. The third was furnished as the first, but it was much more luxurious. He opened a corner cupboard and took down an ordinary glass stopper bottle, unlabelled and containing a colourless liquid.

"'That is it,' he said smiling; 'that is what makes all things new.'

"Of course, by this time I knew he was cracked, but I asked him how.

"'After frequent inhalations of this scent,' he said, 'one loses all sense of limitations or conditions. One believes that one can walk straight through a brick wall, or fly in the air, or live in the year one, or in the year two million, or in any intervening year. One is sure that he can do anything which it occurs to him that he would like to do. One has a feeling of complete omnipotence, and that means a feeling of complete happiness. No one conscious of a limitation can be completely happy. At present the effects are very transient, but I may be able to improve upon that.'

"'One moment,' I said. 'This scent does not really remove limitations and conditions.'

"'Subjectively, yes, objectively, no; but that matters little. Nothing can be unreal to us at the time that we fully believe it to be real. It is because the effects are illusive that I now refrain from experimenting with myself unless there is someone in the room with me. It is a hard struggle to keep off it. Frankly, I was very glad when you suggested that you should come here. Now, watch me.'

"He removed the stopper, and for perhaps two minutes continued to inhale the perfume. Then he put the stopper back again in the bottle and set it down on the table by his side. He did not change in appearance in the least. Half-jokingly I asked him if he could now write stories like Mr Rudyard Kipling.

"'Better,' he said, 'infinitely better. They are nothing. I will show you one very short thing.'

"He took paper, pen and ink, and covered one sheet with feverish haste. Then he handed it to me with an air of triumph. It was absolute nonsense from beginning to end, and absolutely incoherent. There were phrases in it which we had used in our conversation, phrases which he might have seen in advertisements on hoardings, two or three lines of a song which is very popular just now, the whole strung together anyhow. I looked over it.

"'Capital,' I said; 'and can you fly?'

"'Of course.' He got up and opened the window, I let him climb up on the ledge, where a nervous man would certainly have fallen. I saved him only just in time, and he was angry with me. As I told him unfortunately, I was not able to fly and wished for his company, he sat down and talked rubbish about the things which he said he could do for about five minutes. Then he stretched himself and yawned.

"'It has passed off now,' he said. I had a long argument with him, but it was of no use. He would not give up the bottle and he would not promise to leave it alone in the future, and he would not tell me what he called it. To irritate him I said that the whole thing was a fraud from beginning to end; the bottle contained water, and nothing else. I picked it up, took a long sniff at it, and went out.

"In the street a moment later, I called a cabman and told him to drive to Downing Street. I wanted to show Lord Salisbury the means of destroying any nation. I had the power of destroying any nation, and I wished to use it for the benefit of England. Long before the cab reached Downing Street, I also stretched my arms and yawned, and knew that the effect had gone off. I drove back to my chambers.

"Today I read of the suicide. He had tried to fly and he did it because I suggested it to him when he was in that state the other day. It was my fault, really."

He picked up his second glass of brandy and began sipping it. He talked it over for a long time, but he would not contradict himself or be shaken in any way.

It is at any rate perfectly true that at the sale of the suicide's property he made some large purchases. I found that out afterwards from the auctioneer.

He is living abroad now.

The Unknown God

The air of the primitive and remote island was soft and languorous. Its population consisted of a man and woman, brown-skinned, and without any of the blessings of education and religion. This afternoon the population had been bathing, and now lay on the sand in the sun.

"Presently," said the man, "we will go and look at the boat which has drifted ashore."

"Presently," said the girl, lazily. "It is a good boat."

"Very good boat," echoed the man. "It will be useful to us." And immediately he fell asleep.

In a moment or two the girl awakened him. She was in a philosophical humour, and there is not much fun in being philosophical all by yourself.

"Are you happy?" she asked.

"I do not know," said the man. "I have never thought about it."

"Then you are happy," she said with decision. "People who think about it are not. I, for example, am not."

"If we now roused ourselves a little and caught a few fish—"

"No," said the girl, decisively, "I wish to talk."

The man sighed.

"Do you not know what it is to wish to be taken out of yourself, and to become somebody else—to be full of inspiration from the gods? These days and nights that are always the same are becoming a burden to me. I want to be different for a little while."

"It is not possible," said the man. "There are gods undoubtedly. It was always the opinion of our forefathers that there were gods, but the gods never interfere with us and we cannot get at them. Therefore, they do not concern us, and it is much better to catch a few fish."

The girl, looking as if she might burst into tears at any moment, said that she hated fish, and that she hated her island, and that she hated herself.

"I wish to meet with one of the gods," she said. "I wish to talk with someone who is more than mortal. Tell me what the gods look like."

"As to that," said the man, "more than one opinion has been expressed. There are some who say that the gods are like big men, taller than the palm-trees, of gigantic strength. There are others who say that the gods cannot be seen, and that it is only by their influence within us that they may be recognised. To talk of things which we do not know is very foolish. If you will not catch fish, let us go and look at the boat."

The woman arose rather sullenly, and followed him.

They found in the boat a tin containing biscuits. They had never seen biscuits before, but a little investigation showed them the use to which they should be put. They bored holes in them and hung them round their necks.

They found, moreover, a large square bottle, containing a colourless fluid. The girl removed the cork, dipped her finger in the fluid, and touched her tongue.

"Of what does it taste?" asked the man, anxiously.

"Of fire and sleep and sin," answered the girl.

"In that case," said the man, "I will go and fetch our drinking-cups."

The drinking-cups were two halves of the shell of a cocoanut, smooth and polished by much use. The man filled them, and they drank in slow sips. A drink which tastes of fire and sleep and sin cannot be taken hastily. As she filled their cups for the second time, the girl observed that she believed there was a god in that bottle.

★★★★★★★★★★★★

Next morning the girl awoke and zigzagged from the point where she had fallen down the beach to the sea. She kept her head under water for the longest possible time. Then she rose to the surface and swam slowly and lazily. Presently the man's head shot up by her side. He also had been down below.

"There can be no doubt about it at all," said the girl. "We have found the unknown god, and by his influence within us he may be recognised."

"I do not feel at all good this morning," said the man.

"Nor I," said the girl. "But last night was magnificent. Never have I danced so long and so wildly. Never have I laughed so much."

"I had an impression," said the man, as he swam by her side, "that I was being unusually witty."

126

"No," said the girl, "I do not think it was that. Everything was amusing. I laughed at the sea, I laughed at the boat, I laughed at the trees. You also laughed."

"I remember it," said the man. "The entire world had suddenly become ridiculous. But this morning I do not feel at all good." He dived under a wave with the girl after him, and presently they lay side by side on the sand.

"It is about this time in the morning," said the girl, "that we generally catch fish for our breakfast, but today I do not wish to catch fish for my breakfast, and I think I do not wish to eat anything more as long as I live."

"I have the same feeling," said the man. "Why then should this be if indeed it was a god that we found in the boat?"

"Because," said the girl, "if with great force you pull the bough of a tree in one direction and then let go, it will swing with great force in the other direction. Because last night we were exalted, therefore this morning we are abased. I am willing. I pay the price. Why do you get up? Where are you going?"

"I am going," said the man, "to see if by any chance there is still left in the bottle a little of that drink which tastes of fire and sleep and sin."

"Lie down again," said the girl. "There is not any left. I have looked into the matter myself."

★★★★★★★★★★★★

Two days later the man and the girl built up a rough altar of white stones on the beach, and on the top of the altar they placed the bottle in which the god had lived. The perfume of his presence was still there. The man thinks now that the girl spends too much time in the contemplation of it. And what will happen when the missionaries land?

The Reaction

1

Ernest Purdon had served his apprentice ship, passed his examinations with a little luck and not much margin, and was now qualified to dispense medicines. He was now an assistant at one of Myer and Co.'s myriad shops. This particular shop was in Dunnivan road, Whitechapel. It was not a sweet neighbourhood, and hardly a day passed when Mr. Purdon was not asked to do something absolutely illegal. Such a proposal never even tempted him. He flicked the dirty, folded note back across the counter, and told the man or woman to go away. He had a conscience. Why, he went to church every Sunday morning with Ethel and her mother.

During business hours he was pontifical and impressive. He wore a fairly good black coat, and his hands were very white. He took care of his fingernails, and his signet-ring was genuine. He was under thirty, but when he assumed his gilt-rimmed *pince-nez* you felt at once that he had only to look into it. He even had a local reputation. Clumsy, ill-dressed men, earning more money than our Mr Purdon ever did or could, lumbered up from the docks and addressed him with great respect. John Mace, ship's steward, was a walking testimonial.

"You go up to Myer's in Dunnivan Road," he would say, "and get a fair-haired bloke with eyeglasses. Can't miss him. He knows. Cured my leg. Took a pal of mine and sobered him up, so that he was fit to go aboard, in about record. Beats the doctors, to my mind."

It had been Mace himself and not a pal of his whom Mr Purdon, fear and suggestion concurring, had sobered with such rapidity. But Mace was not a pedantically accurate man in any respect.

Out of business hours Ernest Purdon was much less pontifical and impressive. Myer and Co. did not overpay their assistants. Purdon lived at a cheap boarding-house, run by an experienced iron-faced lady who had worked out to a small fraction what was the least she could possibly give for the money she took, and never gave more. The food was of the worst quality, the rooms were not clean. Purdon, who had no expensive vices, managed to put by a very little money. Also, though he did not know it, he was heartily afraid of the iron-faced lady. He would not have dared to say that he was dissatisfied. He had once ventured to complain that the window of his bedroom would not remain closed.

"You surprise me," said Mrs Bowes. "I should have thought that if there was one gentleman in my house to appreciate the value of fresh air, it would have been you, Mr Purdon, being practically on the borders of the medical profession."

He gave up. But the nights in November were cold, and he made a device of his own with a piece of stout wire to keep that window closed.

He had been engaged to Ethel nearly a year. Sometimes he wondered if he were really engaged to Ethel, or to Ethel and her mother, for they were inseparable. He was well aware that Ethel was much more attached to her mother than she was to him. The mother, Mrs Ratton, with Ethel's help ran a stationer's shop in Hampstead, which she had inherited from her deceased husband. They lived over the shop and did fairly well out of it. Every Sunday Ernest Purdon called for them, went to the morning service with them, and returned to their home for the midday meal. When it was finished, the same conversation nearly always took place, the responses coming with much the same regularity as the responses in the church.

Purdon said: "Matter of fact, this is the only decent meal I get in the week."

Mrs Ratton said: "If not comfortable where you are, why not change?"

Ethel said: "That's what I always tell him."

And finally, Purdon said: "Oh, well you never know."

Once a month he took Ethel and her mother to the theatre. They always chose the piece, and he found to some dissatisfaction that it was only too often Shakespeare. He had once ventured to suggest that he should take Ethel alone.

"Why," said Ethel brightly, "what has poor Mamma done?"

And Purdon protested lamely that of course he had taken it for granted that poor Mamma would come too. She did.

Purdon found life dull, but was not very discontented. It was of no use to cry over the moon, and if he lost Ethel, he might not get another. He recognised that he was not popular with the ladies—not like his friend Harry Bates. Bates was a man of good appearance and manner, knew how to talk, and was sometimes dryly humorous. He was in the same profession as Purdon and no better qualified. But he was making considerably more money. Bates was not employed by Myer and Co., but by a man who kept a very well-known and very discreet druggist's shop in Mayfair. Wealthy young men, suffering from the night before, consulted Bates, took what he gave them, and were not ungenerous. Some of Bates's caustic sayings were quoted in the West End clubs. Well, Bates had promised that if ever he saw an opening, he would give his friend Purdon a lift. That might happen at any time—it had not happened yet.

2

It was growing dark on a November afternoon, and the lights in Myer's shop in Dunnivan Road were already lit. John Mace peered in. At the moment, Ernest Purdon was talking to an old woman with a shawl over her head. He held a phial of tablets in his hand. The old woman spoke of a sense of tightness in the chest, and Purdon tapped his own chest with his white fingers sympathetically. He quite understood. Then he tapped the phial. Two of those before each meal would probably remove the inconvenience. She purchased the phial and left the shop. Mace entered at once.

"Back again, Mr Mace," said Purdon genially.

"Yes, sir. Got in the day before yesterday. There was a little thing I wanted to see you about."

"Well, well, what's the trouble?"

"It's not trouble exactly," said Mace, pulling out a bulky pocketbook and taking from it a small package in oiled paper. "It's this sample. I don't know what it is, and I want to know. I was wondering if you could tell me."

"We're pharmaceutical chemists here," said Purdon, "not analytical. If you want to know just what this stuff is, you'll have to take it to an analytical chemist, and I may as well warn you that you may have to pay a pretty stiff fee for it."

"I don't want to do anything beyond five shillings," said Mace. "I've reason to know that you're a good deal cleverer than the usual, Mr Purdon. I've no doubt if you cared to take that home with you, you could tell me something about it tomorrow evening. I don't say everything. I only want a general idea. Because I've reason to believe it might be pretty good."

"How do you mean? Where did you get it from?"

"Got it from a man who died of pneumonia this trip and was buried at sea. He wasn't the ordinary sort. Mr E. Mathews he was on the passenger-list and letters after his name. An educated man I should say, and got money. Traveling in the first-class, he was. There weren't a lot of people wanted to talk to him, and he talked to me. Showed me this powder, and said he was going to make a fortune with it. That was all I could get out of him, and he was taken ill the next day. If you'll take that home with you and look into it, Ill go to five shillings and chance it. You might find out something, or you might not."

"Very good," said Purdon, and slipped the little packet into his waistcoat-pocket. "See you tomorrow evening."

When he got back to the boarding-house he went to his bedroom and hung his overcoat and hat behind the door. He might have hung them up downstairs, but the boarding-house was one in which mistakes frequently happened, and Purdon was taking no risks. He took off his black business coat, brushed it and hung it in the wardrobe, and put on a light jacket. Then he took from his pocket the little packet which Mace had given him, and opened it. It contained a brown powder which was not of a regular consistency. Some of it was the finest dust, and some of it was much coarser, and there were even little unbroken lumps in it. The smell of it was terrific and unrecognisable. He had not the slightest notion what the stuff was. He tried a couple of simple tests, in order that he might have something to talk to Mace about. He found that the powder was easily soluble in water, and that it was alkaline. The whole thing did not take him five minutes.

He did not propose to investigate any father. The stuff simply stank, and he wanted to get it out of his small bedroom. Even when it was gone, he would have to leave the window open for half an hour before the place was fit to sleep in. The window looked out at the back of the house, over a small blackened yard that Mrs Bowes called a garden. Purdon picked up the paper with the remainder of the powder, intending to throw it out of the window.

And then accident came in. As Purdon tried to undo that wire device of his which kept the window shut, he scratched the thumb of his left hand deeply, so that the blood came. And as he pushed the window open, a gust of wind blew a little of the fine powder over his bleeding thumb.

"Damn!" said Purdon. He went to his washstand and washed his

132

thumb carefully. He heard the church clock outside strike eight. Ten his eyes grew dark and his head swam. He groped his way to his bed and flung himself on it. And there for an hour he lay unconscious of his actual surroundings.

And in that hour, he lived a whole year of the most perfect happiness.

It was nine o'clock when he became aware that he was lying on his bed in his own sordid room at the top of the boarding-house. But for a minute or two a thought persisted that he might have been unconscious for a year. Then he reflected that, if that had been so, he would have been found in his room, and would have been removed. He pulled out his watch; it was still going. He could only have been there an hour. It was marvellous, that time extension. In that one hour he had been through the countless incidents of a wonderful year—a year in which quiet bliss and triumphant ecstasy had alternated.

At a quarter-past nine Purdon saw it all, and began to be frightened. That brown powder was dope, and the accident to his thumb had practically given him a hypodermic injection of it. There was no dope like that in the world. Any man would spend his last penny—would give his soul—for a year such as Purdon had just been through.

But Purdon had never taken any form of dope before and, in his profession, he had seen something of it, and the ghastly effects of it. That very day a little, shivering old lady with untidy hair had come into the shop with a prescription that was obviously and preposterously bogus, and had burst out crying when Purdon had tossed it back to her and told her not to come there again unless she wanted to be handed over to the police. Dope was appalling. Even now, with the memory of that great year still vivid in him, he had not the slightest inclination to renew the experiment. He could not have renewed it. He had no more of the drug in his possession.

Perhaps a man who had by accident taken a hypodermic injection of uncertain strength, of an unknown and potent drug, may be pardoned for feeling nervous. Purdon felt nervous. He did not now what the stuff might do to him. He might be taken ill in the night. Locked up in his room he had an ordinary eight-ounce medicine bottle filled with brandy. He kept it for emergencies, and had had it for two years. He got it out now and put it on the table by his bedside. He undressed quickly and got into bed. He did not suppose he would be able to sleep Even if he did, he felt sure that he would awake on the following morning with a splitting head and tremulous nerves, possibly even unable to go to business. And that would not do him any good with Myer and Co.

He fell asleep almost immediately and slept quite peacefully til seven on the following morning. He had no headache at all. He took his pulse and temperature and found them normal. If anything, he felt better than usual. It was almost as though some of the happiness and confidence of that wonderful dream-year still lingered in him. His recollections of the dream-year had grown very vague. He could recall that several beautiful women had been very much in love with him, that men had respected him, that crowds had cheered him, that he had done many things exceedingly well which in real life he could never have done at all. But the picture was blurred. The very effort of trying to recall it seemed to make it more indistinct.

He went downstairs with a very good appetite for a very bad breakfast. It as in the train on his way to business that the great idea came to him. He must get the rest of that drug away from Mace. The man had been quite right—there was money in it.

3

Throughout the day Purdon kept a very close eye on himself. He took his pulse and temperature frequently. He could find no departure from the normal at all. He had never been better. He did his work well and easily. And all through the day that scheme grew rapidly in his mind. He was going to get the stuff away from Mace. At any rate, he was going to get some of it. Enough for his purpose.

It was shortly after six that Mace came in.

"Well, sir," said Mace eagerly. "Got any news for me? Spotted what it is?"

"Well," said Mr Purdon, "there's not been much time. For that matter, you didn't give me nearly a big enough sample for a proper analysis. Still, I can tell you something. The stuff's in a very crude state, and full of impurities."

"Full of——?" suggested Mace.

"Impurities. Dirt. That would have to be put right before it could be used. The thing is a gum-resin—like gamboge or asafoetida, you know." (Purdon had not done much in the way of analysis, but he had enough to show him that the stuff was not a resin.) "How many hundredweight of it have you got?"

"Hundredweight? Didn't I tell you? He carried it about with him in his hip-pocket. He'd got it in an old half-pound, flat tobacco tin.

There's just over six ounces of it. What would that be worth?"

"In its present state, probably nothing. If it had been properly man-ufactured, it might have been worth a shilling or two. But you would never find a buyer."

"Then what did the man mean by telling me he was going to make a fortune with it?"

Purdon laughed.

"Well, your friend was a sick man, and may have been light-head-ed. Besides what does he know?"

"But I told you he was an educated man. Letters after his name."

"There are quite a number of people who have letters after their name, to which they are not entitled. I've known it happen in my own profession. Besides, all these people are superstitious. If you want me to tell you what I really think, it looks to me as if it were some kind of a crazy charm that he was carrying for luck. Not that it seems to have brought him much. But what made him give it to you?"

Mace appeared slightly embarrassed.

"Between ourselves, he didn't give it to me. I took a fancy to it. I wouldn't touch his money or jewellery. I never do. But a little thing like this that would never be missed, that's different. I expect you're right about it. The stuff's no good to me now I've got it. Worse than no good because I've got to settle with you. What do I owe you?"

"Look here," said Purdon. "As a chemist, I don't like to be beaten. If you'll hand over the tin to me, that will give me enough to make a complete analysis, though in any case a crude gum-resin like that wouldn't be worth much. If you like to hand it over, I'll charge you nothing for my time and the drugs I've used so far, and I'll slip you a couple of shillings for yourself. You'll get a drink out of it anyway."

"Suppose I can't do better," said Mace hesitatingly.

"I know you can't," said Mr Purdon lightly. "But if you like to try, I'm not stopping you."

"All right," said Mace, and drew the tin from his pocket and pushed it across the counter.

Mr Purdon opened the lid and glanced at the contents. "Two shil-lings," he said, and dropped them into Mace's hand. "Good evening, and don't forget to drink my health."

Outside in the street, Mace paused and looked back into the shop. He saw Purdon take up the tin, wrap it in paper, and put it in the pocket of his overcoat, which hung behind the screen. Mace did not like the expression on Purdon's face. As he walked slowly away, the truth dawned on him. That blighter in the black coat had done him.

Why, there could not be a doubt of it. Purdon had wanted the stuff for himself. Chemists' assistants had no money to burn. Purdon didn't throw away two shillings on buying a little puzzle for his amusement. Oh, no, not in this life. Purdon knew all about it. He said he didn't, but he did. Why, you only had to see his face as he put the tin in his pocket. That man knew what he was talking about. There was money in it, and Purdon had found out where the money was.

Mace turned into the aristocratic seclusion of the private bar of a public-house. He ordered a drink and thought things over. Purdon had got the stuff now, but Purdon left his shop at seven, and Mace was not dead yet. That clever young man might not have it all his own way. Mace himself was clever enough in one or two little things.

Meanwhile Purdon's scheme went on rapidly. It seemed one dose of this new drug produced no bad after-effects at all. No doubt if the dose were repeated many times, it might be injurious. Indeed, Purdon felt sure that it must be. But that drug would never go out of his own possession. It would be for him to say how many doses a customer might have. There was nothing illegal about it, for the law did not even know of the existence of such a drug. There was nothing even immoral about it. Purdon meant no harm. He would sooner sacrifice some of his profits than do ay harm. All the same, the profits would be enormous. Ethel and her mother would be surprised. They would not have to be told everything, of course. Ethel's mother would be certain to ask questions. He would not tell her to mind her own business; he would simply say that in the course of chemical study and research he had come upon a discovery of commercial value, bout which he was not at liberty to say more. It would make a difference. Ethel's mother had seemed at times almost patronising. There would be an end to anything of that kind.

The first thing to do, of course, was to get into touch with Harry Bates. Through him he would be able to get just the right *clientele*. The shop where Bates was employed had a great reputation with the big racing men and the stars of the theatrical world. Such people had money to spend and were willing to spend it. Purdon felt confident that they would have to spend it if they made but one experiment with the dope that gave you a year of paradise in an hour. Yes, as soon as he got back to his boarding-house he would write to Bates and make an appointment with him. It might not be wise to put down too much in actual writing.

At seven o'clock Purdon left the shop and made for the tube train. The crush on the platform as usual at that hour, was terrific. As he struggled into the carriage, he caught sight of Mace close beside him, and tossed him a little joke on the crowd. Once in the carriage he looked round for him again, but Mace had apparently been unable to fight his way in. And that was unlike Mace.

4

Purdon hung up his overcoat, brushed and put away his business coat according to his usual routine, and turned to go downstairs again to write his letter to Bates.

But after all the night was not cold. It was a muggy night—unusually warm for the time of year. If he went downstairs the chances were that he would find the writing-tables all occupied. Even if he found a place, there were men and women in that boarding-house who were too much interested in other people. They found themselves accidentally in such a position that they could glance over the shoulder of the letter-writer. Purdon decided to write his letter in his own room. He took his writing-block and fountain-pen, sat down, and began as follows:

Dear Harry,
I want to see you tomorrow if possible. I want your help. And when I say help, I don't mean money. On the contrary, I shall be able to pay very handsomely for——

Why, some of that powder must have been spilt in the room. He could smell it. He had not noticed it when he first came in. But now there could be no mistake. It grew in intensity. He would have to open the window before he could finish the letter.

He looked up from his writing-block. Outside the church clock struck eight, and at the same time there was a rattle of a chair being moved in the room.

As he looked up, he saw opposite to him a gigantic negro, wearing a light tweed suit, sitting astride a chair with his arms on the back of it, and his chin on his arms, watching Purdon intently.

For a moment Purdon was not much perturbed. Mrs Bowes was not averse to making money from all nationalities and all colours. And this might be a boarder who had recently arrived and had mistaken his room.

"Begging your pardon," said Purdon firmly, "I think you've made a slight mistake. This is not——"

He stopped because the man had suddenly vanished. And then in a flash, he knew the truth. That paradise dope had its reaction. This was the beginning of the reaction.

He put down his writing-block, put his fountain-pen back in his pocket, and crossed over to the tiny looking-glass on his dressing-table. He could see that he looked ill. It seemed to him that his face had perceptibly changed. And then in the looking-glass he saw brown fingers come slowly round his throat. He felt them touch him and begin to press tightly. He made an effort and broke away. The negro in the light suit was standing opposite to him, laughing noiselessly.

Purdon decided on his line of action. The thing to do would be to lie down on his bed, close his eyes and remain absolutely quiet until the whole thing had passed off. The only thing was that he dared not go past that man in the light suit who stood opposite him.

Once more the he vanished. Now was his time.

He approached the bed, and from under it an arm shot out, and a hand gripped him by the ankle. This time he tried in vain to break away. He stood there sweating with terror.

This lasted for some seconds. And then suddenly the man shot out from under the bed and sprang to his feet. He was not laughing now. He was breathing hard, and he looked like murder. Purdon noticed that the giant wore a double watch-chain, with a bunch of seals pendent from it, over his protuberant stomach, and that there was an enormous diamond in his emerald-green necktie. There were diamond rings, too, on the brown hands that now slowly approached Purdon. Purdon felt himself unable to move.

The hands clutched him by the waist, raised him in the air, and then hurled him forward.

He fell with a crash and did not dare to get up again. He lay there with his hands pressed tightly over his eyes, in order that he might not see anything more. And deep in his mind was the conviction that he was lost—lost forever—lost in this world and the next. He could still hear the man's panting breath.

Then all was still. Slowly and timidly, he raised himself and looked round the room. It seemed to be quite empty. A picture had been torn from one of the walls and lay on the floor with the glass broken. He supposed he must have clutched at it as he was hurled through the air. He waited some little time before he dared to cross the room to the locked drawer in which he kept his brandy. He took the glass from his washstand, poured out the entire contents of the bottle, and drank it at a draught. If only that would steady him sufficiently, he would be able to go downstairs and send somebody to fetch a doctor for him. He would have to tell the doctor everything. That could not be helped.

Again, the awful stench of the drug filled the room. Sickened with it, Purdon staggered to the window and tore it open. Instantly a furry hand shot across the window ledge, a great chimpanzee lumbered into the room and crouched. Another followed, and another, and another. One of them was crouched before the door, so that there was no escape that way. They all had old, philosophical, weary expressions, and they all had their impartial eyes fixed on him.

The largest of the apes picked up a piece of the broken picture-frame, looked long at it as though he were trying to probe its secret, smelled it, broke it in two, sighed deeply, and as he scratched himself with one of the pieces fixed his eyes again on Purdon.

Purdon was backing along the edge of the table. It chanced that his hand knocked over the empty medicine-bottle.

The sound seemed suddenly to break up the melancholy calm of the chimpanzees. Their eyes became animated and angry. Their mouths twisted. One after another they put their hands on the floor, swung their bodies through their long arms, and advanced upon him.

Purdon tried to scream for help. His mouth opened wide, but no sound came. Desperate with terror, he flung the water-jug and the looking-glass at them. He picked up a chair and lashed out wildly with it till it broke in his hands. They leaped at him and got him down.

"Death—thank God!" thought Purdon.

And instantly he was sitting up and listening to Harry Bates. Harry Bates was not there. Purdon saw nobody in the room but himself, seated amid the furniture wreckage.

But the voice of Harry Bates was there—a resonant, confident bass.

"A thousand pities you didn't come to me at the very first," said Bates. "I could have warned you. I know about the stuff, and have seen two cases. Cocaine is a baby's toy to it. After one hypodermic, the reaction lasts as long as life lasts. Life doesn't last long, because suicide is inevitable. The sooner the better. No human being can stand the damned torture of it. No known drug touches it. Nothing can alleviate it. Goodbye, Ernest. The window's open. It's a seventy-foot drop. It won't take more than a few seconds."

Purdon rose and walked as a doomed man towards the open window. It chanced that he nearly slipped upon a fragment of the broken picture-frame. He staggered into the closed door of his room, and clutched at his overcoat hanging there to save himself from falling. Why, there it was. The drug itself would save him. For a time, at any rate. And he had a tin full of the stuff in the pocket of that overcoat. In a few moments he would be back again in a year of paradise. He began to search in the pockets of the overcoat. Through the open window he heard the clock strike nine.

He searched very carefully, but the tin was not there. His pocket had been picked, and Purdon knew just when it had been done. Mace had taken it. That was why Mace had never got into the train. Mace was welcome to it. Purdon had no wish ever to see the stuff again. He went to the open window and drew in deep breaths of the cold, refreshing air. He was still feeling very shaky. He had knocked himself about, and was sore and bruised, but it was nothing that could be called real suffering. The awful depression had gone. There was no more delusions and his mind seemed clear and logical. The reaction was over, and he knew it. His dream that he would make a fortune out of the drug was over too. And it did not seem to him to matter. He decided to sit down for half an hour or so and rest. After that, he would clear up his room, as best he could, and get a long night's sleep.

But now he heard his voices and footsteps coming up the stairs. The loudest voice was that of Mrs Bowes, enjoining silence on the others. Purdon could also recognise the whining voice of William, a weak old man who did the boots and knives, and looked as if all his life he had never done anything else.

There was a pause, and whispering on the landing outside the door. Then Mrs Bowes's bony and decisive knuckles rapped twice.

"Come in," said Purdon. He recognised that the chance was coming to him to be quit of Mrs Bowes forevermore, and he welcomed it.

Mrs Bowes entered alone. She left the door ajar, and her reserves were marshalled outside to rush to her support if necessary. Purdon caught the suppressed giggle of a nervous maid. Mrs Bowes looked— it was almost habitual with her—like avenging justice.

"What am I to understand by this, Mr Purdon?" she said.

"Understand by what?" said Purdon, with a sudden calm courage.

"Pandemonium, Mr Purdon. Ladies and gentlemen, living under my roof, saying that murder was being done upstairs. You ought to be ashamed. Look at the state of the room. Oh, look at the breakages."

"The breakages will be paid for at a fair valuation," said Purdon. "If you want to know, I have been experimenting upon myself with a potent and unknown drug—my own discovery, by the way. Men of science must make these sacrifices."

Mrs Bowes picked up the empty medicine-bottle and sniffed at it.

"Potent and unknown drug," said Mrs Bowes sardonically. "Not so very unknown. I could put a name to it. Just what I expected. Well, this is a respectable house, and———"

"You had better be careful, Mrs Bowes. If you dare to imply———"

"Oh, I'll tell you what I imply fast enough. I imply that I'm giving you notice to quit this house at the end of your week."

"That all?" said Purdon. "I've been thinking for weeks past that the place was a bit low class for me. Of course, I'll go. Let me remind you that the law knows how to deal with slander. And now Mrs Bowes, I should be obliged if you would get out of my room."

"Nothing but my strong sense of duty could ever have induced me to enter it," said Mrs Bowes, and retired in good order.

Purdon was pleased. The right words had come slick to the tip of his tongue. He had told that old girl off properly. He wondered a little how he had done it. He need not have wondered. Reaction also has its reaction. Sudden cessation of acute suffering raised the spirit of a man.

5

"Well," said Ethel's mother, "you've given Mrs Bowes notice, and I'm glad you have. But as to seeking other lodgings, what I say is, why need you?"

"Well," said Purdon, "one's got to live somewhere."

"No doubt. But I've talked this all out with Ethel. It's for you to say, of course. I think you said £79 13s. 4d. was what you'd put by, and no doubt it does not seem much on which to face the responsibilities of life. But look at the facts as they stand. There need be no question of setting up a second establishment. This house is big enough. Besides Ethel's room, there's the spare room which is never occupied. You see, you have been engaged for a year. Ethel is an attractive girl, though I say so. But naturally she does not get any younger. At present there are two young men who are after her, madly in love with her."

"If you'll kindly give me their names and addresses," said Purdon, "I think that's a matter that I'm competent to—"

"Oh, don't you worry. Ethel knows how to take care of herself. She can put a man in his place alright. But there's the advantage to yourself from an immediate marriage. You'd be better fed, better looked after, and it would cost you less money. I should be glad to have you here too. Often and often Ethel and I have thought of spending the evening with friends, and hardly liked to, leaving the house empty. Of course, if we were leaving a man here, there would be no cause for anxiety."

"And Ethel agrees?"

"You know as well as I do how shy the girl is. I'll say this much—I think you could persuade her."

"I'll try," said Purdon.

He was entirely successful.

Not on the Passenger List

I had not slept. It may have been the noise which prevented me. The entire ship groaned, creaked, screamed and sobbed. In the state-rooms near mine the flooring was being torn up, and somebody was busy with a very blunt saw just over my head—at least it sounded like that. The motion, too, was not favourable for sleep. There was nothing but strong personal magnetism to keep me in my bunk. If I had relaxed it for a moment I should have fallen out.

Then the big trunk under my berth began to be busy, and I switched on the light to look at it. In a slow and portly way, it began to lollop across the floor towards the door. It was trying to get out of the ship, and I never blamed it. But before it reached the door a suit-case dashed out from under the couch and kicked it in the stomach. I switched off the light again, and let them fight it out in the dark.

I recalled that an elderly pessimist in the smoking-room the night before had expressed his belief that we were overloaded and that if the ship met any heavy weather, she'd break in two for sure. And then I was playing chess with a fat negress who said she was only black when she was playing black pieces; but in the middle of it somebody knocked and said my bath was ready.

The last part turned out to be true. My bath was even more than ready, it was impatient; as I entered the bathroom the water jumped out to meet me and did so. Then, when the bath and I had finished with each other, my steward came slanting down the passage, at an angle of thirty degrees to the floor, without spilling my morning tea, and said that the weather was improving.

There were very few early risers at breakfast that morning, but I was not the first. Mrs Derrison was coming out as I entered the saloon. I thought she looked ill, but it was not particularly surprising. We said good-morning, and then she hesitated for a moment.

"I want to speak to you," she said. "Do you mind? Not now. Come up on deck when you've finished your breakfast."

She was not an experienced traveller, and had consulted me about various small matters. I supposed she wanted to know what was the right tip for a stewardess or something of that kind. Accordingly, after breakfast I went up, and found her wrapped in furs—very expensive furs—in her deckchair. I could see now that she was not in the least seasick, but she said she had not slept all night. I moved her chair into a better position, and chatted as I wrapped the rug round her.

I confessed that with the exception of an hour's nightmare, I had also not slept. As a rule, she would have smiled at this, for she smiled easily and readily. But now she stared out over the sea as if she had heard the words without understanding them. She was a woman of thirty-four or thirty-five, I should think, and had what I generally called an interesting face. You noticed her eyes particularly.

"Well," I said, "the wind's dropping, and we shall all sleep better tonight. Look, there's the sun coming out at last. And now, what's the trouble? What can I do for you?"

"I don't think that even you can help," she said drearily, "though you've done lots of kind things for me. Still, I've got to tell somebody. I simply can't stand it alone. Oh, if I were only the captain of this ship!"

"I don't think you'd like it! Why, what would you do?"

"Turn round and go back to New York."

"It couldn't be done. The ship doesn't carry enough coal. And we shall be at Liverpool the morning after next. But why? What's the matter?"

She held out one hand in the sunlight. It looked very small and transparent. It shook.

"The matter is that I'm frightened. I'm simply frightened out of my life."

I looked hard at her. There was no doubt about it. She was a badly frightened woman. I resisted the urge to pat her on her shoulder.

"But really, Mrs. Derrison, if you'll forgive me for saying so, this is absolute nonsense. The boat's slower than she ought to be, and I'll admit that she rolls very badly, but she's as safe as a church all the same."

"Yes, I know. In any case that's not the kind of thing that would frighten me. This is something quite different. And when I have told you it, you will probably thin I am insane."

"No," I said, "I shall not think that."

"Very well. I told you that I was a widow. I wear no mourning, and

I did not tell you that Alec, my husband, died only three months ago. Nor did I tell you, which is also the truth, that I am going to England in order to marry another man."

"I understand all that. Go on."

"Alec died three months ago. But he is on this boat. I saw him last night. I think he has come for me."

She made that amazing statement quietly and without excitement. But you cannot tell a ghost story convincingly to a man who is sitting in the sun at half-past nine in the morning. I neither doubted her sincerity nor her sanity. I merely wondered how the illusion had been produced.

"Well," I said, "you know that's quite impossible, don't you?"

"Yesterday I should have said so."

"So, you will tomorrow. Tell me how it happened, and I will tell you the explanation."

"I went to my room at eleven at night. The door was a little way open—fixed by the hook arrangement—the way I generally leave it. I switched on the light and went in. He was sitting on the berth with his legs dangling, his profile towards me. The light shone on the bald place on his head. He wore blue pyjamas and red slippers—the kind that he always wore. The pocket of his coat was weighed down, and I remembered what he had told me—that when he was travelling, he put his watch, money, and keys in there at night. He turned his head towards me. It came round very slowly, as if with an effort. That was strange, because so far, I had been startled and surprised but not frightened. When the head turned round, I became really frightened. You see, it was Alec—and yet it was not."

"I don't think I understand. How do you mean?"

"Well, it was like him—a roundish face, clean-shaven, heavily-lined—he was fifteen years older than I was—with his very heavy eyebrows and his ridiculously small mouth. His mouth was really abnormal. But the whole thing looked as if it had been modelled out of wax and painted. And, then, when a head turns towards you, you expect the eyes to look at you. These did not. They remained with the lids half down—very much as I remembered him after the doctors had gone. Oh, I was frightened! I fumbled with one hand behind me, trying to find the bell-push. He knew I had rung—I could see that. His lips kept opening and shutting as if he was trying hard to speak. When the voice came at last, it was only a whisper. He said 'I want you!' when the stewardess tapped at the door, and I did not see him anymore."

"Did you tell the stewardess?"

"Oh, no! I did not mean to tell anybody then. I pretended o be nervous about the ship rolling too much, and managed to keep her with me for a long time. She offered to fetch the doctor for me, so that I could ask him for a sleeping-draught, but I wouldn't have that."

"Why not?"

"I was afraid to go to sleep. I wanted to be ready in case—in case it happened again. You see, I knew why it was."

"I don't think you did, Mrs. Derrison. But I will tell you why it was, if you like. The explanation is vey simple and very prosaic."

"What is it?"

"The cause of the illusion was merely seasickness."

"But I've not felt ill at all."

"Very likely not. If you had been ill in the ordinary way, the way in which it has taken a good many of our friends, you would never have had the illusion. Brain and stomach act and react on one another. The motion of the boat, too, is particularly trying to the optic nerves. In some cases, not very common perhaps, but quite well-known and recognised—it is the brain and not the other organ which is temporarily affected."

I do not know anything about it really, and had merely invented the seasickness theory on the spur of the moment. It was necessary to think of something plausible and very commonplace. Mrs. Derrison was suffering a good deal, and I had to stop it.

"If I could only think that," she said, "what a comfort it would be!"

"Whether you believe it or not, it's the truth" I said. "I've known a similar case. It won't happen to you again, because the weather's getting better, and so you won't be ill."

She wanted to know all about the "similar case," and I made up a convincing little story about it. Gradually she began to be reassured.

"I wish I had known about t before," she said. "All last night I sat in my room, with the light turned on, getting more and more frightened. I don't think there's anything hurts one so much as fear. I can understand people being driven mad by it. You see, I had a special reason to be afraid, because Alec was jealous, very jealous. He had even I suppose, some grounds for jealousy."

She began to tell me her story. She had married Alec Derrison nine years before. She liked him at that time, but she did not love him, and she told him so. He said that it did not matter, and that in time she would come to love him. I dare say a good many marriages that begin that way turn out happily, but this marriage was a mistake.

He took her to his house in New York, and there they lived for a year without actual disaster. He was very kind to her, and she was touched by his kindness. She had been quite poor, and now she had plenty of money to spend, and liked it. But it became clear to her in that year not only that she did not love her husband but that she never would love him. And she was, I could believe, a rather romantic and temperamental kind of woman, by whom many men were greatly attracted. Alec Derrison began to be very jealous—at that time quite absurdly and without reason.

At the end of the year Derrison took her to Europe for a holiday. And there, in England, in her father's country rectory, she met the man whom she ought to have married—an artist of the same age as herself. The two fell desperately in love with one another. The man wanted to take her away with him and ultimately to marry her. She refused.

There is a curious mixture of conscience and temperament which is sometimes mistaken for cowardice and is often accompanied by extraordinary courage. She went to her husband and, so to speak, put her cards on the table.

"I love another man," she said. "I love him in the way in which I wished to love you but cannot. I did not want this and did not look for it, but it has happened to me. I am sorry it has happened, but I do not ask you to forgive me, for you have nothing to forgive. I want to know what you mean to do."

His answer was to take her straight back to New York. There for the eight years before he died, he treated her with kindness and gave her every luxury, but all the time he had her watched. Traps were laid for her, but in vain. He had reason to go to England every year, but he never took her with him.

When he was away, two of his sisters came to the house and watched for him.

And yet, because in some things a woman is cleverer than a man, and also because the feminine conscience always has its limitations, during the whole of those eight years she corresponded regularly with the other man without being found out. They never met, but she had his letters. And now she was going back to marry him.

It was, perhaps, a little curious that she should tell all this to a man whom she had known only for a few days. But intimacies grow quickly on-board ship, and besides she wanted to explain her terror.

"You see how it was," she said. "If a dead man could come back again, then certainly he would come back. And when one begins to be frightened the fear grows and grows. One thinks of things. For instance, he crossed more than once in this very boat—I thought of that."

"Well, Mrs. Derrison," I said, "the dead cannot and do not come back. But a disordered interior does sometimes produce an optical illusion. That's all there is to it. However, if you like, I'll go to the purser and get your room change for another; I can manage that all right."

It was not a very wise suggestion, and she refused it. She said that it would be like admitting that there was something in it beyond seasickness.

"Good!" I said. "I think you're quite right. I thought it might ease your mind not to see again the room where you were frightened, but it is much better to be firm about it. In fact, you had better take a cup of soup and then go back to your room now, and get an hour's sleep before lunch."

"I wonder if I could."

"Of course, you can. You're getting your colour back, and there's much less motion on the boat. You won't have another attack. You've had a sort of suppressed form of seasickness, that's all. And I can quite understand that it scared you at the time, when you didn't know; but there's no reason why it should scare you now when you do know."

She took my advice. A woman will generally take advice from any man except her husband—because he's the only man she really knows. She was disproportionally grateful. Gratitude is rare, but when found, it is in very large streaks. She had also decided to believe that I knew everything, could do everything, and had other admirable qualities. When a woman decides to believe, facts do not hamper her.

She was much better at lunch and afterwards. Next day she was apparently normal, and was taking part in the usual deck-games. I began to think my seasickness theory might have been a lucky shot. I consulted the ship's doctor about it, without giving him names or details, but he was very non-committal. He was a general practitioner, of course, and I was taking him into specialist regions. Besides, naturally enough, a doctor does not care to talk his own shop with a layman. He gave me an impression that any conclusions to which I came would necessarily be wrong. But it did not worry me much. I did not see a great deal of Mrs. Derrison, but it was quite obvious that she had recovered her normal health and spirits. I believed that the trouble was over.

But it was not.

On the night before we arrived, after the smoking-room had been closed, old Bartlett asked me to come to his rooms, for a chat and a whisky and soda. The old man slept badly and was inclined to a late sitting. We discussed various subjects, and amongst them memory for faces.

"I've got that memory," he said. "Names bother me, but not faces. For instance, I remember the faces of seventy or eighty in the first class here."

"I thought we were more than that."

"No. People don't cross the Atlantic for fun in February. It's a pretty light list. It's a funny thing too—we've got one man on-board who's never showed up at all. I saw him for the first time this morning—to be accurate, yesterday morning—coming from the bath, and I've not seen him since. He must have been hiding in his state-room all the time."

"Ill, probably."

"No, not ill. I asked the doctor. I supposed he don't enjoy the society of his fellowmen for some reason."

"Well, now," I said, "let's test your memory. What was he like?"

"You've given me an easy one as it happens, for he was rather a curious chap to look at, and easy to remember in consequence. A man in the fifties, I should say; medium height; wore blue pyjamas with a gold watch-chain trickling out of the pocket, and those red slippers that you buy in Cairo. But his face was what I noticed particularly. He's got a one-inch mouth—smallest mouth I ever saw on a man. But the whole look on his face was queer, just as if it had been painted and then varnished."

"He was bald, round-faced, wrinkled, and clean-shaven. He walked very slowly, and he looked as if he were worried out of his life. There's the portrait, and you can check it when we get off the boat—you're bound to see him then."

"Yes, you've a good memory. If I had just passed the man in a passage, I shouldn't have remembered a thing about him ten minutes afterwards. By the way, have you spoken about the hermit passenger to anybody else?"

"No, Oh, yes, I did mention it to some of the ladies after dinner! Why?"

"I wondered if anybody besides yourself had seen him."

"Well, they didn't say they had. Bless you, I've known men like that. It's a sort of sulkiness. They'd sooner be alone."

A few minutes later I said goodnight and left him. It was between one and two in the morning. His story had made a strong impression upon me. My theory of seasickness had to go, and I was scared. Quite frankly, I was afraid of meeting something in blue pyjamas. But I was more afraid about Mrs. Derrison. There were very few ladies on board, and it was almost certain she was in the group to whom Bartlett had told his story. If that were so, anything might have happened. I decided to go past her state-room, listening as I did so.

But before I reached her room the door opened, and she swung out in her nightdress. She had got her mouth open and one hand at her throat. With the other hand she clutched the handle of the door, as if she was trying to hold it shut against somebody. I hurried towards her, and she turned and saw me. In an instant she was in my arms, clinging to me in sheer, mad, helpless terror.

She was hysterical, of course, but fortunately did not make much noise. She kept saying: "I've got to go back to him—into the sea!" It seemed a long time before I could get her calm enough to listen to me.

"You've had a bad dream, and it frightened you, poor child."

"No, no. Not a dream!"

"It didn't seem like one to you, but that's what it was. You're all right now. I'm going to take care of you."

"Don't let go of me for a moment. He wants me. He's in there."

"Oh, no! I'll show you that he's not there."

I opened the door. Within all was darkness. I still kept one arm round her, or she would have fallen.

"I left the light on," she whispered.

"Yes," I said, "but your sleeve caught the switch as you came out. I saw it." It was a lie, of course, but one had to lie.

I switched the light on again. The room was empty. There were the tumbled bedclothes on the berth, and a pillow had fallen to the floor. On the table some toilet things gleamed brightly. There were a pile of feminine garments on the couch. I drew her in and closed the door.

"I'll put you back into to bed again," I said, "if you don't mind.

"If you'll promise not to go."

"Oh, I won't go."

I picked her up and laid her on the berth, and drew the clothes over her. I put the pillow back under her head. With both her hands she clutched one of mine.

"Now, then," I said, "do you happen to have any brandy here?"

"In a flask in my dressing-bag. It's been there for years. I don't know if it's any good still."

She seemed reluctant to let go of my hand, and clutched it again eagerly when I brought the brandy. She was quite docile, and drank as I told her. I have not put down half of what she said. She was muttering the whole time. The phrase "into the sea" occurred frequently. All ordinary notions of the relationship of a man and a woman had vanished. I was simply a big brother who was looking after her. That was felt by both of us. We called each other "dear" that night frequently, but there was not a trace of sex-sentimentality between us.

Gradually she became more quiet, and I was no longer afraid that she would faint. Still holding my hand, she said:

"Shall I tell you what it is?"

"Yes, dear, if you like. But you needn't. It was only a dream, you know."

"I don't think it was a dream. I went to sleep, which I had never expected to do after the thing that Mr. Bartlett told us. I couldn't have done it, only I argued that you must be right and the rest must be just a coincidence. Then I was awakened by the sound of somebody breathing close by my ear. It got further away, and I switched on the light quickly. He was standing just there—exactly as I described him to you—and he picked up a pair of nail-scissors. He was opening and shutting them. Then he put them down open, and shook his head. (Look they're open now, and I always close them.) And suddenly he lurched over, almost falling, and clutched the wooden edge of the berth. His red hands—they were terribly red, far redder than they used to be—came on to the wood with a slap. 'Go into the sea, Sheila,' he whispered. 'I'm waiting. I want you.' And after that I don't know what happened, but suddenly I was hanging on to you, dear. How long was it ago? Was it an hour? It doesn't matter. I'm safe while you're here."

I released her hands gently. Suddenly the paroxysm of terror returned.

"You're not going?" she cried, aghast.

"Of course not." I sat down on the couch opposite her. "But what makes you think you're safe while I'm here?"

"You're stronger than he is," she said.

She said it as if it were a self-evident fact which did not admit of argument. Certainly, though no doubt unreasonably, it gave me confidence. I felt somehow that he and I were fighting for the woman's life and soul, and I had got him down. I knew in some mysterious way I was the stronger.

"Well," I said, "the dream that one is awake is a fairly common dream. But what was the thing that Bartlett told you?"

"He saw him—in blue pyjamas and red slippers. He mentioned the mouth too."

"I'm glad you told me that," I said, and began a few useful inventions. "The man that Bartlett saw was Curwen. We've just been talking about it."

"Who's Curwen?"

"Not a bad chap—an electrical engineer, I believe. As soon as Bartlett mentioned the mole on the cheek and the little black moustache, I spotted that it was Curwen."

"But he said he had never seen him before."

"Nor had he. Curwen's a bad sailor and has kept to his stateroom—in fact, that was his first public appearance. But I saw Curwen when he came on board, and had a talk with him. As soon as Bartlett mentioned the mole, I knew who it was."

"Then the colour of the slippers and—"

"They were merely a coincidence, and a mighty unlucky one for you."

"I see," she said. Her muscles relaxed. She gave a little sigh of relief and sank back on the pillow. I was glad that I had invented Curwen and the mole.

I changed the subject now, and began to talk about Liverpool—not so many miles away now. I asked her if she had changed her American money yet I spoke about the customs, and confessed to some successful smuggling that I had once done. In fact, I talked about anything that might take her mind away from her panic.

Then I said:

"If you will give me ten seconds start now, so that I can get back to my own room, you might ring for your stewardess to come and take care of you. It will mean an extra tip for her, and she won't mind."

"Yes," she said, "I ought not to keep you any longer. Indeed, it is very kind of you to have helped me and to have stayed so long. I'll never forget it. But even now I daren't be alone for a moment. Will you wait until she's actually here?"

I was not ready for that.

"Well," I said hesitatingly.

"Of course," she said. "I hadn't thought of it. I can't keep you.

You've had no sleep at all. And yet if you go, he'll—Oh, what am I to do? What am I to do?"

I was afraid she would begin to cry.

"That's all right," I said. "I can stay for another hour or two easily enough."

She was full of gratitude. She told me to throw the things off the end of the couch so that I could lie at full length. I dozed for a while, but I do not think she slept at all. She was wide awake when I opened my eyes. I talked to her for a little, and found her much reassured and calmed. People were beginning to move about. It was necessary for me to go immediately if I was not to be seen.

She agreed at once. When I shook hands with her, and told her to try for an hour's sleep, she kissed my hand fervently in a childish sort of way. Frightened people behave rather like children.

I was not seen as I came from her room. The luck was with me. It is just possible that on the other side of the ship, a steward saw me enter my own room in evening clothes at a little after five. If he did, it did not matter.

★★★★★★★★★★★★

I have had the most grateful and kindly letters from her and her new husband—the cheery and handsome man who met her at Liverpool. In her letter she speaks of her "awful nightmare, that even now it seems sometimes as if it must have been real." She has sent me a cigarette case that I am afraid I cannot use publicly. A gold cigarette case with a diamond push-button would give a wrong impression of my income, and the inscription inside might easily be misunderstood. But I like to have it.

Thanks to my innocent mendacity, she has a theory which covers the whole ground. But I myself have no theory at all. I know this— that I might travel to New York by that same boat tomorrow, and that I am waiting three days for another.

I am suppressed the name of the boat, and I have said nothing by which she could be identified. I do not to spoil business. Besides, it may be funk and superstition that convinces me that on every trip she carries a passenger whose name is not on the list. But, for all that, I *am* quite convinced.

The Unseen Power

Winter walked restlessly about the room as he told his story. He was a slender young man, with very smooth hair worn rather too long, a gold-mounted *pince-nez*, and an expression which showed that vanity was not wholly absent from his composition. It was the story of a heisted house. The man who owned it, and was now unable to let it, had asked Winter to investigate.

"And the whole point of it is that you've got to come along and help me," he concluded.

"Thank you," said Mr Arden, "but I will not go."

Arden was a man of fifty, white-haired, thin, heavily lined.

"Well, why not?" said Winter, peevishly. "I want to know why not. It seems to me it would be rather interesting. You can choose any night you like, and—"

Arden waved the subject away with one hand. "It's useless to talk about it," he said, "I'm not going."

"But what do you mean?" said Winter. "You are not going to tell me that you're superstitious or afraid?"

"I should say," said Arden, "that I am what you would call superstitious. You, I presume, are not." "Emphatically not," said Winter.

"Nor afraid?"

"Nor afraid," Winter echoed.

"Then why don't you go alone?" said Arden. Winter murmured of sociability; it was no great fun to sit up all night by one's self. Besides, in the detection of a practical joke, which was probably all that it was, two would be better than one. Arden must see for himself that—

Arden broke in impetuously. "Look here," he said. "Stop wandering about the room and sit down. I'll tell you why I won't come. Did you ever hear of Minnerton Priory?"

"Of course, I've heard about it. I don't know the whole story, and I don't suppose anybody does. A man lost his life over it, didn't he?"

"Two men lost their lives. I was the third man. Now, you know why I won't play with these things anymore."

"Tell me about it," said Winter. "I've only heard scraps here and there, and reports are always inaccurate. So, you were actually one of them. I should never have guessed it."

"I will tell you the story if you wish. Will you have it now, or will you wait till you have finished your investigation of the house at Falmouth?"

"I will hear it now," said Winter.

This is the story that Arden told.

★★★★★★★★★★★★

"In 1871 my aunt, Lady Wytham, bought Minnerton Priory. The place had been uninhabited for the best part of half a century, and was in very bad repair. It was cheap and it was picturesque, and both cheapness and picturesqueness appealed to Lady Wytham. Of the original Priory there was very little left standing. Frequent additions had been made to it at different periods, and the general effect of the place when I first saw it was rather grim and queer. Lady Wytham was very energetic, had the place surveyed, and in a few months had got her workmen down there.

"In one wing of the house a secret chamber had been found. It was on the ground floor, and it was a small room of perhaps twelve feet square. There was one window to it, placed very high up, and this window had been built up on the outside. Opposite to the window was a small fireplace, and the only entrance to the room was from the big dining-hall. The hall was panelled, and one of the panels formed the door into the secret chamber. I believe this kind of thing is fairly common in old houses dating back to the times of religious and political trouble, when hiding-places were constantly wanted.

"The builders had not been at work many months at the Priory before there was trouble. I cannot say exactly what it was. It began with the unbricking of the little window in the secret chamber. I know that the men refused point-blank to do any work whatever in the great dining-hall. Many were dismissed and new hands were taken on, but the trouble still persisted, till finally Lady Wytham herself went down to interview the clerk of works and a foreman or two. On the following day she wrote to me. She said that an idiotic story was being told with reference to the newly-discovered chamber of Minnerton Priory, and she was anxious to have it satisfactorily knocked on the head. Would I, and any friends that I might care to bring down, spend a few nights in the secret chamber? It would probably be very uncomfortable, but she would send over furniture and a servant to wait on us. The postscript explained that the servant would not sleep in the house.

"The idea rather appealed to me, but being, unlike yourself, a little nervous over the business, I determined to take a couple of men down with me. One of them was an intimate friend of mine, Charles Stavold, a good-natured giant, but a useful man in a row. He and I talked it over together, and finally selected as the third man a young doctor, Bernard Ash. Ash was a remarkably brilliant young man, and we looked to him to supply the brains of the trio. If any practical joke were attempted, he would be quite certain to find it out, and both Stavold and myself were quite sure that some practical joke would be attempted, Minnerton Priory lies in a very conservative county.

"The rustics of the village were quite capable of resenting Lady Wytham's intrusion into the Priory. It had always been uninhabited in their father's time, and that would be quite reason enough to determine them that it should not be inhabited now. There were some objections to our choice. Ash led an extremely dissipated life, and Stavold and myself were a little inclined to doubt his nerves. This doubt, by the way, was not justified by results.

"We reached Minnerton in the afternoon. A large staff of men was busy at work at the place, but the only person in or anywhere near the great dining-hall was Lady Wytham's servant, Rudd. She could not have sent us a better man. He could turn his hand to anything. He had already unpacked the beds and other furniture that had been sent and put them in place, and was at present engaged on getting dinner for us. We went through the dining-hall and into the secret chamber.

"'This won't do,' said Ash at once,

"'What don't do?' asked Stavold.

"'Why, there's no furniture in here of any kind. One can't sleep on these stone flags.'

"'Are we going to sleep in here?' I asked.

"'One of us is,' he said.

"I called up Rudd and gave my directions. He brought mattresses and made up a bed on the floor. Then we went round and examined the walls carefully, for, as Ash observed, where there is one trick panel there may be another. But we could find nothing that seemed in any way suspicious.

"We came back into the great hall, and sat down there and talked the thing over. It was now growing dusk. Already the tapping and hammering of the workmen had ceased, and we had heard them laughing as they passed the window on their way home. Right away at the other end of the hall came the chink of plates and the hiss of a frying-pan where Rudd was busy with his preparations. He had brought four big lamps with him, and these he now lit, but there seemed to be something impenetrable about the darkness of this vast room. The light was still dim, with masses of dark shadow waving in the far corners and in the vaulted roof above us.

"'Who's going to sleep in the haunted chamber?' Stavold asked.

"'I am,' said Ash.

"We squabbled about it, and finally decided to toss for it. Ash had his own way. He was to sleep there that night, Stavold was to sleep there the second night, and I myself was left the third night. By this time, we had little doubt that we should be at the bottom of the mystery.

"Rudd gave us an excellent dinner, and had shown wisdom in his choice of the wine which he had brought with him. The wine made glad the heart of man, and before dinner was over, we were treating the whole thing more as an amusing kind of spree than as a serious investigation. At ten o'clock Rudd inquired at what hour we should like breakfast in the morning, and asked if there was anything further, he could do for us that night.

"'Aren't you going to stop and see the ghost, Rudd?' I asked.

"'I think not, sir,' he said quietly. 'Her ladyship had arranged, sir, that I should sleep at the inn.'

"So, we let him go, and I had a curious feeling that with him went the most competent man of the four. Perhaps the same idea had occurred to Ash.

"'He's a perfect wonder,' said Ash. 'Fancy being able to turn out a dinner like that here, with no proper appliances of any kind. I don't call it cooking; I call it conjuring tricks.'

"Perhaps you'll see some more conjuring tricks a little later,' said Stavold, grimly.

"After dinner we played poker for an hour or so and then turned in. One of the lamps was left burning in the big hall, and Ash took a candle with him into the secret chamber. But he did not propose to leave it lighted. It wouldn't be playing the game, he said.

"Some time after I had got into bed, I could hear Ash tapping on the panels and trying them again, and I could see the light under the door. Stavold was already heavily sleeping. I knew nothing more till I was awakened by him early on the following morning. Rudd had already returned, and was preparing breakfast. Naturally our first move was to the secret chamber. We opened the panel door and went in. Ash's clothes were hung on the only chair in the room. The bed had been slept in, but there was no one there now. I noticed that the two candlesticks had also vanished. For a moment or two neither of us spoke, and then I asked my companion what he made of it.

"'That's all right,' he said, 'Ash woke early, and has slipped down to the river in his pyjamas to get a swim. It's ten to one we find him there.'

"It was not impossible, but I was surprised that he had not awakened either of us in passing through the hall. We picked up our towels and went down to the river. We called and got no answer, but we had not at this time begun to be anxious. Possibly after his bath he had gone off for a stroll through the plantations. We took a long swim, lit our pipes, and walked up to the house. The workmen were busy now on the new part far away from the big hall. In the hall itself we found breakfast laid for three.

"'Dr Ash has come back then?' I said to Rudd.

"Rudd looked puzzled, 'I have not seen him this morning, sir,'

"'Drowned himself?' I suggested to Stavold.

"'Not a bit of it. Why should he? This is a little practical joke of Ash's. We'll see if he doesn't get tired of it before we do. Hunger will bring him back at lunchtime.'

"Late in the afternoon he had not returned, and we sent word up to the police-station. The police-station sent us the usual idiot, who made his notes and did his best to look as if he knew what to do. We spent the rest of the day in searching for Ash with no success. At ten o'clock we gave it up, and Rudd went back to the inn. We did very little talking, and I had some curious and inexplicable feelings as I sat there in the silence. My tobacco pouch lay on the table at arm's length, and I found myself thinking that I might have an impulse to take it up in my hand but that as I did not want the pouch at the moment, I should resist the impulse. Then my hand shot right out to the pouch, gripped it, and shook it.

"'What the devil are you doing?' said Stavold.

"I flung the pouch down and got up from my chair. 'Dropping off to sleep, I fancy,' I said.

"'You didn't look it.'

"'Well, I ought to know, oughtn't I? Help me to drag another bed into that chamber there. We'll see it through together tonight.'

"'Oh, no, we won't,' said my companion. 'If we did that, we should leave this hall here for the use of the practical jokers, if there are any. You will sleep here tonight. I shall take my turn in the secret chamber; only, if I can help it, I shan't sleep.'

"'I wonder where on earth Ash is,' I said.

"'We don't know and it won't improve our nerves to imagine. Yours seem a bit jumpy anyhow. We've done all we can to find him. Leave it at that.'

"I did not expect to sleep that night, yet sleep came to me in fits. I had wakened many times, and at last I determined that I might as well get up. In half an hour the grey dawn would be beginning, I remembered that Stavold had told me that he did not mean to go to sleep. I whistled softly as I slipped on my clothes, so that he might hear that I was moving about and join me. As he did not come, I listened at the door of the chamber and heard no sound. In a moment I was standing inside it with the lamp shaking in my hand. The room was exactly as we had found it the morning before. There was nobody there. The bed had been slept in, and was now empty. The clothes lay on the chair. The candlestick had gone. I was horribly frightened.

"I did not wait for Rudd to come back. I went on to the village police-station at once and told my story. There was no doubt that this was a serious matter, and before breakfast-time an inspector had arrived from Saltham. Accompanied by a sergeant and myself he came over to the Priory and into the dining-hall.

"'I think I'll take a look round by myself first,' he said. 'You can wait here.' He went into the chamber, and I could hear his heavy boots on the flags and the useless tapping on the walls. I was confident that nothing could be found there. There were a few minutes of silence, and he opened the door and said, 'Will you come in here, Mr Arden?'

"I went in and saw that the bed had been pulled out from its usual place in the corner. He pointed to a large flagstone which the bed had covered.

"'I should like to show you, sir, a curious optical effect there is in this room. Would you mind standing on that flagstone there?'

"I came round the bed to it, and my foot had just touched it when I was jerked backwards and fell to the floor.

"'Beg your pardon, sir,' said the inspector behind me. 'I had to satisfy myself that you didn't know of the trap. See here.'

"He knelt down beside the big flagstone and touched it lightly with his fingers. It was exactly balanced by a big iron pin through the centre, and it now swung open, showing a dark shaft going far down into the earth.

"'You mean that they are down there?' I said.

"'Not a doubt. Each of them, as is only natural, tried the floor as well as the walls, and moved the bed for the purpose. That finished them. It's the merest chance that I didn't go down the shaft myself.'

"'Well,' I said, 'the sooner we go down there the better. Where can we get a rope?'

"The inspector picked up a small tin match-box and emptied out the matches into the palm of his hand. 'Listen,' he said. He flung the box down the shaft. We listened, and listened, but heard no sound. 'See?' he said. 'That's deep. No use to get a rope there. Anyone who fell down there is dead. That's been a well, I should say.'

"I was angry with the man's cock-surety, and said that I was going down in any case. A rope was brought and attached to a lighted lantern. The lantern was lowered, and in a few yards went out. The experiment was tried again and again, and each time the lantern was extinguished by the foul air.

It was hopeless. No human being could have lived for five minutes down there.

"I rose from the floor, put on my coat, and turned to the inspector. 'This explains nothing,' I said. 'On the morning that Dr Ash was missed I went in here with Mr Stavold, and we found the bed placed as it had been the night before, immediately over this trap. If Dr Ash fell down it, how did he put the bed back after him? The same thing applies to Mr Stavold; again, the bed was left over the trap.'

"'They did not move the bed back again, but somebody else did.'

"'Who?'

"'That is what I hope to find out tonight? Are you yourself willing to sleep tonight in the big hall alone?'

"'Certainly. I don't exactly see what the idea is.'

"'Never mind about that. It may come to nothing. One can but try. You say that Rudd locked the door to this hall when he went out at night?'

"'Yes. A modern lock had been fitted, and the door locked itself as soon as it was shut. It could only be opened from the outside with a latch-key.'

"'And no one but yourself, that you know of, had a key?'

"'No one that I know of.'

"'Very well. I have a few things to see after. I must speak to this man Rudd. I shall see you before nightfall.'

"I spent a horribly long day. I had to telegraph to the relatives of my two friends. I sent Rudd for books, and tried in vain to read. Rudd was aware that the police had a suspicious eye upon him and was in a state of suppressed fury. While Rudd was away, I again examined the inner chamber. The window was too high up to be reached by anyone within the room, and too closely barred to admit of anyone passing through it. The chimney was equally impassable. No vestige of hope was left to me. At ten o'clock the inspector came in and told me that he had given up for the night. He looked thoughtfully towards the whisky decanter. I gave him a drink and mixed one for myself. Then he said goodnight and went off.

"I had not expected to sleep, but an insurmountable drowsiness came over me. I flung myself down on the bed as I was, without undressing, hoping that in this way I should wake again in an hour or so.

"When I woke the room was brightly lighted. The inspector, two of his men, and Rudd himself were all there. I was startled.

"'What's the matter? What's up?' I said.

"'Nothing much,' said the inspector, 'but I know who put the bed back in its place.'

"'Who was it?'

"'It was yourself, sir. You did it in your sleep. It had occurred to me that this was just possible, and I had a man watching through the window of the room.'

"'It is impossible,' I said. 'I should know something of it. I am sure I have been here ever since you left me. Your man must have made a mistake.'

"'My man made no mistake,' said the inspector, drily, 'for my man happened to be myself. You came in, set the lamp down, pushed the bed over to one corner, and then went to the chair, where you seemed to be folding up imaginary clothes.'

"The bodies were recovered two days later, and the whole story of course got into the papers. I was away from England for some years after that. It was one of the things that one wishes to forget. You ask me to take part in another of these investigations. In all probability there is nothing to investigate but a practical joke, or a chance noise, or something equally explicable, but you will understand that I will not take the risk that there may be something else."

★★★★★★★★★★★★

"But, my dear Arden," said Winter, balancing the pince-nez in his hand, "there is nothing whatever in the story that you have told me. What could be more natural than that your two friends should examine the floor, should do so with too little care, and should reap the consequences? The repeated dream is itself quite natural; I should imagine there are few people who have not had it. At the most it is a coincidence that the dream, accompanied by somnambulism, should have come three nights in succession, but there is nothing supernatural there."

"Never mind that word supernatural. Do you think there is anything inexplicable? You are forgetting that the bed in that chamber had been slept in both nights. The sleeper had been awakened by some sound. What was it? What drew him to the trapdoor? What was it that took possession of my will and my body so that my own personality was as blotted out as if I had been dead? But," he added, impatiently, "I do not want to convince you. When you are brought in touch, as I have been, with the unseen power you will be convinced. As your friend, I hope you never will be."

The Undying Thing

1

Up and down the oak-panelled dining-hall of Mansteth the master of the house walked restlessly. At formal intervals down the long severe table were placed four silver candlesticks, but the light from these did not serve to illuminate the whole of the surroundings. It just touched the portrait of a fair-haired boy with a sad and wistful expression that hung at one end of the room; it sparkled on the lid of a silver tankard.

As Sir Edric passed to and fro it lit up his face and figure. It was a bold and resolute face with a firm chin and passionate, dominant eyes. A bad past was written in the lines of it. And yet every now and then there came over it a strange look of very anxious gentleness that gave it some resemblance to the portrait of the fair-haired boy. Sir Edric paused a moment before the portrait and surveyed it carefully, his strong brown hands locked behind him, his gigantic shoulders thrust a little forward.

'Ah, what I was!' he murmured to himself—'what I was!'

Once more he commenced pacing up and down. The candles, mirrored in the polished wood of the table, had burnt low. For hours Sir Edric had been waiting, listening intently for some sound from the room above or from the broad staircase outside. There had been sounds—the wailing of a woman, a quick abrupt voice, the moving of rapid feet. But for the last hour he had heard nothing. Quite suddenly he stopped and dropped on his knees against the table:

'God, I have never thought of Thee. Thou knowest that—Thou knowest that by my devihsh behaviour and cruelty I did veritably murder Alice, my first wife, albeit the physicians did maintain that she died of a decline—a wasting sickness. Thou knowest that all here in Mansteth do hate me, and that rightly. They say, too, that I am mad; but that they say not rightly, seeing that I know how wicked I am. I always knew it, but I never cared until I loved—oh, God, I never cared!'

His fierce eyes opened for a minute, glared round the room, and closed again tightly. He went on:

'God, for myself I ask nothing; I make no bargaining with Thee. Whatsoever punishment Thou givest me to bear I will bear it; whatsoever Thou givest me to do I will do it. Whether Thou killest Eve or whether Thou keepest her in life—and never have I loved but her—I will from this night be good. In due penitence will I receive the holy Sacrament of Thy Body and Blood. And my son, the one child that I had by Alice, I will fetch back again from Challonsea, where I kept him in order that I might not look upon him, and I will be to him a father in deed and very truth. And in all things, so far as in me lieth, I will make restitution and atonement. Whether Thou hearest me or whether Thou hearest me not, these things shall be. And for my prayer, it is but this: of Thy loving kindness, most merciful God, be Thou with Eve and make her happy; and after these great pains and perils of childbirth send her Thy peace. Of Thy loving-kindness. Thy merciful loving-kindness, O God!'

Perhaps the prayer that is offered when the time for praying is over is more terribly pathetic than any other. Yet one might hesitate to say that this prayer was unanswered.

Sir Edric rose to his feet. Once more he paced the room. There was a strange simplicity about him, the simplicity that scorns an incongruity. He felt that his lips and throat were parched and dry. He lifted the heavy silver tankard from the table and raised the lid; there was still a good draught of mulled wine in it with the burnt toast, cut heart-shape, floating on the top.

'To the health of Eve and her child,' he said aloud, and drained it to the last drop.

Click, click! As he put the tankard down, he heard distinctly two doors opened and shut quickly, one after the other. And then slowly down the stairs came a hesitating step. Sir Edric could bear the suspense no longer. He opened the dining-room door, and the dim light strayed out into the dark hall beyond.

'Dennison,' he said, in a low, sharp whisper, 'is that you?'

'Yes, yes. I am coming, Sir Edric.'

A moment afterwards Dr. Dennison entered the room. He was very pale; perspiration streamed from his forehead; his cravat was disarranged. He was an old man, thin, with the air of proud humility. Sir Edric watched him narrowly.

'Then she is dead,' he said, with a quiet that Dr. Dennison had not expected.

'Twenty physicians—a hundred physicians could not have saved her. Sir Edric. She was——' He gave some details of medical interest.

'Dennison,' said Sir Edric, still speaking with calm and restraint, 'why do you seem thus indisposed and panic-stricken? You are a physician; have you never looked upon the face of death before? The soul of my wife is with God——'

'Yes,' murmured Dennison, 'a good woman, a perfect, saintly woman.'

'And,' Sir Edric went on, raising his eyes to the ceiling as though he could see through it, 'her body lies in great dignity and beauty upon the bed, and there is no horror in it. Why are you afraid?'

'I do not fear death, Sir Edric.'

'But your hands—they are not steady. You are evidently overcome. Does the child live?'

'Yes, it lives.'

'Another boy—a brother for young Edric, the child that Alice bore me?'

'There—there is something wrong. I do not know what to do. I want you to come upstairs. And, Sir Edric, I must tell you, you will need your self-command.'

'Dennison, the hand of God is heavy upon me; but from this time forth until the day of my death I am submissive to it, and God send that that day may come quickly! I will follow you and I will endure.'

He took one of the high silver candlesticks from the table and stepped towards the door. He strode quickly up the staircase. Dr. Dennison following a little way behind him.

As Sir Edric waited at the top of the staircase he heard suddenly from the room before him a low cry. He put down the candlestick on the floor and leaned back against the wall listening. The cry came again, a vibrating monotone ending in a growl.

'Dennison, Dennison!'

His voice choked; he could not go on.

'Yes,' said the doctor, 'it is in there. I had the two women out of the room, and got it here. No one but myself has seen it. But you must see it, too.'

He raised the candle and the two men entered the room—one of the spare bedrooms. On the bed there was something moving under cover of a blanket. Dr. Dennison paused for a moment and then flung the blanket partially back.

They did not remain in the room for more than a few seconds. The moment they got outside, Dr. Dennison began to speak.

'Sir Edric, I would fain suggest somewhat to you. There is no evil, as Sophocles hath it in his "Antigone," for which man hath not found a remedy, except it be death, and here——'

Sir Edric interrupted him in a husky voice.

'Downstairs, Dennison. This is too near.'

It was, indeed, passing strange. When once the novelty of this—this occurrence had worn off. Dr. Dennison seemed no longer frightened. He was calm, academic, interested in an unusual phenomenon. But Sir Edric, who was said in the village to fear nothing in earth, or heaven, or hell, was obviously much moved.

When they had got back to the dining-room. Sir Edric motioned the doctor to a seat.

'Now, then,' he said, 'I will hear you. Something must be done— and tonight.'

'Exceptional cases,' said Dr. Dennison, 'demand exceptional remedies. Well, it lies there up-stairs and is at our mercy. We can let it live, or, placing one hand over the mouth and nostrils, we can——'

'Stop,' said Sir Edric. 'This thing has so crushed and humiliated me that I can scarcely think. But I recall that while I waited for you, I fell upon my knees and prayed that God would save Eve. And, as I confessed unto Him more than I will ever confess unto man, it seemed to me that it were ignoble to offer a price for His favour. And I said that whatsoever punishment I had to bear, I would bear it; and whatsoever He called upon me to do, I would do it; and I made no conditions.'

'Well?'

'Now my punishment is of two kinds. Firstly, my wife. Eve, is dead. And this I bear more easily because I know that now she is numbered with the company of God's saints, and with them her pure spirit finds happier communion than with me; I was not worthy of her. And yet she would call my roughness by gentle, pretty names. She gloried, Dennison, in the mere strength of my body, and in the greatness of my stature.

'And I am thankful that she never saw this—this shame that has come upon the house. For she was a proud woman, with all her gentleness, even as I was proud and bad until it pleased God this night to break me even to the dust. And for my second punishment, that, too, I must bear. This thing that lies upstairs, I will take and rear; it is bone of my bone and flesh of my flesh; only, if it be possible, I will hide my shame so that no man but you shall know of it.'

'This is not possible. You cannot keep a living being in this house unless it be known. Will not these women say, "Where is the child?"'

Sir Edric stood upright, his powerful hands linked before him, his face working in agony; but he was still resolute.

'Then if it must be known, it shall be known. The fault is mine. If I had but done sooner what Eve asked, this would not have happened. I will bear it.'

'Sir Edric, do not be angry with me, for if I did not say this, then I should be but an ill counsellor. And, firstly, do not use the word shame. The ways of nature are past all explaining; if a woman be frail and easily impressed, and other circumstances concur, then in some few rare cases a thing of this sort does happen. If there be shame, it is not upon you but upon nature—to whom one would not lightly impute shame. Yet it is true that common and uninformed people might think that this shame was yours. And herein lies the great trouble—the shame would rest also on her memory.'

'Then,' said Sir Edric, in a low, unfaltering voice, 'this night for the sake of Eve I will break my word, and lose my own soul eternally.'

About an hour afterwards Sir Edric and Dr. Dennison left the house together. The doctor carried a stable lantern in his hand. Sir Edric bore in his arms something wrapped in a blanket. They went through the long garden, out into the orchard that skirts the north side of the park, and then across a field to a small dark plantation known as Hal's Planting. In the very heart of Hal's Planting there are some curious caves: access to the innermost chamber of them is exceedingly difficult and dangerous, and only possible to a climber of exceptional skill and courage. As they returned from these caves. Sir Edric no longer carried his burden. The dawn was breaking and the birds began to sing.

'Could not they be quiet just for this morning?' said Sir Edric wearily.

There were but few people who were asked to attend the funeral of Lady Vanquerest and of the baby which, it was said, had only survived her by a few hours. There were but three people who knew that only one body—the body of Lady Vanquerest—was really interred on that occasion. These three were Sir Edric Vanquerest, Dr. Dennison, and a nurse whom it had been found expedient to take into their confidence.

During the next six years Sir Edric lived, almost in solitude, a life of great sanctity, devoting much of his time to the education of the younger Edric, the child that he had by his first wife. In the course of this time some strange stories began to be told and believed in the neighbourhood with reference to Hal's Planting, and the place was generally avoided.

When Sir Edric lay on his deathbed the windows of the chamber were open, and suddenly through them came a low cry. The doctor in attendance hardly regarded it, supposing that it came from one of the owls in the trees outside. But Sir Edric, at the sound of it, rose right up in bed before anyone could stay him, and flinging up his arms cried, 'Wolves! wolves! wolves!' Then he fell forward on his face, dead.

And four generations passed away.

2

Towards the latter end of the nineteenth century, John Marsh, who was the oldest man in the village of Mansteth, could be prevailed upon to state what he recollected. His two sons supported him in his old age; he never felt the pinch of poverty, and he always had money in his pocket; but it was a settled principle with him that he would not pay for the pint of beer which he drank occasionally in the parlour of The Stag. Sometimes Farmer Wynthwaite paid for the beer; sometimes it was Mr. Spicer from the post-office; sometimes the landlord of The Stag himself would finance the old man's evening dissipation.

In return, John Marsh was prevailed upon to state what he recollected; this he would do with great heartiness and strict impartiality, recalling the intemperance of a former Wynthwaite and the dishonesty of some ancestral Spicer while he drank the beer of their direct descendants. He would tell you, with two tough old fingers crooked round the handle of the pewter that you had provided, how your grandfather was a poor thing, 'fit for nowt but to brak steeans by ta rord-side.' He was so disrespectful that it was believed that he spoke truth. He was particularly disrespectful when he spoke of that most devilish family, the Vanquerests; and he never tired of recounting the stories that from generation to generation had grown up about them.

It would be objected, sometimes, that the present Sir Edric, the last surviving member of the race, was a pleasant-spoken young man, with none of the family wildness and hot temper. It was for no sin of his that Hal's Planting was haunted—a thing which everyone in Mansteth, and many beyond it, most devoutly believed. John Marsh would hear no apology for him, nor for any of his ancestors; he recounted the prophecy that an old mad woman had made of the family before her strange death, and hoped, fervently, that he might live to see it fulfilled.

The third baronet, as has already been told, had lived the latter part of his life, after his second wife's death, in peace and quietness. Of him John Marsh remembered nothing, of course, and could only recall the few fragments of information that had been handed down to him. He had been told that this Sir Edric, who had travelled a good deal, at one time kept wolves, intending to train them to serve as dogs; these wolves were not kept under proper restraint, and became a kind of terror to the neighbourhood. Lady Vanquerest, his second wife, had asked him frequently to destroy these beasts; but Sir Edric, although it was said that he loved his second wife even more than he hated the first, was obstinate when any of his whims were crossed, and put her off with promises.

Then one day Lady Vanquerest herself was attacked by the wolves; she was not bitten, but she was badly frightened. That filled Sir Edric with remorse, and, when it was too late, he went out into the yard where the wolves were kept and shot them all. A few months afterwards Lady Vanquerest died in childbirth. It was a queer things John Marsh noted, that it was just at this time that Hal's Planting began to get such a bad name. The fourth baronet was, John Marsh considered, the worst of the race; it was to him that the old mad woman had made her prophecy, an incident that Marsh himself had witnessed in his childhood and still vividly remembered.

The baronet, in his old age, had been cast up by his vices on the shores of melancholy; heavy-eyed, grey-haired, bent, he seemed to pass through life as in a dream. Every day he would go out on horseback, always at a walking pace, as though he were following the funeral of his past self. One night he was riding up the village street as this old woman came down it.

Her name was Ann Ruthers; she had a kind of reputation in the village, and although all said that she was mad, many of her utterances were remembered, and she was treated with respect. It was growing dark, and the village street was almost empty; but just at the lower end was the usual group of men by the door of The Stag, dimly illuminated by the light that came through the quaint windows of the old inn. They glanced at Sir Edric as he rode slowly past them, taking no notice of their respectful salutes.

At the upper end of the street there were two persons. One was Ann Ruthers, a tall, gaunt old woman, her head wrapped in a shawl; the other was John Marsh. He was then a boy of eight, and he was feeling somewhat frightened. He had been on an expedition to a distant and foetid pond, and in the black mud and clay about its borders he had discovered live newts; he had three of them in his pocket, and this was to some extent a joy to him, but his joy was damped by his knowledge that he was coming home much too late, and would probably be chastised in consequence. He was unable to walk fast or to run, because Ann Ruthers was immediately in front of him, and he dared not pass her, especially at night. She walked on until she met Sir Edric, and then, standing still, she called him by name.

He pulled in his horse and raised his heavy eyes to look at her. Then in loud clear tones she spoke to him, and John Marsh heard and remembered every word that she said; it was her prophecy of the end of the Vanquerests. Sir Edric never answered a word. When she had finished, he rode on, while she remained standing there, her eyes fixed on the stars above her. John Marsh dared not pass the mad woman; he turned round and walked back, keeping close to Sir Edric's horse. Quite suddenly, without a word of warning, as if in a moment of ungovernable irritation, Sir Edric wheeled his horse round and struck the boy across the face with his switch.

On the following morning John Marsh—or rather, his parents—received a handsome solatium in coin of the realm; but sixty-five years afterwards he had not forgiven that blow, and still spoke of the Vanquerests as a most devilish family, still hoped and prayed that he might see the prophecy fulfilled. He would relate, too, the death of Ann Ruthers, which occurred either later on the night of her prophecy or early on the following day. She would often roam about the country all night, and on this particular night she left the main road to wander over the Vanquerest lands, where trespassers, especially at night, were not welcomed. But no one saw her, and it seemed that she had made her way to a part where no one was likely to see her; for none of the keepers would have entered Hal's Planting by night.

Her body was found there at noon on the following day, lying under the tall bracken, dead, but without any mark of violence upon it. It was considered that she had died in a fit. This naturally added to the ill-repute of Hal's Planting. The woman's death caused considerable sensation in the village. Sir Edric sent a messenger to the married sister with whom she had lived, saying that he wished to pay all the funeral expenses. This offer, as John Marsh recalled with satisfaction, was refused.

Of the last two baronets he had but little to tell. The fifth baronet was credited with the family temper, but he conducted himself in a perfectly conventional way, and did not seem in the least to belong to romance. He was a good man of business, and devoted himself to making up, as far as he could, for the very extravagant expenditure of his predecessors.

His son, the present Sir Edric, was a fine young fellow and popular in the village. Even John Marsh could find nothing to say against him; other people in the village were interested in him. It was said that he had chosen a wife in London—a Miss Guerdon—and would shortly be back to see that Mansteth Hall was put in proper order for her before his marriage at the close of the season.

Modernity kills ghostly romance. It was difficult to associate this modern and handsome Sir Edric, bright and spirited, a good sportsman and a good fellow, with the doom that had been foretold for the Vanquerest family. He himself knew the tradition and laughed at it. He wore clothes made by a London tailor, looked healthy, smiled cheerfully, and, in a vain attempt to shame his own head-keeper, had himself spent a night alone in Hal's Planting. This last was used by Mr. Spicer in argument, who would ask John Marsh what he made of it.

John Marsh replied, contemptuously, that it was 'nowt.' It was not so that the Vanquerest family was to end; but when the thing, whatever it was, that lived in Hal's Planting, left it and came up to the house, to Mansteth Hall itself, then one would see the end of the Vanquerests.

So, Ann Ruthers had prophesied. Sometimes Mr. Spicer would ask the pertinent question, how did John Marsh know that there really was anything in Hal's Planting? This he asked, less because he disbelieved, than because he wished to draw forth an account of John's personal experiences. These were given in great detail, but they did not amount to very much. One night John Marsh had been taken by business—Sir Edric's keepers would have called the business by hard names—into the neighbourhood of Hal's Planting. He had there been suddenly startled by a cry, and had run away as though he were running for his life. That was all he could tell about the cry—it was the kind of cry to make a man lose his head and run.

And then it always happened that John Marsh was urged by his companions to enter Hal's Planting himself, and discover what was there. John pursed his thin lips together, and hinted that that also might be done one of these days. Whereupon Mr. Spicer looked across his pipe to Farmer Wynthwaite, and smiled significantly.

Shortly before Sir Edric's return from London, the attention of Mansteth was once more directed to Hal's Planting, but not by any supernatural occurrence. Quite suddenly, on a calm day, two trees there fell with a crash; there were caves in the centre of the plantation, and it seemed as if the roof of some big chamber in these caves had given way.

They talked it over one night in the parlour of The Stag. There was water in these caves. Farmer Wynthwaite knew it; and he expected a further subsidence. If the whole thing collapsed, what then?

'Ay,' said John Marsh. He rose from his chair, and pointed in the direction of the Hall with his thumb. 'What then?'

He walked across to the fire, looked at it meditatively for a moment, and then spat in it.

'A trewly wun'ful owd mon,' said Farmer Wynthwaite as he watched him.

3

In the smoking-room at Mansteth Hall sat Sir Edric with his friend and intended brother-in-law, Dr. Andrew Guerdon. Both men were on the verge of middle-age; there was hardly a year's difference between them. Yet Guerdon looked much the older man; that was, perhaps, because he wore a short, black beard, while Sir Edric was clean shaven. Guerdon was thought to be an enviable man. His father had made a fortune in the firm of Guerdon, Guerdon and Bird; the old style was still retained at the bank, although there was no longer a Guerdon in the firm.

Andrew Guerdon had a handsome allowance from his father, and had also inherited money through his mother. He had taken the degree of Doctor of Medicine; he did not practise, but he was still interested in science, especially in out-of-the-way science. He was unmarried, gifted with perpetually good health, interested in life, popular. His friendship with Sir Edric dated from their college days. It had for some years been almost certain that Sir Edric would marry his friend's sister, Ray Guerdon, although the actual betrothal had only been announced that season.

On a bureau in one corner of the room were spread a couple of plans and various slips of paper. Sir Edric was wrinkling his brows over them, dropping cigar-ash over them, and finally getting angry over them. He pushed back his chair irritably, and turned towards Guerdon.

'Look here, old man!' he said. I desire to curse the original architect of this house—to curse him in his down-sitting and his uprising.'

'Seeing that the original architect has gone to where beyond these voices there is peace, he won't be offended. Neither shall I. But why worry yourself? You've been rooted to that blessed bureau all day, and now, after dinner, when every self-respecting man chucks business, you return to it again—even as a sow returns to her wallowing in the mire.'

'Now, my good Andrew, do be reasonable. How on earth can I bring Ray to such a place as this? And it's built with such ingrained malice and vexatiousness that one can't live in it as it is, and can't alter it without having the whole shanty tumble down about one's ears. Look at this plan now. That thing's what they're pleased to call a morning room. If the window had been *here* there would have been an uninterrupted view of open country. So, what does this forsaken fool of an architect do? He sticks it *there*, where you see it on the plan, looking straight on to a blank wall with a stable yard on the other side of it. But that's a trifle. Look here again——'

'I won't look any more. This place is all right. It was good enough for your father and mother and several generations before them until you arose to improve the world; it was good enough for you until you started to get married. It's a picturesque place, and if you begin to alter it you'll spoil it.' Guerdon looked round the room critically. 'Upon my word,' he said, 'I don't know of any house where I like the smoking-room as well as I like this. It's not too big, and yet it's fairly lofty; it's got those comfortable-looking oak-panelled walls. That's the right kind of fireplace, too, and these corner cupboards are handy.'

'Of course, this won't *remain* the smoking-room. It has the morning sun, and Ray likes that, so I shall make it into her *boudoir*. It *is* a nice room, as you say.'

'That's it, Ted, my boy,' said Guerdon bitterly; 'take a room which is designed by nature and art to be a smoking-room and turn it into a *boudoir*. Turn it into the very deuce of a *boudoir* with the morning sun laid on for ever and ever. Waste the twelfth of August by getting married on it. Spend the winter in foreign parts, and write letters that you can breakfast out of doors, just as if you'd created the mildness of the climate yourself. Come back in the spring and spend the London season in the country in order to avoid seeing anybody who wants to see you. That's the way to do it; that's the way to get yourself generally loved and admired!'

'That's chiefly imagination,' said Sir Edric. 'I'm blest if I can see why I should not make this house fit for Ray to live in.'

'It's a queer thing: Ray was a good girl, and you weren't a bad sort yourself. You prepare to go into partnership, and you both straightway turn into despicable lunatics. I'll have a word or two with Ray. But I'm serious about this house. Don't go tinkering it; it's got a character of its own, and you'd better leave it. Turn half Tottenham Court Road and the culture thereof—Heaven help it!—into your town house if you like, but leave this alone.'

'Haven't got a town house—yet. Anyway, I'm not going to be un-suitable; I'm not going to feel myself at the mercy of a big firm. I shall supervise the whole thing myself. I shall drive over to Challonsea tomorrow afternoon and see if I can't find some intelligent and fairly conscientious workmen.'

'That's all right; you supervise them and I'll supervise you. You'll be much too new if I don't look after you. You've got an old legend, I believe, that the family's coming to a bad end; you must be consistent with it. As you are bad, be beautiful. By the way, what do you yourself think of the legend?'

'It's nothing,' said Sir Edric, speaking, however, rather seriously. 'They say that Hal's Planting is haunted by something that will not die. Certainly, an old woman, who for some godless reason of her own made her way there by night, was found there dead on the following morning; but her death could be, and was, accounted for by natural causes. Certainly, too, I haven't a man in my employ who'll go there by night now.'

'Why not?'

'How should I know? I fancy that a few of the villagers sit boozing at The Stag in the evening, and like to scare themselves by swopping lies about Hal's Planting. I've done my best to stop it. I once, as you know, took a rug, a revolver and a flask of whisky and spent the night there myself. But even that didn't convince them.'

'Yes, you told me. By the way, did you hear or see anything?'

Sir Edric hesitated before he answered. Finally, he said:

'Look here, old man, I wouldn't tell this to anyone but yourself I did think that I heard something. About the middle of the night, I was awakened by a cry; I can only say that it was the kind of cry that frightened me. I sat up, and at that moment I heard some great, heavy thing go swishing through the bracken behind me at a great rate. Then all was still; I looked about, but I could find nothing. At last, I argued as I would argue now that a man who is just awake is only half awake, and that his powers of observation, by hearing or any other sense, are not to be trusted.

' I even persuaded myself to go to sleep again, and there was no more disturbance. However, there's a real danger there now. In the heart of the plantation there are some eaves and a subterranean spring; lately there has been some slight subsidence there, and the same sort of thing will happen again in all probability. I wired today to an expert to come and look at the place; he has replied that he will come on Monday. The legend says that when the thing that lives in Hal's Planting comes up to the Hall the Vanquerests will be ended. If I cut down the trees and then break up the place with a charge of dynamite I shouldn't wonder if I spoiled that legend.'

Guerdon smiled.

'I'm inclined to agree with you all through. It's absurd to trust the immediate impressions of a man just awakened; what you heard was probably a stray cow.'

'No cow,' said Sir Edric impartially. 'There's a low wall all round the place—not much of a wall, but too much for a cow.'

'Well, something else—some equally obvious explanation. In dealing with such questions, never forget that you're in the nineteenth century. By the way, your man's coming on Monday. That reminds me today's Friday, and as an indisputable consequence tomorrow's Saturday, therefore, if you want to find your intelligent workmen it will be of no use to go in the afternoon.'

'True,' said Sir Edric, 'I'll go in the morning.' He walked to a tray on a side table and poured a little whisky into a tumbler. 'They don't seem to have brought any seltzer water,' he remarked in a grumbling voice.

He rang the bell impatiently.

'Now why don't you use those corner cupboards for that kind of thing? If you kept a supply there, it would be handy in case of accidents.'

'They're full up already.'

He opened one of them and showed that it was filled with old account-books and yellow documents tied up in bundles. The servant entered.

'Oh, I say, there isn't any seltzer. Bring it, please.'

He turned again to Guerdon.

'You might do me a favour when I'm away tomorrow, if there's nothing else that you want to do. I wish you'd look through all these papers for me. They're all old. Possibly some of them ought to go to my solicitor, and I know that a lot of them ought to be destroyed. Some few may be of family interest. It's not the kind of thing that I could ask a stranger or a servant to do for me, and I've so much on hand just now before my marriage——'

'But of course, my dear fellow, I'll do it with pleasure.'

'I'm ashamed to give you all this bother. However, you said that you were coming here to help me, and I take you at your word. By the way, I think you'd better not say anything to Ray about the Hal's Planting story.'

'I may be some of the things that you take me for, but really I am not a common ass. Of course, I shouldn't tell her.'

'I'll tell her myself, and I'd sooner do it when I've got the whole thing cleared up. Well, I'm really obliged to you.'

'I needn't remind you that I hope to receive as much again. I believe in compensation. Nature always gives it and always requires it. One finds it everywhere, in philology and onwards.'

'I could mention omissions.'

'They are few, and make a belief in a hereafter to supply them logical.'

'Lunatics, for instance?'

'Their delusions are often their compensation. They argue correctly from false premises. A lunatic believing himself to be a millionaire has as much delight as money can give.'

'How about deformities or monstrosities?'

'The principle is there, although I don't pretend that the compensation is always adequate. A man who is deprived of one sense generally has another developed with unusual acuteness. As for monstrosities of at all a human type one sees none; the things exhibited in fairs are, almost without exception, frauds. They occur rarely, and one does not know enough about them. A really good text-book on the subject would be interesting. Still, such stories as I have heard would bear out my theory—stories of their superhuman strength and cunning, and of the extraordinary prolongation of life that has been noted, or is said to have been noted, in them. But it is hardly fair to test my principle by exceptional cases. Besides, anyone can prove anything except that anything's worth proving.'

'That's a cheerful thing to say. I wouldn't like to swear that I could prove how the Hal's Planting legend started; but I fancy, do you know, that I could make a very good shot at it.'

'Well?'

'My great-grandfather kept wolves—I can't say why. Do you remember the portrait of him?—not the one when he was a boy, the other. It hangs on the staircase. There's now a group of wolves in one corner of the picture. I was looking carefully at the picture one day and thought that I detected some over-painting in that corner; indeed, it was done so roughly that a child would have noticed it if the picture had been hung in a better light. I had the over-painting removed by a good man, and underneath there was that group of wolves depicted. Well, one of these wolves must have escaped, got into Hal's Planting, and scared an old woman or two; that would start a story, and human mendacity would do the rest.'

'Yes,' said Guerdon meditatively, 'that doesn't sound improbable. But why did your great-grandfather have the wolves painted out?'

4

Saturday morning was fine, but very hot and sultry. After breakfast, when Sir Edric had driven off to Challonsea, Andrew Guerdon settled himself in a comfortable chair in the smoking-room. The contents of the corner cupboard were piled up on a table by his side. He lit his pipe and began to go through the papers and put them in order. He had been at work about a quarter of an hour when the butler entered rather abruptly, looking pale and disturbed.

'In Sir Edric's absence, sir, it was thought that I had better come to you for advice. There's been an awful thing happened.'

'Well?'

'They've found a corpse in Hal's Planting about half an hour ago. It's the body of an old man, John Marsh, who used to live in the village. He seems to have died in some kind of a fit. They were bringing it here, but I had it taken down to the village where his cottage is. Then I sent to the police and to a doctor.'

There was a moment or two's silence before Guerdon answered.

'This is a terrible thing. I don't know of anything else that you could do. Stop; if the police want to see the spot where the body was found, I think that Sir Edric would like them to have every facility.'

'Quite so, sir.'

'And no one else must be allowed there.'

'No, sir. Thank you.'

The butler withdrew.

Guerdon arose from his chair and began to pace up and down the room

'What an impressive thing a coincidence is!' he thought to himself. 'Last night the whole of the Hal's Planting story seemed to me not worth consideration. But this second death there—it can be only co-incidence. What else could it be?'

The question would not leave him. What else could it be? Had that dead man seen something there and died in sheer terror of it? Had Sir Edric really heard something when he spent that night there alone? He returned to his work, but he found that he got on with it but slowly. Every now and then his mind wandered back to the subject of Hal's Planting. His doubts annoyed him. It was unscientific and unmodern of him to feel any perplexity, because a natural and rational explanation was possible; he was annoyed with himself for being perplexed.

After luncheon he strolled round the grounds and smoked a ci-gar. He noticed that a thick bank of dark, slate-coloured clouds was gathering in the west. The air was very still. In a remote corner of the garden a big heap of weeds was burning; the smoke went up perfectly straight. On the top of the heap light flames danced; they were like the ghosts of flames in the strange light. A few big drops of rain fell. The small shower did not last for five seconds. Guerdon glanced at his watch. Sir Edric would be back in an hour, and he wanted to finish his work with the papers before Sir Edric's return, so he went back into the house once more.

He picked up the first document that came to hand. As he did so, another, smaller, and written on parchment, which had been folded in with it, dropped out. He began to read the parchment; it was written in faded ink, and the parchment itself was yellow and in many places stained. It was the confession of the third baronet—he could tell that by the date upon it. It told the story of that night when he and Dr. Dennison went together carrying a burden through the long garden out into the orchard that skirts the north side of the park, and then across a field to a small, dark plantation. It told how he made a vow to God and did not keep it. These were the last words of the confession:

Already upon me has the punishment fallen, and the devil's wolves do seem to hunt me in my sleep nightly. But I know that there is worse to come. The thing that I took to Hal's Planting is dead. Yet will it come back again to the Hall, and then will the Vanquerests be at an end. This writing I have committed to chance, neither showing it nor hiding it, and leaving it to chance if any man shall read it.

Underneath there was a line written in darker ink, and in quite a different handwriting. It was dated fifteen years later, and the initials R.D. were appended to it:

It is not dead. I do not think that it will ever die.

When Andrew Guerdon had finished reading this document, he looked slowly round the room. The subject had got on his nerves, and he was almost expecting to see something. Then he did his best to pull himself together. The first question he put to himself was this: 'Has Ted ever seen this? Obviously, he had not. If he had, he could not have taken the tradition of Hal's Planting so lightly, nor have spoken of it so freely. Besides, he would either have mentioned the document to Guerdon, or he would have kept it carefully concealed. He would not have allowed him to come across it casually in that way.

'Ted must never see it,' thought Guerdon to himself. He then remembered the pile of weeds he had seen burning in the garden, He put the parchment in his pocket, and hurried out. There was no one about. He spread the parchment on the top of the pile, and waited until it was entirely consumed. Then he went back to the smoking-room; he felt easier now.

'Yes,' thought Guerdon, 'if Ted had first of all heard of the finding of that body, and then had read that document, I believe that he would have gone mad. Things that come near us affect us deeply.'

Guerdon himself was much moved. He clung steadily to reason; he felt himself able to give a natural explanation all through, and yet he was nervous. The net of coincidence had closed in around him; the mention in Sir Edric's confession of the prophecy which had subsequently become traditional in the village alarmed him. And what did that last line mean? He supposed that R.D. must be the initials of Dr. Dennison. What did he mean by saying that the thing was not dead? Did he mean that it had not really been killed, that it had been gifted with some preternatural strength and vitality and had survived, though Sir Edric did not know it? He recalled what he had said about the prolongation of the lives of such things.

If it still survived, why had it never been seen? Had it joined to

183

the wild hardiness of the beast a cunning that was human—or more than human? How could it have lived? There was water in the caves, he reflected, and food could have been secured—a wild beast's food. Or did Dr. Dennison mean that though the thing itself was dead, its wraith survived and haunted the place? He wondered how the doctor had found Sir Edric's confession, and why he had written that hue at the end of it. As he sat thinking, a low rumble of thunder in the distance startled him. He felt a touch of panic—a sudden impulse to leave Mansteth at once and, if possible, to take Ted with him. Ray could never live there. He went over the whole thing in his mind again and again, at one time calm and argumentative about it, and at another shaken by blind horror.

Sir Edric, on his return from Challonsea a few minutes afterwards, came straight to the smoking-room where Guerdon was. He looked tired and depressed. He began to speak at once:

'You needn't tell me about it—about John Marsh. I heard about it in the village.'

'Did you? It's a painful occurrence, although, of course——'

'Stop. Don't go into it. Anything can be explained—I know that'

'I went through those papers and account-books while you were away. Most of them may just as well be destroyed; but there are a few—I put them aside there—which might be kept. There was nothing of any interest.'

'Thanks; I'm much obliged to you.'

'Oh, and look here, I've got an idea. I've been examining the plans of the house, and I'm coming round to your opinion. There are some alterations which should be made, and yet I'm afraid that they'd make the place look patched and renovated. It wouldn't be a bad thing to know what Ray thought about it.'

'That's impossible. The workmen come on Monday, and we can't consult her before then. Besides, I have a general notion what she would like.'

'We could catch the night express to town at Challonsea, and——'

Sir Edric rose from his seat angrily and hit the table.

'Good God! don't sit there hunting up excuses to cover my cowardice, and making it easy for me to bolt. What do you suppose the villagers would say, and what would my own servants say, if I ran away tonight? I am a coward—I know it. I'm horribly afraid. But I'm not going to act like a coward if I can help it.'

'Now, my dear chap, don't excite yourself. If you are going to care at all—to care as much as the conventional damn—for what people say, you'll have no peace in life. And I don't believe you're afraid. What are you afraid of?'

Sir Edric paced once or twice up and down the room, and then sat down again before replying.

'Look here, Andrew, I'll make a clean breast of it. I've always laughed at the tradition; I forced myself, as it seemed at least, to dis-prove it by spending a night in Hal's Planting; I took the pains even to make a theory which would account for its origin. All the time I had a sneaking, stifled belief in it. With the help of my reason, I crushed that; but now my reason has thrown up the job, and I'm afraid. I'm afraid of the Undying Thing that is in Hal's Planting. I heard it that night. John Marsh saw it last night—they took me to see the body, and the face was awful; and I believe that one day it will come from Hal's Planting—'

'Yes,' interrupted Guerdon, 'I know. And at present I believe as much. Last night we laughed at the whole thing, and we shall live to laugh at it again, and be ashamed of ourselves for a couple of supersti-tious old women. I fancy that beliefs are affected by weather—there's thunder in the air.'

'No,' said Sir Edric, 'my belief has come to stay.'

'And what are you going to do?'

'I'm going to test it. On Monday I can begin to get to work, and then I'll blow up Hal's Planting with dynamite. After that we shan't need to believe—we shall *know*. And now let's dismiss the subject. Come down into the billiard-room and have a game. Until Monday I won't think of the thing again.'

Long before dinner. Sir Edric's depression seemed to have com-pletely vanished. At dinner he was boisterous and amused. Afterwards he told stories and was interesting.

★★★★★★★★★★★★

It was late at night; the terrific storm that was raging outside had awoke Guerdon from sleep. Hopeless of getting to sleep again, he had arisen and dressed, and now sat in the window-seat watching the storm. He had never seen anything like it before; and every now and then the sky seemed to be torn across as if by hands of white fire. Suddenly he heard a tap at his door, and looked round. Sir Edric had already entered; he also had dressed. He spoke in a curious, subdued voice.

'I thought you wouldn't be able to sleep through this. Do you re-member that I shut and fastened the dining-room window?'

'Yes, I remember it.'

'Well, come in here.'

Sir Edric led the way to his room, which was immediately over the dining-room. By leaning out of window they could see that the dining-room window was open wide.

'Burglar,' said Guerdon meditatively.

'No,' Sir Edric answered, still speaking in a hushed voice. 'It is the Undying Thing—it has come for me.'

He snatched up the candle, and made towards the staircase; Guerdon caught up the loaded revolver which always lay on the table beside Sir Edric's bed and followed him. Both men ran down the staircase as though there were not another moment to lose. Sir Edric rushed at the dining-room door, opened it a little, and looked in. Then he turned to Guerdon, who was just behind him.

'Go back to your room,' he said authoritatively.

'I won't,' said Guerdon. 'Why? What is it?'

Suddenly the corners of Sir Edric's mouth shot outward into the hideous grin of terror.

'It's there! It's there!' he gasped.

'Then I come in with you.'

'Go back!'

With a sudden movement, Sir Edric thrust Guerdon away from the door, and then, quick as light, darted in, and locked the door behind him.

Guerdon bent down and listened. He heard Sir Edric say in a firm voice:

'Who are you? What are you?'

Then followed a heavy, snorting breathing, a low, vibrating growl, an awful cry, a scuffle.

Then Guerdon flung himself at the door. He kicked at the lock, but it would not give way. At last, he fired his revolver at it. Then he managed to force his way into the room. It was perfectly empty. Overhead he could hear footsteps; the noise had awakened the servants; they were standing, tremulous, on the upper landing.

Through the open window access to the garden was easy. Guerdon did not wait to get help; and in all probability none of the servants could have been persuaded to come with him. He climbed out alone, and, as if by some blind impulse, started to run as hard as he could in the direction of Hal's Planting. He knew that Sir Edric would be found there.

But when he got within a hundred yards of the plantation, he stopped. There had been a great flash of lightning, and he saw that it had struck one of the trees. Flames darted about the plantation as the dry bracken caught. Suddenly, in the light of another flash, he saw the whole of the trees fling their heads upwards; then came a deafening crash, and the ground slipped under him, and he was flung forward on his face. The plantation had collapsed, fallen through into the caves beneath it. Guerdon slowly regained his feet; he was surprised to find that he was unhurt. He walked on a few steps, and then fell again; this time he had fainted away.

The Octave of Claudius

CHAPTER 1

Mrs. Wycherley was not quite old. She seemed always to be keeping one foot on the tail of her youth; the poor thing squeaked, but could not quite break away. In her conversation she would often drag you, all tremulous, with her into the confessional, where you found, to your disappointment, that she had no sins, only errors of diet. She was by way of being a woman of the world, with the world left out. Its place in her Erciston Square *salon* was taken by the world's understudies. Henry Burnage, who for years had made her *salon* a habit, would torture himself at times with the thought that he was only a fashionable man's understudy; but the torture did not persist, for his opinion of himself was high and on the whole stable.

Of the understudies there were many; her rooms were full on Sunday evening. Mr. Wycherley would be seen there sometimes; he sat in corners, and was mildly disapproving; he made the money, and Mrs. Wycherley spent it. Still, he acknowledged that his daughter Angela must have every chance, and the *salon* was in some sense a chance. More often Mr. Wycherley did not show himself. He liked to take a walk on Sunday evenings, and he frequently took it. He had a dislike, not wholly irrational, to the *salon*. Reason was a strong point with him.

"Be rational, Jessica," he would frequently say to his wife. "I only ask you to be rational."

When he went his walk, she alluded to his headache. Nobody minded. He was not the attraction, neither was she, and they both knew it; but Angela wore pink, and understudies attract one another. Angela petted her papa a good deal; and, in return, he never mentioned anything in which he was seriously and commercially interested. In public she would sometimes talk to him with endearing facetiousness; this mildly puzzled him—he only dealt in the milder sensations—because in private she rarely tried to talk brightly to him.

Mrs. Wycherley's drawing-room was not in itself wonderful. The walls were covered with a paper that had a dado to it; she had ordered it some years ago herself, and she regretted it. She knew now that it had been premature, and that a paper-with-a-dado did not constitute art's last word with regard to wall-decoration. Mr. Wycherley did not think the times were yet ripe for it to be superseded. He had said so more than once.

Mrs. Wycherley rather believed in what she called "those pretty trifles that make a room look bright;" so she concocted some flower-holders out of Japanese fans and some velvet that had been on the dress that she had worn when Maria was married. These things afterwards were transferred to a spare and permanently unoccupied bedroom. It was thought that Angela had been responsible for their removal. Angela considered that the room was irredeemable, and thought that cheap attempts at redemption humiliated her.

It was late one evening. Mrs. Wycherley's guests had all gone; she had interviewed the hired man in the hall, paid him, swung back into the room again with a declaration that Jameson was invaluable, and now sat down in her rocking-chair, facing her daughter, fanning herself rather vehemently with a fan that had been mended.

"Oh yes, Angela, you may say what you like, but there's never any need to tell Jameson anything. Why he goes on the job instead of taking a permanent place is more than I can imagine. He's just the picture of the perfect butler."

"All right, mamma, all right!" said Angela, rather irritably. "He does, but you needn't think that he deceives anybody."

"I don't wish that he should, dear; far from it. The queen herself may know that he's hired for the evening for all that I care. When one is entertaining a great number of people, one supplements one's staff. The very best people have to do it."

"Yes," drawled Angela, "but they have a staff to supplement. Ah, if we were only *quite* poor."

"Angela, that is really wicked! If you dislike our means—our moderate means—you would dislike poverty still more. We do our best, and it's too ungrateful of you. Mind, I don't say that I am not fond of a little society myself—"

"Oh, mamma, dear! don't be intolerable!"

"I don't know what you mean. But I do know that it's chiefly for your sake that your father consents to these Sunday evenings. And you know that it's the dream of our lives to see you happily married—like Maria. Poverty would be to you Life's Greatest Curse."

"Mr. Burnage told me tonight that he thought families whose income just touched the four figures really had the hardest fight against vulgarity; but he added, from conjecture and a subsequent politeness, that all things were possible to genius. We have the fatal income without the genius, I fancy."

"Ah, Mr. Burnage is one of these rather clever young men. I don't understand 'em. But he looks very well in a room. Angela, my dear, I must hunt myself up a little supper. I hadn't any, I dare not eat when I'm feeling nervous. It only means that I wake with a fluttering in my side and feel as if the angel of death had summoned me. I'll just go into the dining-room and see what I can rescue."

She returned in a minute with a champagne-bottle—still loyal to the third of its contents—and a plate and small tumbler. On the plate was a cold cutlet in aspic, and a silver fork; on the portion of the plate which still remained untenanted were two chocolate *éclairs*. She was careful to keep the aspic clear of the *éclairs* until their turn came; she ate rather greedily. Angela looked genuinely distressed.

"Honesty is a poor word for Jameson," Mrs. Wycherley remarked as she filled her glass. "Any other man would have finished the bottle. You can trust him; that's what I feel so much about Jameson. As a tonic for the stomach, I believe that there's nothing—"

"Oh, mamma, mamma!" said Angela suddenly, "why do we keep on fighting? I used to love our parties once, but I'm getting to know things. We're ridiculous. We aren't quite what we want to be, and we are the more absurd because in some things we are so very near it. I don't think I want to marry. I used to, but I don't now. I certainly don't want to marry any of the underbred young men who come to this house and fall in love with me. I often wonder why I go on trying to be bright and amusing to them, and why I do my best to cover up the rough places and make things go smoothly, and cajole papa, and dress as well as I can. The hell—the awful hell of this London life!" And poor Angela buried her head in a recently purchased cushion, and began to sob a little.

"You distress me," said Mrs. Wycherley, excitedly; "I can't bear to see you like this, Angela. I insist that you shall not sob. I cannot digest when my mind is disturbed. Poor Angela! do be comforted!"

Angela sat up, and dried her eyes in silence. Her brief storm had passed.

"You're feeling low," Mrs. Wycherley continued decisively. "Now, be guided by me, and take something. There are some of these *éclairs* still left, you may just as well have one; you know what things with cream in them are like on the second day. And chocolate's sustaining—now do. And that," she said, suddenly breaking off as she heard a sound at the front door, "is your father's latch-key. Don't let him come in and find you like this."

By the time that Mr. Wycherley had entered, Angela had composed herself. Mr. Wycherley was short and bald, with a slight tendency towards rotundity.

"I have had such a walk," he said, with enthusiastic satisfaction, as he took a distinctly uncomfortable chair, "I went as far as Putney by an omnibus, just as I said I would, then I struck across the common—wonderful place!—round by the mill (thinking about Richmond, you know), and then off to the left into Wimbledon (changed my mind, you see). From Wimbledon I took train to Waterloo, and walked to the club. I found Bodgers there, and we split a bottle of old port. Bodgers would pay. I hope you've all enjoyed yourselves as much as I have."

"It's been a most successful evening," said Mrs. Wycherley.

"Do you like the new champagne, Jessica?"

"On the whole I think it an improvement."

"Sixpence a bottle cheaper—that's what it is. Be reasonable, Jessica, and don't pretend to know anything about anything. There kiss me, and goodnight, Angela; it's time you were off to bed." His lips smacked on her forehead, hers brushed his cheek "Sixpence a bottle cheaper," he murmured to himself again, and went off with a mild approach to hilarity.

Mrs. Wycherley turned once more to her daughter. She was feeling quite optimistic.

"I notice, Angela, that you talk a good deal to Henry Burnage."

"Do I? I'm glad you mentioned it, mamma. I won't do it in future. As a rule, I talk to anyone who isn't talking to anyone else."

"I haven't a word to say against your manner. It isn't the old-school, stately manner exactly."

Angela leant forward, her elbows resting on her knees, her pretty face—she was not nearly as pretty as she looked—framed by her warm little hands. At this point she interrupted her mother—

"Dear mamma, I'm a flirt. When you can't be what you want to be, it's a kind of baby's consolation to be the thing you hate most. But you must not deceive yourself. It occasionally seems to me that Henry

Burnage is less foolish and rather better bred than the average here; but don't imagine that I love him. And he's not in the least in love with me."

"Well, he's been here, off and on, for years. He must be a good deal taken by us. I don't say that, as a rule, I would recommend a girl to marry a young commencing barrister. No, no! I'm not so unwise as that. But Mr. Burnage has means, independent means. I ask you to look at the way his rooms are furnished. You may call them what you like, but I call them gorgeous. And then he entertains—not so frequently as we do, nor on so large a scale."

"But so infinitely better," said Angela, fervently.

"There! you're defending him; what does that mean?"

"It does mean that I tolerate him, and it does not mean that I love him. I know what you want, and it couldn't be done. "Why, if he kissed me, or if I thought even that he wanted to kiss me, I should go quite mad—mad with disgust."

"Oh, Angela, darling!" said Mrs. Wycherley. "You know that I wouldn't force you into anything. There, goodnight! We must not sit up any longer, or what will your father say? You'll come directly, won't you?"

At the drawing-room door she paused a moment, and looked almost beseechingly at her daughter.

"Angela," she said, "I believe that I've had one *éclair* too many."

Chapter 2

If Mr. Wycherley had taken his stroll over Wimbledon Common later in the evening, he would have had an opportunity to play the part of the Good Samaritan. There is no role which is more popular; the feelings of self-satisfaction and superiority help to make life enjoyable, and in consequence it is delightful to rescue. But to be rescued is quite another affair. The thing which is condemned as ingratitude is often a very natural resentment of one who has been placed compulsorily under an obligation. Most men, given a certain amount of sensitiveness, would sooner fall among thieves than among good Samaritans.

The chance which Mr. Wycherley lost was taken by Dr. Gabriel Lamb. The doctor was returning home rather late; it was already beginning to get dark. When he was within a few yards of the garden-gate of his own house, he noticed a young man lying in an awkward position on the grass by the roadside. Dr. Gabriel Lamb bent over him, found him half-conscious, and made a cursory examination of him.

The young man was clad in a well-cut tweed suit, worn to utter shabbiness. His boots were in holes. He was lying where he had fallen when he found that he could go no further; his hat was off, and had received from the fall a damage with which it was already familiar. His face was thin, and at present quite colourless, but it had the tokens of refinement and strength.

Dr. Lamb's examination lasted less than a minute. "I shall be back directly," he said, and began to run towards his own house. He was a middle-aged man. His head, save for a fringe of reddish hair all round it, was bald; but he was very active. He dashed up the garden drive and into the house; here he gave one or two rapid orders to servants, and hurriedly prepared what he wanted. In a very few minutes he was out on the roadway again, with a glass in his hand, bending over the young man. The doctor's servant had accompanied him, and stood at a few yards' distance, waiting.

The young man's eyes were half closed. When the doctor held the glass to his lips, he turned his head away impatiently.

"Drink it at once!" said the doctor, sharply. "Do you want to die?"

The young man spoke in a faint whisper, and with some difficulty.

"Not a beggar. I'm much obliged—very natural mistake of yours. I—I'd rather you left me alone."

"I won't, then. Whoever heard such nonsense? Any man who is taken suddenly ill accepts help from the first stranger who is not too much of a brute to give it him. It's no question of begging. Damn it!" he went on, getting furious, "you shall pay for the ha'porth of brandy, if you like—but drink it."

The young man shook his head. "No money," he murmured, "that's why I'm—"

The effort at explanation seemed to be too much for him, and he stopped.

"All right, then, I'll take your clothes, or you shall work for me; at any rate, I promise you that I will put you under no obligation which you cannot repay. I swear it. Now then."

The young man drank the contents of the glass; in a moment or two his eyes opened wider. He looked reflective.

"That wasn't brandy," he said. His voice was already a shade stronger.

"Not brandy alone. There were other things in it. I'm a doctor, you know. Now, do you see that house?"

The young man raised himself into a sitting position, looked at it,

194

and nodded his head.

"That's my house, and I'm going to take you there, with the help of my servant. Then you'll be put to bed. In a day or two you'll be all right. Now, you must place yourself entirely in my hands and trust to me. I'm not going to put you under any obligation. You shall work out your debt. You look like an educated man."

"Eton and Cambridge—but you couldn't believe it."

"I believe it entirely. Now then, you shall get up. Steady!—there, that's it! Now, slowly."

Supported—almost carried—by the doctor and his servant, the young man was taken into the house. It was a house which seemed to have an old quiet in it—a quiet that had long been there. The colours in the interior were low; it was lit softly and without glare; one's footsteps were not heard on the thick carpets. The house was of red brick; but the red had been softened and shaded by time, and the walls were partly covered with ivy. At the back of the house there was a modern addition, which Dr. Lamb had erected for his own purposes. It was a long, low building, and had a separate entrance into the garden.

The young man found himself in a large and very comfortable bedroom. At one end f the room there was a door into a bathroom, at the other end the room communicated with a dressing-room and a small study. Here the doctor's servant did for him all that a valet could do for a man. Soon he was lying in bed, refreshed by a bath, soothed by the luxuriousness that he had missed so much and for so long, dreamingly wondering whether it could be all true. He had suffered very much, and this sudden change for the better seemed so strange. He thought half-amusedly that the doctor had done a foolish thing; he had taken into his house a man of whom he knew nothing, except that he had found him, a mere vagrant, shabby and fainting from exhaustion and want of food. But the young man reflected that in the course of his life he had frequently been trusted like this—on sight. Certainly, in some way or other, he must repay the doctor. How, he could not imagine. It did not matter—the doctor had promised to find a way for him. But the doctor's kindness and trust were, he felt, beyond repayment.

He began to wonder if they would bring him something to eat; he hoped so. The valet had left the lamp and the candles by his bedside alight, so it seemed certain that he would return. The valet had treated him with the utmost respect, as an honoured guest, and not as a relieved vagabond. If he ever got any money, he would remember the man. Presently the door opened, and the doctor and the servant entered. The servant carried a small tray, on which were a cup of chocolate and two sandwiches, made of toast and some kind of meat-jelly. While the young man was eating (he was ordered to eat slowly) the doctor sat down by the bedside and began to talk to him. At first, he was merely medical, then he said—

"My name, you know, is Lamb. I'm Dr. Gabriel Lamb. May I ask what your name is?"

"Mine is Claudius Sandell. I really don't know how to thank you."

"Not a word, not a word, if you please."

"Words would certainly be of very little good. I hope that I have not been keeping you from any other patients."

The doctor smiled. "Oh, I don't practise," he said. "It was lucky for you—and I think it lucky for me also—that you chose a Sunday evening for your collapse. I only walk on Sunday evenings—chiefly because it is not church. Ah, yes—quite true—there is church also on Sunday morning, Sunday afternoon, and on certain occasions in the week! My wife—to whom I hope soon to introduce you—attends every service; she also stays for the after-meetings. You must not, by the way, think that I am an unbeliever. I am not; at one time I always went to church on Sunday evenings, and there was much in it that I enjoyed. But the curate's banalities, the superstitiousness of the people, and the perfectly evil singing of the choir vexed me. Then it occurred to me that if I went for a walk on Sunday evening instead, I could get the service without the church. I could have the sunset and the aspirations, the longings for the far-away that it produces."

He stopped abruptly, and noticed that the servant was listening with rather a puzzled face. He turned to him.

"Wait outside, Francis," he said.

When the man had retired, the doctor began to pace the room, and went on talking. Under his very thick sandy eyebrows and long lashes his grey eyes grew luminous.

"Sometimes it's in the spring. Damn it! there's nothing like a spring evening. I'm in earnest about it. The poetry of it is so strenuous and yet so quiet; so full of fresh life, and yet so full of the old peace that still passes all understanding. But it's always as the service of God that I take my Sunday evening walk. I love the lime-trees—trees of the Pentecost—with their leaves turning to tongues of fire as they shake under the strokes of wind and sunlight. I love the cold purity of the sky on winter evenings that get dark so soon. How all the stars look at one! The heavens declare the glory of God. Ah! I'm talking far too much!"

Claudius was watching him with keen interest. "No, no," he said, "go on, I'm beginning to understand."

"That really is all—only on Sunday evenings do I walk, because it is not church but is service. The rest of my time is given to work."

"To work, doctor? But you said that you did not practise."

"Quite so, I do not, although, when I was a younger man, I had a practice for a time. It did not content me. One night I was rung up by a woman; I went downstairs and found her hysterical on the door-steps. She pulled herself together, and prayed me to come at once to see her son who was dying. She lived about a mile off. We ran a good deal; she was distressed and I was sympathetic. When we got there, I found that the boy was not dying, but was slightly bilious. Then I asked myself if that kind of thing was science as I loved it—if it really assisted the great cause of humanity for which alone I live. I gave up my practice. I study the individual man only when he is likely to throw light on the aggregate. I never work on behalf of the individual. But I tire you."

"No, I am not tired."

"Pardon me, but you are. It is merely the effect of the restorative that makes you feel strong, and that effect will pass off. You are very much run down, and yon need rest. You would perhaps like something more to eat; I shall not give it you. Tomorrow you shall be better treated. Goodnight, Mr. Sandell, goodnight!"

When he got to the door, he paused a moment, and said, "Do the clothes you were wearing fit you perfectly?"

"Very fairly—it's about all you can say for them. I have got thinner since they were made."

"That's all right. A tailor can make others from them, I suppose: it will save you the bother of measurements. Goodnight, again."

Before Claudius could answer, the doctor had gone. In the passage, outside the room. Dr. Lamb was detained for a minute by the valet.

"Excuse me, sir, but I've seen this Mr. Sandell before."

"Where?"

"At Cambridge. I was a gyp at Trinity, sir, you remember, before I came to you. This Mr. Sandell was really there; it's quite true what he said."

"Don't make that mistake again," said Dr. Lamb, somewhat impressively, "When I told you, a few minutes ago, that Mr. Sandell was my guest, it ceased to be necessary for you to give him a character for truthfulness, or sobriety, or early rising, or anything else. You will sleep in the dressing-room, in case Mr. Sandell should want you during the night. If he is unable to sleep, or turns faint again, you know what to do, but he won't. I shall want you to go to town tomorrow for me; you must go early. I will give you your orders immediately after breakfast."

As Dr. Lamb was coming down the stairs, a carriage drove up to the door. Mrs. Lamb had come back from the after-meeting. She placed on the hall table two or three devotional books: amongst them was her Bible, fastened by an elastic band, and bulged with sheets of written notes. She was rather a short woman, with dark hair, and plain anaemic face and ecstatic eyes. She looked very young, twenty years younger than the doctor.

"I'm late," she said to him, "but I've been very happy—so happy! We had Mr. Catcome as usual—Elijah and the believer's hope."

Dr. Lamb looked at his wife, and said nothing; then he smiled slightly. When he smiled his thin lips showed rather large white teeth. She saw the smile, and a nervous expression came into her face; she appeared to be slightly afraid of her husband.

They went into the dining-room. At a small table supper was laid; and they both sat down. Mrs. Lamb said grace audibly, while her husband stared pensively at a mayonnaise.

CHAPTER 3

Mrs. Lamb's want of tact was so pronounced that it even overcame her fear of her husband, and she still spoke about the service of the church and the great good that she had received from it; he listened politely with attention, occasionally looking up from his plate at her, almost inquisitively. At each glance from under the thick sandy eyebrows, and at each slight smile that showed the big white teeth, she faltered. The glance and smile had a kind of reserved meaning in them; they forced her into the exasperating belief that she was being treated with superiority. She was half-inclined to lose her temper—did, indeed, for one moment cut the chicken-wing on her plate as if it had been an enemy—but commanded herself. She was not a very clever woman, emotional, half-fanatical, with the pathetic want to be good.

Dr. Lamb said very little until supper was over, and his few remarks to his wife were commonplace enough. As she rose from the table, he said—

"I've told them to take the coffee to my room tonight. I can't talk comfortably in these big rooms, and I've got some news for you. Will you come, Hilda?"

"Yes, dear, in one minute."

He held open the door for her, she passed into the hall. He stood a moment reflective; his brows were slightly wrinkled. He did not like the substitution of a late cold supper for dinner at the usual time; but it marked Sunday for Hilda. He did not like Hilda to sit down to an evening meal in an afternoon dress, with her hat on; but it marked Sunday for her. This interested him slightly; he wondered how her observation of Sunday would work out when her day came. There had been signs lately (he had noted them all as they came) that her day was very near.

He crossed the hall and went down a corridor to the two rooms which constituted the addition which he had made to the house. The first of these rooms was furnished as a study; the walls were covered with books, most of them, books of the advanced scientist, some of them, books that even an advanced scientist would have classed as heterodox, the work of charlatans.

It was brightly lighted; on a side table the coffee and liqueurs had been placed all ready. At one end of the room was a door leading into the laboratory. The doctor opened the door and looked in; the laboratory was in darkness, but he reached his hand upward to a button in the wall and switched on the electric light.

The lamps reflected themselves on polished mahogany cases and on the bell-glass that protected a large microscope from the dust. There was rather an unpleasant smell in the room. Shelves and cabinets were ranged all round the walls; in one corner stood a lead-covered table; on another table stood two or three bottles and a measuring glass. The doctor put the bottles back in their places on the shelves, and washed the glass at a square stone basin. He had used the things in preparing the restorative. Then he switched off the electric light and went back into the study again, closing the door behind him. Here he sat down, poured out his coffee, tilted a little glass of Cognac into it, lit a cigarette, and began to think.

He really had a very great deal to think about that night.

He was interrupted, however, almost immediately, by the entrance of his wife. She had changed her dress, and was wearing a loose black tea-gown. It suited her fairly well, and her pale face had now a pretty tinge of colour in it. Dr. Lamb looked at her critically.

"You've changed," he began.

199

"Yes, I saw you weren't liking the other."

"Ah!" said Dr. Lamb, "that's good of you. It's the curse of the individual that such trifles should matter to him. There's nothing so small in the impulses of collected humanity, the aggregate. Mankind," he continued, speaking more to himself than to her, "is so great, and isolated man's so small."

"You had something to tell me," Hilda said timidly.

"Ah, yes." He told her how he had found Claudius Sandell, and taken him into the house. It was his intention to keep him for a few days—perhaps weeks— to provide him with clothes, and so on. "He says that he must repay me—cannot bear the obligation—is very strong on that point."

"Gabriel, this is one of the queerest things you have done. Of course, it is very kind of you, and I must say that many professing Christians would have been quite content just to have given the man a copper—or a sixpence."

"He would not have taken it; and in that condition it would have been no good to him if he had taken it."

"No? It was so silly of him not to want to be helped; I rather like him for that. Quite dark hair, you said—and tall, I imagine him. Well, I hope it will turn out all right. But you have done almost more than you need. The best suite of rooms in the house, and in every way the treatment of an honoured guest!"

"Quite so. Apart from the fact that a gentleman cannot very well take advantage of another gentleman's poverty in order to humiliate him, there are reasons. You will oblige me by treating him exactly as I have done—as an honoured guest."

"I will do anything to please you," she said humbly.

"And I must confess that I like you better in this docile mood than in the mood which it has replaced. When you came back to the house tonight, you addressed me as if I were an atheist, which was incorrect of you—as I have frequently explained. You also spoke to me about the curate and Elijah, and the believer's hope, and you are quite aware that I do not discuss such subjects with you. Your God is the projection of the curate upon the average feminine intelligence; you believe in your heart that your God wrote the whole Bible in English and got it published by Bagster.

"I cannot share your conception or your view; but I am not an atheist. I love God; that is the reason why I love and serve to the uttermost His humanity, and would sacrifice any unit of it in the cause of the aggregate. Now this must be the last time. I leave you your intellectual freedom and you may go to church, but you shall not talk church."

"Gabriel, did you love me when you married me?"

Her downcast eyes were raised and looked full at his.

"I am a man of like passions to others."

"You made me happy, you know. It was a life of sordid drudgery at home—papa was always overworked and mamma was always tired, and there was that trouble with my sister Matilda. You gave me all that money could give. And then"—she gasped and caught her breath—"our child!"

"Well, go on!"

"Now I don't know whether you love me or not—I don't even know whether I love you, because I am afraid of you so. But I know that there's a change. You used even to go to church with me. You were not always locked up in the laboratory. Even now you are good to me; you give me more money than I can spend; you give me presents; you are considerate for me, and do things to please me. But I'm shut out of your real life. Oh, Gabriel, I hate science!"

"You should not do that, dear," said the doctor, blandly. "My interest in you is largely scientific."

"Don't!" she said, pathetically, not irritably. "Don't look at me as if I were a specimen. Don't be just interested in me. I'm a woman. It wasn't for the money and comfort that I married you. I loved you. You loved me once, Gabriel; science did not stand first; you used to make concessions to me."

"I am making concessions now."

"By listening to me politely? Yes, you regard all the smaller conventionalities."

"I do. I have no pretence to transcend humanity. My contempt for the individual includes my individual self. I try to regard all the smaller conventionalities, and to some of them I am really attached. I get vexed at trifles. I am particular about some quite unimportant things. For that reason I prefer the conventional dinner to the Sunday supper, which is one of my concessions to you; to which you sit down, perspiring and religious, in a hat. And I despise myself for ever thinking about such light things, when I realise the greatness of the work before me. Do I love you? My dear Hilda, I do not even love myself My point of view has been changed by—"

"Don't talk," she broke in passionately, bursting into tears, "don't go on talking! It doesn't comfort me. Love me again, Gabriel! Love me! Else I shall hate you."

"Excessive emotion," said the doctor, "is not good for you, and will probably hasten your day. You must go to bed at once."

She rose like a whipped child. "I'm sorry," she said, in a low husky voice; "I forgot, I know you don't like scenes, and I'm wanting to try very hard to please you in everything. I'm going; goodnight, dear."

The doctor raised one of her hands and kissed it, and opened the door for her. She passed out. Halfway up the broad staircase that led to her room she paused a moment, thinking. What had he meant by "hasten her day"? He had said once before that "her day would come." She knew instinctively, that it would be useless to ask him, and put the question by with a kind of despair. In her room she stood before the glass, surveying herself. The colour on her cheeks was slightly disordered. She took a sponge and washed it all off. She made up her mind not to use it again.

It was of no good for her to try and make herself look pretty anymore; and, even if rouge had given her beauty, that would not have made her husband love her again. "Love!" she whispered to herself, panting. Then she remembered that it was wicked to use rouge. She had but just come from church, and had painted her face like a bad woman: it was wicked of her. She knelt and prayed God to forgive her. Then she rose, and took a candle and stepped across the passage to another room. It had been her baby's nursery. She unlocked the door and entered.

The room was neatly kept. A little cradle stood in one corner, bedecked and empty. She walked over to it, and rocked it a little. Then she opened a drawer, and turned over piles of tiny clothes that were not wanted now. "My little baby!" she whispered. Her eyes were strained, and aching, and dry. But she cried again in bed that night.

It was long before Dr. Lamb came to bed.

He had not been working in his laboratory; he had been thinking about Claudius Sandell. The doctor had not had much opportunity to observe him; but, nevertheless, he summed him up: a man whose pride was greater than his instinct of self-preservation, a truthful man.

The doctor thought for a long time. "Oh, I shall use him— I shall certainly use him," he said to himself at last. "A great find; he will quite repay me."

Upstairs Claudius Sandell slept peacefully.

CHAPTER 4

"Yes," said Harry Burnage to himself, "I must marry Angela." He paced up and down the soft carpet, thinking about it. He was alone in his well-ordered chambers, smoking a cigarette that was not to be bought in shops. It was a good cigarette, but its flavour was as nothing to the fact that it was not to be bought in shops. It seemed to fill the room with that atmosphere of uniqueness, distinction, speciality, that Henry Burnage believed that he loved. He had arrived slowly at his resolution; he rarely hurried important things; he liked to act correctly; and, though he would say a passably brilliant thing about the commercial spirit and the middle classes, he very much liked to get on in the world. He had been considering marriage with Angela Wycherley as one might consider anonymous journalism—in a critical spirit, weighing the arguments for and against. That was the way he had begun at least.

Angela's mother was barely possible. She was too large, too obvious, too good-tempered, and she gave too much publicity to that side of her which should have been reserved for the specialist in dyspepsia. Her circle included too generously. Well, once married, Henry Burnage felt that Mrs. Wycherley could be deleted altogether. Then there was her father—a mildly commercial person, whose Sunday night anxiety (unless he had one of those headaches) seemed to be first to find the background, and then to sit in it. He would not need to be deleted, he would delete himself. He would probably do something for Angela. The commerce was only mildly successful, but Angela was the only unmarried child; it was almost certain there would be something for her. Besides, Henry Burnage's own father had made him a very liberal offer—if he got married. The elder Burnage did not believe that young men kept straight unless they married—besides, he wanted to see a grandchild.

Then there was Angela to be considered. Just here the merely critical consideration became touched by emotion—the material side of Henry Burnage was in love with Angela, he had come under her charm. Now, this charm was not peculiar to Angela; many other girls have it, and it is more easily described in its result. Angela made the men that she met imagine her secrets; she inspired fascinating reverie. Burnage, with all his business qualities, was much given to fascinating reverie.

A catalogue's justice would have been unjust to her looks, for her features were slightly irregular. The ebb and flow of colour on her dusky cheeks, or a chance movement of her long eyelashes, or the curve of her figure in some chance position that she had taken would baulk dispassionate criticism; she had a store of trifles to throw into the scale against classical beauty, and apparently outweigh it. She had seemed at one time to Burnage to be a flirt; but now he was inclined to think that she had grown serious-hearted, and was being hurt by it. He wondered if she cried sometimes at night, just before she went to sleep, because of her thoughts. That would be terrible.

She should tell him about it—just give him her warm little hands to hold, cast her eyes down, and make shy confidences. His vanity, caught by his imagination, soared grandly upwards, like thistledown riding the wind. He began to picture things; her rapt eyes seemed to look at him, and her low voice to tell him how good he was. He seemed to hear music; the wedding march took its memorable downward sweep, curled over the key-note, and broke at his feet. It moved upwards again, changed to a slow, straining waltz that beat its great wings regularly—upwards into the rarefied atmosphere of the passionate lover, where the whole world stopped, and one kiss continued.

He had arrived slowly at his resolution—beginning with criticism and ending in ecstasy, just at the last, warming a cold ambition by the fires of love, or the nearest that he could get to love. He was glad that the resolution was taken; it had been hovering in his mind for some time. He felt a kind of importance in consequence of it; he seemed to himself to be embarking on a fresh epoch in his existence.

He dined at his club, and dined well. Thoughts of a love-touched future, black coffee, a small glass of *kirsch*, and another of the cigarettes that could only be obtained by favour occupied him for the next two minutes. Then he proceeded to write two letters.

His first letter was to his father, and Henry Burnage's letters to his father were exceedingly unlike his letters to anybody else. The elder Burnage had started life with a small shop, and although he had long ago retired from his business, he had never been able to feel properly ashamed of it; and he never said even a passably brilliant thing about the commercial spirit and the middle classes. This alone made him different from the kind of man that his son was.

The father was somewhat Puritanical, and quite uncultured; here again the son was different. In a more humorous moment, the father would sometimes say: "Have you been buying any aesthetic things lately, Henry?" What was to be done with such a man—a man who could never succeed in forgetting the back numbers of *Punch*—a man who was quite crude and point-blank—a man who could never be convinced that he misunderstood another man's point of view, and yet always did misunderstand it?

Henry could only sigh drearily, and try to read the essays of Matthew Arnold without noticing that their severest thrusts went straight through his own father—happily ignorant of the assault, and quite contented. Just as a mean motive and a more generous motive had made Henry decide to marry Angela, a mixture of motives influenced him in the treatment of his father. He was not without filial affection, but he also wondered, occasionally, in what proportion his father would, in his last will and testament, divide his property between him and his very plain and unattractive sister. He tried to write to his father the kind of letter that his father would like, but he spent as little time as possible on the composition of it, knowing that his father was not critical in such things. Tonight his letter ran as follows:—

My dear Father,

You may be assured that your last letter—stating that you have had no return of the sciatica—gave me great pleasure. I was delighted to hear that you managed to get as far as from our house to the cemetery. You must be careful not to overdo it, but I suppose you would not walk that distance without permission from the doctor. Certainly, the embrocation which he prescribed seems to have done wonders. So, you have got the main drainage at last, and are compelled to connect with it; I always said that it would come, and after the initial expenses you will probably find the arrangement much more satisfactory. I am sorry that the new vicar is not to your liking; his adoption of the eastward position and other ritualistic practices in face of so many protests seems to me very silly.

It is, as you say, a great pity that the living should be in the gift of Sir Constantine Sandell—a man who has belonged at times to almost every conceivable religious sect. By the way, I am almost certain that I saw Claudius Sandell in the Fulham Road about a month ago, just after I sent you my last letter. It was getting dark, and I cannot be positive; but, if I am right, he has very much come down in the world. The man I saw was dressed in the seediest clothes, no stick or gloves, smoking a clay-pipe, and peering into the window of a small eating-house.

As I had two other men with me, I was naturally not anxious to claim the acquaintance of—apparently—a half-starved tramp; so, I hurried on to avoid recognition. Otherwise, I should have been glad to have lent him a few shillings for the sake of old times together at Cambridge. Of course, we do not know what the quarrel was between Sir Constantine and Claudius. You think that Sir Constantine was in the wrong; he may have been. At the same time, I do not think that a father—however hot-tempered, and however eccentric—entirely breaks with his only son for nothing.

Why was it that Claudius, who was quite by way of being my friend at Trinity, never told me one word of the reason for the quarrel, and parried my questions on the subject? Why is it that, although he has been in London, and knew that he could get my address at the Temple, he has never been to see me, and has never sent me his own address? It must mean that he is ashamed of something.

It is strange that he—who was always thought so wonderful—should have been compelled to leave Cambridge without taking a degree, and should then have gone completely under; while I—who was nobody in particular—took a second in my tripos, and am already beginning to get on at the bar. By the way, is that curious woman, Miss Comby, still at Sir Constantine's?

In conclusion, I have something important to say. I feel that you are right, and I accept your very generous offer. You will not be surprised to hear that the lady whom I intend to marry is Angela Wycherley, of whom I have often spoken to you. I am now only waiting my opportunity to make a formal proposal; and I think I may say, without conceit, that I know what her answer will be. Before I do so, I shall be glad to hear from you if you think the alliance suitable.

> Your affectionate son,

> Henry Burnage.

His next letter was to Luke Monsett. And to him Henry Burnage employed a sort of sham literary style, with a good deal of affectation, short paragraphs, and capital letters in it.

Dear Luke,

Action and reaction make me distrust all. The swing of the pendulum in one direction seems to take a man so far: it also returns as far. There is no Stability. How we clung to the expression of culture through furniture—environment. Nay, I still cling to it. Yet always I shift my around from time to time. Even now it is better to employ aniline dyes with a duchess than to like the art flower-pot that has penetrated Bloomsbury. Stability!

If you knew—if you could only know—how I long to get to it! Now comes some hope at last. You ask what? A woman's eyes, that are more beautiful because they are now grown serious; on my part, nights in which I do not sleep, but think entrancingly. Is there not hope of stability there? The *bourgeois* marry to perpetuate their very indifferent species; and I to find anchorage for my soul in calm waters. If so—then, at last, stability. Of other news, nothing—save that I hear that our friend, Claudius Sandell, is now definitely gone under. And you thought him very great. All, well, it will teach you to distrust!

Of your own life, what??

Write soon.

Yours in these bonds of flesh,

Henry Burnage.

He did not write in this style to his father, because his father was not sympathetic, would not have understood, and would certainly have called him an ass. But Henry Burnage fancied the style, and probably would have believed that his letter to Luke was rather good.

But in one point he was mistaken: Claudius was not yet definitely "gone under."

In fact, not very long after this date. Dr. Gabriel Lamb wrote a letter to his bankers, asking them to place eight thousand pounds to the credit of Mr. Claudius Sandell (of whose signature he enclosed examples) during a period of eight consecutive days, to commence on the following Saturday morning. The circumstances which led to this order may now be recorded.

CHAPTER 5

Three days after the curious arrival of Claudius Sandell at the house of Dr. Gabriel Lamb, the two men stood together in the garden, one morning after breakfast. Claudius was smoking a delicious cigar, the first that he had smoked for over a year. He had drunk good coffee; his memory contrasted it with the "cup o' thick" that he had been compelled to take a few days before at an early-morning stall. He remembered the sharp eyes of the man who had handed it him, and the furtive Jew boy that had rubbed shoulders with him, and the bad green smell of everything.

And now he was looking out on a well-kept garden, noting the fruit trees as they spread themselves to the sun along the wall. He heard the sleepy hum of the mowing-machine, where at a little distance a gardener was busy on the lawn. He had been refreshed by a long sleep and a cold bath; he was wearing good clothes; he had fed well and been well treated. It was hard for him to realise that all this was the result of charity, for the kindness that had been shown him had come in the guise of hospitality. Dr. Lamb had acted up to his principle, that it was impossible for a gentleman to take advantage of the necessities of another gentleman in order to humiliate him.

"Come down to the end of the garden," said the doctor, cheerily. "You haven't half seen the place yet."

The doctor was wearing a short holland jacket and no hat; in one hand he swung a small empty canvas bag. As they went down the paths Claudius happened to make some remarks, with almost boyish *naïveté*, on the perfection of the house and garden. He had, he said, never seen a place which was so complete in small details—trifles.

"Now, my dear Sandell," said the doctor, putting one hand on his arm, "I am not going to contradict you, but I am going to correct an impression that I believe you must have formed of me. I own that I have taken great care lest there should be anything wrong in even the minutest domestic matters, but you must not think, that because I am particular about trifles, I admire them or take an interest in them. I assure you that I hate them; I hate them so much that I cannot bear to have them in my mind. If the details of my house and domestic life were wrong, they would always be obtruding themselves upon my attention: I should think about them, and I should detest that. It is the same with money. If a man really hates money, he takes good care that he has enough of it for all his needs, in order that he may not think about it.'"

"You found me," said Claudius, "without a penny in my pocket and fainting from exhaustion. But, all the same, I assure you that I do not love money."

"Do not," said the doctor, pleadingly, "be so ultra-sensitive, my clear fellow. I like fine feelings, but to be ultra-sensitive is so—so altogether damnable. I assure you that your case was not in my mind when I spoke. And my remark would not apply to you in any case, because you are too young. You will make money yet, because you hate it; there is plenty of time before you."

"You're much too good to me, doctor," Claudius said rather seri-ously. "I am inclined to agree with you: one of the greatest curses of poverty and privation is that they make a man who is not used to them sensitive and bad-tempered. I never used to be bad-tempered."

"There's good enough evidence of that."

Claudius looked as if he did not quite understand, and the doctor went on—

"I mean, of course, in your physiognomy. You are, on the whole, very good-tempered; you can lose your temper badly, for all that. In that you are not exceptional at all. But it is queer that you have never told a lie, and couldn't tell one if you wanted to."

"Why," said Claudius, "I've told any amount of the usual—"

"Quite so—the ordinary social fib, that has no other motive but to spare somebody's feelings. We may leave that out; that is not dishon-ourable. You have never told the dishonourable lie—the lie that would get you out of some scrape or be of some advantage to you."

"But, of course," Claudius answered, "one doesn't do that."

"No? I've told dozens of dishonourable lies myself. But there, my system of ethics is different and simpler: there is one great purpose, and all else is subordinate to it. But men, in other respects, like your-self, do, as a matter of fact, tell mean lies, or would, if the occasion were urgent enough. Now, no occasion, however urgent, would make you break your word."

"Well, one never knows."

Claudius found this open praise, as it seemed, of himself very em-barrassing; and he hastened to change the subject.

"If it comes to that, doctor, I have noticed one exceptional point in you."

"I had flattered myself," the doctor said, "that I was composed chiefly of exceptional points. Which do you mean?"

"You talk a great deal of your work, and profess to be devoted to your work, and call it the enthusiasm of your life; and yet you really *do* work very hard. I've only been here a few days, but I've noticed that. I happened to wake at three o'clock this morning, and looked out. There was still a light in your laboratory. Now, at Cambridge it was different: the men who talked much about their work, as a rule, did least; and to keep an average of your number of hours' work *per diem* was simply a preliminary step to being spun in your tripos."

"Well, the case is so different. The ordinary man at Cambridge works, I suppose, for the purpose of his tripos, and with the involved purposes of pleasing his people and providing himself with a profession. Oh yes, those are very good things, of course—but they are not great. If you try to simulate an enthusiasm for work with such purposes, you are likely to use up all the energy for the simulation, and have none left for the work. Yes; I did work late last night." The doctor's eyes grew brighter, and his manner more excited; he gesticulated a little with the hand that held the canvas bag.

"Last night, Sandell, I stood before the gate—the locked gate that stands between the living and the mystery of life. I tampered with the lock, but I could not force it. I could not get in. But, Sandell, I assure you—I am speaking seriously—last night I caught a glimpse between the bars. It makes me breathless. Can you wonder that I am enthusiastic and—Lord! I do keep talking about myself. I wish I did not. I shall become a bore."

"Will you?" said Claudius. "If I may speak as frankly of you to you as you have done of me to me, I will say that I have never met anyone who interested me so much, and I do not suppose that I shall ever meet anyone who will be half so kind to me."

"Oh, kindness is not in the question at all. For all that I give you, I intend to receive as much again. Practically, you are in a hotel, and have the means to pay your bill, only it does not quite suit either of us to treat each other just like that. No, not a word. I won't be thanked—I assure you that I shall come out of this under a great obligation to you. Now, look here, we won't talk of this; I want to show you, my rabbits."

They had reached the end of the garden. Here there was a row of twelve small rabbit hutches, standing about two feet from the ground. The hutches were kept very clean and dry, and it was evident that good care was taken of their occupants.

"I didn't know you were a fancier," said Claudius.

"Oh, I'm not; these are all of the common kind. They hardly remain here long enough for me to make pets of them, and in a pet one would prefer a little more intelligence. Still, these hutches are well planned, I think, and I like to have them properly fed and cared for until they are wanted. Research, you know, would be impossible without experiment; one is as humane, of course, as it is possible to be under the circumstances. By the way, I want one of these this morning for my work."

He opened one of the hutches, and a black doe that had been nibbling green stuff at the entrance scurried away to the far end of the cage; pressed close to the boards she watched the two men with soft, furtive, frightened eyes.

"Pretty creature, isn't it?" said the doctor.

"Now then, my common rabbit, you're wanted. Why didn't you stand erect, and have articulate speech, and wear white ties in the evening? Then you would have had a God and lost Him, and worried yourself about it at nights, when you had no one to talk to, and never got any further; and also, you would have bragged about it—people always do. You weren't consulted, neither was I. Now you are going to die in a dream, but first you have got to tell me what you know, but don't know that you know." He stretched his great hand into the hutch, and grasped the doe by the neck. "Come, now," he said, pleasantly, as she kicked and struggled, "don't you be frightened, my little dear." Then he dropped her into the canvas bag.

The two men walked on to the garden entrance of the laboratory. Vivisection had been the subject of debates at which Claudius had been present; they had not been, as a rule, very well-informed debates: it had been a case of brutality against sentimentality, and had not interested him very much. One of the most potent arguments for vivisection that he had yet come across was that Dr. Gabriel Lamb practised it. He mentioned this to the doctor. Dr. Lamb put down his canvas bag in the garden path, and fumbled for the key of the laboratory door.

He was an astonishing grotesque figure; the short holland jacket did not seem to go well with the bald head, with its fringe of auburn hair. Curious traces of scientist, sensualist, and poet, seemed to flit across his face, hopelessly inconsistent and passing in a moment. Between the box-edging on either side of the path the black doe rabbit jumped and struggled in the bag that imprisoned it.

"Vivisection? I am not, of course, opposed to it; at the same time, I realise its limitations. It has taught us what we know of physiology, and it will teach us more; but it will never teach us everything, as practised at present, and nothing less than everything is of much good to myself. I have got to pass through that gate of which I spoke to you. See here—you know, of course, that a pig is internally much the same as a man. But the pig's nervous constitution—a very important factor, mark you—is as different from a man's—" Once more he broke off abruptly. "You are provoking me to become a scientific bore," he went on; "and all bores are hateful; and the scientific bore is the worst of the lot."

"Well, doctor," said Claudius, "I can only say again that I am not bored. Now, by the way, I could not, perhaps, do a good hard day's work. But I am so far recovered that a few hours' secretarial work would not hurt me. May I not undertake your correspondence for you, or copy your scientific memoranda? You have already decided that I am to be trusted—that I should not abuse your confidence—and I need not tell you that I should be careful. I should give you the best of such ability as I have."

"That is quite so," said the doctor. "If I were the usual philanthropist, I should probably fake up some secretarial work for you to do. But I am not; and the work for which I want your assistance is far more serious and important. I will tell you about it when the time comes. In the meantime, if you would order the victoria and take my wife for a drive, I know she would be delighted. No; you'd rather drive yourself, I think. Have the dogcart and the bay mare. Oh yes—and you'd better ask for her, or they will give you 'Peach-blossom,' who's a good horse, but not so amusing."

Claudius drove the bay mare, and she did not give him much leisure for conversation. She was a beauty, but she needed driving. Mrs. Lamb watched him earnestly all the way, and only spoke to praise him. The doctor never drove the mare himself. It is curious that even the cleverest man will fail to notice when things are significant, if they concern himself. Claudius had that morning omitted to notice several things.

CHAPTER 6

It was a comfortable house to live in, Claudius decided, but there were some queer points about it. In the first place, there were no visitors: it suited the doctor, apparently, to live in a certain style—dinner, for instance, was distinctly a formal function—but he evidently did not think there was any necessity for witnesses of his severe taste in appointments, or of his conversation, which at times was brilliant, or of the excellence of his chef and his cellar. In a word, he did, merely to suit himself, what most people do in order to keep up appearances. No stranger apparently, with the exception of Claudius, ever trod those soft carpets, or tasted those exquisite wines, or heard the doctor on those few occasions when it pleased him to put his great ideas aside and be merely eccentrically witty. Mrs. Lamb must have realised that Claudius would notice this. She took particular pains to tell him that the doctor was a recluse and would see no one—and so on.

There was something queer, too, about Mrs. Lamb. She was religious—ardently religious, but yet she was an untameable woman. Religion might inspire her, Claudius thought—and he was angry with himself for such analysis of his hostess—but it would never hold her. Her eyes looked searchingly at him out of her pale face, and he saw in them this much, at least, that she was not a woman to be taken lightly and easily. With regard to her feelings towards her husband, he was very much in doubt; but he was certain that she was afraid of him.

And what was the doctor's own position? He was formally courteous to his wife in public; further, he did not talk her over with Claudius; further, he took an evident interest in her. But, for all that, Claudius could not persuade himself that the interest which the doctor took in his wife was the same as the interest which a man takes in the woman whom he loves; it seemed a colder, more scientific, thing. Claudius could not explain it: he could only wonder.

But one point seemed stranger to him than all—the curious way in which he was taken for granted. He had been in the house for days, and he had come into it as a broken-down tramp; the Lambs had only his word for it that he was not a broken-down tramp: yet the days went by, and no question was put to him about his past, and very little was said about his payment of his obligation—nothing, in fact, except the doctor's indefinite assurance that it would be all right. As a rule, he spent the greater part of the day with Mrs. Lamb: he drove her out, read to her, educated her taste in music. She began to make some sort of confidences to him; she told him that she had had a very great sorrow, and that religion had been a consolation to her in it.

Once she began to talk about the doctor—with her eyes fixed nervously on the door of the room, lest he should enter suddenly. Claudius did not like this. Gabriel was very clever, she said, but it was too awful—he despised religion. He seemed to be entirely given up to one thing. She did not know whither it was leading, but she had an uncomfortable sensation that it was leading somewhere—that they were on the verge of things. Then she hesitated, and looked shyly down at her own knees, and said, with seeming irrelevance:—

"I want you, Mr. Sandell, to be very careful."

"In what way? In my dealings with the doctor? Why surely—" He broke off and laughed. "You must not have these presentiments; there is nothing to be afraid of in a scientific enthusiasm."

"Isn't there?" she said, rather drearily.

Claudius had no desire whatever to make confidences—if anything he was inclined to reserve; but he felt that his host and hostess had a claim to know something about him, and it was characteristic of him that he had to satisfy all claims of which he was conscious, whether they were pressed or not. He chose his opportunity one night after dinner. The dining-room was large and irregular in shape. The table—an oval oak table—was laid in a square recess, and brightly lighted with wax candles; the rest of the room was almost in shadow. It had been rather an interesting dinner.

The doctor, starting from a case in the papers that morning, had gone on to a theory that suicide was largely the result of a sense of humour. People killed themselves because they saw that any further existence would be ridiculous. It was a pity—but those who had a sense of humour generally had it over-accentuated. Had Claudius ever noticed that? And had it never occurred to him how much better things must be on the moon? Yes, of course, there were the usual shilling-manual baby's arguments to show that the atmosphere and temperature of the moon did not permit the existence of human beings. It was the common confusion of beings with bodies.

There were certainly beings on the moon, and the bodies did not matter. Things would be much better there, because nothing there would be over-accentuated. The consuming passion of love that we men and women feel would be on the moon a mild preference. Our Athanasian Creed would be there a hesitating assent to Matthew Arnold's definition. Dinner would be afternoon tea, and afternoon tea would be no more than one transient, dreamy glance at the thinnest possible bread-and-butter. Everything would be toned down.

"My own enthusiasm," he concluded, "would be nothing more than the feeling which makes a boy buy the sixpenny chemical cabinet, do lour tricks, break one test tube, and swop the remainder for a specimen of common quartz with which to initiate a new geological passion."

Claudius took up the idea, and went on with it mirthfully. He and the doctor combined their suggestions—the wildest suggestions—of what this under-accentuated, toned-down moon-life would be like. Mrs. Lamb, consciously well dressed, watched them in silence, sometimes with anxious eyes, as she wondered if all this was quite religious, sometimes with quite a different expression as she thought what a good thing it was to look at Claudius and hear his musical voice, and then grew afraid of the thought. The doctor said that the moon-life would be heavenly.

"Why not have it? Why not reconstruct your existence here? Why not reduce your enthusiasm to the schoolboy's whim?"

The doctor became suddenly serious. "That is my own fault for speaking inaccurately," he said. "I spoke of my own enthusiasm, and I was wrong. The enthusiasm is not mine, but I am its. I belong to it; I am its slave. Body and soul I am claimed by the service of humanity, and given up to it.'"

"But a willing slave?"

The doctor did not answer for a moment. He went on peeling a peach, his white nervous fingers and the knife in them suggesting the rapid neatness of a surgical operation. He seemed to be thinking deeply.

"I really do not know," he said at last. "I never wanted it to come, and I never resist it. It is, I should say, that some powerful tendency has absorbed my will into it. I feel like part of a natural law. Yes, that's absurd, but I really grope for words to describe my sensations, and I do not get them very well."

"And your work is for the good of humanity?"

"Ultimately."

"I wish I had some part in it. My end in view in my own work was so much more selfish. Perhaps that was why I failed. I have never told you about it."

Dr. Lamb shot a rapid glance at his wife, and it was she who answered.

"Yes? You must not speak about it, Mr. Sandell, if the subject hurts you."

"On the contrary," he protested, "I am anxious to tell you. The one thing I can do, apparently, is to prevent you from being generous in the dark."

"No, no!" said Mrs. Lamb, leaning back in her chair, "You must not imply that we could possibly mistrust you. That is hard on us." She spoke earnestly.

The doctor looked at her significantly. She was saying just what he wished, but he was very well aware that she was not saying it because he wished it, nor from mere politeness, but because she really meant it. It confirmed a vague notion that had crossed his mind that day. It enabled him, as he thought over his future plans, to see where there was a possible weak spot. The whole thought went through his mind in a flash.

"Quite so," he murmured, as he passed the tips of his fingers gently through the rosewater in the bowl beside him. "Quite so."

"I should really like to tell you," said Claudius. "I think it would interest you."

Mrs. Lamb leant her elbows on the table, and her head on her hands, and looked at him intently.

"Ah! That is undoubted; it would be very good of you," said the doctor.

At this moment a servant came forward with the coffee, and Dr. Lamb gave a rapid order,

"The coffee and—and everything we are likely to want—on the lawn. At once,"

"You would rather?" the doctor went on inquiringly, turning to the others. "The night is so hot, and I thought it would be pleasanter to talk out there,"

They both thought it a capital idea, Mrs. Lamb's maid had entered the room, with an Oriental shawl in her hands, Mrs. Lamb adjusted it carefully over her head and shoulders. She was a curiously grotesque figure in that shawl. Her dinner-dress had all that Madame Ellice could do for mortal woman. The pallor of her face and the darkness of her hair were noticeable. She missed being beautiful. She looked like an Egyptian dissenter that had known Bond Street. The world had chosen her dress; the flesh and the spirit showed alternately in the expression of her face.

Outside it was growing dusk. A big rug had been spread over the grass; on it were lounge chairs and a low table. On the table were the smoking apparatus and the wonderful Madeira that the doctor liked to taste after dinner. The tiny Roman lamp gave a minute weird flame. The servant handed the coffee, and withdrew. The two men lighted their cigars from the lamp.

"Now," said the doctor, "if you are ready, Mr. Sandell."

Claudius began. "I think," he said slowly, "that the thing I have wanted most all through life has been freedom—the absence of limitation. I have often thought that I would be willing merely to taste it and then die. Yet I have never tasted it. As for my birth, I am the only son of my father, and my recollection of my mother—who died when I was a child—is very vague. My father, Sir Constantine Sandell—his knighthood was one of the birthday honours in the year that I was born, and it is an honour that he has since regretted—would have been considered, in some respects, an indulgent man. At Eton—I know now—I had very much more pocket-money than was good for me. At the age of sixteen I got the parental sanction to the use of tobacco—well, my father is himself a smoker. At Cambridge, again, my allowance was very generous. But in important points I was never free. Now, religion is, I suppose, an important point."

Mrs. Lamb looked up at the grey sky, and then slowly down again. Claudius continued—

"Religion was, is, and always will be, a most important point to my father. Unfortunately, it is a point on which he has never been able to satisfy himself. He has changed his religion times without number. He is about due into Buddhism by now," he said with a bitter laugh, "for I do not see what else is left. No, I am not joking. And I was always compelled to follow any sect with which he happened to be in sympathy.

"I myself have been a Scotch Presbyterian, an English Low Churchman, and an English Ritualist; I have found that the truth was in the Greek Church alone; I have been a Roman Catholic; I have followed my father into the religion of 'three persons and no God,' which has its dwelling somewhere off Fetter Lane; I have tried with him to find consolation in metaphysics that neither of us could quite understand; then I listened to the sermons of Parker, and after that to Voysey.

"I did not mind, I was only a boy; fellows always believed what their fathers believed; it was all in the day's work. It was at the call to spiritualism that I rebelled; by this time, I was at Cambridge, and had begun to think. Now, my father had invited to our place a professed medium from London— a Miss Matilda Comby."

At this moment the doctor and Mrs. Lamb exchanged glances, as though the name of Miss Matilda Comby were significant. It was almost dark. Claudius noticed nothing, and continued—

"For all I know to the contrary, Miss Matilda Comby may be there still. With all that I have against her, I must own that she is a distinctly clever woman. I began to study conjuring tricks; I paid—with my father's money—for lessons from professors. When I thought that the time was ripe, I exposed Miss Matilda Comby, and showed to my father that the absolute proof—as he called it—was ingenious, but that they did better at the Egyptian Hall. I might as well have spoken to the Pyramids. Miss Matilda Comby was clever and plausible; she had warned my father against the very explanations that I offered. He considered that her position was confirmed, and told me, in so many words, that I was a blasphemer."

"And that was the cause of your quarrel with your father?" said Dr. Lamb, dreamily.

"No, he still had hopes of me. We did quarrel, of course, but the real reason is much more difficult to tell. One day, at Cambridge, I had a letter from him that surprised me and distressed me a good deal. I knew that this woman, Matilda Comby, had a great influence over my father, but I did not guess how great—until I read that letter. Briefly, it peremptorily ordered me to marry Matilda Comby—a woman ten years older than myself—a woman whom I had always had the greatest difficulty to treat with even the barest civility—a woman whom I knew to be a fraudulent charlatan. During the whole of a year, I had been doing my best to get this woman turned out of our house—and now I was calmly told that I was to marry her. The spirits had willed it; the spirits were very anxious for it; the spirits had foretold that it would be 'a singularly blessed union.' It sounds like madness; yet in all business matters my father, at this very time, was showing himself particularly sane, particularly judicious."

"That," said the doctor, "is not uncommon."

"Matilda Comby also must have had some talent for speculative business. My father is, I suppose, a very wealthy man. With all her influence she doubted at first if she could persuade him to leave his entire property away from me. On money matters he was too sane. But it had probably occurred to her that she might marry me, and come into the money that way. The spirits had suggested the marriage, but there was never any doubt that the spirits were merely Matilda Comby."

"One moment," said Mrs. Lamb, rather shyly. "Matilda—I mean Miss Comby—was a charlatan, of course. I think myself that spiritualism is wicked. But has it not occurred to you that possibly she was really—it is so hard to be certain—really in love with you?"

"Impossible, Mrs. Lamb. I had always made it fairly clear that I despised her."

"Sometimes, you know, that does not make any difference."

"Well, I do not think that her subsequent behaviour showed that she was very fond of me. At first, I treated the thing as a joke; but I soon saw that my father was in earnest: then I refused point-blank. Now, my father does not take point-blank refusals nicely as a rule, and I expected a storm. On the contrary, I got a very patient letter. The spirits had been at it again. They had told him that I was secretly engaged to another woman, and that it was for this reason I had refused, but that it would be to the advantage and happiness of the other woman if I gave her up.

"I replied that there was no other woman in the case at all—as a matter of fact, although it is not a particularly interesting fact, I have never been in love in my life—and I repeated my refusal. His next letter accused me of having trifled with Matilda Comby's affections. Oh, it was the wildest business! Matilda Comby never appeared directly in it at all. But it was obvious that her hand guided my father's in every letter that he wrote. I need not give you details of all the correspondence.

"At last, he called me a liar, and I sent him a letter, which I now regret—for, after all, I am his son. That finished it. I had a brief communication from him to the effect that he did not wish to see me or hear from me again. He enclosed me a cheque for one quarter's allowance in advance, and told me that I was to expect nothing further from him, either during his lifetime or after his death. I sent the cheque back. Well, there I was with a bank balance of fifty pounds and the world before me."

"It was very cruel of him," said Mrs. Lamb. "It was very cruel and unjust." She shivered slightly.

"Ah," the doctor said, "it has turned a little chilly, hasn't it? Let us finish the story indoors—in my study, Sandell. I have got some of that tobacco about which you were speaking, if you care to try it."

"Thanks very much," said Sandell. "I should be delighted to try the tobacco, but I must get my pipe first from upstairs."

As soon as he had gone upstairs, Doctor Lamb turned brusquely to his wife.

"Matilda Comby?" he said. "Your sister?"

"I—I fear so."

"Why is she going by her maiden name? Oh, I see—yes, her husband."

"I thought she would go back to it after her husband—went away, but I know no more for certain than you do. She had stopped writing letters to us, you know, Gabriel, even before my marriage. It is possible that her husband may have died in—died there."

"Ah, yes. My wife's sister originally ran away with a fraudulent company promoter; he married her, and got into difficulties; he is now, if alive, doing a term of penal servitude; so, your sister resumes her maiden name, becomes a common swindler, and attempts bigamy. What trifles these things are! They ought not to concern me. And yet, Hilda, I should prefer that you did not mention these facts to Mr. Sandell."

"But they give him the means of reconciliation with his father."

"He will never take the first step in that direction. Besides, why sacrifice any man's good opinion of you? How will you be regarded if you say that you are the sister of Matilda Comby? With involuntary dislike and distrust."

"But I might write to Sir Charles—anonymously—giving proof of my statements."

"Quite so! Admirable! But you must get proof. Unless you know that the convict is still alive, you have no case. Find that out first. How? I have not the least idea. Be clear on your facts, before you sacrifice sisterly affection to your passion for—" he paused a moment, and added, "your passion for justice and reconciliation."

"I will do that, Gabriel. I won't say anything to Mr. Sandell. How happy he will be to get back in his right place again!"

"There, run along, Hilda. He will be down in the study by now. Join him, and say I will be there in a moment. I have a short note to write, which must go tonight."

When she had gone, he sat down before the fire, with his head in his hands, thrusting fingers into the fringe of hair. His brow wrinkled, and then cleared; he smiled horribly to himself

"Hilda's letter cannot go for three or four days. I *think* that I can finish my business with Claudius Sandell tonight, tomorrow at latest. After I have got him—once got him—bound him by his word—after that, there may be as much reconciliation as you please, my dear Hilda, because it will not make any difference. Praise God!" He rose and paced the room excitedly. "Praise God in the highest!" he said with fervour.

He sat down and scribbled a brief note, and gave it to a servant. Then he crossed the hall, and went down the passage to the study. "I wonder," he thought to himself, "does Hilda think that I notice nothing—nothing at all? She is falling in love with Sandell—I use it. He is entirely honourable—I use it. I have been kind to him—and I use that, and now—we really progress."

CHAPTER 7

The rest of the story Claudius had to tell need not be told in his own words. He had come to London with his fifty pounds in his pocket, and had taken cheap lodgings in Bloomsbury. He meant to live economically, but he did not quite know how to do it; he also meant to write, and he did not quite know how to do that either. It was probably his acquaintance with Burnage and Monsett at Cambridge that had given him this idea of making a living by literature. These two men had been actually printed in a London paper—Burnage once, and Monsett twice. In all three cases it was poetry, and unremunerated.

Claudius did not think that he could write poetry; he cheerfully acknowledged in Burnage and Monsett their superior talents. But, in common with most men, he wanted to tell a story—and, unlike most men, he had a story to tell. He had had it for a long time. He remembered vaguely what had started it. He had been one summer evening on a country railway-station; and as he waited for the train, he had read the advertisements, and some chance line of the merest foolishness had been whimsical enough to give him a suggestion. Looking up, he saw at the further end of the platform a woman standing silhouetted against the sunset sky, and the sight of her had carried the suggestion on.

It had all been forgotten next day, and all remembered many days afterwards. Since that time, it had gone through a long period of change and growth in his own mind, until he knew all the people of his story intimately, and its incidents had become like incidents in his own career. Now, when he had to make his own livelihood, he thought he would write his own novel. Both Burnage and Monsett had drawn for themselves brilliant pictures of literary success, and Claudius had listened. He knew that such success was not for him; he merely hoped to write a passable, readable, and consequently saleable story. There was nothing else that he cared to do.

While he was learning how to write—he was surprised to find there was so very much to learn—and learning how to live economically, the fifty pounds slipped away. There came a day when he left his Bloomsbury lodgings and took all his personal belongings to a shop in the Fulham Road. Nominally and externally, it was a second-hand furniture shop, but there was really nothing that its proprietor would not buy and sell. He was an obese man, with a little voice, and a quick, narrow eye, and a watch-chain like a golden snake that suns itself on a hillock. To this man Claudius sold all his books and almost all his clothes, leaving himself hardly enough to keep himself warm—it was late winter.

"Now, sir," said the man, when the last iniquitous bargain had been completed, "is there nothing else? I buy anything and sell anything. Think now, sir. Any little bits of furniture? Old carpets or rugs? Fetch 'em away in my own cart and give you no trouble. Or bedding now—

I give a fair price for that."

Claudius being in rather a mad and bitter mood, had answered that he would sell himself, body and soul, for one thousand pounds and one year to spend it in.

"Come now, sir," the man went on, "joking apart—"

"I'm not joking; I've nothing else to sell, and I mean what I say."

"Supposing," the man said, rubbing his fat chin, "the law allowed it and I could tie you up somehow: I might risk two hundred pounds and give you your year. It 'ud be a speculation. But there—there—where'd my security be? No, that's all nonsense."

Claudius went off with something under ten pounds in his pockets. Instead of two rooms in Bloomsbury he now took one small and dirty room in a back street in the Fulham neighbourhood. Here he almost starved himself and constantly overworked himself. He had intended at one time to write his novel to make his living; now he chiefly wanted to live in order to write his novel well. It was, as it were, a race against time, to get the novel finished as he would have it before the little money that he had gave out. Hopelessly improvident and unpractical, he made no calculation for a possible future when the novel might be finished and prove a failure.

His experiences in those lower *strata* of London in which he now lived had helped to make him bitter and angry with the world, so that he told himself that when his novel was finished, he would no longer want to live in the world at all. It seemed to be a world in which there was no generosity, and no sense of what was really valuable. To guess the motives of those with whom he came in contact, he persuaded himself that he had only to guess the meanest possible in order to be always right. The struggle for life hardly seemed worthwhile. Sore as he still was at the treatment he had received from his father, his depression was further increased by his miserable surroundings, his semistarvation, his occasional loss of his belief in his power to write at all, and his terrible loneliness.

This latter was his own proud and foolish fault. It is true that the friends he might have had in London were quite singularly few, but still there were some. Partly from the belief that he would work best if he worked alone, and still more from a reluctance to meet in his adversity those whom he had known in his prosperity, or to discuss the quarrel with his father, Claudius had kept to himself. Otherwise, Burnage, to do him justice, would have been willing—staunch and loyal—to have walked hand-in-hand with this lonely embryo-novelist until that point when Claudius really needed a friend.

Lady Verrider, an old friend of the Sandell family, a kindly and worldly woman who was fond of Claudius, would have gone with him much further; and there were others, of less importance, who would have been glad to see him. But Claudius would have none of them. The lower he sank in poverty and dejection, the more obstinate he became on this point. He had much the same instinct that makes the wounded animal hide itself.

On the day that the novel was finished, Claudius sent it off to a publishing firm. It came back almost directly, and he sent it to another. He paid his landlady, and had one shilling left in his pocket. And now he thought that he could die quite easily, and soon found that he could not. He was young, and unable to rid himself of the instinctive love of life. There were many ways in which a man of good character and education and some abilities could make a fair livelihood. None of them appealed to his tastes particularly but he determined to adopt one of them—any one; only it was necessary to have a little money first: he must be able to buy an outfit and pay a railway fare, or he could do nothing.

If the publishers accepted his novel, he determined to sink his pride and ask for an advance from them. This was his only chance; he had in his letter to them asked them to let him have their opinion as soon as possible, and somehow or other he must hang on until their letter came. He had only one shilling on which to wait; to speak accurately, he had only eleven pence, for the landlady had intimated that she would charge one penny for taking in the letter for him when he was no longer her lodger. As it was necessary to make his eleven pence last as long as possible, he considered that it would be absurd to spend any of it on a bed; the early summer had begun now, fortunately, and the nights were just warm enough to make it possible to keep in the open air without killing one's self.

He had found a spot away on Wimbledon Common, where it was unlikely that anyone would interfere with him. There he slept for nine successive nights; indeed, he spent most of the days there too, for he found himself too weak to do very much walking about. On the morning of the tenth he had only one penny left out of the shilling, which the landlady would want if there was a letter for him. He walked slowly to his old lodging in Fulham, and inquired if there was a letter.

There was a letter, and the novel had come back again. The landlady refused to take his penny, and said that he could leave the parcel with her. His first sensation was one of intense delight that he would now be able to buy something to eat. He hurried off; when he got to the baker's shop, he was so breathless that he could hardly ask for what he wanted. He bought a penny loaf and hid it under his coat, breaking bits off it and eating them as he went along. It was very beautiful bread, he thought.

When he had finished half the bread, he put the rest in his pocket. He had a vague idea that when he had come to the end of the bread, he would have come to the end of everything. It was with the greatest difficulty that he walked back to Wimbledon Common. There, among some furze bushes, out of sight, he lay down. Late in the evening he finished his bread. He did not sleep that night, but in the early morning he dozed off for an hour or two. When he awoke, the world seemed to be very far off; nothing that he had ever said or done seemed to him to be quite real.

There was no gnawing of hunger now, and even the instinctive craving for mere life had left him. He did not think about his novel at all, but he noticed very small things: he picked a big leaf and counted the veins in it carefully. A gradual drowsiness came over him, and he had moments when his consciousness seemed to go, and he was not sure whether he was walking or lying down.

It was on that night that— as has already been described—the doctor found him.

★★★★★★★★★★★★★★★★

Claudius did not tell all this. He gave the bare facts without comment, and hardly recorded at all what his sensations had been. When he had finished, Mrs. Lamb rose, and said quietly—

"That has been very interesting to me, Mr. Sandell. I am sorry that you suffered so much. You must not suffer any more—life must be made easy for you."

"It has been already—too easy, I'm afraid."

"I am tired, and must say goodnight."

She gave him her hand. It shook visibly, and even Sandell noticed that she seemed to be with difficulty concealing some emotion. He reproached himself.

"Ah, Mrs. Lamb," he said, "you must not believe too much in my own story of my own sufferings. One is ignobly tempted to make the most of such things when one is speaking to sympathetic people."

"No," she said, "you did not do that. But I certainly am sympathetic. Goodnight, Mr. Sandell; goodnight, Gabriel."

Dr. Lamb looked at her curiously from narrowed eyes. He looked like a chess-player, hovering over a great and final move, whose attention has been for a moment distracted.

"Goodnight, my dear," he said.

When she had got upstairs that night, she hesitated a moment before the door of the room that had been her dead baby's nursery.

Her thin white hand touched the handle of the door and then left it. She dared not go in. In her own room, she flung herself on the bed; after a minute or two she rose and knelt down. There were prayers which she said in a certain formal order every night. She began the first of them in a low voice.

"Almighty and most merciful—"

Then she stopped suddenly, her whole body shaken by a dry sob.

"God help me!" she wailed. "God help me! I'm a wicked woman. I hate Gabriel! I hate him—hate him! Make me love him again. Take away my sin—my sin that I can't help or fight against anymore!"

Even in the moment of her prayer she felt no faintest hope. This sudden, awful love for Claudius that had come upon her seemed to have entered too deeply, to be part of her, so that not even the fires of torment could burn it out. In great anguish she prayed on.

"Was I not tried enough and hurt enough? Every day I see women in the street that have their babies with them, and they're laughing. They don't know that they're driving me mad. They don't know it, but they are. I bore it all when my darling was taken away from me. I bore it all when I lost Gabriel's love, too. Only have mercy now! Do not let me be wicked! Oh, God!"

Once more she stopped suddenly. This time she rose to her feet.

"It's no use," she said. "God has left me!"

She did not sob any more at all; she was perfectly quiet.

When the dawn stole into her room, hours afterwards, she still lay with eyes wide open. Her hands rested quietly by her side; all through her sleepless hours she had hardly moved. It was such a little thing to lose one's sleep, when one had lost one's child, and love, and God.

CHAPTER 8

Downstairs in the study the two men went on talking, long after Mrs. Lamb had left them. Claudius felt himself to be just a shade above his normal state. The difference was very slight—a feeling of unusual contentment, almost of exaltation. Perhaps it was no more than the pleasure that comes in telling of trouble past.

"Sandell," said the doctor, "in some respects I observe that you are a practical man."

Claudius laughed. "I've never been accused of that before," he said. "Do you mean it?"

"Well, perhaps I should have put it that, according to my view, you are practical. The world would think otherwise; it would consider that you should have gone to your friends in London, and bothered them to find you work of some sort; it would rebuke you for your foolishness in having written a novel when you ought to have been earning money; it would have asked you why you did not take a post as a master in a private school, or become a cab-driver—my wife tells me that you drive well—since either profession would have brought you a certain income."

"For that matter," said Claudius, "they would both have brought about the same income. Well, when I come to look back on my life now, I honestly think that the world would be right."

"Do you? Is life, for mere life's sake, worth living? Could you, for instance, live on in a state of continual humiliation and obligation?"

"Do not forget that I am living in a state of great obligation at this moment. It is true that I will not—"

"There, there—I wasn't referring to that. If it is any comfort to know it, I will give you the chance tonight to end all the obligations—even to place me under an obligation to you."

"I accept it at once!" said Claudius, impulsively.

"No; you must hear about it first. Oh, don't let's bother about it just now! Let me see, I was speaking of life for its own sake. There I entirely agree with what must have been your own belief. Life for its own sake is without value. I do not want it. You reached a point in your career in which you lived for your work alone. Believe me, whatever your future fate may be, you will always look back on that period with a great and legitimate elation. For myself, I always live for my work alone. I also should be elated, only I haven't the time; besides, my work makes me humble."

"Your work," Claudius said, "is different from mine. It is so much finer. I suppose that my novel is very bad. I have been too close to it, worked too long on it, to be able to form any opinion about it myself. Now that it is written I hardly ever think about it. But if it were good, and deserved reward, I should have it. The days of the unappreciated are over. The unseen blush is gone out. I work for myself and get a reward, if I deserve it. You work for humanity at large, regardless of rewards."

"Pioneers are seldom rewarded," the doctor answered. "Ideas don't pay; the improvements on ideas do, and the tinkers are kings nowadays. But I certainly have my reward. You have noticed, perhaps, that only people with imagination lay down wine. The old man in his cellar, storing the vintage that he knows he cannot live to drink, tastes in that moment all its unborn perfections that one day his grandson overhead will praise. The man that plants trees, sleeps in imagination under their grateful shade."

He began to pace slowly up and down his study. He went on—

"And I have at least imagination enough to picture the humanity that might be, if my own line of research would do all that it promises. Ah, Sandell, it is well enough that we should look backward—from man to the anthropoid ape, from the ape to the original bird or reptile: but to look forward is better. We are not at the end yet. I see—yes, in my mind's eye, I actually see—this new humanity. It walks erect, cringing to no mystery. It holds the keys of life or death—of heaven and hell. It is the master of its fate, makes its character, moulds its physique, has just what intellect it wills. And all that may happen if I will tell it, as I hope to tell it, some two or three things."

He opened the window, and looked out in the direction of the lights of London.

"There!" he exclaimed. "There they are, millions of them, away in the smoke, laughing, sweating, living, dying! Each man of them is nothing as an individual. Charles Peace and William Shakespeare were both accidents. Yet how I am compelled— as by some blind force—to love them in the mass! They don't know where they came from or whither they go; they have their hopes about it, or their fears, or their complete indifference, but not one of them knows."

"Not one," echoed Claudius.

"They don't know their own potentialities. And most of them are half afraid to push the limits of their knowledge. Yes, that is really pathetic—unspeakably pathetic."

"I should have thought," said Claudius, "that the tendency nowadays was the opposite of that—a thirst to find out all that one possibly could."

"Yes, yes—in certain directions."

"Not in all?"

"Not for the average man. He believes in his divine genius and his devilish criminal. He does not want to have them explained away; he

227

does not want to find their origin traced otherwise than directly to God or devil. He will let the doctor give him pills for his body; but he believes that his mind and his morals are exclusively in the hands of God and fate."

"And you do not believe in any of that?"

"At any rate, I substitute 'very indirectly' for 'directly.' If there is any antagonism between religion and science, it is the fault of religion. It will defend untenable positions, and then—when the positions are lost—assert that it was unnecessary to have defended them, as they were immaterial. That kind of thing makes any man angry who loves truth. At the same time, I do not rail against religion. While your raw medical student is making himself objectionable about the doctrine of the Incarnation, I am studying parthenogenesis. True, I sneered just now at the divinity of genius and the devilishness of the criminal. Neither has the inevitability which belongs to one's idea of a super-human power. Bring me a genius, and permit me to hit him on the head; if I hit him hard enough, but not too hard, he will not die; but his genius will leave him, his books will remain unwritten, his pictures unpainted."

"But the reverse process," said Claudius, "to make a stupid man intelligent."

"By the simple operation required for the removal of a post-nasal growth, a stupid child may be made intelligent; the administration of a simple purge may preserve the sanity that a man would otherwise have lost; by the—but why should I quote these commonplaces? You know that the connection between mind and body exists—the con-nection between fear and the heart, for instance; between hope and the respiratory organs; between anger, or melancholy, and the diges-tive apparatus, is as well-known as the connection between thought and the brain. After all, why should I bother you with the starting-points of medical psychology—of my own beliefs, and my own line of research?"

"Really, doctor, I am more eager to find out than you are to tell. I want to know how this research is going on, and how it will end."

"It will go on and end in the service of humanity. If I gave you the details, I think that you would regard me rather as a quack than as a doctor—a quack with the restless ambitions of a mad man. Yet remember that the heterodoxy of today is the orthodoxy of tomorrow. What the charlatan falsely pretends to do, the man of science sneers at as impossible; but the man of science of the next generation actually does what that charlatan falsely pretends to do. If I have been ambitious, at any rate I have not been reckless. I have worked—I have won my way step by step.

"If I was ever tempted to make a theory, and one little fact stood in the path, I have either accounted for the fact or modified the theory, or abandoned it altogether. I have proved theories, on the other hand, that I should have never dared to imagine—they have been forced upon me by the chain of facts—theories that have never even been propounded before. As far as I have got, I could write my discoveries on half a sheet of note-paper; but though they may be few, they are vital. I tell you solemnly, Sandell, that the whole future of humanity depends upon them and what will follow them."

"Will it be long before you reach the end?"

"I cannot say. At present I cannot get on properly. I am in a position of the greatest tantalisation and difficulty. If I had not learnt from my work the utmost patience and humility, this tantalisation would be enough to drive me mad. I told you how—the other night—I almost forced the gate. That word 'almost,' it comes in and spoils everything. There is one thing that I want."

"What is it?"

"I want a man whom I can trust implicitly—who will trust me implicitly."

"I am at your service, doctor," Claudius answered. "I mean it. You said the other day that you knew I did not tell lies: I would keep your secrets."

"Ah, yes; it is proverbial, of course, that it is better not to show children or fools half-finished work! I should be reluctant to have one of my discoveries known at present, because it could be so easily misused. Still, you must not think that I'm the victim of scientific jealousy. Lord, what a lot there is of that! Let me do the work, and get the knowledge—and anyone else may have the glory of it. But you must hear more."

"Well?"

Doctor Lamb sat down again, his great hands interlocked, his eyes fixed steadily on Claudius. You must have had your finger on his pulse to know that he was going through critical and exciting moments,

"Sandell," he said, "do you remember that when you sold all your personal property, to get enough money to enable you to finish your novel, that you made one offer—ironical, I suppose—which the shopman was foolish enough not to accept."

"Yes. But my offer was more foolish than his refusal."

"Your offer was foolish for two reasons. You asked too little. You have probably thirty efficient years before you in the ordinary course of things." The doctor pulled out a pocket-pencil, and did a rapid sum on his shirt-cuff. "The entire command of your body and soul must be worth to any man more than £33 6s. 8d. a-year. Even you must see that. You would get more if you simply worked for a few hours a day as a bricklayer's labourer. Then, again, you asked for a year in which to spend that money."

"Yes, too little."

"Too little, my dear Sandell? It was too much—very many times too much. Think what may happen in a year— the countless ties that one may form and find it difficult to break; the entire change that may come over one's opinions, the entire alteration in one's views of life. How could you go back at the end of a year? The temptation to break your word would be almost insuperable."

"Yet, if I had made the senseless arrangement, I should have gone back."

"You would—but you would have rendered it difficult. Besides, that year—that pleasant holiday in which you would have said farewell to the world and your own past—should have been characterized by freedom, as far as freedom could possibly be obtained. You said tonight that you had never tasted real freedom. You would certainly not have had it if you had lived for a year on a thousand pounds; you would have found yourself constantly exercising common care to avoid a pecuniary indiscretion. In that last holiday of your life, you should have no common care—at any rate, no thought of money."

"Yes, it sounds reasonable. It always interests me to discuss imaginary conditions of life—the moon-life of which we were speaking at dinner, for instance."

"Sandell," said the doctor, seriously, "the conditions which we are discussing now need not be imaginary. I told you that I wanted a man who would trust me implicitly. I want a man who will trust me so far that he will make over to me, asking no questions, the remainder of his life, for the consideration —eight thousand pounds—that I am prepared to offer. He must come to me as he would come to death itself, putting his past behind him and away from him, giving up himself, body and soul, to me. Twice recently have I found a man who would have been willing to have placed that trust in me; but in neither case could I have trusted the man. Sooner or later, he would have gone back on his bargain, and, of course, the law would not have helped me. But I trust you. If you give me your word of honour, I do not want other security. I do not offer you more than you are worth to me—indeed, I am not wealthy enough to offer you as much as you are worth. You would leave me under an obligation. I offer eight thousand pounds, and I give you eight days."

"Are you really meaning this?"

"Yes."

"I am to ask no questions about the future?"

"It would be better not. For your own sake, it would be better that the eight days of holiday and farewell should be without anticipations—that you should be able to shut the future out of your mind. And for my sake—you must place yourself in my position, you know—it, at any rate, shows me that you place the same confidence in me that I do in you. Perhaps it is for that reason I ask it. Remember that I risk eight thousand pounds on your word alone."

"True. Why eight days? And I could not possibly take the money."

"On that point you must let me decide. The money is not too much. A thousand pounds a day will make it unnecessary for you to exercise common care; besides, it will be a satisfaction to me to feel that I have paid it. In eight days, you will not have time to form new ties, or make new opinions—only time to taste freedom for once in your life, to enjoy deeply, and yet not to that pitch of nausea which comes to those who follow enjoyment for a long period; to say farewell in happiness instead of saying it—as you would have done on the night that I found you—in abject misery. For me the eight days is too long. I am impatient for—for your co-operation. Eight days—the Octave that the Church gives to its saints—do not ask for more."

"Well, if I refuse, is there no other way by which I can repay my obligations to you?"

"Oh, why speak of them? If you refuse, there is an end of it, and I am charmed to have been able to give my medical advice, and my poor hospitality, to such a good fellow as yourself. That is all; that ends it so far as you are concerned. Of course, there remains for myself a considerable disappointment."

The doctor's voice was careless: his expression was one of geniality and generosity.

"It is a tremendous thing," said Claudius, slowly. "Yet I do not see why I should refuse. As you say, you found me when—if you had not found me —I should have died, probably. I really speak the truth without affectation, when I tell you that I was perfectly ready and willing to have died then. Very little has changed since. I have been away from all friends for so long, that I have got used to doing without them. I am still cut off from my father and my home. I have never been in love in my life. I am alone in the world. If I gave my mind to it now, I could probably make a livelihood—enough to give me bare life, without the things in it that I should like.

"But possibly I couldn't; if I could, I should be serving no good end. If I come to you, you use me, as you use yourself, for the service of man. I have no scientific training, and I do not see how I can help you. But you know that. What you say suggests to me that you may require my assistance in some—well, you know, doctor, it is inevitable that in your research there should be experiments, and I dare say some of them are singularly repulsive. You may require from me good nerves, laboriousness great that it takes no account of health, and complete secrecy and devotion, rather than scientific attainments. I do not see why I should not leave these things to you.

"I have myself had some experience of your unusual knowledge— the rapidity with which I recovered my strength under your treatment was almost miraculous. Still more have I reason to trust your kindness and humanity—it is not merely the material kindness that I have had from you. I think under difficult circumstances you have shown more delicate regard for the feelings of a foolishly sensitive man than ever I experienced before. You showed no trace even of unkindliness when I spoke of refusing your offer, proving, if proof had been wanted, that your generosity was spontaneous, without a second motive."

Claudius was not looking at Dr. Lamb at this moment; the doctor half closed his eyes, and smiled slightly.

There was a short pause. Claudius sat with his eyes fixed on one point of the carpet, then he drew a long breath, and said—

"I put the responsibility for myself in your hands, doctor. I accept. I will take my eight days of freedom, and then come back to you."

"You understand that you give me your word of honour," said the doctor, "and that the arrangement once made will not be revoked? It will be terminated only by your own death or mine."

"Yes."

A deep-toned clock struck the hour of midnight. The doctor stretched himself, picked up a cigarette, and lit it. "Extraordinary thing, Sandell," he said, "the difficulty that two men have who are not used to business experience in concluding a money bargain with each other. They shirk it, and get awkward in their manner, and clumsy in their speech. Well, it's over, I'm glad of it."

"The day's over too," said Claudius, glancing at the clock. "Personally, I'm not sleepy. But it seems to me that I must be keeping you either from your work or your sleep."

"From neither, I assure you. The day was made for working, and the night was made for talking, whenever one wants to talk. If you care to discuss the details, by all means let us do it."

"Well, doctor," said Claudius, "there is very little to say. I shall spend the eight days in London, probably. When would you like them to begin?"

"Now," said the doctor, laughing. "Of course, I don't mean that. Let me see, tomorrow's—no, today's Friday. That's the worst of sitting up past midnight; tomorrow becomes today, which is damnably confusing. I really don't see why you shouldn't leave me at midnight on Friday, returning, consequently, at midnight on Saturday—eight days afterwards. Then you begin your new career with a new week. One's always despicably hungry to secure these dirty little coincidences."

Both men laughed. "I should like, of course," Claudius said, "to see my friends again in London in these eight days—the two or three friends that I have there. True, I didn't see them when I might have done so; I felt too poor to see anybody, which—now I come to think of it—was vulgar of me. But, still, friends are friends. Besides, how can I say farewell unless I have someone to say it to? And my father decides that I have already said it as far as he is concerned."

"By all means see your friends," the doctor replied, cheerfully. "Have as good a time as you possibly can. Remember that for eight days you are absolutely free. In the morning Francis shall go into London for us. He will take the necessary letter to my banker for me, and he will do anything for you that you want—secure you the best rooms in the best hotel, take letters to your friends and bring back their answers, order your box at the opera, carry out any commission you like."

"Thanks, very much. A thousand pounds a day! It is tremendous. What couldn't one do with it?"

"Let us hope that you won't find out the answer to that question, Sandell," the doctor went on. "We are neither of us drinking anything. The formal, necessary, unpretentious whisky-and-seltzer is here, but it doesn't seem to me to be suited to the occasion. I may be old, but I am young enough to want to drink champagne now. The servants are all in bed, but no matter. Where are my keys? Ah, here! It's a wise man that knows his own cellar. Don't you trouble to come, I'll find what I want."

He was back in a minute or two with the bottle in his hand. "The last," he said, "the very last of a wine that I have reverenced." With deft fingers he began to uncork it. Both men had for some unexplained midnight reason got into the highest spirits, and they jested like boys over the operation. The doctor filled two tumblers, handed one to Claudius, and raised his own.

"Success to your eight days!" he cried.

"Success to the Octave!"

CHAPTER 9

Claudius breakfasted late and alone on Friday morning. The doctor had breakfasted long before, and Mrs. Lamb did not leave her room. The doctor excused her on the ground of ill-health, and said that when Claudius returned, they would probably be leaving England. "She needs a change."

After breakfast Claudius wrote two notes—one to Burnage and the other to Lady Verrider. Francis was to take them to town and bring back answers. He was also to execute various other commissions for Claudius, and make the necessary arrangements at the bank. Dr. Lamb was much more fertile than Claudius in suggesting what might be done. The doctor had a keen appreciation of the various luxuries and pleasures that eight thousand pounds would procure. To Claudius the chief point was that the eight thousand pounds would free him from the necessity for thinking about pounds at all. He did not want nearly so much money, but the doctor insisted, and only by this arrangement, carried out exactly as the doctor proposed it, would he be allowed to free himself of his obligations. The doctor had told him very little, and it was useless for him to make conjectures. Possibly he had done a very foolish thing, but there had seemed to be nothing else before him.

It was just before dinner that Francis returned from London. He brought back with him two notes for Claudius. The first was from Henry Burnage. It contained this "Of course I shall be delighted to lunch with you at your hotel tomorrow. I need not inquire after the material prosperity of anyone who can afford to patronise such a place, and I am glad to think that all goes well with you. But why have you hidden yourself like this for so long? It was such an exceedingly bad thing to do, that there is probably a woman at the bottom of it. And why are you leaving England? But we can talk about that tomorrow.

"Yes, I still write. My work is not of a class that could be called popular, nor should I wish it to be. I am writing a series entitled *Inward Incidents* every week, in a new journal called *The Latest Light*. They are impressions of some emotional experiences in the life of a young and sensuous girl. I will bring you a number or two to see, but I dare say you won't make much of them. 'Are you married, or engaged, or anything?' you ask. No, my dear Sandell. Art is my only mistress. It is unaccountable to me, and I do not say it out of any spirit of boasting, but the fact is that I seem to have a horrible gift of seeing right through every woman I meet—an absolute incapacity for being illusionised. The wonder to me is that every other man does not show a similar incapacity. But they do not. Poor Luke Monsett—you remember him—has just engaged himself to his principal's daughter."

It is, perhaps, unnecessary to add that Henry Burnage had carried out his intention and proposed to Angela Wycherley, and that Angela had in the kindest and most considerate way refused him. It had been a great sorrow to Mrs. Wycherley, but her husband, who was not without shrewdness, had quite approved of the refusal.

The other letter was briefer. It was from old Lady Verrider.

My good Claudius,

I've half a mind never to speak to you again. I've quarrelled with your father about you; and, by way of showing your gratitude, you leave me severely alone for over a year. Well, you always were erratic, and, honestly, I shall be very glad to see you again. Young men always do as they like. Now, I am going to be at home to you on Saturday afternoon, if you will come and have a talk and account for yourself a little, and, in any case, you must dine with me on Saturday night. You shall take in to dinner a good and sufficient reason for changing your mind about leaving England. I've recently discovered her, and love her, and her name's Angela.

Always your friend,

Jane Verrider.

Claudius saw but little of the doctor during the day. He had been busy in his laboratory. But shortly before dinner he came into the library where Claudius was reading.

"Your carriage will come for you at twelve precisely tonight," he said. "You forgot to tell Francis when you wanted it, and so I took the liberty. You see I am not going to let you off one single minute of your imprisonment here. At twelve exactly the Octave begins."

"Imprisonment!" said Claudius. "Good Heavens! what a word for it. Why didn't you let me go to town today instead of Francis? I've been dying for want of occupation except when I was driving your bay mare, and then pretty nearly died for other reasons. You'd better sell her before she kills somebody."

"I shall be selling all three horses before I leave England. You couldn't have gone to town, anyhow. You haven't the genius that Francis has for doing a whole lot of uninteresting things in the quickest and most practical way, without forgetting any of them. I'm afraid, though, you've been having a rather solitary time of it. I was at a point in my work when I simply couldn't leave it, and my wife—"

"Oh, I hope she's better tonight!"

"She says she is. She will dine with us." The doctor's shaggy eyebrows contracted a little. "A curious case," he said, almost as if he were speaking to himself, "a very curious case."

Claudius did not like to hear the doctor speak of his wife as a "case." He had a vague idea that to doctors all sick persons were cases, but this seemed to be in bad taste. He changed the subject.

"Doctor," he said, "Francis brought me back from town a note from a man called Burnage, whom I used to know at Cambridge. I won't say that he was an absolutely intimate friend of mine, but certainly I thought I knew him fairly well. I wrote to ask him to lunch with me tomorrow—a half-chaffing letter. Well, he sends me back a long and serious reply—the most preposterous stuff—and it puzzles me. Has Burnage changed altogether since I knew him at Cambridge, or have I?"

"Both," said Doctor Lamb. "As far as character is concerned, it is pretty certain that the boy is not father to the man. It was the ambition of my life at one time to be an evangelical preacher. I fainted on the first occasion when I went into a dissecting-room, and I wrote a letter attacking vivisection to an evening paper. I fell in love several times, and I certainly wanted to make money. Do you mean to tell me that the man who did these things is the man who speaks now? Of course not. Is the girl who flutters under a first kiss the same as the wearisome mammal who's the mother of your seventh? Of course not."

"That sounds brutal. But this man Burnage, he wasn't particularly popular at Cambridge; he went in for despising athletics, which was a stupid kind of thing to do. But he wouldn't have written that letter then. He went in for being distinctly the man of taste."

"Certainly. *Corruptio optimi pessima.* Carry precision in literary style too far, and you may get the precious and emasculated. Carry truth too far, and, as you observe, you may get brutality. The worst possible taste is the result of an attempt to grow the best possible taste from anything but the best possible feeling."

"I don't fancy that the belief in the change of individuality could be carried to its logical conclusions," said Claudius. "For instance, now, doctor, when I was a boy of fourteen, I, in company with another boy, surreptitiously procured a bottle of whisky. We put a lot of sugar into it to make it more palatable, and even then, we didn't like it; and, of course, we had no previous experience of spirits. However, we both of us got completely drunk. We weren't discovered, as it happened, but we suffered punishment for all that. Well, I laugh about this, and yet for the life of me I can't help feeling ashamed of it. The boy that got so badly intoxicated on cheap whisky wasn't the man I am now. Then why should I feel ashamed of his notions?"

"Why, indeed! To me it seems that it is no more logical to be ashamed of one's past than to be ashamed of one's waste tissues. Be ashamed of your present, if you like, but what has the past got to do with you? You are illogical because you are influenced by a long-formed habit. Habits of thought are just as hard to break off as other habits."

"After all," said Claudius, "it's only a question of a point of view. The illogicality does no actual harm."

"In your case possibly not. But take our method of dealing with the criminal. We tie him tight down to his past, and we do our best to destroy his self-respect, which is the most important factor in the production of self-improvement. In fact, if we can make the man heartily ashamed of himself, we call him penitent, and we are very glad. When we do these things, we say that we are repressing crime or punishing crime—as a matter of fact, we are making crime. One night a clerk—in the ordinary way a respectable clerk—allows the utter pig within him to come uppermost. There may, perhaps, be some exceptional combination of temptation and opportunity.

"Well, the utter pig is so outrageous that the man is imprisoned. His name is in all the papers. When he comes out, he finds not only that his self-respect is gone, but that the conditions of his life have been so altered that it is more difficult for him to get work and be decent and upright. Of course, it should be much more easy. Equally, of course, the man's self-respect should be strengthened in every possible way."

"That's all very well, doctor, but what about the habitual criminal? Would it be of any use to take the habitual criminal, slap him on the back, tell him that there was plenty of good in him after all, and put him into a position of trust?"

"Possibly not. I was not speaking of the habitual criminal. When the criminal has really ceased to be responsible—as in the case of some of the habitual female drunkards that you come across in the police reports—I think medical treatment might be good, occasionally. And in cases where medical treatment could do nothing, obviously the really moral and humane thing is to kill the criminal."

"No one would hear of it."

"No one ever will hear of the obviously right thing to do—they mistrust it just because it's obvious. So, we kill the man who has committed one murder. Often, he is a man of talent and activity; with strong potentialities for good, a man who might do his part towards human happiness and human improvement. But we let the confirmed sot live and breed more sots. Remember, too, that it is under your penal system that the hardened criminal occurs, and that method which you considered ridiculous has at any rate never been tried."

"Wouldyou try it?"

"Oh no! It's not much less ridiculous than you think it. It would succeed in a greater percentage of cases than you suppose; but even then, the percentage would be very small. It is wrong because it is working at the wrong end. It is dealing with effect instead of cause, and that kind of mistake is a good deal more common than you would suppose. Even Darwin—popularly supposed to be the exponent of a belief that man sprang from the monkey—curious all these popular suppositions are—made the same kind of mistake in a different use. In the question of sex difference, he substitutes a teleological for an etiological explanation."

"Ah," said Claudius, laughing; "it's just as well that we've got to get up and dress! You're taking me too deep."

"Deep! Good heavens, man, we aren't even paddling! Your education—pardon me—was too one-sided. It gave you much that I would like to have and have not. But it was the kind of education which could let you hold a popular and imperfect notion of Darwinism, and could let you be ignorant how far the theories of Darwin have since been modified or corrected."

"And you think that omission very important?"

"Well, yes, for certain reasons. But we will discuss them after dinner."

Subsequently Claudius found Mrs. Lamb in the drawing-room. She was wearing some fine diamonds. They were quite out of place, of course. The doctor raised his thick eyebrows. Yes, it was so—of taste and tact she had very little. Yet the greater things—the things that lie at the back of life—the things that we try to put away because they are too serious—seemed sometimes to rise and at once to claim her for their own, and to justify her. Twice that night she surprised Claudius. At dinner, in the course of ordinary talk, quite suddenly and quite calmly she made a remark that was worse than irreligious: it was virulently blasphemous.

It did not involve the use of any word that a decent woman could not use; but, for all that, it was indescribably shocking even to the two men, who were neither of them orthodox—the more shocking because it was so utterly unexpected. Claudius was staggered; for a moment he hardly knew what was happening, and then he became conscious that the doctor was talking to him about steam-rollers and, at the same time looking at Mrs. Lamb, and that Mrs. Lamb seemed nervous and half frightened. For the rest of dinner, she was almost entirely silent. She seemed to avoid her husband's glance. Her eyes looked hard and dry.

After dinner she excused herself to Claudius on the ground of her health. She felt tired, and must go back to her room; certainly, she looked very pale. Claudius opened the door for her. The doctor stood at the dining-table, some distance away, absorbed in the choice of a cigar.

"You have chosen a queer time for leaving us," she said. "You should have stopped and driven over to London in the morning. However, goodbye."

She said it without the least trace of excitement.

He took her hand. "Don't let us call it goodbye. I am coming back. I must have another opportunity to thank you for all your kindness to me. It is *au revoir*, Mrs. Lamb."

She laughed, said that she was not to be thanked at all, and passed into the hall.

Claudius shut the door, and then noticed Mrs. Lamb's handkerchief lying on the floor. He picked it up, and opened the door again to give it her. As he did so, she called from halfway up the stairs—

"Have I dropped my handkerchief, Mr. Sandell?"

"Yes," he said, "and I'll bring it to you; don't trouble to come down." He went up and handed it to her. Without a word of thanks, she clutched his arm, and said in a low, rapid voice—

"Listen quickly. You must not come back. For my own sake, for yours. I warned you before, and you wouldn't believe me. It's a matter of life or death."

"I'm sorry," said Claudius, "but I must not discuss it at all. The doctor wants me, and I have given my word of honour."

"I shall do all I can to prevent your return; I've had ideas. But Gabriel used to say my day was coming, and I know now what he meant. It may come before I can carry the ideas out, and if I fail you *must* break your word. Ah, if I only had time to tell you! It would be less wrong to break your word—"

"No, no," said Claudius, gently withdrawing his arm, "you must not think about this, Mrs. Lamb. Everything will be all right. You need have no fear. Goodnight again."

She put one hand to her throat for a second, and seemed to be trying to speak again. But she said nothing; she turned and ran upstairs.

"Poor lady!" said Claudius, to himself. She was, he felt sure now, far more ill than he had supposed. She had evidently not known what she was saying.

In the dining-room he found the doctor, leaning back in his chair, smoking placidly.

"Sandell," he said, "there are two alternatives between which every night after dinner I find it difficult to choose. If I perform a simple amputation of the end of my cigar, I find that the draught is good but that the leaf unrolls. If, on the other hand, I make a wedge-shaped incision, at a distance of one-eighth of an inch from the end, the leaf does not unroll, but the draught is less satisfactory. "What am I to do? What do you do?"

"Well," said Claudius, "I've tried both ways, and I've always found both of them answer perfectly. But if your cigars won't work, why don't you try a pipe?"

"Sublime in its simplicity! I will. It's only my own method with the irreclaimable criminal adapted. Have some more wine? No? Then let's go into the study, out of the smell of the mutton."

In the study the doctor suddenly changed his tone.

"Sandell," he said nervously, "I've been thinking it over, and I have an uneasy feeling that I've been taking advantage of you in this business. I hurried you. I rushed it too much."

"No," said Sandell. "When I spoke, I spoke deliberately. The chances of my book are, I am persuaded, worth nothing. As a schoolmaster, or a secretary, I might have scraped up enough to repay you what you have spent upon me, but there would still be much of another kind that could not be repaid, and I have some doubt whether I could stand the life. Doctor, I'm sick of pettiness and struggling; I had so much of it in the months before you found me, and I'm equally sick of working for merely selfish and ignoble reasons. Let me be some good to somebody. The work that you do is great, and if I can help you at all in it, I ask nothing better. No, my one objection is that I do not in the least want eight thousand pounds."

"No more of that," said the doctor. "See here—I don't want reputation. I only want to get the knowledge. But the reputation will come, and you will not share it. Money too will come, though I shall take no steps to acquire it. You will not have any of it. You are merely taking your share in advance, and you must see your own point of view, the law does not recognise any such arrangement as we have made together. By the law I am wrong, but there are grades in wrongness, and if I did not carry out my side of that arrangement I should he more wrong. If I allowed you to give yourself to me and gave you nothing in return, I should stand condemned by my own moral sense. Curious thing my own moral sense is.

"Owing to my disregard of individuals, it is never affected by any personal bias, and is always perfectly just. It will let me use any means, however wrong, that are requisite for the great end that I have in view; but it will not let me use means that are more wrong, than is really requisite. I don't ask or expect you to listen to this, of course. If any man talked to me, after dinner, about his moral sense, I'd go to sleep under his very eyes, and tell him afterwards why I did it. But—"

"Oh, I'm not going to sleep. Very well, then—we let things stand just as we arranged last night."

"I was more or less in a hurry," said the doctor, "and consequently I hurried you. But there is some excuse for me. When you first came here, my wife was—for her—unusually well. She—well you saw for yourself tonight. I must get her abroad as soon as possible. And—"

"Yes, yes, I understand," said Claudius.

They fell to chatting of other subjects. The doctor was, as usual, sometimes enthusiastic, sometimes bitter, and sometimes blasphemous, and sometimes showed the clearest judgment and sense. He began by saying how glad he was that Claudius had friends in London who would help him to enjoy his eight days.

"Otherwise, you'd have died of *ennui*. One can enjoy nothing alone—except solitude."

"And now I come to think of it," said Claudius, "I suppose I must make rather a point of not dying?"

"To die intentionally," the doctor said, smiling, "would, of course, be fraudulent. Otherwise, your death would merely end the bargain—I take the risk of that—just as I take the risk of my own death. By the way, death isn't altogether uninteresting."

"What *is* death, doctor?"

"Good heavens, man! if I could define it, I should know enough about it to avoid it for ever. To be out of harmony with one's environment is to die, if you can stand a definition that tells nothing and means nothing. Death is the price we pay for being multicellular. That's rather better. The happy protozoan, with his single cell, never dies—never, at any rate, by natural death. The strength of wind blows down the tower, but does not damage the single brick."

"Yes," said Claudius, rather impatiently. "That accounts for the body—looks at the mechanical side. One knows all that, our bodies are 'roll'd round in earth's diurnal course, with rocks, and stones, and trees.' But I have a personality, feel sure of it—what becomes of that?"

The doctor altered the position of the lamp, and spread out the fingers of his great hand.

"You observe," he said, "the shadow of my hand on the wall. I take away the hand—the shadow goes. That's the second analogy I've used tonight, and I might as well be a curate. However, no matter! Take away the body and the personality goes. We find them always together—not connected, but simultaneous. Is it unreasonable to suppose that if the body breaks up the personality suffers some similar dispersion? And," he added, with sudden passion, "is there the least comfort, the least satisfaction, in finding that that conclusion, or any other conclusion, is 'not unreasonable to suppose'?

"Damn it, man! why do you take me on to the subject of my greatest difficulties? The questions that you ask are just the questions that you may ultimately help me to answer. The thing that most surprises me in man is his lethargic, contented ignorance about some essential points. He has been here so long, and he does not yet know how he gets here, how he goes, or how to influence with certainty and to a really appreciable extent his moral character or his intellectual abilities. There are moments when he cares, and gets very nervous. But, as a rule, he is quite comfortable—sits before the fire, reads the daily papers, and says he is 'master of his fate.' Master of his fate, indeed! Never was there a more astounding and audacious lie."

"Yes," he said at another point in the conversation, later in the evening, "that is, put in a few words, the aim of my work—to make man master of his fate. Ah, Sandell, I've been ordinary enough! I've loved a woman. I loved my child, and my child died. I have had delight out of good books and good wine. I've felt fear, envy, sorrow, hate—gone through every experience which could show that I do not transcend humanity. But my work is not ordinary; it is on a higher plane. The time has come for man to hasten his own evolution. For the slow, crude modifications of Nature he must substitute his own thought, his own researches. He must put truth into that boast that he is master of his fate."

"Doctor," said Sandell, "you told me once that you believed in God, without giving any definition. Do you believe in the will of God?"

"The phrase," Dr. Lamb answered, frowning slightly, "is anthropomorphic. To ascribe will to God is to ascribe a limitation which, except to a theologian with his talk of the self-conditioned, must seem futile."

"Well, put it in other words: Do you believe that there is something which you cannot thwart—"

"I dislike the word 'thwart,'" interrupted the doctor. "I believe that there is a tendency which man can neither retard nor accelerate.

"All!" said Claudius. "Now, a moment ago, you said that the time had come for man to hasten his evolution."

"I am not illogical. The time has come—the tendency is here. Thanks to the primitive instincts of reproduction and self-preservation, we have arrived slowly at what we are. Thanks to the evolved mind of man, we shall arrive more quickly at what we shall be. Evolution itself has provided that which will accelerate evolution. The tendency is not accelerated by man, but by itself acting through man."

"I see what you mean, but how will it happen?"

"If I said that I myself was the point of the new departure, you would probably consider me a megalomaniac; but then you are not yet in possession of the facts. Possibly I may only live to see the bare commencement of the results of my own work, if even that. But I trust I shall not die until I am assured that those results must ultimately follow."

"Is there any satisfaction to be got out of being the slave of a tendency?"

"Can one be said to be the slave of a master that is doing all that the slave wishes? The tendency is but part of the manifestation of God, and to the man of science in my position the love of God has passed from a religious duty into a logical necessity. God, so far as God is revealed by our knowledge of Nature, is taking man 'to the haven where he would be.' Sandell, you've often thought me brutal, and once said so.

"It is because I do not regard the individual, but the race, and what the race may ultimately be. But think whether my view or yours is most in accord with the laws of Nature, the manifestation, if you like the term, of 'the will of God.' It is on the just and the unjust alike that the sun shines or the tower of Siloam falls. There is no regard there of the individual. A moment ago, you spoke of your personality as though it were so precious a thing that you could not bear to lose it. No, I am not sneering at you. The instinct for self-preservation is almost universal; but do not let it make you lose your sense of proportion.

"Read a manual of astronomy, read Darwin—We all crib his facts even when we correct his theories—familiarise yourself with great tendencies, great numbers, great space. You may still believe that you are something; but to give that up when your time comes will seem to you—in a delightful obedience that is no slavery—to be far better."

The doctor, who had paced up and down the room as he was talking, now seated himself, facing the fireplace. He had seemed to speak with sincerity, enthusiasm, almost excitement. But with him excitement did not slowly die; it vanished like a flame blown out. As he filled another pipe, he remarked, in a matter-of-fact way—

"Look here, Sandell, if you'll write me a cheque for fifty, with tomorrow's date, I'll cash it for you now. You may want small sums tomorrow before it is convenient for you to change a cheque."

"Thank you," said Claudius. He did not quite seem to be hearing and understanding. However, he wrote the cheque, took the notes and thrust them into a pocket, and thanked the doctor again. For a few moments there was silence, and then Claudius said—

"And I'm going away to spend eight thousand pounds—or as much of it as I can—in eight days. When I think of all you've been saying, I feel like a bibulous coster, who has come into a little money, and means to go on the burst with it."

"You will do in your way what he would do in his, but the ways are widely different. Don't frighten yourself with phrases. Enjoy! Enjoy!"

Before Claudius could answer, Francis opened the door:—

"Mr. Sandell's carriage is here."

Both men glanced at the clock; it was five minutes to twelve. As Francis shut the door, the doctor said—

"Don't be impatient. You have tried to earn what you are now going to have, but you have failed. I know the feeling that you are going through. But remember you will earn fully, afterwards, all the enjoyment that eight days can bring you. Ah! you will do far more than that. Words cannot express the obligation under which I shall be to you, or the delight which I feel in having found you."

They had passed into the hall, as the doctor talked. Claudius smiled drearily.

"How do you know that I shall come back? You must have me watched."

"I know it, because you have truth and courage. You will not be watched, of course. The greater your freedom—and the law will not recognise our contract—the more such a man as you will feel bound."

For a minute or two they chatted; the clock had begun to strike the hour as they shook hands and Francis opened the carriage door. The doctor waved his hand as Claudius stepped into the carriage.

"*Au revoir*, Sandell! Saturday after next, at the same hour. Hope you will have a good time; I'll give your message to my wife. . . ."

The carriage drove off. In the window above the entrance doors there was a light. It was the window of the room that had been the nursery. The blind was held back a little; Mrs. Lamb was watching the lights of the carriage passing down the drive. As the carriage turned on to the road, Claudius thought he heard a cry; the coachman must also have heard it, for he almost pulled up his horses, and then—probably with a reflection that, after all, it was none of his business—drove on again.

The doctor standing alone in the hall heard that cry very distinctly; it was the scream of a hysterical woman, and it came from the room overhead. He wrinkled his brow a little, and his lips drew back showing his great white teeth. He crossed the hall and took down a light riding-whip. Then he went slowly upstairs, humming to himself. He opened the door of the nursery. On a chest of drawers stood a couple

245

of lighted candles, in tall candlesticks, that Mrs. Lamb had brought from her own room. On the floor against the window she lay, face upwards—chuckling, panting, sobbing—occasionally speaking incoherently.

Gabriel Lamb closed the door behind him. "Get up!" he said curtly.

"No, no!" she moaned. "Don't come near me, Gabriel; don't touch me."

In four quick steps he had crossed the room and was by her side. She began to scream again. He dragged her to her feet, and as she went staggering away from him with arms widespread, he struck her savagely across the back again and again with the whip. The immediate effect of this brutality was that the hysterical fit stopped suddenly. She reached the mantelpiece, and stood clutching it and facing her husband. Her bosom rose and fell, quickly and deeply, with anguish in her eyes. But her self-control had partly returned, and when she spoke it was in a subdued voice.

"Why—why have you done this awful thing?"

"For two reasons. When you come to think over it, you will see that you know them both."

She could think of nothing. The blows that he had given her stung and throbbed; from sheer physical pain she began to cry—quietly.

"Oh, Gabriel, you have hurt me so! you have hurt me so!"

"You had better go to bed now." He opened the door for her. "I will put the lights out here. Be careful not to drop your handkerchief as you go out this time."

Without another word she went into her room. The doctor went downstairs, through his study and into the laboratory. He switched on the electric light, flung the riding-whip into a corner, and began work.

CHAPTER 10

As Claudius dressed for the dinner at Lady Verrider's on the following night, he felt that, so far, he had had a pleasant day. He had breakfasted late, had had a delightful ride in the park, an amusing luncheon with Burnage, and a friendly talk afterwards with Lady Verrider at her house, and had just left her in time to dress and return to dinner. It did occur to him once that it was not perhaps worthwhile to barter the rest of his life for eight such days—but still it had been pleasant enough.

Burnage had been full of questions at first, and Claudius had evaded them. Burnage did not press his inquiries, for a chance was offered him of talking about himself, and he could not bear to miss it. He apologised at intervals for egotism. He referred rather slightingly to his 'Varsity days. "One is so young, you know, when one is young," he said. He was fond of saying that kind of thing; it was not difficult. He knew that if he only adopted the form of the epigram, a humble and stupid world would always give him credit for the point of it.

Finally, at the request of Claudius, he read out one or two of the *Inward Incidents*, those passages in the life of a "young and sensuous girl." If Claudius had taken them seriously, he would have been of the opinion that Burnage must have lived a very moral life, but have been afflicted with a very indecent imagination. But he did not take them seriously; he chaffed him good-naturedly about them, and regarded them as evidence of merely a passing phase. Burnage served to remind Claudius of the good times he had had at Cambridge, and merely for that Claudius was grateful to him. Burnage's irrepressible superiority was not to be overcome by good-natured chaff.

"My dear fellow," he said, "you have given me an excellent luncheon. The wine has been beyond reproach. Consequently, I am sorry to have to be rude to you. But I fear that you are a sojourner in the land of Gath. You have told me that you don't like my cigarettes. They're quite perfect. It's only by the greatest—well, the Turkish Ambassador happens to—. However, I needn't go into that. The dislike of those cigarettes is a mark. Then there is the way in which you receive my little *Inward Incidents*. You don't understand them. You have gone backward. At Cambridge, I remember, you used to think about writing—to take an interest in literature. Now, if you wrote at all, you would turn out—let me see—a novel with a plot to it, with adventures in it."

Claudius chuckled. "That's just exactly what I have done," he said.

"Ah! Where is it?"

"To tell you the truth, I exactly know but don't in the least care."

"Then you can have given no trouble to it."

"I gave too much, and that's why I want to forget it, please."

"Well, doing anything tonight?"

"Yes, dining out."

"I was to have dined tonight at Lady Verrider's. But I had to send an excuse the other day, I happened to find out that—well, it's nothing of importance, but a girl's dining there who ought not to meet me."

"Why not? It isn't as if you talked as you wrote."

"You misunderstand. Poor little thing—pretty too, in her way! It would hardly be fair to tell you more; and besides, it's nothing, I say."

In the afternoon Lady Verrider had been a little puzzled by Claudius. He had been charming to her as ever; his looks, she thought, had improved as they had passed from boyishness to manliness—most faces, she noticed, coarsened in the process, or else became effeminate. But there had been a certain reserve; he had not told her all she had expected. He had explained freely his long absence from her house—he had wanted to give himself up entirely to his work; and he had, besides, been too poor to see anyone. It was with reference to the future that he was so reticent. Where was he going to when he left England? With whom was he going? What would he do—if anything—when he went abroad? He would, he told her, earn the money which he was now spending. For the rest he was afraid that his future was not his own secret, and that therefore it must remain a secret.

"Entangled!" cried Lady Verrider. "A woman! I see it all."

"No," said Claudius, "there is no woman in the case at all. It's almost a matter of business. Be as kind to me as you always are, and don't ask me any more about it, or mention to anybody that there is any mystery. It's embarrassing. I can't be mysterious. I couldn't look the part."

"Yes, you could, do, and always did," Lady Verrider answered snappishly, "However, young men always have their own way—I've known that for a long time. Unless, of course, you marry her. M'yes, Angela."

"I beg your pardon?"

"I said Angela. Oh, it's lucky that you're coming here to dine to-night! A man dropped out two days ago, and you've got his place. Otherwise, there might not have been, as far as you're concerned, any Angela at all. She's your reason for not leaving England, as I told you in my letter."

"Might we hear more?" Claudius asked.

"The father's invisible, and the mother ought to be. No; that's sheer spite and worldliness. The mother's a good mother, with social aspirations—I believe they're chiefly for the daughter's sake, and that, as soon as she's married, the aspirations will be folded up and put away, and the poor old lady will go to bed tired. Looks as if she dressed too youthfully, and always had done—even in her cradle. Homeopath, I fancy—talks pills, anyhow. But quite a good heart."

"And if you had *not* set aside all spite and worldliness," said Claudius, "how would you have described her then?"

"My dear Claudius, haven't I said that she's got a good heart?"

Claudius smiled. "When it comes to mentioning *that*—— But, however, with regard to Angela?"

Lady Verrider's grey eyes lit up with enthusiasm.

"A wayward lamb. Eyelashes, So wrong, and sweet, and rather discontented, and good! Oh! I can't describe her!"

"Ah," said Claudius, "I've not deserved these treasures! I'm an outcast."

Lady Verrider sighed. "If only I could be anything half as romantic as that! But no—I simply must not talk about your dear father. Temper upsets me. In his last letter he said that he 'Utterly, absolutely, and altogether declined' to receive any further communication from me. Think of it!"

"I recognize the idiom," said Claudius. "Then you've no recent news, I suppose?"

"Fairly recent; but there's no change. That Comby woman has a cottage in your father's place now. The spiritualistic business goes on. I got that, by the way, from my maid, whose cousin is in service there. I didn't ask her anything, of course, but sometimes one has to give her the run of her tongue."

Lady Verrider's husband had been long dead. At her dinners her brother acted as host, if he was in London. He was a dried-up little man, who drank water during dinner, and one glass of claret afterwards. He knew nothing about horses, something about men, and quite a great deal about women; so, he liked best to talk about horses—at any rate, in the first stage of acquaintanceship. In the last stage—there were with him about sixteen of them—you would perhaps find out that he had lived much abroad, fought three duels, killed one man, and regretted exceedingly that he had not killed the other two. He was good-tempered, rather absent-minded, and lived chiefly at his club.

"He's a nice little nan, Geoffrey," Lady Verrider used to say, "and kind and obliging to me, though we don't know each other very well." Lady Verrider looked brilliant that night. She could no longer be beautiful as in her youth, but she had such pearls and old lace as can be had for money, and always seemed more dignified than she felt.

"Don't hurry away tonight," she murmured, as she shook hands with Claudius, "otherwise I shan't have a chance of seeing you. One never sees anybody in one's own house if there's anyone else there."

With this enigmatical utterance she turned to shake hands with a member of parliament, who believed that he had rescued her from a bore; everybody who shook hands with Lady Verrider at once believed that he had done something great and right.

Geoffrey Severn emerged from behind a palm to greet Claudius.

"Delighted to meet you again, old man," he said. "Saw you in the park this morning, on the top of a horse. You were in the distance, or I'd have saluted you before. Going abroad, I hear. Well, well—you'll get tired of it. I did—at least, I think I did. At any rate, I came back to England—and mind you do the same. And, by the way, you're taking in Miss Wycherley, if you would. Know her? Come along, then."

Silhouetted against a shaded lamp, Claudius saw the face of a young girl. She turned as Geoffrey spoke to her, presenting Claudius. She smiled prettily; but as the smile died away her eyes looked rather sad. She was the image of sweet discontent. There had certainly been some fog that evening; the real question was whether it would or would not become any worse. He thought and said with due gravity, that he feared it would. She half opened her fan, and looked down at it caressingly. Then she said, a little shyly, that she hoped it wouldn't.

"We're going out of the land of fogs on Monday," she added, as he gave her his arm; "mamma and I are going down into the country."

"Really? So am I," he said. "But can you bear to part with London in the season?"

"We shan't be there for more than a few days. Do you know Guilbridge at all?"

"Yes; very well. (Here are our places—why *must* one always go to the wrong side first?) You don't mean to tell me that it's to Guilbridge that you're going?"

"Y-yes." Rather humbly, "Do you mind?"

"It's a coincidence, because I happen to be going there myself."

"Still, there's plenty of room, isn't there? I hoped you wouldn't mind. You see we've taken our rooms there now, and I don't think we can afford—"

Their eyes met and understood. They both laughed.

"Don't you think," Claudius said, "that you're being a little severe?"

"Then," she answered, somewhat inconsequently, "why did you say that I couldn't bear to part with London in the season? Do I look merely worldly? Has somebody traduced me?"

"I believe," he said seriously, "that I asked the question for much the same reason that I feared the fog was getting worse. It's a humiliating confession to have to make. As for the rest, no one has traduced you. Lady Verrider adores you, and spoke of you to me. You don't look merely worldly."

She drew a long breath. "Ah! please say the last part of that again—slowly."

"As for the rest, no one has—"

"No; go on after 'You don't look merely worldly,' and say some more."

"You don't look merely worldly. You look—but I'm afraid I've not known you long enough to say that."

"Let me see," she said meditatively, "how long *have* you known me?"

"Either five minutes, or five hundred years."

"Well"—with conscious audacity—"make it years, then."

"In that case I may say that you look like—like your first name, grown a little tired of paradise."

"Oh, stop! you must go back at once. Away with those years! You've only known me minutes, just three minutes, Mr. Sandell."

"Pardon me. Miss Wycherley, but it must be at least six—probably more. You observe that we are eating salmon."

Angela laughed. "What a nice idea to measure time by the menu. Now observe, when it's half-past the caramel pudding, we may possibly speak about myself again. Until then—no. You've been to the Academy, of course?"

"Certainly not."

"A great theatre-goer?"

"Hardly ever. Come soon—soon—caramel pudding."

"You ought not to say that. Here's another chance for you. The lady in black satin is my mamma, and Lady Verrider's a dear too. But you can say anything you like about anybody except those two—and me."

"Then," said Claudius, "I shall talk about myself, and at some considerable length. I've made up my mind to it, and it's your fault."

She lowered her voice and looked mischievous.

"Do you think, Mr. Sandell, that you ought to neglect that quite nice lady on your other side all through dinner? Oughtn't you to—to—give her some of it?"

They laughed again. "Not at all, she's very busy, telling Mr. Severn all about herself. She doesn't wait for any caramel puddings. And as he knows a great deal more about her than she does, he's amused and she's interested. It would be brutal to interrupt them."

"Very well. Why are you going to Guilbridge?"

The moment that Angela had said that she was going down into the country Claudius had decided also to go down into the country. To know that she was going to Guilbridge was to know that he also was going there. He had changed all his plans, suddenly, gladly, without the slightest hesitation, and now he was asked why, why was he going? He hardly knew. He was a little dazed, like a man who is suddenly wakened from sleep and with his eyes half-closed vaguely feels that it is a glorious morning. But he knew, quite clearly, that the reason, whatever it was, was not one that could be told—now, at any rate.

"I think London's at its worst in the hot weather. I've been to Guilbridge before—had the quaintest lodgings there. It's so jolly to be near the river in the summer."

"Most lodgings are quaint," said Angela, meditatively. "The people who let them have always had more bereavements than other people, and everything looks too clean at the beginning of the season and too dirty all the rest of the time. And the furniture is of a type. Our rooms at Guilbridge are of the normal hideousness, I believe. But they look out over the heath. You know it?"

"Ah—it's lovely, that heath!"

They talked on of the heath, of boating, of riding, of many things— not more seriously than a dinner-table permits, but just a little confidentially, happy in a kind of tacit understanding that each pleased the other.

"Ah!" said Claudius suddenly, "the moment has come. It is exactly half-past the caramel pudding."

"Yes," Angela answered, "that is the time by your plate. But your plate's a little fast."

"Miss Wycherley," said Claudius, "you may think that I eat too quickly. You may regret it. But you really can't mention it—not to me. You're now going to talk about yourself."

"I only said I might There's nothing to say, too. Oh yes, why did you say that I was like my first name? How could you even know that I had a first name?"

"As for the last question I may answer that I conjectured it. I do these brilliant things at times."

"But, listen: you said that I was like my first name. Now my first name is Laura."

"Ah!"

"What did you think it was?"

"Angela."

She had wanted to hear how it sounded when he said it. She had just what she wanted, and straightway blushed slightly.

"It is Angela, really. But I wouldn't be discontented with paradise, or tired of it—if only I could find it."

"Does anybody ever find it? I haven't."

"Some do. Don't look at the girl opposite to you, because I'm going to talk about her. Know her? No? Her name's Eva Murray, and of no importance. To look at, she's pretty but commonplace."

"I noticed her a few minutes ago. I grant you the commonplace."

"Well, most of the time her face has had the usual expression—the expression that a woman puts on with the powder for social purposes. But I caught her just now at a moment when she was neither talking nor listening; she allowed herself a moment's absent-mindedness. Her story seemed to come up into her eyes; her face was transfigured, ecstatic, and pathetic. It only lasted a moment, and it was not very becoming—made her look seven years older. She was quite right to change it for that metallic, insincere brightness. But none the less if we were in possession of Miss Murray's private history, we should fine a paradise-period in it."

"Really, Miss Wycherley? If you can tell as much as that from a momentary change of expression, I shall be very much afraid of you. Suppose, for instance, that you were to guess all my horrible past."

"One can only guess such things vaguely and occasionally. I—I don't think you've had a horrible past, but—" she stopped short.

"Well?"

"Isn't it quite absurd that we should have a fog at this time of year? I call it perfectly preposterous."

"Perfectly. Well? You had a sentence to finish."

"I'm not quite sure how I was going to finish it: you must let me think."

At that moment the matronly lady on the other side secured Claudius.

"Now, Mr. Sandell, I haven't seen you for an age, and when we *do* meet, you *don't* talk to me."

"Ah!" said Claudius, "Mr. Severn has given me no chance. A selfish man, I'm afraid, Lady Dunwich."

"Very nicely put. On a French model, "should say. Now, do you know anything about guinea-pigs? I am *most* anxious to find out about them, and Mr. Severn knows nothing. My daughter Ella (you remember the child) keeps them, or I should say *did* keep them. There were thirteen. They died at intervals—I mean they died one after another, beautifully kept, died perfect, everything all right—and yet they died. So very annoying to poor Ella. Can you explain it?"

"It looks to me like foul play. It is mysterious—even romantic. Has Ella an enemy? Had the guinea-pigs an enemy?"

"You really suggest the most horrible things. You don't think a good vet?"

"Oh, his evidence would be useful. You want the police, detectives, the vengeance of the law."

"But, Mr. Sandell, I assure you I do not; I refuse, positively, to go to law about anything. I am *not* going to stand up in a public witness-box with a young man in a foolish wig paid to be impertinent to me."

The hostess was already making her preparations for departure when Claudius got free from Lady Dunwich and turned again to Angela.

"You have a moment in which to finish that sentence. Please do it. You do not think I have a horrible past, but—"

"It's only a conjecture. You'll laugh at it, I think—I'm inclined to think you have something very important at stake just now."

She rose with the rest of the women. She had dropped a glove; Claudius picked it up, saying, as he gave it to her—

"No, I'm not amused at your conjecture—it is right."

Then followed what seemed to Claudius a waste of time. The man who chatted with him over the coffee thought him slightly absent-minded, as indeed he was. The days of the Octave had suddenly acquired a value for him far beyond the value of material luxury and enjoyment. Plans formed themselves rapidly, one after another, in his mind.

When the men entered the drawing-room afterwards, Angela Wycherley wondered what Claudius would do. She did not want him to come and talk to her just at first. He did not. She saw him go up to Lady Verrider and chat with her for a few moments. Then, at his request, Lady Verrider took him up to Mrs. Wycherley and presented him to her. Claudius was not always reckless. He could do wise things at times.

Mrs. Wycherley found him delightful. He had known their old friend Mr. Burnage at Cambridge. She was the soul of indiscretion, and he heard with a flickering smile that Angela had refused Burnage. On the question of her own health, however, Mrs. Wycherley showed what was for her an unusual reticence. But he understood that she was a sufferer, and was quite sympathetic. He was mildly amazed to find that this was the mother of Angela, but he recognised that she really had the good heart of which Lady Verrider had spoken.

She spoke of her daughter Angela with pride but slightly concealed, and told stories of her childhood. The wayward Angela had had rather a naughty childhood. Mrs. Wycherley was expecting to have a few friends at her house on the following evening—the Sunday evening. She wondered many things, and apologised too much; but Claudius was delighted and said that he would come. Mrs. Wycherley was equally delighted to find that he was going to Guilbridge. He was so considerate, so interesting, had such a pleasant manner. She decided to find out more about him from Lady Verrider. She glanced across at her daughter Angela, and for the moment her imagination ran riot.

The drawing-room gradually emptied. Lady Dunwich and several other guests were going on to a dance. Mrs. Wycherley began to be a little uneasy. The hired brougham (it was never less than that when she dined with great wealth or slight title) had not come, and was already twenty minutes late. It was not the first time that it had defected. Claudius crossed the room and sat down beside Angela.

"I have been making your mother ask me for tomorrow night," he said. "It was very good of her."

"It was kind of you," said Angela, demurely.

"Yes," he said smiling, "I am never unnecessarily severe with myself, Miss Wycherley. May I say how glad I shall be to meet you again? I think we have some—some explanations."

"Yes," she said, looking down, "we have. And yet—well, you must not think that my unfortunately right guess compels you at all to tell me anything that you would rather not tell."

"Nor to believe that it would be of the least interest to you."

"Mamma is going I see. Goodnight, Mr. Sandell." She gave him her pretty hand. "And"—she hesitated a little—"it would interest me."

Mrs. Wycherley wished to know if she might have a cab called—a four-wheeler, please. For some reason or other her brougham had not come, and it was really most annoying.

"One moment, Mrs. Wycherley," said Claudius. "My carriage is waiting, and I shall not be going yet for some little time. It would be pleased and proud if you would allow it to take you and your daughter home, and then come back for me."

Mrs. Wycherley was infinitely obliged. It was very kind of Mr. Sandell, and really if it was not giving trouble, she thought she would. Reassured on this point, and with her hand warmly shaken, she and

Angela departed.

"Son of Sir Constantine Sandell," she thought to herself, "keeps his own carriage, and is a very charming young man. Obviously much attracted by Angela. Ah! if it could only be!" The poor lady had given up hoping much. To her feminine and most intimate friends and contemporaries she said frankly that Angela simply would not look at a man.

Lady Verrider, Geoffrey Severn, and Claudius were left together.

"I say, Jane," said Geoffrey, "if you've done with me now, I've got a sort of half-appointment at the club. You might come there too, Sandell."

"You may go," said Lady Verrider. You've behaved very nicely, and I'm very grateful to you. Shan't let you take Claudius though, because I want him myself. Goodnight, Geoffrey, and thanks again."

When they were alone, Lady Verrider went to the fireplace, rested an arm on the mantelpiece and gazed into a quaint Venetian mirror. Her back was turned on Claudius as she spoke—

"Well, Claudius, I'm not blind. I have eyes and see. I don't want you to tell me what you think of my Angela. I know. What difference does it make?"

"The future is not in my own hands. Nothing can alter that—after next Saturday."

"You mean that seriously?"

"Yes."

"I would give worlds to know what hideous trouble you have got yourself into. I have been a friend to you since you were a baby, and you tell me next to nothing. Why do you stop at a hotel, and why don't you stop here with me? Why should I lose your confidence?"

She stamped her foot impatiently.

"My dear lady, you have not lost my confidence in the very slightest. I should be very glad to accept your hospitality, but my plans are changed. I am going into the country on Monday."

"Are you going to the Wycherleys on Sunday night?"

"Yes."

"Is it to Guilbridge that you are going on Monday?"

"Yes."

"Knowing that she will be there?"

"Yes."

Lady Verrider turned round and faced him.

"Claudius, my good friend, I'm going to speak to you very plainly. There is a chance that the girl may get fond of you. I think she will.

And then? And then you suddenly leave her without a word, pass out of her life, drop her, leave her humiliated and puzzled. You cannot do that."

"I do not think there is much chance of what you say. But I propose to tell her as soon as I decently can, at least as much as I have told you."

"Your intimacy with her seems to have progressed sufficiently rapidly. I know that you cannot do anything dishonourable. I have the utmost faith in you, but you're human—a man, and not a god; and she is human—poor, pretty Angela. You may explain to her that you cannot marry, but that will not prevent the chance that she may fall in love with you."

"And," said Claudius, rising, "I am unwilling to risk on so slight a chance the utmost happiness I have ever had. Do I not speak frankly to you now? The days are so few that are left me. Trust me a little further."

"I hope the best," Lady Verrider said. "Women go by siege, man by assault. The days are few, certainly, and it is possible no harm may be done to her. But I'm anxious."

"Tell me," she added, "is this a money matter?"

"No, dear lady," he said. "Money could not help me. I know your kindness though, and do believe that I am very grateful for it. Goodnight."

"Goodnight, then, Claudius. Let me know if I can help you in any way, and in any case write to me."

As he stepped from his carriage into the hotel, he heard above the sound of the traffic, the clang and chime from many steeples. The first day of the Octave was over.

Chapter 11

Claudius slept ill and rose early. From his brief sleep he had been awakened by a horrible dream. He dreamed that he saw the doctor's face bending over him; the eyes were wolfish and eager, the lips drawn back a little, the whole expression diabolical. He tried to speak, but could not. As the face came nearer and the horror of it grew on him, he tried to raise his arms and thrust it away, but he was unable to move. Then he awoke; it had merely been ordinary and typical form of nightmare.

Yet long after he was awake something of this horror from his sleep haunted him. For the first time a suspicion of the doctor and a dread of the future entered his mind. He banished them at once as reasonless. What the doctor required, he told himself, was an assistant absolutely devoted; there might be experiments which would require constant watching night and day; secrets that could be trusted only to one who first forfeited his right to use them for himself.

A thousand explanations occurred to him. He had been told that he was to regard himself as a slave, body and soul; it had been said seriously, and he must be prepared to accept it literally. Yet it was always possible that there had been in the doctor's use of the phrase much of that whimsical exaggeration which was habitual with him. It seemed even probable, and the suspicions vanished. Before the Octave was over, they were to return again.

After breakfast Claudius chose the inexpensive pleasure of an aimless walk through the London streets. He had much to think about. His point of view had changed. The doctor had been right in saying that a year of freedom was too long, if it was to be one's last year; much might happen in that time to bind one to earth and make the farewell bitter. But eight days, one day, even one hour might also be too long.

It was little more than an hour that had made the change in Claudius, placed him in the position of one who with the strongest possible motive for living sees the end of life very, very near. He loved Angela though he had seen her but once.

"*Quant à nous*," wrote Theophile Gautier, "*notre avis est que si l'on n'aime pas une personne la première fois qu'on la voit, il n'y a aucune raison pour l'aimer la seconde et encore moins la troisième.*"
("As for us," wrote Theophile Gautier, "our opinion is that if you don't like a person the first time you see them, there is no reason to like them the second time and even less third.")

If Claudius had met Angela but one hour before the doctor spoke of their strange contract, that contract would never have been made. If life meant Angela, then it would be worthwhile to undergo poverty, sordid struggles, many humiliations, in order to live. Life would then be beyond price. Claudius saw now that among the many mingled causes which had resulted in the contract under which he was bound there was one which he had not suspected at the time.

Yet, in this tragic position, he had no feeling of tragedy and no unhappiness. He loved, and it was enough. True, it seemed that the ordinary end of love was not for him, but then no lover at first thinks of marriage or possession. Lady Verrider's word of warning was vaguely in his mind—the dim memory of one who was wise from her point of view. He could not bring himself to think that Angela would love him like that. The nauseous vanity of such a supposition was insufferable. He hoped that she would be kind to him and let him see her often. On his part he knew that he was not free to—he hated the banal words—to make love to her.

Doctor Gabriel Lamb seemed a shadow, and all the previous incidents of Claudius's life seemed obscure and unsubstantial when he thought of Angela. She was the light. In the joy of thinking that for these few days he would often be with her, he could forget that when those days were passed, he was to leave her for ever. On one point he forced himself, however, to be clear—doing this much justice to Lady Verrider. He would take advantage of the strange guess that Angela had made at dinner the night before to tell her everything. He did not believe that in this point it mattered one straw whether he deceived her or not, but all the same he would not deceive her.

She should know exactly how he stood. Until he met her, he had decided not to tell anyone the story of his contract with the doctor. But if anyone could possibly think that he ought to tell Angela, then he would tell her. He would leave it for the night to settle how much and how little he should tell her then. But certainly, she should know all as soon as might be managed.

In the afternoon he went to Guilbridge, and took three rooms at the hotel there. He returned and dined in town. Halfway through dinner it occurred to him that he would have preferred another wine, but he did not commit the extravagance of ordering it. Of course, he might have taken the entire hotel at Guilbridge, and ordered the entire wine-list in London. But, perhaps, one of the best proofs that it was not for the thousand pounds a day that he had sold himself, was that he constantly forgot that he had a thousand pounds a day. The doctor had strangely insisted on his side of the contract—it had little or no interest for Claudius.

Mrs. Wycherley had not a thousand pounds a day, but she had no doubt that her husband had been making money lately—within the last fortnight. He had. In his mild and unpretentious way, he had been practically gambling and gambling for far more than he could have afforded to lose. It is a pity to have to record it, because its effect may be deplorable on those—if any—who hear about it, but Mr. Wycherley had won.

Having won, he had decided not to gamble any more, but to stick to his legitimate business. He kept to that decision. Once only in his life did, he sell shares which he did not possess in a mine which practically did not exist; once only did he buy shares for which he would have been unable to pay from people who had not got them to sell. These two speculations, although they may not look promising when stated baldly, put money into Mr. Wycherley's pocket, and left him quite satisfied that dabbling in mines was a dangerous business, and he must never touch it again. He did not tell his wife any of this. He did not want to make her anxious. Besides, in matters masculine and commercial, Jessica did not know anything about anything, and explanations were tedious.

But still she noticed things. Mr. Wycherley one day tasted the party-champagne. On inquiry he found that he had six dozen of it. He sent that six dozen off to a hospital, remarking dryly that it ought to be drunk in some place where the doctors were handy. Also, he thought that, after all, he might as well have some wine that he could drink himself. And he ordered that wine.

Then, again, he suddenly discovered that the house needed to be re-decorated. Jessica and Angela were to go to Guilbridge while it was being done, and Jessica might have those Oxford Street people she was always thinking about to do it. No, he wouldn't go to Guilbridge himself. When a man leaves his business, his business leaves him. Besides, there ought to be somebody in the house to keep an eye on the workmen.

Mrs. Wycherley was delighted. "Things are looking up in the city, then," she said.

"We get along somehow," he answered, with a sigh. It was his invariable reply to that question.

He would not let Mrs. Wycherley keep her own carriage.

"Be reasonable, Jessica. In people in our position that would be ostentatious—"

"Mrs. Bodgers," Jessica began. Bodgers, by the way, had joined Mr. Wycherley in that speculation.

"Bodgers is a fool—a fair judge of port, but in many ways sadly wanting in discretion. No; you may have that hired brougham sometimes—well, pretty often. You can fetch me from the office at five, now and then, if you like."

The first time that Mrs. Wycherley and Angela fetched him from the office, he inquired of them vaguely—

"What's the name of the place where you get your clothes?"

They suggested several places.

"Ah!" said Mr. Wycherley. "This is more comfortable than the 'bus. Mustn't do it every day though." Then he relapsed into silence. But presently he added, "I don't like your clothes, Angela, and I don't like your mother's either. We'll go and get some more."

On this occasion he was wildly generous, insisting on Bond Street and the best of everything. On the next afternoon he came back on the 'bus though, and—not to make a penny fare into twopence—walked the last quarter of a mile.

Mrs. Wycherley had a few people to dinner that night, and the invaluable Jameson assisted. After the dinner, Jameson retired to the basement, and spoiled a previously immaculate career by getting drunk on about equal parts of kitchen beer and upstairs *curaçoa*. He did not appear again, fortunately, until the guests were gone, and then he attempted to leave the house surreptitiously. That is to say, he took off his coat, folded it neatly over his arm, opened his umbrella, and came up into the hall. Here he paused, possibly to add some further touches to the disguise, and was discovered by Mr. Wycherley. Mr. Wycherley had been inquiring the reason for Jameson's absence, and had been told by a euphemistic parlourmaid that "Mr. Jameson had come over very strange in his manner." Mr. Wycherley was, in fact, looking for Jameson.

"Mister Wy'l'ly," said Jameson, with dignity, "I've know your family many yearsh, and I'm man as liksh to shee ev'rythin' tidy roun' 'bout me. Ev'rythin' qui' tidy, and then I'm—I'm as I ought to be." He lowered himself into one of the hall chairs. "You'll 'shcuse me for speakin', bur when thingsh are understood, then they're—they're ash they ought to be. And ev'rythin' ought to be ash it ought." With which remarks on the *comme il faut*, Jameson immediately fell asleep. He was removed from the house in a four-wheeled cab, and he never returned to it.

Mrs. Wycherley, aghast and much upset, said she was deeply and truly thankful that this shocking scene had not taken place when the guests were still there.

Mr. Wycherley said, "Get a permanent man, Jessica—good, but not too expensive. Get him tomorrow."

It was the crowning extravagance. It was this permanent and perfect person who hovered at the doors of Mrs. Wycherley's *salon* when Claudius entered. Claudius, generally self-possessed, felt himself almost trembling with excitement tonight. He could not, however, see

Angela at first. Mrs. Wycherley—breaking in waves on a black velvet shore—shook his hand and was so glad. She handed him on to a clever girl in the wrong pink, with the smudgy complexion that almost always goes with much soul. She talked vivaciously, and so did Claudius. The buzz of conversation around them made most of their remarks inaudible to each other, but neither minded it much.

As Claudius was talking, he caught a glimpse of Angela. She was standing at some distance away in the window, and an undersized young man with yellow hair and a make-up tie was openly and rather nervously adoring her. He was one of the world's understudies, and there were many of them there. However, Lady Verrider had almost promised to come and bring her title. Mrs. Wycherley did not despair of the evening's brilliancy.

Angela was in white satin and silver, and the dress had cost a great deal of money. She was feeling quite all right about herself, as far as appearance went. But her eyes were sad and thoughtful. She knew that Claudius was in the room—had glanced once rapidly at him, found him looking intently at her, and not dared to glance again until she heard his voice and he was shaking hands with her.

"May I be introduced to nobody and talk to you all the rest of the evening?" said Claudius. "Thy servant is the daughter of the house," she said, "and has duties."

"Which I am sure Mrs. Wycherley performs to perfection. Has the daughter of the house also had supper?"

Angela rose, put her hand under his arm, and the two joined the stream flowing supperwards.

"Isn't that a charming dress?" said Angela. "I mean the lady right over there in the corner."

"I should have thought so."

"You must think so."

"I have seen one I admired more."

"Which? What colour?"

"If my audacity may be forgiven, white and silver."

"Oh, this! Yes, it's pretty. I tried to dress like an angel, and I've come out like a wedding-cake. I didn't dare to go into supper before, for fear someone would cut a slice."

"I will protect you."

"Me? No; protect them. Think of their disappointment. It's true, though, those that go often to dances and things always become gradually exactly like some dish in a ball-supper. Their dresses are no longer trimmed, they are garnished. Their expressions alter too—get creamy like a mayonnaise, luscious like a macedoine, virulent like a boar's head, patient and vacuous like a cold fowl. Every chaperone looks like a cold fowl. I know one of them will get carved by accident one of these days."

Their talk at supper-time was not much more serious. Angela was happy, bewitching, and in rather mad spirits, apparently. She introduced Claudius maliciously to several people. She had a way of making others fall into her mood. Many dull and heavy people sprang into wit at her end of the table that night, and wondered, when they got home, with approving wonder at the things they themselves had said.

Afterwards Claudius took Angela out on to the balcony. Here striped canvas made a sweet seclusion for two lounge chairs, a tiny table, a shaded lamp, and a potted palm.

"Well," he said, "and now we are out of the crowd."

"My crowd, please. Poor little struggling crowd! I must go back to it soon."

"Before you go, I have something to tell you."

She leaned right back in her chair, a graceful creature, her pretty white hand playing with her ivory fan. Her eyes had grown sad again, almost plaintive under the long lashes. Her red lips had lost their garb of raillery.

"Yes," she said, "you have. But there is one thing, tell me nothing if you would rather not. We met by chance. I guessed something by chance. I ought not to have guessed—shall we leave it?"

"It would be kind of you if you would let me tell you."

"Yes, then, tell me. I am interested. I guessed that you had something of importance at stake, and—why should I not say it? I have thought a great deal about it since."

"Have you?" he said eagerly. "Have you? I have myself, my life, at stake. No doubt it is chiefly important to myself; but it is more important to myself than I thought once. By a promise given—a contract made—after a few days I become body and soul the property of another man, his to kill or to keep alive, his to do just as he likes with, his utterly until one or other of us dies."

There was a moment's silence. Angela's eyes were wide open.

"You astonish me!" she said. "It is a fairy story. I cannot understand."

"It is literally true."

"Yes; that—of course. But I do not understand how it happened—

how it *could* happen."

"The story is long. I don't want you to think too badly of me. When I gave my promise I thought—I thought I was right. I'm sure enough now—God knows!—that I was wrong. It is a long story, but if you have the patience to hear it, I will tell it you."

Angela rose from her chair and clasped her hands. She was thinking.

"I cannot hear it now," she said, "because we must go back. I am not quite sure whether I want you to tell me it or not. That has nothing to do with patience or interest, of course. I am interested—it is all so strangely romantic! My possible reason for not hearing it would be—be different. Did you not say that you expected to be at Guilbridge?"

"Tomorrow. Your mother has promised to bring you to dine with me at my hotel that night. I am hoping to see you very often."

"I wonder why you spend your last days there? No; don't tell me—not now. Perhaps one day at Guilbridge I shall ask you for the whole story. Will you tell it me then?"

"Yes; whenever you wish it."

"You have given me the impression that you are a lonely man, and sometimes that you are unhappy."

"I ought to be unhappy. I do not think I am, strangely enough."

"I want," she faltered quickly and suddenly, "to give you, my sympathy."

She stretched out both her hands, and he held them for a second. Her face had grown pale; she looked to him unspeakably beautiful. He checked an impulse, and they passed back into the crowded room together. A formal farewell followed. On his way home he felt glad that he had not made love to Angela Wycherley. Better men have had similar illusions.

After all the guests had gone, Mrs. Wycherley had a talk with Angela.

"We met him last night," said Mrs. Wycherley, with fat gaiety, "and again tonight, and we're to dine with him tomorrow; and he means to see us often at Guilbridge, he tells me. I'm sure I don't know what it means. Perhaps you could tell me, my dear."

Angela sat down beside her. "Mamma, dear," she said, "I am going to be serious."

"What? Is it? At last?"

"Tonight Mr. Sandell told me something of his private affairs. He

264

will not and cannot marry—"

"Then why—"

"I wish to see a good deal of him during the next few days. I am grown-up. You must trust me completely."

"Yes, darling Angela, I *do* trust you. But is this right in him? And is it—is it, dear—for your own happiness?"

"Yes, I think so. The circumstances are strange. You know me, mamma dear, and you trust me. That is sweet of you. Leave this to me, and don't ask me any more questions now. I will tell you all one day, if Mr. Sandell lets me; and I am sure he will."

"My dear, this is terribly upsetting. I wonder—no, I won't ask any questions. Of course, he does not make love to you."

"Don't say those words, mamma dear. I do *hate* them so. No, no; he has not."

She honestly believed it. Better women have had similar illusions.

Mrs. Wycherley allowed herself to be persuaded on every point. In her heart she supposed that there was but some temporary obstacle, exaggerated by Angela's imagination, and that, although Angela might not think it now, she would yet be happily married to Claudius Sandell.

CHAPTER 12

Before Claudius left for Guilbiidge on the following morning he sent a messenger to his old lodgings, to recover the manuscript of his novel. The motive of living had come now, and come too late. It was his whim to see if the means of living would not come also now, and with a similar irony. The book had been refused, when refusal meant despair. Possibly it would be accepted when acceptance could bring with it no hope. He sent the manuscript off to another publisher. In the note that accompanied it, he said that as he was leaving England, an early decision would greatly oblige him.

At the same time, he despatched another messenger with a note to Dr. Gabriel Lamb. It was only after long consideration that he had decided to send it. The question which he wished to ask was, indeed, one which practically, had been asked and answered before. Yet there seemed to him just the barest possibility that the doctor might change his mind, and—if not—it would be something definitely to know the worst. Besides, it was possible that the doctor's answer might throw some light on the future—on what was to come when the Octave was over. In the course of the letter Claudius wrote:

"Is there any consideration which would make you rescind our contract? If, for instance (though I cannot imagine anything of the kind could happen), some stroke of luck made it possible for me to repay to you twice or three times the sum that you have advanced to me, would you then—if I asked it—give me back my promise? Or is there any other way?"

There were several arrangements besides that Claudius had to make before his departure, to supplement the resources of a provincial hotel, and make things more worthy of Angela. She had mentioned that she had meant to ride, when she was at Guilbridge, if she found that she could hire a horse that was suitable; Claudius had to make it certain that that horse would be forthcoming, and without any necessity for hiring it. Just as he was leaving for Guilbridge, the man who had taken his note to Wimbledon returned with a verbal message that the doctor would send his reply by post that night.

At the last moment, Mr. Wycherley decided that he would accompany his wife and daughter down to Guilbridge, see them safely established in their lodgings, and then return to dine at his club.

"You don't understand about trains, Jessica," said Mr. Wycherley; "and you might let these lodging-house people be too—too independent. I'll just come down with you and see that you really get there."

So Mr. Wycherley put on a light tweed suit; he had bought it and paid for it, but it did not look in the least as if it belonged to him—guided his wife and daughter safely through the intricacies of Waterloo Station, and finally conducted them to their lodgings at Guilbridge. There he explained to the landlady that a variety of things which she was sure she had never been asked for before would be both asked for and insisted upon. Then, with a consciousness of duty done, he took Mrs. Wycherley and Angela for a stroll on the heath previous to his return to the station.

Here Claudius chanced to meet them, and he would not hear of Mr. Wycherley going back to the station. He had been told that Mr. Wycherley was not coming to Guilbridge, but as he had come he must certainly stop and dine with him.

Angela seconded the appeal. "Do stop, papa, there are lots of trains after dinner, and you can't eat your poor little dinner all alone in a solitary club."

"There was a chance—well, half a chance—of my meeting Bodgers at the club. I said something about it, and he said something about it—but nothing definite."

266

"Mr. Bodgers must dine alone," said Claudius. "A telegram to the club, in case he goes there, and the thing is settled. You really must not disappoint me."

"And," added Mr. Wycherley, "I've no clothes with me except what I stand up in."

"That doesn't matter in the least. I also will dine in this very identical suit, if you like. There's the last excuse shot dead."

"Oh, well!" said Mr. Wycherley, with mild geniality. "I'm sure I'm not anxious to make excuses. If you'll take me as I am, I'll come with pleasure. Very kind of you."

The pleasure was quite real on Mr. Wycherley's part. Young people did not as a rule make much fuss with the little man, or seem particularly desirous for his society. He felt rather flattered.

The hotel proprietor did not feel flattered at all. Claudius had taken some trouble about this dinner; there had been various importations from London which seemed to the hotel proprietor to cast imputations on the quality and extent of his resources. He ventured respectfully and grandiloquently to remonstrate with Claudius, and he did not obtain a lengthy hearing.

"Go away, and don't bother," said Claudius. "I know that what I've done is unusual, but no slight to you is intended by it. I must have my own way, and I expect to pay you for the privilege."

The actual dinner was short and simple. But the wine, the Venetian glass, the linen, the silver and cutlery, the flowers and fruit, even the oak table on which the dinner was served, had all come from London, and the arrangement of the table had been wrested from the hands of the hotel head waiter and given to an imported, superior, and professional person. And this was all done for the entertainment of a mature lady in a tea-gown that looked like a dressing-gown—or it may have been a dressing-gown that looked like a tea-gown— a young girl in pink, a young man in a tweed suit, and another tweed suit with an older man lurking in its interior. But then the girl in pink had eyelashes, and very pretty ways, and was sympathetic. Even the hotel proprietor could see this.

And he was stirred to emulation. He himself stood in the kitchen, closely inspecting, wisely directing, even with his own hands adding last touches, while the dinner was being prepared. He himself decanted a bottle of port, that was one of a remaining three, long ago taken out of the wine list and reserved for the most rare and exquisite occasions. The dinner was short and simple, but it was perfect.

"You know," said Mr. Wycherley, mildly, "I was once at this hotel before—came over with Mr. Bodgers one Sunday. But they didn't do me like this. Yet we ordered our dinner carefully—very carefully. Bodgers is always careful about that. This—this is miraculous."

"You flatter me," said Claudius, laughing. "Hotels won't trouble themselves for mere men, I believe: you should have brought your wife and daughter with you."

"No, no," cried Angela, "I protest against that, I'm not going to be taken about the country as a decoy-dinner even for my own starving father. It's too sordid a role."

Claudius changed the subject. "Now," he said, "I do take to myself some credit for the view from this window. I think I've arranged that very well. Will you please look?"

Through the open window one saw a big yellow moon and a clear night sky, in front the tops of the dark trees in the garden outside and beyond the dim low hills.

"Now that *is* nice," said Mrs. Wycherley.

"You don't think," asked Claudius, "that it would have improved the composition of the picture if I had put my moon a little more to the right?"

"Don't be irreverent, Mr. Sandell," said Angela, reprovingly. "It's two far-awayly lovely!" She sighed. "I don't think any of us deserve it, except, perhaps, me."

"Ah, well," Mr. Wycherley said, "views are not a thing that I'm much of a judge of. Now this port—"

"That is to remind us that we are to leave them to drink it, Angela," said Mrs. Wycherley. They passed into the next room.

Mr. Wycherley settled himself again and filled his glass.

"This port," he continued, "is not the port that they gave my friend and myself when we were here, Mr. Sandell. Shouldn't have believed a country hotel, had got any of it."

"I seem to be particularly lucky," said Claudius.

Mr. Wycherley rolled the wine round in his glass meditatively.

"Luck," he said, "I wish there wasn't such a thing. It's the ruin of legitimate business."

Claudius led him out on this subject. It was Mr. Wycherley's own subject, and he talked exceedingly well upon it. In a dry and unpretentious way, he gave Claudius glimpses of the romantic side of commerce. He had stories of the mining market that were worth telling, and he told them. When he paused Claudius started him afresh.

On the subject that he thoroughly understood Mr. Wycherley became fascinating and interesting. He was, it appeared, strongly opposed to avoidable gambling.

"Of course," he said, "all business is nowadays more or less of the nature of a gamble. But there is avoidable speculation, and the number of men that go in for it is astounding. Some make fortunes, more get broken. I won't touch it myself."

Mr. Wycherley, it will be observed, did not say that he never had touched it.

"A man came to me today," he went on. "It was that friend of mine, Bodgers, I spoke to you about, he wants me to buy some shares that are at present on the rubbish heap. He's seen the last report from the mine, not yet published, and it's very favourable. He knows that a syndicate is just being formed in Paris to deal with the shares. I'm convinced that his information is as good as it can be, and I can trust him as I can trust myself. But for all that I'm not going to touch it."

When they had rejoined Mrs. Wycherley and Angela in the next room, Angela told her father that he had been behaving very badly, and she had a great mind to send him to bed at once.

"Dear me!" said Mr. Wycherley, "what have I done?"

"You have been talking business after dinner, which is wicked of you. No, I didn't listen at all. You raised your voice once, and I couldn't help hearing the words, 'three hundred *per cent.*' I won't have any 'three hundred *per cent.*' after business hours."

"I never have it during business hours," replied Mr. Wycherley. "I confess I've been talking 'shop,' but it is really Mr. Sandell's fault. When I stopped and apologised, he made me go on again."

"Oh—oh! How cowardly!"

"But perfectly true," added Claudius. "I can't understand this prejudice against talking 'shop,' Miss Wycherley. If a man speaks of something that he really and specially knows, and makes it exceedingly interesting, why should he be stopped with the word 'shop'? Everybody ought—at times, at any rate—to talk his regular 'shop.'"

"Very well," said Angela. "If he really has been interesting, he may sit up a little longer. I wonder what my own particular 'shop' is?"

"You professed," Claudius said, "to have a special gift for appreciating the moon. I don't know whether there was anything in it."

"And, by the way," Mrs. Wycherley remarked, "what a pity it is we can't see it from this room! So pretty it was."

Claudius suggested the hotel garden. The night was fine and warm, and Mrs. Wycherley was sure it would be most pleasant. All four went downstairs, and out into the gravel walk. Here Claudius and Angela passed on in front. When they were out of hearing Mr. Wycherley said—

"Don't know when I've enjoyed an evening so much, Jessica. Most pleasant and sensible young man, that. Who is he, by the way?"

"Son of Sir Constantino Sandell, my dear, and a great friend of Lady Verriider's. She speaks most highly of him. And money—as you see."

"Does he want to marry Angela?" asked Mr. Wycherley, bluntly.

"Ah, my dear, that's where I'm puzzled! There may be a certain something, though Angela doesn't say there is; but there's something else rather in the way at present. I don't know whether you see."

"I don't," said Mr. Wycherley, laconically.

"And I don't know that I do either, exactly. Angela was really most mysterious. If the child has a fault, it is that she won't discuss things enough. She wants me to take no step at all, to leave things to her, and one day she will tell me."

"It sounds all wrong, and rather shady," said Mr. Wycherley. "If he's entangled with some other woman—"

"Oh, I don't think it's that!"

"It generally is that, Jessica. You see, you don't know about things. If it is, he has no business here—for he's obviously here for Angela."

"Shall I speak to her firmly—take her away?"

"No; it is not necessary."

"But, my dear, you said it was all wrong."

"I said it sounded all wrong. You were never exact enough in your language, Jessica. As a matter of fact, it's all right, I believe. It sounds as if he were entangled with another woman, and had no business to be after Angela. On the other hand, Lady Verrider, who is devoted to Angela, introduces him. Also, Angela is independent, and takes care of herself. Girls have more freedom now than they had when you and I were young—they've got used to it—don't lose their heads over it. Also, there may be nothing in it; and as it's a question of a few days only, we'd better not interfere—unless something fresh and different happens."

"How you do see the reasons of things!" said Jessica, admiringly.

"Besides, I'm much inclined to like the young man—and I don't often like anybody on sight. If dining out were always like this, you'd get me to dine out more often. Small dinner, no crowd, no tinn'd

270

humbug to eat, and good wine to drink—that suits me."

Mrs. Wycherley was switched into her favourite topic at once.

"I never had a better appetite," she observed. "It may be the country air, or it may be the railway jerking being good for the liver, which Maria *always* said. But, for me, I had a capital dinner. And, afterwards, not a touch—not a twinge. You know how it is sometimes."

Mrs. Wycherley expatiated with some plainness of speech on how it was sometimes. Her husband listened, or appeared to listen, patiently. He was smoking an excellent cigar, and placidity came easily to him.

On ahead, Angela and Claudius walked together. They saw the golden moon through gently swaying branches. The summer night was lavish of its poetry. Angela's voice was soft, and touched with emotion. She spoke of the most matter-of-fact commonplace things, but her personal glamour made them beautiful to Claudius. She wondered if she would be able to find anything to ride in Guilbridge— perhaps the hotel let out horses. Did Claudius know?

Claudius said that he himself had a little mare there—had bought her because she was beautiful and cheap, though he didn't know what to do with her beyond selling her again. He would be very glad if Angela would try her. On the following afternoon perhaps, they might ride together over to Deepwater. Mrs. Wycherley might drive and meet them there. There was a picturesque inn by the river, where they could get tea. It was arranged. And it was all commonplace, and yet it brought back to Claudius's mind echoes of a poem that every one knows and loves—

I and my mistress, side by side,
Shall be together, breathe and ride,
So, one day more am I deified.

And the possible days were few and flying with terrible swiftness.

CHAPTER 13

After breakfast on Tuesday morning, Claudius took the morning papers out into the garden, and stretched himself comfortably under the mulberry tree on the lawn to glance through them. He had had a long swim in the river before breakfast, and had eaten a breakfast that would not have discredited a criminal on the morning of his execution. As he lay there in a light flannel suit, with his pipe in his mouth, and the *Times* open before him, he felt perfectly placid and contented. The day was glorious. In a few hours he would see Angela again and be riding by her side. He was so absorbed in feeling that life was good that he could forget that for him it was so brief. He glanced up for the first time in his life, over a report of the mining market.

He wondered which out of the long list it was that Mr. Wycherley had been told to buy. His eye was attracted by the name Martenhuis Deep. That might be it or might not. Possibly it was not even in that list at all. He flung the paper down and picked up another. He opened it casually, and once more the same name caught his eye—Martenhuis Deep. He noted that the shares were to be bought at 13-16. He recollected at the same time that he knew personally his father's broker. For a few minutes he lay back and reflected. Then he got up and walked briskly back into the hotel.

He wrote a hurried note to the broker, asking him to purchase four thousand Martenhuis Deep, and giving the name of his banker. He sent this off at once by a messenger to town. He had never transacted any business of the kind before. He was not even clear if his note was correct, and the commission would be executed, or if he had omitted any necessary formality. By the second post came a letter from Dr. Gabriel Lamb, written in a small neat hand on thick white paper. It ran as follows:—

My dear Sandell,

How on earth did you get the preposterous notion that I entered into our contract in a commercial spirit, and would be likely to close it for a consideration of one hundred, or more, *per cent.*? You really do me an injustice. Remember that you were positively reluctant to take the sum that you will fully earn. I had, to satisfy my own conscience, actually to insist. Should I, if I had been commercially-minded, have spent eight thousand pounds on what I might have obtained with equal ease for eight hundred or merely as a return for such poor hospitality and attention as I was able to show you—a consideration of no value whatever except for the pleasure your company gave us. It is a pity, of course, that you have met her—you obviously have met her, you know.

Under these circumstances I waited to reply to your letter until I had once more thought the matter over. The notion had occurred to me that you might perhaps (in the event of that 'stroke of luck') be able to find and purchase a substitute. I had to decide whether I would accept a substitute. Speaking quite frankly, any young man of a normal type would, if I could only trust him, suit me just as well as yourself. But I am afraid that I cannot trust anyone as well as I trust you. Mind, I have nothing but the word of the other party to the contract. He has but to break his word and he can go. I have no legal hold.

For the matter of that, you have only to break your word. You are not watched. I do not know whether you have left London for Guilbridge in order to be with her or in order to avoid her—I think the former and hope the latter. Even if I had you watched I should have no power to compel you to come to me next Saturday at midnight and to be mine, to do as I please with. It remains with you—if you break your word, you will not come. Otherwise only the death of one or other of us will end the contract. I need not point out again that murder or suicide would have for you—in addition to the conventional objections—the objection that either act would be dishonourable. But although I can hold out no hope to you—the enthusiasm of my work which requires you is stronger than myself—I can honestly sympathize with you.

You entered into that agreement when you had no motive for living—you have now found the motive. It is possible that within the few remaining days you may have that motive strengthened—possible, even, that you may find yourself in a position to offer me absurd sums to free you, as you suggest. This will make you feel bitter against what the story-teller calls fate, and, though unjustly, bitter against me.

Believe me, my dear Sandell, the best romance is the briefest. Though I am acting in the interests of my work and without the least regard to your own private interests, I do you a service in saving you from satiety. Come away from life while it is still giving you youth, and poetry, and romance, and possibilities. I myself should have left it long ago had not my work detained me.

It may interest you to hear that the bay mare, whose temper has daily grown more damnable, has killed the coachman. Did not you say that she would kill somebody? I have never driven her myself—my life is valuable to humanity. The coachman was not a perfect coachman. But his widow has already called twice at the house, apparently with no other motive than to tell me that he would have preferred to live (which I could have conjectured for myself) and to have hysterics on the door mat.

We leave England next Sunday, and, of course, you with us. I have sold the house, and preparations for departure are already being made. If you happen to come across any really fine madeira, would you let me know, or better still, order twelve dozen to be packed for shipping and sent to me here. I have nearly finished my own wine, and my wine merchant seems to think that I will buy disease and disappointment at a hundred and twenty the dozen. This is quite above the current market quotation for such commodities.

As I have explained to him. I would pay double that to get exactly the wine I want. By the way, there is no earthly likelihood of your finding anything of the kind, but I thought I would mention it on the barest of chances, as you have a palate and understand my taste.

If my wife were in the room, I am sure she would join me in sending kind regards. Her health is at present a subject for the gravest anxiety. *Au plaisir.*

Cordially yours,

Gabriel Lamb.

Claudius read this letter through twice, and put it in his pocket. He walked up and down thinking about it. Certain phrases in it haunted him. His suspicions of the doctor came back again—came back with more force and would not be dispelled. He had strange and horrible fears for the future before him. He could not put them from him till he was cantering over the turf with Angela beside him. Angela was not a very experienced horsewoman, but she was not nervous. A child would have been safe with the mare she was riding—perfectly made and as kind and easy as possible. In the exhilaration of the ride and the presence of Angela, the worst could be easily forgotten.

From the heath their way lay through a gate into a grassy lane with high hedges on either side. As they approached the gate at a walking pace two youths—humorous louts apparently—shut the gate, latched it, and then ran off laughing down the lane.

"Please wait here a moment," said Claudius to Angela, quietly.

He wheeled his horse round and then put it at the gate. Over he went and down the lane after those louts.

He returned in a minute, literally driving them before him, with a pleasant smile on his face. Men who smile pleasantly when they have lost their temper are mostly dangerous. Possibly the two louts knew this. Their choice lay between going back to the gate, being ridden down, and pulling Claudius off his horse; they decided to go back to the gate.

"Open it," said Claudius, curtly, "and hold it open until we're through."

"It was only a joke," said one of them rather sheepishly, as he pulled the gate back.

"So's this," replied Claudius. "Don't let it go any further than that."

Claudius rode up to Angela, laughing, and returned through the gate with her. His fit of temper had completely vanished. He flung a coin to the youths as they passed.

"To show them that their civility will pay them better than their humour," he explained.

"That was rather pretty," said Angela,

"And rather silly, I'm afraid," said Claudius. "I don't know exactly why, but I feel a little like a circus rider in consequence. I expected a bad brass band to begin as I came down the lane, and was rather disappointed that it didn't."

"Oh no!" Angela answered. "You were in a very bad temper. Many a poor child has had its pudding and its pocket-money cut off for less."

"Leave me my pudding, and I will apologise."

"I've got the nastiest possible temper myself."

"I can't pretend to believe it," said Claudius. "You ask too much. But look, here we are at the inn!"

Mrs. Wycherley had not yet arrived. Angela said that she would order tea, while Claudius saw that the horses were properly looked after. They met in the garden of the inn—a picturesque garden, dotted about with tables and chairs and arbours.

"Have you ordered a very good tea?"

"Well," said Angela, "I've done my best. The place looked so tumble-down and old, and out of the world, that I had great expectations of it. I hoped that there would be a surly landlord who would say that he never had been asked for tea and wouldn't give us it. Then I should have persuaded him, and bribed him, and helped to cut the bread-and-butter, and gradually he would have got to like me."

"It's not impossible," said Claudius.

"But the place is different, spoiled by the patronage of the tripper—ruined by civilization. I gave my orders to a trim little person in a clean London apron, with a lot of nasty little hotel ways. And there was a tariff, mark you, Mr. Sandell, a horrible fixed tariff with three kinds of tea on it—plain tea, tea with eggs, and tea with meat."

"Tea with meat would be extravagant and ostentatious. If you have ordered that, I refuse to pay for my share, or to countenance it in any way except by eating it."

"But I didn't, neither did I order the plain tea, because it sounded dull, and also because I thought it would make the trim person think that we were not wealthy. I went in for the golden mean, which takes the form of eggs."

"And where are we going to have the golden mean?"

"Out here in the garden. I insisted on honey and cream. I prayed the trim person if only for a few hours to be as pastoral and unsophisticated as possible. And she said, 'Oh, you'll find us quite punctual!' So possibly she hasn't caught the spirit of the thing."

"Possibly not. Why this hunger and thirst after pastorality?"

"Because I'm in the country," she said impetuously; "because all of a sudden, I hate horrible, vulgar, complex, social, dirty, striving, mean London life. It has made me so bad, and I want to be better again. Oh, I'm much more in earnest than you think! Really, really, I am! It's been coming upon me lately—and quite suddenly, I know it. I'm a changed girl."

There was a whimsical smile on her face, but her eyes were serious and looking out for sympathy.

"Yes! tell me all about it."

"It would be a heavenly thing to confess everything. You confessed to me a little, didn't you, at our house the other night? I haven't been criminal in spots—no murders or burglaries, or things of that kind. I've only been mildly always and altogether wrong. I believe I would have been good if the world and circumstances had not spoiled me. I was very vulgar in one way, and very angry with anybody who was very vulgar in the other way. I didn't know the right value of things. I ran after straws that were worth nothing. I see now that nothing's more vulgar than to think much about vulgarity and to use the word."

"This is subtle."

"Subtle! Ah, believe me, I am fairly crying for simplicity. If I could get work as a dairy-maid, not the stage dairy-maid but the real thing, I might save my soul alive. As it is I"—she made a movement of her hands to her throat—"I am choked in London. It's all one game of brag—silly, undignified brag. I've played at it—loathed it—and gone on playing it. Everyone tries for an effect, and most of them miss it, and are laughed at for their failure, and those who get it find that it is not worth getting. One manages and schemes and does humiliating things to secure—what?—less than the fluff on that seeding dandelion."

"Is this all quite serious?"

"Yes. If you like, it is the cynicism of extreme youth, and therefore counts for nothing. But it's not assumed, at any rate. I'm being very honest this afternoon."

With the arrival of Mrs. Wycherley and tea, Angela suddenly changed her tone. She was no longer mournful; her eyes brightened, her talk was full of the brightest and maddest raillery. But as Claudius and she rode back again together, she as suddenly became very quiet.

They had ridden for some time, side by side, without a word, when Angela raised her head and said—

"Mr. Sandell, what are you thinking about?"

"I had the presumption to be thinking about you."

"What are you thinking about me?"

"That you have as many moods as an April day."

"Do you mind?"

"I would have nothing altered."

"You enter into all my moods. When I am in good spirits, you are in good spirits too. How can you do it with the end so near for you? I think I shall ask you to tell me the rest of your story very soon. I have not forgotten it."

There was a pause, and then she added, "I am in a sad mood now." Their eyes met, and she read the sympathy that he did not speak. He found himself wishing that the ride might last for ever, on and on in a perpetual quiet summer afternoon. He desired nothing better than the strange exaltation that he felt just now. The ride lasted exactly until half-past six. Angela praised Jeannie, the mare that she had been riding. She thanked Claudius.

"You must ride her again if you like her," said Claudius.

"She's an adorable beauty and too good for me. Perhaps. And thank you again, Mr. Sandell. Goodbye."

Even as he left her, he knew that he was to see her again that night. He felt sure of it. After dinner he strolled out on to the heath. It was growing dark, and the twilight was cool and fascinating. He was not surprised to see her standing silhouetted against the sky, a slender grey figure. Nor did she seem surprised as she turned and saw him.

"Are you not afraid to be out alone?"

"No—no, thank you. When we are in the country, I often do this.

Mamma writes one letter, and then goes to bed early—and I, if I'm restless, walk until I'm tired. See—I have my own key."

"Would you rather be by yourself, Miss Wycherley, or, may I?"

"If you would walk with me, and tell me the rest now—the rest of the story."

He began at once. He told the story as briefly as possible, wasting no word on apologies for telling it. He told how, an outcast from his own home, a failure in the work he had attempted, with no tie to life, and no motive for living, worn out by privations and disappointment, he had been found by Dr. Gabriel Lamb. He dwelt at length on the kindness of the doctor and his wife, and tried to indicate the character of the man. He described how the agreement came to be made, and told the precise terms of it.

"Thank you for telling me," she said quietly, when he had finished. "It's worse than I had feared. Is there no other way? Can he not be bought?"

"I thought of that—only yesterday I wrote and asked him. Early this morning I ventured on a mining speculation—your father had spoken of such things the night before. I do not care in the least for gambling of any kind—it doesn't amuse me. I know nothing whatever of the shares I have bought, except their name and present price. I somehow felt sure—it was a silly presentiment, but a strong one—that I was right, and that I should make a profit large enough to buy my release. I had hardly sent off the order to the broker, before the second post came in. The doctor refuses to cancel the agreement for any money consideration whatever. I believe that he really does not care for money in the least—or for anything very much except his work."

"Is the name of the mine Martenhuis Deep?"

"Yes—why? How do you know?"

"Because, as we were coming here yesterday, papa asked me jokingly if I should like him to make a fortune. He said he could make one in less than a week by buying Martenhuis Deep, but that he wouldn't do it, because it was outside his legitimate business. As you were speaking, the name flashed into my memory again. Wait, there is another thing I want to ask you. Will you let me see the manuscript of your novel?"

"I would, but I have sent it off to another publisher."

"Why—why," she exclaimed impatiently, "did you not do that before the agreement?"

"The book had been refused twice, and I was quite hopeless about it. But if I had known that the agreement was coming, I think I should have tried again first. I did not know. It came suddenly—time was apparently of great importance to the doctor, and he would not have waited for the publisher's decision. Then I was under great obligations to him. He had saved my life, clothed me, fed me, treated me with the most delicate kindness and perfect trust. By accepting, I repaid him; if I refused, I saw nothing before me."

"It is too soon to say yet. But if everything came now—now in these few days—now when it is too late, that would be terrible. Do not be angry with me, Mr. Sandell, for what I am going to say. You tell me that the doctor has no legal hold on you. I think he has no moral hold—that he is not acting in good faith. Have you thought of the possibility of—of breaking your word?"

"I am not angry with you," said Claudius, with a dreary smile. "I'm no better than other men, and I've thought of it. If I did it, I dare say for a few days I should feel nothing but relief, freedom, pleasure. The other thing would come though—I should feel that I had broken my promise, betrayed a man who trusted me. I should feel that I had done it through cowardice. It would not be possible to live like that. Perhaps it would be easier to break my word, if he had a legal hold upon me— if I ran the least risk in breaking it—if it were not mere cowardice."

"Yes, yes; I see," said Angela. "I had not guessed what the story would be; and very often when I have been laughing and—generally silly—you must have hated it, and thought me unsympathetic. You know, when you were at your house, I gave you my sympathy, and I meant it. Only, I did not know that it was quite so horrible or quite so hopeless then, and so, sometimes—"

"Ah! Do not alter! Let me be happy for the little time that is left!"

Angela laughed a little mirthless laugh. "I feel," she said, "as if I had been playing the fool at a funeral."

"No, no. If you must reproach anyone, reproach me for having done a reckless and suicidal thing, and for having distressed you by telling you about it. I have told no one else."

"I wanted you to tell me about it—I would not have that different. Will you please let me go home alone, Mr. Sandell? Now, please, goodnight."

Her small cold hand touched his a moment, and she had turned and gone. As he stood still watching her as she walked away, he heard through the still night a faint sound, and knew that she was sobbing.

He went back to the hotel, cursing himself for all he told her, cursing that excellent Lady Verrider for her well-meant advice that had led him to do it. He spent a wretched and sleepless night.

In the letter which Mrs. Wycherley wrote to her husband, she said—

Angela has gone for one of her favourite evening strolls—just after dinner—but the young never think of these things. A good daughter she always was, but really she improves. Never corrects me now if I do or say anything that isn't quite as it should be. Less strict she seems to be, and fonder. We have much to be thankful for. Not one touch or one twinge since I've been here— country air and plain food account for it. The cooking is good here with the exception of the gravies—no richness or strength in them; but I've not spoken about it yet.

CHAPTER 14

Wednesday morning brought two letters for Claudius. One of them was merely the contract note for four thousand Martenhuis Deep purchased at thirteen-sixteenths. In the report in the morning paper Claudius read:

The chief feature in the mining market was the demand for Martenhuis Deep on Paris buying. After quickly springing to two and five-eighths, there was a slight relapse owing to profit taking. This, however, was nearly recovered in the street, the last price reaching two and a half."

Claudius had thought of wiring to Mr. Wycherley, to ask whether he should sell or hold. Then he decided for himself to hold and leave it to luck. Whether he won or lost could not matter to him now.

His other letter was a friendly and informal note from the senior partner in the publishing firm, to which he had sent his novel.

Mr. Arragon wrote:

It is not a common thing, for a novel to be sent us on Monday, and accepted on Tuesday. That, however, is the case with your book. On Monday afternoon, I happened to want something to read in the carriage as I drove home from business, and picked up the first few pages of your novel. There were several manuscripts on the table waiting to be sent off to my reader— it is seldom that I read anything myself, and it was the merest chance that I picked up part of your book rather than one of the others. Well, I read these few pages on my way home; and, as soon as I got there, I sent the carriage back again for the rest of it. I finished it after dinner. That was quite enough to decide me. If the book took hold of me like that—and I am fairly hardened—it is certain to interest others. We shall be very glad to publish it.

The terms offered were fair and business-like—neither unjust nor wildly generous. Claudius wrote to thank Mr. Arragon and accept them. That also could not matter to him now—save that it added to the irony and bitterness of the fate that held and mocked him.

He sent round a note to Mrs. Wycherley, offering her his carriage. Jeannie, too, was at Miss Wycherley's disposal if she preferred to ride. He waited impatiently for the reply. He picked up a book and tried to read—then found that he was turning the pages mechanically, without being in the least conscious of what he was reading. He flung the book down and went out into the road, pacing up and down impatiently. It seemed as if the messenger would never come.

He came in sight at last, sauntering leisurely along until he saw Claudius. The note that he brought was from Mrs. Wycherley. It was brief: it thanked Mr. Sandell very much for his kindness, but neither she nor her daughter would ride or drive that day. It gave no reason, and suggested no meeting. Claudius at once read into that letter more than poor Mrs. Wycherley had ever intended to put there. It vexed him with a certainty that there was something behind, and an uncertainty what that something was. It seemed cold. Was Angela ill?—Mrs. Wycherley distrustful? What could it be?

To remain still was impossible. He had his horse brought round, and started out. He rode past the house where Mrs. Wycherley and Angela were lodging. He had some faint hope that they might come out or in as he passed—that, if only for a moment, he might speak to Angela. He saw nothing of them. He noticed though that the blinds were drawn in the upstairs rooms. Again, the fear came to him that Angela might be ill. His mind was a torture-chamber. Anxiety for her, self-reproach, impotent rage at his fate, burning and stifled passion goaded and maddened him. The Octave was drawing near to its end, and the hours were flying wasted away—wasted without Angela. He turned on to the heath and rode, as a man rides, who would fain get away from himself—from his own thoughts.

It was three o'clock when he returned. He had come back by the same way he went. Once more he had failed to see Angela. Once more he had noted the drawn blinds. At four o'clock he could endure it no longer. He had decided to call at the house, expecting only to be refused admission.

But Mrs. Wycherley was at home. She was in the garden. If he would walk through the house, he would find her there. He found her seated in the shade, in an easy-chair, propped up with cushions that she took with her when she went away from home. She looked benevolent. She was reading a shilling paper-covered book that she had purchased at the station book-stall—*Dainty Dishes: How to Cook and how to Serve them*. "It might give me some ideas," she had said to Angela. She laid aside the book (with the title downwards) as she saw Claudius.

"Now this is very kind of you," said Mrs. Wycherley, "not to have got tired of us."

Claudius looked for satire in her voice or expression, and found none.

"It was so good of you to send round this morning too," Mrs. Wycherley continued. "But Angela seemed so tired. No—not ill—merely tired. I thought a quiet day would be the best thing for her. They are bringing you a chair, aren't they? Yes, I see, that's right. Oh, Angela—yes! I was speaking about her. A short walk—that really has been all we have done. In this heat, you see, everything is so—so hot. And that induces lassitude. Angela, in fact, is lying down upstairs now. I insisted upon it."

"I ought to have proposed the river this morning; it would have been cool there."

"For Angela, yes; for me, I am afraid it would not do. I suppose I am a curiously constructed person, but the rocking of the boat sadly interferes with—with my being perfectly well. As my doctor once said to me, putting it as I thought very neatly, 'You have not,' he said, 'got a delicate constitution, but you *have* got a sensitive constitution.' Angela is not a sufferer at all. She adores the river. Now to my mind there is nothing pleasanter than to be driven through beautiful green country in a comfortable carriage. That drive to Deepwater and back really did me good."

"You must try it again." Claudius spoke at intervals, as her babble demanded it of his civility. All the time he was looking towards the house.

And Angela came at last—contemporaneously with the tea-things. She stepped slowly through the French windows and down the lawn towards them. She walked gracefully, her head thrown back. She was pale, and dark under the eyes; her expression was one of patience— new to her, wonderfully appealing.

She shook hands hurriedly with Claudius, and busied herself with the teacups.

"I am sorry to hear that I tired you out yesterday, Miss Wycherley," said Claudius.

She smiled and shook her head. "I wasn't tired, and you didn't do it if I was, and besides I've got over it—modelled on the housemaid's excuse for the broken vase." She seemed afraid to meet his eyes; in her manner she was strangely shy.

"And I had meant to tire you again tomorrow," he said. "I thought the river—"

"Ah! the river—I love it—but mamma—"

Mrs. Wycherley would not hear of that objection.

"We might arrange something," she said. She had just been reading in that yellow-covered book a descriptive passage entitled, "The Pic-nic Pie." A picnic was in her mind. Her imagination built up a lovely entertainment, with the pie as its chief corner-stone, and seated her on emerald moss under an azure sky.

Angela refused the suggestion of a picnic. "Unless you leave the picnic part out," she added, "I don't mind the sward so much, but I dislike the sandwiches. Then there's bother and discomfort, and one always tears one's dress," she sighed. "Give me peace and a public-house," she said earnestly.

Claudius laughed. Mrs. Wycherley said that Angela was really too shocking.

"But the idea is excellent, Mrs. Wycherley. We go by the river to the inn at Deepwater. You go in the carriage and meet us there. Then luncheon—peace and a public-house."

That was settled. Soon after Claudius left, with some, at least, of his troubles over. Mrs. Wycherley and Angela were not angry with him for anything. Angela was not ill—he would be alone with her on the morrow. All that was good. But each time that he saw Angela made it harder to part with her, and harder to love in silence.

★★★★★★★★★★★★★★★★

That night Mrs. Lamb dined downstairs with her husband. She said that she felt better and she looked better, though the extreme pallor of her face was still noticeable. Her eyes were restless and unsteady, and she was very talkative. Throughout dinner he took his own part in the conversation genially enough, admired her dress, told her a good story or two, and answered readily her questions as to their departure from England. As dinner progressed, she seemed to grow rather more excited, and as soon as the servants had gone, she turned abruptly to the doctor, and said, "I want to be forgiven, Gabriel." He looked critically at her, and did not answer. She avoided his gaze, and rambled on—speaking vaguely, at times almost incoherently.

She wanted to be forgiven. She had saved him from himself, or believed she had, and he knew nothing about it. She said that she felt that she had to tell the truth now, and that she was compelled to say that she hated him, but she had saved him from himself all the same. She knew he was clever, but it was better to be good, and she was trying to be good again. He might trust her.

Dr. Lamb gave a long, slow yawn. "This," he said, "is becoming tiresome, Hilda. However, as you insist, I will go through it all once, quite plainly, and get it over. You should not try to be mysterious with me, for you are not good at mystery. You have said more than once that you want me to forgive you. You do not tell me why."

"I cannot."

"I can tell you, though."

"No! no!" she cried, "I will not hear it."

"You will understand your own position, and mine, better if you hear it. You want me to forgive you for your desire to be a much worse woman than you will ever have the chance to be. Claudius Sandell—"

She rose, gasping, looking round her with agonised eyes. She took two or three steps to the window. A heavy curtain was drawn over it. She stood there with her back to the doctor, holding on to the curtains with both hands, her white face pressed against its folds.

"Claudius Sandell does not and never will love you. You are saved from being bad by being—pardon me—insufficiently attractive. Even if he cared for you, it would make no difference, because he is an honourable man, and also—but I need not go into that. Your own position is, therefore, contemptible, and my position is perfectly secure. His position, by the way, is unfortunate. I had a letter from him the other day, from which I understand that there is another woman. Hopeless, of course. As I have not quite finished, I would suggest that you should sit down. Standing will tire you."

She sat down, covering; her face with her hands.

"I pass to the next point. You say that you have saved me from myself—a pulpit phrase, I should imagine. Strange that though you have suddenly passed from a somewhat crude religion to a somewhat crude atheism, you still use the phrases of the religion. If you mean that you have written to Sir Constantine Sandell, I am perfectly well aware of it—could have easily stopped it, but did not care enough about it. Your letter may bring about a reconciliation between father and son, but that will not prevent Claudius Sandell from keeping his word and returning here; and it will not alter my subsequent treatment of him—your guess as to what that will be is, roughly speaking, correct.

"It will turn Miss Matilda Comby—a fraud, but your sister—out of a very comfortable berth, and make Sir Constantine miserable. Nothing more than that. Lastly, you say that you hate me. I pass over the impropriety of it. I merely ask you to consider the possibility that the fact—if it is a fact—though apparently of great interest to you, may not be of the least interest to me. Have I made everything clear?"

She nodded her head.

"Then we need not refer to these matters again. That will be in every way better. I am exceedingly sorry to use language to you which is positively rude, and excitement is very bad for you. After tonight there need be no occasion for either. As to your future conduct, I should prefer that you did not tell me I was clever, and also that you did not treat me as if I were a fool—that is to say, do not plot, be mysterious, or undertake the guidance of my actions, especially where my work is concerned. Always speak to me as if there were a servant in the room. Great though my contempt is for every individual, including myself, I find that my tastes can be best disregarded when they are entirely satisfied, and my tastes are not in favour of Clapham-Villa squabbles with you. I cling, positively cling, to the conventionalities of decent life.

"There are many men in my place who would have killed you, or tried to divorce you. I myself gave you a certain remedial punishment that you have not forgotten. But violence and scandals, though the violence was necessary in that instance, offend my love of conventionality. I only ask to live (until your day comes) as almost every man of the world lives—on perfectly friendly and civil terms with a woman in whom he has ceased to be interested. You understand? Is there anything you would like to ask?"

Hilda Lamb slowly raised her head. Her fit of excitement and volubility had passed; she looked beaten and suffering. There was blood on her lower lip, where she had bitten it.

"Ah, God!" she wailed, "if I could only die tonight!" Once more she rose, and paced up and down the room. Then she stopped and said—

"Am I free to do what I like—to write letters if I like? Are you having me watched?"

"How could you suspect me of such abominable vulgarity? Of course, you are free, and of course you are not watched. By all means write your letter to Scotland Yard to say that your husband intends to murder Claudius Sandell, and has told you so, and will Scotland Yard please come and stop it. If you succeed in making your story sufficiently probable to induce the police to investigate it—which I do not for one moment, think—the police will discover that I am about to employ an amanuensis, a Mr. Sandell, as my poor afflicted wife is no longer able to help me."

"Yes," she said, drearily, "I believe that I am going mad. Sometimes I am mad already. I could do nothing. But I was right then, and it will be murder."

"My dear child," said the doctor, "we do not use these coarse, crude, inappropriate terms. That word 'mad,' for instance. Consider rather that you are in a state of unstable equilibrium. I apply a certain force, notice, to the saucer of my coffee-cup. It moves slightly, but returns to its original position. Its equilibrium is stable. The same force or stress applied to this wine-glass would knock it over and break it—its equilibrium is unstable. You must guard against stress—against excitement. Avoid violent emotion of any kind. There is no occasion to think or speak of madness.

"As for the other word equally melodramatic, murder, it is out of place. Supposing that an experiment ends in death—in this case death merely means the conclusion of a commercial transaction. I might also point out that the loss of life to one individual is nothing, as compared with the gain to the race—but I know that you do not take these broad views. Say to yourself that Claudius Sandell has, for a consideration, agreed to help me to verify much which at present is merely theory, and that you hope all will be satisfactory. Be optimistic—be euphemistic—and you may yet be happy."

Mrs. Lamb half closed her eyes.

"Gabriel," she said, "did he—did Mr. Sandell—know about me?"

"About the—tacit but unfortunate compliment that you paid him? He did not—and I should not tell him."

"Can you tell me the name of the other woman?"

"I do not know it. But in any case, he must leave her on Saturday, and he will not see her again. She does not concern any of us."

"Gabriel, one cannot help thoughts and feeling. One can only try to check them; and, at first, when I could pray, I did."

He made a little impatient gesture. She went on.

"I have not said or done anything wrong. The rest I could not help; and, perhaps, if you had gone on loving me, or if my baby had not died, it would not have happened. But you are my husband, and you pay for everything for me, so it was wicked; and so I asked you to forgive me. And now I want to ask you a favour."

"Well?"

She spoke very slowly. "Let Mr. Sandell go, and use me instead. I can bear things, and I would not let anyone suspect, and I should be glad to die."

"Do you think it probable," the doctor asked, "that I should allow you the exquisite pleasure of dying for him? Surely it is not to me that you should offer evidence of such devotion. But in no case could I have thought of it, as you are not suitable, not what I want. Is there anything else that you want to ask? No?" He gave a deep sigh of relief. "That is capital; we have been through it all, and got it over. It is half-past nine, and you should get as much sleep as possible." Mrs. Lamb rose obediently. "And after this, no more scenes. We meet tomorrow on ordinary terms—the most ordinary possible—perfectly ordinary. Goodnight, Hilda." He opened the door for her, and she passed out.

He sat down again, lit a cigar, and smiling as he sat there, smoking, he made two observations. The first was—

"Typical—that connection between religion, self-sacrifice, and the sexual instinct!"

The second was—

"Wonder why I told her to avoid excitement and not think about her mental state? Professional habit, I suppose."

CHAPTER 15

Mrs. Wycherley supposed that it must have been in consequence of her sitting out in the garden. She did not see how it could have been that; but, at the same time, if it was not that, what else could it have been? Anyway, there it was—a slight chill—not so much a cold, she explained, as the beginning of a cold.

"Deal with these things promptly," she said to Claudius, "and you get them over in a day. Keep indoors and in one room as much as possible. Spirits of camphor, light diet, and a little champagne in the evening—that is my rule, and I do not know what it is to have a cold last more than one day. You nip it in the bud, before it really gets hold of the system."

Claudius was properly sympathetic. Mrs. Wycherley must not, of course, dream of going out. The visit to Deepwater could easily be postponed until the morrow.

But the good-natured lady would not hear of this.

"Why," she said, "should three people sit indoors for one cold—or, rather, the beginning of a cold—on a glorious morning like this? if you don't mind conducting Angela, alone and unchaperoned, I am sure you would take good care of her, and for that matter I think she is quite capable of taking care of herself. I told her I should insist, and she's putting her hat on now."

"But won't you be wretchedly dull all done?"

"My dear Mr. Sandell, if I thought that I was spoiling everybody's pleasure, then I should indeed be dull. But I assure you I have much to occupy me. I'm working for a bazaar. I don't know if you ever—"

At this moment Angela entered. She wore white muslin, and it was quite a new dress.

"Mamma won't let me nurse her," she said, "and has turned me out-of-doors. I am going back to live with papa."

Mrs. Wycherley smiled, protested, fluttered, fussed. There were a few moments of amiable and aimless small talk, and as much opposition to Mrs. Wycherley's plan as civility demanded. And then Claudius and Angela started out.

"This is your own boat," said Angela, as she stepped into the stern of it and took the lines.

"Yes; it's mine. Why did you think so?"

"I thought it looked too new for a hired boat; and the cushions are too good; and it's got several little treats in it that one does not get in a hired boat."

They spoke further of the difficulty of steering with the sun blazing on the water, of dragon-flies, and of certain popular beliefs as to the bad temper and physical strength of swans. And of all these they spoke with that appearance of great interest that one always shows when one is being more interested in something of which one is not speaking.

After a little while they came to a backwater, and went down it. Here they were quite alone. The dragon-flies flashed across the river over the floating water-lily leaves. The midges in fevered shoals danced out their way. From the high white road in the distance, where a man was driving cattle, and having trouble with them, came the faint echo of an angry shout. In a shady place, with trees meeting over the water, Claudius drew the boat into the bank, and Angela, nestling more comfortably into the silken cushions, thanked him for having found so lovely a spot.

They had both known through all their impersonal talk that the personal question was for them the inevitable question—that on that day, sooner or later, in one way or another, it would arise.

"I have been thinking a good deal," said Angela, suddenly, looking away from Claudius, and over the water.

"I was afraid so," said Claudius. "I was wrong, but I know it now, and I'm very sorry or it."

"In what way wrong? I do not understand."

"For telling you, even though you asked it, all that I told you on Tuesday night. I knew that you were sensitive, tender-hearted—that the story must hurt you. I knew that by telling you I was not materially benefited. The only thing that can be said for me—"

He paused.

"Yes?" said Angela, in a low voice.

"Why should I not say it? I could not endure to be in a false position with you."

A slight flush came and died in her cheeks.

"And, besides," he continued, "I felt—I think it was the first time in my life—that I needed sympathy."

"Why should tender-hearted people be cowards?" said Angela. "In order to give sympathy, one must first feel pain, but in giving it there is pleasure: the greater that pain the greater that pleasure. No, you must not reproach yourself. I should be glad if you would tell me more—if there is any more."

"We shall soon be at the end of that story. Last night I laid awake an hour and seemed to hear all the clocks in the world ticking out the minutes left to me. There is little that is new since I spoke to you that night on the heath, and what is new is very prosaic. A publisher has accepted my novel. Before I came to you this morning, telegrams passed between my broker and myself. I have sold my Martenhuis Deep—they were up again yesterday—at a profit of twelve thousand pounds. I could repay Dr. Lamb twofold, if there were the remotest chance that money would tempt him."

"Your book accepted," murmured Angela, "and fortune come to

you—and all too late!"

"If that were all," said Claudius, passionately. "If that were only all!"

"Isn't it?" she said.

"You know that it is not. You must know what I have no right to tell you—except it be the right of a dying man. It is the love which comes too late— it is that which hurts: Angela, I love you—I who have no right to say it—I love you."

"I think I knew," she said. She spoke with quiet serenity, but her bosom rose and fell more deeply and quickly. Her pathetic eyes looked fixed away from him. "And it all goes on," she said after a moment's silence, "the shadow of the clouds drifting over the water, and little bits of things floating down stream, and that thrush there singing—just the same. And—in a few hours you will have gone away, and I shall not hear you speaking to me anymore, and—"

Just then she broke down. Suddenly she covered her face with her hands—

"I can't bear it, Claudius!" she sobbed. "I can't bear it!"

"Forgive me, dear Angela."

She let her hands drop, looked at him with tears in her eyes, and spoke, catching her breath here and there—

"But no— if you had not spoken—that would have been harder. Now there's happiness coming through it all."

He was as one dazed. "It's so hard to believe," he said. "Do you mean that you care—that you love me?"

"Yes—oh yes!" She said it almost proudly, with her sad eyes still looking full into his.

"Though I die tonight," he said, "I shall have seen Paradise. Do you remember saying that?"

"Yes, I remember."

"That was the first evening I met you and loved you."

"Oh, Claudius!"

"All my life through I must have been looking for you."

"Only two days more. I too—I seem to hear all the clocks in the world ticking out the minutes. Have you no hope at all, dearest?"

He smiled. "I have but to break my word, and I am free."

She shook her head. "You know," she said, "I could not ask that. Is there no other hope?"

"So little," he said drearily, "that I had no right—"

"Don't," she broke in impetuously—"Don't say that any more. You must not reproach yourself. You have done right in telling me—I feel it, know it. It cannot go on to—to the conventional end, but it's good that you have loved me even this very little while."

Away in the distance a church-clock chimed out the hour. Then near at hand they heard the regular turn of oars in the rowlocks; another boat was approaching; voices and laughter grew gradually more distinct. Claudius pushed out from the bank. They were not far now from the inn at Deepwater, and he rowed towards it in silence. Angela lay back on the cushions, watching him.

Beyond the garden of the inn, with its sly, commonplace, sentimental arbours, was an old orchard. They had their coffee brought here after luncheon. Angela sat, playing with her coffee-cup; Claudius lying on the grass at her feet, looked up in her eyes and praised her. Their talk was enraptured, full of those endearing words and phrases that lovers use and the rest of the world derides. After a while they spoke of the past, each wanting to know what the other's life had been like.

"Full of the smallest things," said Angela, "until—until this."

"Until I loved you," said Claudius, "my life was worthless—not worth what Dr. Lamb gave me for it—not worth anything."

They praised love—love was the light in life, the stars in the night, the scent in the flowers, the soul in the music. All the truisms come out new when one is living the truth of them. To the dying man *Tempus fugit* is no commonplace.

As they rose, at last, to go homewards, Claudius took her by the hands and drew her towards him. She half-whispered something—he could not hear the words.

"I love you!" he cried. "If you knew how I loved you!"

"I love you!" Her gentle voice came like an echo.

He held her closely in his arms now. Her head fell backward, her eyes fainted, her breathing quickened. He kissed her beautiful mouth.

Together, in silence, they passed back through the orchard, through the garden, to the inn and the river.

In the boat, too, for some time they sat in silence.

"If," said Claudius at last, "by some means—by some means that I cannot foresee now—I can get back my liberty, I shall come back to you. I am bound to you. But you must not think yourself bound to me. You are free."

She held her little hands together like a chained captive.

"I shall never be free again," she said; "I would not be."

"Will you come to me tonight on the heath?" said Claudius. "I will be by the white beeches—you remember, where I found you that night when I told you my story—and wait for me there. The time is so short, and I must see you again before the day's over."

"Yes," she said, "I will come to you, Claudius."

★★★★★★★★★★★★★★★★★

Once that afternoon Angela had said, "I do not think we need tell anyone about this. No one else could understand."

Lovers love secrecy, and Claudius would fain have given in to her wishes, but he felt that he had no right in this matter.

"I am afraid," he said, "that you must tell your mother our secret; but not, of course. Dr. Lamb's."

Perhaps no one could have understood. Certainly, when Angela tried to do as Claudius had said, poor Mrs. Wycherley was mystified extremely. She sympathized. She said that she could have wished for nothing better than an engagement between her daughter and Claudius Sandell—who was a kind and honourable gentleman, if Mrs. Wycherley had ever seen one. But was this an engagement? If not, what was it? Oh! couldn't Angela explain a little more? Angela, on the verge of tears, could not. Mrs. Wycherley thereupon roamed into a wild field of hypothetical explanations on her own account. Some of them sounded likely, some were very wild, and all were quite wrong. Then she became expostulatory. Until this obstacle, whatever it was, was removed, Angela ought really not to see Mr. Sandell.

"Well, as you have promised, I shall let you go tonight, just for five minutes—or shall we say four?—well, five then. But, after that, no more—no more at all, until he is free to—to go on as he ought to go on."

"But, mother," Angela pleaded, "you've told me that you like him and trust him. If I do not see him again after tonight, perhaps I shall never see him again at all, never as long as I live. You can't understand.

The difficulty is not any of the things you think—not anything he can escape or alter. If not tomorrow, let me see him on Saturday before he goes. It will only be like saying goodbye to a dying man. Oh, I will be good and do what you tell me, but I'm so unhappy, and—" Here Angela, not ineffectively, though the poor child was not acting, burst into tears.

Mrs. Wycherley was sure that she was more distressed than she could express. She blamed herself that it had ever come to this; and how, she asked, was she to know what to say, when she only wanted to act in the way that was best for Angela? What she said at last was that they would be back in London on Saturday, that Claudius might call on them in Erciston Square on Saturday evening, and Angela should be allowed to see him alone then.

When they met on the heath that night, Angela told her sorrows breathlessly, and asked what was to be done.

"I had meant to ask you that," he replied.

"See—can you read this? I found it waiting for me when I got back this afternoon—it is from Lady Verrider."

By the light of the wax match that Claudius held in his hand, Angela read the telegram.

"Your father wires me nothing wrong with him, but he would like to see you at once. Do please go to him. Am sure it would be best."

"What does it mean?" said Angela. "The telegram says that he is not ill."

"It may mean reconciliation," said Claudius thoughtfully, "or it may mean that the spirits have advised Matilda Comby to send for me. It may mean anything."

"Claudius, I think you must go to him."

"Yes, I think so too, now. If I cannot be seeing you, I will go there—indeed, if it does mean reconciliation, I shall be glad to go. I should love to be on good terms with him again before the end. But, Angela, to think that we have only two days left and that we are to lose almost the whole of them!"

"Dear love!"

As best they could they comforted each other, yet parted with heavy hearts.

Chapter 16

That night, immediately after leaving Angela, Claudius took the train from Guilbridge to London, and then went on by the night-mail north. It was a hideous journey. The man was in a fever, and could not sleep. In following the Wycherleys to Guilbridge, he had acted as those weak fools act who shut their eyes and deceive themselves. It was a bitter reproach to one who had in him the makings of a strong man. He had before him, horribly and vividly, the certainty that he would lose his life, and that life—since now he knew that life meant love—was immeasurably valuable. And above reproaches and above horror, came the exaltation of mutual love. Angela's words seemed to speak themselves again to him. The dawn, coming pale through the carriage windows, seemed to him symbolical of her farawayness. His life had been like a grey day, working and commonplace; and its sunset was like the gate of heaven; and the night was inevitable.

It was little wonder that he could not sleep.

A servant in livery was on the platform when he arrived—in a slow local train from the junction—and the carriage was waiting for him, although it had been too late for him to telegraph that he was coming.

It was a wearisome drive to Sir Constantine's place. In the hall he found a servant whom he remembered—the old butler.

"Yes, sir, Sir Constantine is in very good 'ealth, sir. He'd expected you'd come by this train. Well, this *is* a pleasure, if I may say so, sir."

Claudius chatted with the old man for a minute or so; they had always been friends, and it is pleasant to be welcomed.

"Well, now, Gunning," he said, "what's the news here? How's Miss Comby?"

Gunning dropped his voice. "Gone, sir. Went Wednesday night, after telegrams had been comin' and goin'. Marchin' orders, I fancy. And if I might take the liberty, we're all of us—well, we can live through the loss of her. We'd a fire, too, last night, while you were in the train. But that you'll hear about, sir, and it's not for me to speak. Breakfast will be ready directly; but if you'd like to have your bath first—"

Claudius had his bath, and made his way into the dining-room.

Gunning brought a message that Sir Constantine would be down directly, and Claudius was not to wait. Claudius was in love, but he was also physiologically hungry. He had scarcely begun breakfast when the door opened, and Sir Constantine, noticeably well-dressed, with a newspaper in his hand, sauntered into the room.

Sir Constantine had the face of a dreamer, poetical eyes, and rather a weak chin; he had an erratic sense of humour; his forehead was developed in a way that showed he was not such a fool as his chin would have had you believe.

He shook hands with Claudius, calmly and quietly, as if they had parted the night before. Sir Constantine had an admirable talent for ignoring anything which he wished to ignore, and it was very soon apparent that he intended to use it.

"While you were asleep in the train, Claudius," he said, "we were having a little excitement here—a fire. That's why I'm late this morning."

"Nothing serious, I hope, sir," said Claudius. He had been brought up to address his father in this old-fashioned way.

"Just a cottage—burned to the ground, and not insured. I dare say it won't ruin us, but still, it's a loss, of course."

"But your private wire to the fire-station in the town?"

"For some reason or other it wouldn't act."

"That's a pity. Who had the cottage?"

"No one at the time. Up till the night before it had been occupied by a woman called Comby. You know nothing about her. She did not arrive here until sometime after you had left—for your work."

Claudius opened his eyes wider. Sir Constantine quietly repeated this pleasant fiction. Claudius smiled and accepted it. The past was to be ignored—or, rather, it was to be altered to suit the taste of Sir Constantine.

He gave a little more information about Miss Comby. He had thought her a deserving woman who had seen trouble, with some knowledge of philosophy—"in which, as you know, my boy, I have always taken an interest." He was willing to own that he had been deceived. An anonymous letter had arrived—he had telegraphed, and had received telegrams. It was a shocking;—a most deplorable and shocking case. He "utterly and altogether declined" to go into it.

But he might say that the anonymous letter had stated the actual facts, and in consequence the woman had gone. He dwelt with an ill-concealed satisfaction on the fact that in the fire at the cottage the whole of the furniture assigned to Miss Comby's use, and even the books which Sir Constantine had lent her, were completely destroyed. He spoke of a poacher seen lurking about the grounds, but Claudius had little doubt who the incendiary was.

After breakfast. Sir Constantine took Claudius round the stables. A pony, he mentioned, had been stolen by gipsies. Then they wandered out into the paddock. At the end of the paddock was a disused slate quarry, deeply excavated, and fenced off some distance from its edge. Sir Constantine climbed over the fence, and Claudius followed; under a tree Claudius saw a neat little governess-cart with a set of plated harness, the cushions, a rug, and a little clock, lying in it.

"What is that doing here, sir?" Claudius asked with some surprise.

Sir Constantine chose to misunderstand the question.

"What is that? Oh, that's the cart that Miss Comby used to drive!" He picked up the shafts, "Neat little thing, isn't it? Runs so lightly."

He pushed it from him. There was a loud crash from a projecting jagged ledge, and a splash in the deep water in the pit below. The cart had gone over.

"Good heavens!" Claudius exclaimed.

"Careless of me," said Sir Constantine. "Really, very careless." He fumbled for his cigarette papers.

"We'd better send a man to see after it," said Claudius.

"Not worthwhile." They retraced their steps to the house. The fire—the theft of the pony—the accident to the cart—were all perfectly obvious. Sir Constantine would not allow one trace of Miss Comby to remain,

"By the way," said Sir Constantine, "as that woman displeased me, it might be as well if her name were not mentioned. In fact, I utterly and altogether decline to have her name mentioned in my presence."

"Very well, sir."

"And now what about yourself? You will be here sometimes, I hope?"

Then came rather a difficult part for Claudius. There was so very little about himself that he could tell. It was unfortunate, but he would have to return to London almost at once—he was leaving England on Sunday.

"You will not be away for long?"

"I do not really know exactly. It does not depend entirely on me."

"Yes, your work," said Sir Constantine, vaguely. "A man ought to be able to support himself by his work—even if it is not necessary it increases his self-respect. I am glad to see you a capable man. I reverence capacity. You used to have, I remember, a tendency towards—er—writing."

"I have written a novel," said Claudius. "It has been accepted, and will be published—and that will be the end of it."

"Let us hope not. From what I know of your abilities, speaking frankly, I do not think your novel will be either good enough or bad enough for a complete failure. But a novel—I could have wished it had been a philosophical work."

"I have not the knowledge."

"Nor I—nor I. But I am taking a great interest in it. I have gone back to my Greek. Aristotle is very difficult—so is Plato. I employ the classical master at the grammar school here three evenings in a week, and I also use translations. That is, I have arranged for the classical master and the translations. I only began on Wednesday. But yesterday—though I had other things to think about—I gave some hours to the subject, and I already have the idea. The Socratic gospel—the gospel according to Socrates—in that lies the only real consolation."

He warmed to his newly-acquired pet.

"Not only for the man of education," he went on. "The Socratic gospel is universal. The bricklayer may leave his crude salvationism. The hysterical woman"—he said it without the least sign of embarrassment—"may leave her silly spiritualistic nonsense. The gospel according to Socrates is the gospel of the future. It may fall to my lot to present it in English—in a popular form. It would be an honourable work. On the title-page, "The Gospel of Socrates. Translated, arranged, and edited for the use of the English-speaking races by—"

And so, he went on, galloping his latest conviction into the land of nowhere. It was half sad and half ridiculous. But the son had known the father for so long now that the exposition neither depressed him nor amused him. It was his father as he had always known him—and now once more his good friend.

Sir Constantine showed very little curiosity. He took it for granted that Claudius would come to see him again—in two or three months, or possibly later. Claudius did not undeceive him. That could be better done by letter, at the last moment.

On the station platform a few minutes before the train came in by which Claudius was to return, Sir Constantine remarked hesitatingly that Claudius looked well—fairly, only fairly, well-dressed, but well-fed, comfortable. He was very pleased to see it. By this route he arrived at what he wanted to say.

"But all the same, my boy, I don't want you to be absolutely dependent on your work—your novels—for the comforts and necessities of life. Now I find from my bankers that there has been a very grave irregularity in paying you your allowance: in fact, for some little time it has not been paid. Even the best of banks seem to make silly mistakes and misinterpret orders sometimes. Now I must have my wishes carried out, and I have made this arrangement. I have made over to you the sum of ten thousand pounds. It's invested, and I shouldn't alter the investment if I were you. But the money is yours absolutely, and if you ever had any pressing need for a large sum, you could of course realise. The interest will be paid into your account at the bank. Strellan, old Strellan, arranged it for me. He thought it the best plan."

Strellan was Sir Constantine's country solicitor, and his opinion of Sir Constantine's plans was generally complimentary.

"Here's your train," the old man went on. "Now take this"—he drew an envelope from his pocket and handed it to Claudius—"it's the particulars about the money. Certainly not—I absolutely and altogether decline to be thanked. Merely my duty, and at the same time my pleasure."

He shook Claudius warmly by the hand, and, without waiting a moment longer hurried from the station, as if escaping from the consequences of a shameful act.

Claudius found in his travelling-bag, placed there by his father's hand, a volume of Grote's *History of Greece*, with certain passages marked. On the fly-leaf was scrawled an injunction to him to read the book on his journey and post it back when he arrived.

Chapter 17

Saturday morning was, fortunately for Claudius, full of business. There were arrangements to be made, bills to be settled, and a really good solicitor to be persuaded to do something in a hurry—and the really good dislike hurry. He had to call at the bank and at the publishers, he had a score of trifles that needed his attention. So far, he had preserved appearances well. On his journey north and on his return, he had spoken and acted in a normal way, had forgotten nothing, given no sign of absent-mindedness, allowed no railway porter or chance travelling companion even the vague idea that there must be "something the matter." He had gone successfully through the ordeal of meeting with his father and parting from him. But this morning it was different.

Every business act was a great effort to him; continually he had to recall his thoughts and to concentrate his attention. Sometimes he would find that he had forgotten to say something of importance, and sometimes that he had repeated some needless commonplace— a remark on the weather, for instance—two or three times. But the flicker of a suppressed smile on the face of the man who happened to be talking with him at the time gave him no annoyance. The same thing that made him capable of small mistakes made him incapable of small annoyances. The excitement overmastered him—the excitement of love returned yet hopeless, of fortune gained yet worthless, of life continued yet worse than death, of fate laughing and the end near.

Two letters had reached him that morning at his London hotel by the first post, one—how often he had read it!—was from Angela. Early on Friday morning Mrs. Wycherley had telegraphed to her husband, and he had come at once. First, he had seen Mrs. Wycherley alone; then he had called Angela down and taken her out in the garden with him. He had seemed serious, but not in the least angry with her; on the contrary, he had never been kinder. He had questioned her, but there had been some questions which she had to tell him she could not answer. Indeed, she had not told him very much.

After that, he had left for London. Angela had heard him say, "I shall certainly call upon Lady Verrider this afternoon." She quoted another remark of his, "It's a case, I think, for a man of business and plain common sense, and I am that and very little else." At the end he had tried to cheer Angela up, and told her that all might be well. He could not say for certain, but he thought the case was not quite hopeless, if Claudius could be got to listen to reason. Her little budget of news, told—poor child!—somewhat incoherently, occupied but a little of her long letter. The rest was quite sacred, and quite human, and to Claudius most lovely, and priceless, and sad.

The second letter, which was from Mr Wycherley, ran as follows:—

My dear Mr. Sandell,

I intend to call at your hotel tomorrow (Saturday) afternoon at five, and take my chance of finding you. I know that you will naturally be much occupied, but I hope you will be able to spare a few minutes in which to see me.

I am far from thinking that you have acted, to say the least of it, with discretion. But I do not want you to suppose that I am calling in order to blame you or oppose you. The happiness of my only child is very dear to me, and any obstacle to that must be removed if I can remove it. Believe me, I am only anxious to secure what you yourself must wish. I may be able to help you, and I hope you will let me try. From the little that I have been able to learn, I think that my business experience may be of service to you.

The letter presented Mr. Wycherley to Claudius as the very image of the completely kind father on the utterly wrong tack; but of course, he determined to see him.

He wished first to see Lady Verrider, but the business of the morning prolonged itself into the afternoon, and it was after four before he arrived at her house. Lady Verrider paced the room. She was beautifully dressed and quite furious, angry and affectionate by turns, and the more angry because she was really fond of him. He had to listen to tirades.

"What did I tell you? What did I warn you? I knew what would happen—what was bound to happen—if you went to Guilbridge.

Oh, I know that devout lover type so well! It's going to love in silence, and it never does. It's going to worship from afar, and it always insists on propinquity. It is determined to be content with very little, and it never is. And if it's good-looking (as I suppose you are) and takes trouble (as I know you did), it may manage to make some poor girl love it and confess her love. Then the devout lover raises his hat politely and says good morning, and how sorry he is that it can never be, and he had never dreamed that it would come to that, and he is not worthy, and so on. Then he walks off. Pretty figure, isn't he?"

"My dear lady, I am not that cur exactly. I told Angela from the first that the rest of my life was not mine. Then the time was so short—just a few days—it did not seem possible that any harm could happen. Angela was, and is, so far beyond me that I did not suppose—"

"No, you devout lovers never do suppose that any perfectly ordinary thing can possibly happen. But why did you say that you loved her—why did you tell her?"

"My God!" said Claudius, with sudden passion. "Do you ask me that? Have you never been in love?"

"Yes, I was in love with the man I married. That is one of the reasons why I am so sorry for the poor girls who are made to fall in love with the men that they can never marry."

"I dare say," said Claudius, "that you will tell me that it is the usual formula of the devout lover; but I can only say again that I did not expect what happened."

"Of course," Lady Verrider continued, "I know in my heart that you don't deserve what I say to you. But I am angry and miserable. You are not a cur, I almost wish you were. What I am afraid of in you is your silly, out-of-date, romantic, high-falutin chivalry. Nothing but that, I am convinced, could have got you into your present impossible position. I have been talking to Mr. Wycherley—a very sensible little man. He quite agrees with me."

There was a pause, and then Lady Verrider asked quickly—

"You went to see your father—are you reconciled?"

"No formal reconciliation took place. The past was ignored—you know his way. But we are on the best of terms. He insisted on giving me money—ten thousand."

"And you also made a small fortune by speculation, I am told."

"Yes, I made some money."

"And your novel has been accepted, and Angela would marry you. And just at this point you disappear, and will not explain why."

"I cannot explain it to you. I have told Angela, and she will tell no one."

"Will you tell me one little thing? You say that your life has been disposed of. To whom? Who is this mysterious man in the background? His name, please—just his real name and nothing more. Tell me that, and the rest I will manage for myself."

"I know you ask it from the kindest motives. I am ashamed not to be able to tell you. If the secret were all my own, it should be yours too, and at once. But it is not only mine. I cannot tell you."

"Oh, I give it up! It is killing me—I am absolutely miserable."

"I am sorry indeed," said Claudius, "that I should distress you in this way."

She stood before the mantelpiece, moving little objects on it restlessly.

"Mind you," she added, suddenly, "you will find Mr. Wycherley far more determined."

"That may be. I am to see him—almost directly. I must be going."

"He has certain rights now. You have given him those rights—yes, I am glad you told Angela—and you cannot get over them."

"Dear Lady Verrider, don't speak as if I wanted to get over them. I'm not a natural martyr. I'm longing to be free and happy. My wishes are just the same as yours and Wycherley's. If without knowing the circumstances—and I cannot tell him them—he can show me a possible solution, I shall welcome it."

Then Claudius said goodbye. He assured Lady Verrider that he would do all he could, and reminded her that some unforeseen chance might possibly favour him. But she would not be assured. She had a presentiment, she said, that she would never see him again.

Claudius found Mr. Wycherley at the hotel. "How is Angela?" Claudius asked eagerly.

"She is very unhappy," the little man replied simply. He was rather nervous at first, observed that the rain still kept off inquired as to the health of Sir Constantine, fidgeted with his hat; then he put down the hat, seated himself, wiped his forehead, and plunged—

"Now, Mr. Sandell, you know that I have seen my wife and daughter. Jessica is, you may have noticed it, a little inclined to be vague. If I may put it so, she never seems actually to know anything about anything. I'm not finding fault with her for it, you'll understand. It's in her nature, and we're none of us perfect. I mention it, to account for any mistakes I have made in forming my idea of the situation. Angela is far more clear in her statements, but she will not go beyond a certain point. She could tell, but won't. My wife would, but can't. Will you let me question you—somewhat plainly—that I may correct myself where I am wrong!"

"Ask anything, and plainly as you will. I will tell you all that I can."

"You love my daughter, and would marry her?"

"Yes."

The simple answer was as effective as a more fervent protest.

"But after tonight you cease to be your own master? Of the remainder of your life some disposition was made before you met Angela?"

"Yes."

"I have known young men—good fellows, really—make for themselves unending trouble. Youth, hot blood, and ignorance—they do a deal of harm. Pardon me, but is there—is there another woman in the case?"

"No."

"Has there been some previous—er?"

"Nothing, nothing. I have never loved, nor ever shall love, anyone else."

"I believe you. Indeed, you tell me what I expected, but I wanted to be quite sure. That finishes with woman. We come to money."

Claudius handed Mr. Wycherley some memoranda and letters— one dated that day from the bank.

"No, no, no!" protested Mr. Wycherley. "It's not necessary."

"I would rather," said Claudius.

Mr. Wycherley examined, and his face fell. "If all this money will not help, then the case is bad indeed."

"No amount of money could help. The case is bad indeed. I want you also to read this. It is my will—by which I leave all unconditionally to Angela. My solicitors are also acting as my executors, and I am just returning it to them."

Mr. Wycherley stared at the carpet. "God help her!" was all he said.

"I knew it was nothing," said Claudius, after a pause. "All that I can do now is nothing. I shall not, at least, die happily."

"Die? Die?" exclaimed Mr. Wycherley, suddenly. "Then you expect to die? Is that so—is it—is it?"

"I cannot tell you."

"But I think you have told me. You leave me to work in the dark. You won't show me the reason, the motive. If it had been woman I could have helped you, for I was once young. If it had been money, I could have helped you, for I am now old. It seems that it's neither. But I have worked in the dark before. In the City—I needn't go into it—but I have had to play the game when I did not know what the game was, or where it would end. But as I have gone on, I have found a glimmer here and a glimmer there, until at last there was light enough. I'm going to work in the dark now, for already, Mr. Sandell, I've seen the glimmer—just the faintest. Now you said that I might question you, tell me under what compulsion you agreed that within a few days you would sacrifice your life?"

"I did not guess at the time "Claudius paused.

"Go on! Go on!" said Mr. Wycherley, excitedly; "you say that you did not guess at the time that there was an actual peril of life. However, you know it now. Go on!

"There was no compulsion whatever. I was broken down at that time, and did not think that my life could ever have any value for me."

"But why to this man? Why give it to him?"

"Mr. Wycherley, it's no use," said Claudius. "I beg you not to ask me any more questions. I've had no sleep, and I'm worn out. I can't think clearly, and I can't trust myself to talk. I'm so afraid of telling you things unintentionally, which I am hound in honour not to tell. Don't think me ungrateful—I am not that. You have been very kind to me when you might with justice have been only very angry."

"Yes," said Mr. Wycherley; "you look tired and ill—I had noticed that. I won't question you any further. On the contrary, instead of asking for an explanation I will give you one. I'm nothing much, you know, only a business man. But Angela is—is a good deal to me. I can't see the rest of her life spoiled, and I won't do it. Nor will I let you be murdered, because from some sense of honour (which as a business man I can't understand) you feel yourself bound by a contract of a nature which the law doesn't allow. I've not been angry with you, though you were in the wrong to go to Guilbridge in the first place—once there, the rest was inevitable. Now, you must not be angry with me if I should seem afterwards to have interfered with you, for I am going on working."

"How? In what way?"

"It is my turn to say that I cannot tell you."

Claudius thought for a few moments. "You are justified," he said. "Mr. Wycherley, there is one more thing to say. I must tell you how sorry I am. The worst that I have to bear is that Angela should suffer;

303

I never dreamed that she would come to care for me. My days were so few—I thought the joy and the sorrow of it would be mine alone. And now, when I think of it, and how you and her mother love her, I see that I have done the worst thing I ever did in my life. I have done a terrible thing that will weigh me down to the end. Angela will not let me ask for forgiveness, and will not bear that there is anything to forgive. You know how much there is."

"I won't say there's nothing to forgive," said Mr. Wycherley. And then very simply and kindly he held out his hand. "But it's all right, Claudius. I believe you're a good fellow—I couldn't have wished for a better for Angela. I should be a harder man than I am if I couldn't forgive you now. I see how you're placed—if you're to be saved, it must be in spite of yourself, and in spite of you I'm going on working. When you come tonight to say goodbye to Angela, remember that she takes things hard. Don't let her think that it's the last time—that she'll never see you again. You understand, of course."

"Perfectly. Thank you, thank you very much."

It was arranged between them that Claudius was to call at Erciston Square at nine o'clock that night. He was to see Angela alone, and only Angela.

Mr. Wycherley was no sooner outside the hotel than his work began; and he was not, he thought, working so completely in the dark now. He remembered all that he had heard from his wife, from Angela, from Lady Verrider, from Claudius himself He pieced his information together rapidly, and formed his conjectures. The commissionaire called a cab for him.

"Where to, sir?" the man asked.

"Ludgate Circus," said Mr. Wycherley.

From Ludgate Circus Mr. Wycherley had not far to go to the office of Mr, Abraham Penny's Detective Agency. It was after six on Saturday night, but that office knows no hours. His business was simplicity itself. A young gentleman (description given) would arrive at Mr. Wycherley's house at nine o'clock that night. He would leave it for some other house before twelve, for he had to be at this other house by twelve. Mr. Wycherley wished to know where this other house was, who its occupants were, and—and all that could be discovered about them, in fact. Mr. Wycherley would like a report to this effect to be on his breakfast-table on Sunday morning, and would then send further instructions; until these were received, a close watch by night and day was to be kept on that other house, and every movement of that young gentleman or of the occupants of the house was to be followed and reported to Mr. Wycherley at once; and Mr. Wycherley hoped that there would be no difficulty.

"Difficulty?" said the assistant manager. "It's the ABC. We see the young gentleman go into your house, and follow him when he comes out. You shall hear from us by eleven on Sunday morning, and anything that turns up further as the day goes on. You don't want the young gentleman or his companions to suspect that they're shadowed, and you'd like the thing to be done thoroughly?"

"Quite so. Put your best men on to it, and don't spare expense. Want a cheque in advance, or a reference?"

"Not from you, sir," said the assistant manager, and thereby showed his astuteness; and he showed it further by not putting his best men on to do work which the less good could do equally well.

Mr. Wycherley was well pleased. He had common sense, and had proved it. As he entered the omnibus that would take him nearest to Erciston Square, he smiled upon his achievement. But common sense is not the gift of prophecy, and Mr. Wycherley little knew what the next few hours were to bring forth.

"How is Angela?" he asked his wife as soon as he got home.

Mrs. Wycherley was troubled and tremulous.

"She doesn't cry any more—not since this morning. She seems to me to try to talk of other things, and cheer me up, and there's nothing breaks me down more than that, coming from her. Takes nothing—a biscuit and a glass of wine that I insisted upon, but nothing more. So, she won't be down to dinner. You saw Mr. Sandell? What have you done?"

"I saw him, and I have done the right thing. Go and tell Angela that Claudius will come to say goodbye to her at nine tonight, that I have been doing what I can, and have good reason to hope that Claudius will not be away long."

"But—one moment—before I go, "What have you really done?"

"Don't tell Angela, for she'd tell Claudius, and he must not know, or it would spoil all."

"Not a word."

"I've put it in the hands of Abraham Penny."

"Penny—what Penny?"

"Private detective."

"Ah!"

And then was Mrs. Wycherley greatly comforted and refreshed.

305

For, like most really good women, she had a faith in private detectives that never reasoned why, and could not be justified by facts.

CHAPTER 18

There was a little back sitting-room in the house in Erciston Square which had been known in the Wycherleys' earlier days as the library. Angela had objected that there were no books in it, and that therefore it was not a library. So Mrs. Wycherley, who could see a point very well when her attention was directed to it, decided that it should be called the breakfast-room, and issued a solemn kitchen decree to that effect. There were relapses into the use of the word "library" on the part of the housemaid—a creature of habit; Mrs. Wycherley took a strong line, and the weeping maiden obtained a fixed idea that the use of the word "library" was indecent. So, the breakfast-room triumphed, and was securely established. Nobody ever breakfasted there, of course.

It was in this room, lit by two red-shaded candles on the mantel-piece, that Claudius said goodbye to Angela. The dim rose light was kind to her pale face. Claudius had no longer any hope at all in his own heart. Mr. Wycherley might attempt something: it did not much matter what he attempted; Claudius knew that Dr. Lamb would be clever enough to foresee that some such attempt might be made, and clever enough to checkmate it.

Yet he spoke to Angela as if he would come back, perhaps, and she, too, spoke as one who hoped. Then at times a hard look of horror came into her soft eyes, and both were very careful not to raise the question of the purpose for which Dr. Gabriel Lamb needed Claudius Sandell.

"Remember," said Claudius, "that as long as I live, I shall always be loving you."

"But not to hear you say it anymore!" cried Angela. "If that should be!"

"It can't be. It can't end like this."

"Oh, Claudius, dear love, what shall I do? Tell me what I shall do? How shall I wait for you?"

Mrs. Wycherley had quite realised that this was an emotional hour in her house, and that for the sake of others she must bear up. To that end she took a glass of coca-wine, and found it a broken reed. The poor, silly affectionate woman loved her beautiful daughter so dearly that the thought of Angela's unhappiness made composure impossible. She was in her bedroom now, with her cap off, all sobs and *sal volatile*.

The undignified love as much as the dignified. This idea of an emotional hour, this sense that there was sorrow in the house, had even permeated into the basement.

Cook sniffed. The housemaid (the one who never said "library" now) observed: "It's my Sunday out tomorrow, but I shan't take it"—a dark saying, a vague, well-meant effort to get into keeping with the general atmosphere. Mr. Wycherley sat bolt upright in a straight-backed chair in the drawing-room. He held the *Times* in his hands, and thought he was reading it, and his face was solemn. He was ready—ready and waiting. He would hear the breakfast-room door open and shut, and the front door open and shut, and the carriage drive away: and at that moment he would emerge with a most cheerful smile and take the broken, crying Angela into his arms, and he would say, "Don't fret, Angela. It's all right. I couldn't tell you before, but I have taken this in hand myself, I have. Tomorrow morning you shall have news of Claudius. I promise it. I absolutely promise it." That would surely do some good.

Her parents had entrusted Angela with comforting messages for Claudius and with their farewells. The messages were easily delivered: the rest was difficult.

"And as they will not see you tonight, and it may be long before they see you again, they asked me to say—Oh, Claudius, I don't want to say goodbye!"

Her breast heaved and her lips trembled. Claudius drew her to him and kissed her again and again. Neither of them spoke anymore now until the moment when Claudius left the house. He could hardly see, his head swam, he staggered like a man that has been drugged.

Hardly had he flung himself back in his carriage before he fell asleep. Nature was exhausted. He did not wake until the carriage entered the drive before Dr. Lamb's house. Waking, he wondered where he was, for he had dreamed that he was back at home. Then he remembered. He pulled out his watch and glanced at the time. It still wanted ten minutes to twelve.

He got out, and just as he was on the point of ringing the bell, paused, changed his mind, and turned round.

"You can put my portmanteau down," he said; "you needn't wait."

"Very good, sir," the man replied.

There were still a few minutes of freedom left. Claudius clung to them.

The coachman hesitated before driving off. Claudius had been very liberal—after all it might be as well to mention what he had noticed.

"I beg your pardon," he said, "but I'm not sure if you know we've been followed?"

"Followed?"

"Yes, sir. I noticed a hansom hanging about when I was waiting in Erciston Square. As soon as I drove off the cab followed. It kept behind me all the way, and when I turned in here, went on a few yards and then stopped. It's there now."

"Anyone in the cab?"

"Two men, sir. I only got a glimpse. Common-looking they seemed."

"Thanks. You were quite right to tell me, though I don't know that it's of much importance."

The carriage drove off. Claudius stood beside his luggage with his watch in his hand. After all, then, he supposed. Dr. Lamb had not trusted him, and had put detectives on to follow him. The black shrubberies stood out clear against the pale sky; a breath of wind woke and rustled and fell again. All was absolutely still. In a moment Claudius put his watch back in his pocket and rang the bell; the sound spoke out, resonant, far back in the house.

And immediately the door opened, almost before the bell sounded. It was opened slowly, and not to the full extent—not as Francis opened it. Mrs. Lamb stood there. She was bare-footed, and in her nightdress; her hair hung loose about her shoulders; her eyes were wild and roaming; she spoke in a horrible whisper.

"I've been waiting behind the door for you. I got up and crept out, and they never knew."

She shivered in the chill night air. Behind her was a chaos of packing-cases. The carpets were up in the hall and on the stairs. The house looked naked. A gas-jet flared without a globe.

"Mrs. Lamb," Claudius began. He was going to persuade her to go in, poor mad woman, but she would not let him speak.

"There is no time. Listen quickly, before they come and take me. I have been sent by Heaven to save you. You are to go away at once, and you must never come here again." She pointed to the passage that led to the study and laboratory. "Gabriel's in there—not the angel Gabriel, but the devil Gabriel. He's getting ready to kill you, sharpening knives. Every night I can hear him sharpen knives, though he does not want me to hear. Always sharpening knives. It goes like this—*b-*

r-r-r-r—b-r-r-r." She made a hideous guttural imitation of the sound of a grindstone.

At the same moment a door opened, and a woman in a plaid dressing-gown came out. She had a cloak over one arm, and she said quietly, "Mrs. Lamb, you must come back to bed." Hilda Lamb flung herself down on the floor of the hall, kicking and screaming. The nurse was a big woman, with a not unkindly face. She would not let Claudius help her, and indeed she needed no help; her strength was enormous. She wrapped Mrs. Lamb in the cloak, lifted her and carried her off. Then Claudius saw that the servant Francis was standing waiting at the further end of the hall.

He now came forward, greeted Claudius respectfully, and began to carry in the luggage.

"Dr. Lamb is in the study, sir," he said.

"My dear Sandell," said the doctor, cordially, coming forward as Sandell entered, "welcome to a half-empty and exceedingly uncomfortable home. I trust that you have been enjoying yourself in your absence."

Claudius shook hands mechanically, thanked him mechanically, and sat down.

"The Octave is over. *Lusisti satis*—how does it go? *Tempus abire tibi est.* You will notice the preparations for departure everywhere here. Indeed, had all been well, we should have gone aboard the yacht on Sunday afternoon. But there has been a sudden change in my wife's mental condition. I'm afraid that when you came in just now you heard—"

"I saw Mrs. Lamb. The nurse took her back into her room. Believe me, I am very sorry."

"Well, this change, though not uninteresting from one point of view, is, of course, exceedingly sad, and it has altered my plans slightly. My wife cannot possibly come with us now, and I have not yet finished the arrangements for her remaining in England. It may be Monday before we can start."

"Where are we going?"

"Sandell, I own you now. I do not want to insist on that ownership more than is necessary for my purpose, and I cannot bring myself to give you an order like a servant. But I ask you, for your own sake, not to put questions to me about the future. Do not ask me where my yacht will take you. Do not ask what I am going to do with you."

Sandell looked the doctor straight in the eyes.

"I know very well what you are going to do with me," he said.

"You believe," said the doctor, "that I intend to use you for the subject of experiment. And yet you keep your word—well, I was sure you would."

"You were sure!" Claudius said. "Yet I have been followed by your detectives tonight right up to your house."

"My good Sandell, I have never employed a private detective in my life. I should think it dishonourable, and it has the additional disadvantage of being almost always useless—they are far from clever, that class, as a rule. At the same time, I can readily believe that you were followed here, and that you are being shadowed now. I can believe that there may be someone in London who has sufficient interest in you to be suspicious of your mysterious disappearance at a time when I understand you have every reason for not disappearing. Is that not so?"

Claudius remembered that Mr. Wycherley had said that he would work on his own account and in the dark. He saw it all now.

"I think you are right—I did you an injustice. I believe I know now who sent them. I have no doubt he believed he was acting in my interests, but it was done without my knowledge and authority. I should not have thought that I had any right to interfere with you in that way. Shall I tell you who I think sent them?"

"No," said the doctor, "I don't think his name would interest me. He can do nothing, of course. His very smart people will hardly come aboard my yacht. They're amusing to watch for a short time, but I don't propose to allow them to take a voyage with me."

"Sandell," the doctor added, after a pause in which Claudius had not replied to him, "you look very tired and broken-down. You are also very depressed. I will not keep you here much longer, for you need sleep. But there is one thing I want to say. You have done me one injustice tonight (perfectly trivial, as it happened), and I am afraid that you also do me another injustice.

"You doubt my humanity. There was a time when you regarded me as a good Samaritan; you now regard me as a murdering devil. The reaction has set in, and, possibly, it has been assisted by the chatter of that mad woman. I heard her talking to you. Now I cannot let you suspect my humanity, and partly for that reason, and partly because I really trust you, I will change my mind and tell you what I have arranged. You are, of course, to be the subject of experiment."

Claudius Sandell looked steadily and contemptuously at the doctor.

"I do not mean it in any offensive sense," the doctor continued, "when I say that you are of no practical use to me for any other purpose. I value your good opinion as I am now showing, and have always found you a most pleasant and interesting companion."

"If I were not yours absolutely, and had any right to suggest, I should suggest that we pass over this part."

"My dear fellow, do not be so humble or so bad-tempered. I am not Legree in *Uncle Tom's Cabin*. You can suggest anything you like, and be sure that your suggestions will always be considered with respect, and adopted wherever it is possible. I do not bask and revel in villainy, and for the purposes of melodrama I am useless. Your attitude towards me hurts me. For days and nights I have been planning how to make everything as easy as possible for you."

"Shall we pass over that also?"

"Certainly, in one moment, I want to tell you how things stand. When the time comes, I shall ask you to allow me to administer an an aesthetic. After a time, you will regain consciousness. Then from thirty to fifty seconds you will suffer. The anaesthetic will be administered again immediately." The doctor paused.

"And when I regain consciousness the second time?"

The doctor lit a cigar, blew out the match, and flung it into the grate. "You will not regain consciousness a second time. That will be—in fact, that will be all."

"That is why you are leaving England?"

The doctor shrugged his shoulders. "There is no privacy in England," he said. "But I ask you to notice that the very most you have to fear is fifty seconds of suffering—probably not acute. All the lurid pictures that your imagination may have conjured up, or my wife in her madness may have depicted, may be dismissed from your mind. I am emphatically a humane man. If it were not for my humanity, for my broad love of the race, for my infinite longing that some future generation might be born, not under the curse which weighs us down, but free and masters of their fate—I would not even ask you for that little thing, your life."

Again, Claudius made no reply.

"Until that moment comes when I begin the experiment, your comfort shall be my first consideration; no indignity shall be put upon you; except for that one purpose, and what is connected with it, you are free."

"I have a considerable fortune," said Claudius.

"I am afraid," said the doctor, "that I cannot consent to accept gratuities."

"You had already told me that money was of no consideration with you. I was not intending to repeat my offer to buy myself from you. I wanted to ask if I were free to dispose of my money now, and to will it after my death, as I wish?"

"Absolutely —perfectly free."

"And I may write letters?"

"Certainly—any letters which do not prejudice my main purpose. After we leave England you will omit the address, of course."

"Thank you," said Claudius. "I have only one more question—is there any consideration whatever which would induce you to terminate our agreement: any consideration apart from money?"

"I had thought that you would be likely to ask the question, and I have no objection to it. My answer is—none, absolutely none."

At that moment Francis entered.

"The nurse would like to speak to you for a moment, sir."

"Excuse me," said the doctor, and went out.

Claudius leant forward with his head in his hands; he felt how easy it would be to fall asleep and to forget.

In a moment or two the doctor returned.

"The nurse," he said, "seems to think that someone should sit up with my wife tonight. It cannot be done. The nurse has not been to bed for two nights, and it would be barbarous to keep her up a third night unless it were absolutely necessary, and I do not think it is. Fortunately, I have to be up all night myself. I have something in the laboratory which requires watching, and I shall be here until six. With the door open I shall hear any sound. My wife sleeps downstairs now, you know,"

"Yes?" said Claudius, hardly conscious of what had been said.

"Yes. It is her idea that her dead baby crawls about upstairs, and would disturb her rest. At any rate, she will not sleep upstairs."

Claudius rose from his chair, "May I go to bed now?" he said, "I am so tired that I am not very good company."

"Certainly. I hope you'll find your room comfortable. Francis will get anything you want. Whisky-and-soda before you go? No! Ah, Claudius, I am sorry I can't give you my philosophy, and I won't insult you by trying! Everybody has the philosophy which is suitable to the situation of somebody else. My philosophy is the very thing for a man in your situation. Well, well—goodnight."

"May I make one request?"

"Again, this Legree business—do, please, ask for anything you want," said the doctor a little irritably.

"I want you to begin this experiment as soon as possible. To wait for it—that is hard to do."

"Be assured," smiled the doctor, suavely, "that I also am impatient. Goodnight again—sleep well, and breakfast just when you happen to feel like it."

Claudius left the room, and went upstairs without a word.

The doctor went on composedly with his work, and two hours slipped by. He had grown drowsy, and, leaning forward with his head on his arms, fell into a doze. He often found that half-an-hour's sleep snatched in this way made a great difference to him, and sent him back to his work as fresh and energetic as ever.

And as he slept, *pit-pat, pit-pat*, across the stone floor of the hall came the sound of naked feet. Past the bare hall, where the windows had stared like lidless eyes since the curtains were packed away, and unfaded patches stood where pictures had been, and the naked gas-light flared—past the hall and down the passage came Hilda Lamb, quiet and cunning as a cat, with all hell awake in her mad eyes. She opened the study door softly; she smiled when she saw that the doctor was asleep.

Without a sound she passed through into the laboratory and switched on the electric light. She opened the big mahogany case of instruments, and was careful not to let the click of steel be heard. She took what she wanted, switched off the light, and came back into the studio again. The bright edge of the thing she held in her hand attracted her attention. "*B-r-r-r-r, b-r-r-r-r, b-r-r-r-r*," she said in her throat, imitating the sound of the grindstone. Doctor Lamb began to move his head. In a moment she flung herself upon him, and thrust and hacked and pulled.

★★★★★★★★★★★★★★★★★

A storm came into the dream that Claudius dreamed that night. The forked lightning split the sky, the thunder cracked and roared. Below were people with white, frightened faces—a dense mass of people, all looking upward. They began to howl with terror, waving their arms. The dream suddenly ceased, and Claudius was awake.

He was awake, and the room was filled with smoke. Someone was knocking violently at the door and crying to him to get up. "Fire! fire!"

And someone outside in the garden was singing—a poor mad woman that had been rescued from the merciful fire. The servants of the house watched her in awe-struck silence as she was dragged away, ceasing her singing from time to time and fighting hard to get back to the flames.

The fire had broken out in the annexe—in the doctor's study. This was completely wrecked before the arrival of the engines. The main body of the building was damaged but not ruined. In the grey, early dawn the police on watch talked confidentially among themselves. "I saw her myself," said one of them, "and there was blood both on her hands and face. It'll be Broadmoor."

At a little distance from the house Claudius stood alone on the road and looked towards London. A four-wheeled cab lumbered slowly up, and Francis, who had gone to Wimbledon to order it, jumped down from the box.

"It's the best they could do, sir."

"Thanks," said Claudius, as he got in. "It will do very well. Tell him to drive as quickly as he can."

"Yes, sir. Where to, sir?"

"Erciston Square."

Francis shut the carriage door. "Erciston Square," he echoed, as he seated himself beside the driver again.